THE RISK OF RETURNING

The Risk
of Returning

Second Edition

A NOVEL

Shirley and Rudy Nelson

WIPF & STOCK · Eugene, Oregon

The Risk of Returning is a work of fiction. The characters and portrayal are
the product of the authors' imaginations, and any resemblance to individuals
living or dead is coincidental. The country of Guatemala is portrayed
fictionally as a location, along with aspects of its history and geography, and
references to public persons, institutions and events.

The quote from *The Magician's Nephew* is from
The Chronicles of Narnia © CSLewis Ptc Ltd 1950-56.
Extracts from the poetry of Emily Dickinson are taken from
Final Harvest: Emily Dickinson Poems ©1961 by Little, Brown & Company, Inc.

Cover and book design, Ed Atkeson, Berg Design
Cover art work by Scott Nelson, ©"The Road"

Printed in the United States of America

Wipf and Stock
An imprint of Wipf and Stock, Publishers
199 West 8th Avenue
Eugene, OR 97401

ISBN 978-1-4982-1922-8
Second edition
First printed by Troy Book Makers, Troy, N.Y.

To order additional copies of this title, contact a local bookstore,
or visit WipfandStock.com

For all the storytellers of Guatemala who have broken through the long crust of silence and fear. This story does not pretend to take a place among those brave disclosures, though it owes a great debt to them, and to the wider, overarching story of the country and its people.

desaparecido -a
noun, masc. or fem.

A kidnapped, missing person
(Latin Amer., political)

Guatemala
August 1987

ONE

We were barely off the ground and on the way when I knew it was a mistake.

It began with Pat Crane. I met him first. No significance to that in itself. Somebody has to be first, and he certainly was. We met in the air, shortly after take-off, 30,000 feet over the Gulf of Mexico.

I had noticed him earlier at the departure gate in Miami, a heavy red-bearded man reading a newspaper. I hardly glanced at him then, or he at me, aside from the way adult males do, with an instinctual check of the territory. But in retrospect it's a wonder he wasn't watching for me there, holding high my name in magic marker, a certain prescient light in his eye.

The flight was delayed, this second leg of the trip. Announcements were made, repairs to something in the instrument panel. The waiting area was full. A big percentage of the passengers were apparently Central American, loaded down with shopping bags bearing the logos of Miami stores. They chattered cheerfully, their voices reaching my ears in a familiar orchestrated sound, the Hispanic lilt. I don't mean I understood it. The language was no longer mine, other than a phrase here and there, an old song I recognized but couldn't sing.

I wasn't taking it well, this delay. It seemed ominous to me, though I knew it was only the state of my mind, that like a lost child was seeing things in every tree and post. Not that I felt lost exactly, more like mislaid, as if someone had set me down and forgotten where I was, a notion that might have struck me funny at another time. I tried to read, paced the corridor, and stared out the windows at our stalled behemoth.

My seat when we boarded the plane was on the aisle next to the portside wing. At the last minute a dozen teen-aged kids swooped on board like a flock of noisy birds, filling spaces in front and on either side of me, chattering across the aisle and singing snatches of songs. All wore the same white T-shirt with the same logo, "Gringos For Jesus." Gringos they were, in a fair-skinned, orthodontal sort of way. Two of them filled the empty seats in my row, a boy in the middle and a girl by the window.

When we were airborne, I removed the headset from the seat pocket, hoping to pick up some decent jazz in the aircraft offerings. As I plugged it into the arm rest, the boy turned toward me confidentially and mumbled something. I unwired myself and asked him to repeat it. He did. Would I like something, I thought he said. Kids had only just begun saying "like" and it still caught me off-guard. "Like what?" I asked. He tried again, still mumbling, his words run together, rapid fire. I leaned closer. "Where would I like to go?" No, wrong. "Where *will* you go," he said. "Where will you go if we all go—like down?" His hand took a dive.

"I go like down, too?" I said. I put on a dead face, eyes rolled back. When in doubt, play the clown.

Not funny. The boy looked frustrated. He mumbled a correction and I had to ask him to repeat it. He raised his voice then, a lot.

"Heaven or hell! I mean like heaven or hell! Where are you going?"

That got attention, everybody's, that is. Suddenly the chatter around us stopped. An audience of young faces peered at us over the seats. I might have been confronting a room full of students on the first day of classes. I felt the same first-day wash of tenderness and panic. The boy was waiting for an answer, his face ruddy with responsibility. I wanted to set him at ease, get him off the hook. Nothing came to my lips. It was not my day for that kind of finesse, but it was his for persistence. His fingers reached for what looked like a tract in his shirt pocket.

Walking away was clearly best for all. I glanced about for a different seat. Nothing empty in front of us. I turned to look behind and found my face mere inches away from another. In a slapstick, it might have been God's own, a fairly young God with a bushy red beard, like the Norse god Thor, but it was only the reader in the waiting room, seated in back of me now and leaning forward to speak.

"There's an entire unclaimed row in the rear," he said. "Shall we go for it?"

Why not? I took up my pack with a wave to the kid. He looked relieved. "Have a good trip," he said.

The man ahead of me in the aisle was big. He wore the rumpled look of a guy who carries an extra hundred pounds and is tired of tucking in his shirt. The bowl of a briarwood curved out of his suitcoat pocket and a faint smell of pipe ashes trailed behind him. When we reached the empty row, he motioned to me to enter first. "Do you mind?" he asked, wheezing a little. "It's easier for me on the aisle." He was in every way wide, his eyes widely spaced, hair abundant over the ears. I felt oddly narrow and colorless beside him, eyes too close set, beard too cropped.

We introduced ourselves, shaking hands over the empty middle seat between us.

"Ted Peterson," I said.

"George Patton Crane," he offered. "But do call me Pat." Not a trace of whimsy. "First time to Wah-day-mallah?" That's how he pronounced it, as I hadn't heard it in years. I mumbled something about "long ago," but he was on another track already, the book he had seen in my hands back there in Miami, that old novel, *The Red Badge of Courage*, which he had noticed especially because his grandfather had been a distant kin to the author, but a copy he suspected could be owned only by an English professor, considering its tattered condition, and who else would be reading it anyway? "Am I right in that decoding process?"

I nodded, smiling carefully.

"And what prestigious institution do you represent?" Crane asked.

"Shawmut Junior College," I told him. "Boston." I was sure he had never heard of it, because neither had I until this second.

He was in sociology himself, he said, before I could ask. In fact, in the course of the next hour I was careful to ask nothing that might be taken as a lead, and couldn't have found an opening if I had tried. He had been working on his doctoral dissertation at NYU for eight years now, he said, and "one might ask—might *well* ask—" why he had not thrown in the towel long ago, considering the roadblocks presented by the needless requirements of a soft and self-conscious science. But at least he had a publisher in waiting, he said, and *Deo volente*, would soon have a book.

He used his hands as he talked, sometimes close to his chest as if conducting a small choral group, sometimes punctuating his sentences with a flourish: quotes, periods, even a semicolon. His advisors kept insisting on a wider statistical base, he said, but lordamercy, his topic was embedded in the unstatistical, the un-pie-chartable spaces of human life. And one might wonder, mightn't one, what all that had to do with the destination of this plane? He answered that with a "drastically stripped down version" of his life story, which took the better part of the next half hour. He was an AB, he said, an army brat. His father had been a military advisor, so as a kid he was dragged around, *ad infinitum, nauseum* and *absurdo,* to various parts of the world.

We were interrupted twice by flight attendants, first with drinks, then with food, a late lunch of sorts. I had no appetite, but Crane apparently did. He stopped talking long enough to feed himself with zest, the little plastic fork in his left hand and the knife in his right, looking like a bear at tea in a British fairy tale. When he began talking again it was to "let me in" on the heart of his thesis, U.S. expats. He was on the way to "Wah-day-mallah" right now to find fresh material among ABs and MKs—missionary kids, "the lost children of Peter Pan"—and he was already on the lookout for a good interview.

"Really," I said, with what courtesy I could muster. If he had tied me to the seat and sat on me, I couldn't have felt more like a hostage. He had been back repeatedly in the last eight years, he said, "in spite of dire travel advisories." Times were when he'd come across dead bodies himself on the street, early morning before they got scooped up.

"Really," I said again.

"Did you happen to be there during those days?"

"What? Oh. No."

"Of course nothing has actually changed. It's just a little sneakier."

"Right. Of course."

"What's yours?" he asked.

"Mine?" I'd lost a thread somewhere.

"Reason," he said. "There are only so many right now. Research, religion, or reconnaissance." He even looked roguish, or tried to. Why was I on this plane, that's what he wanted to know. I considered the "reasons" I could give him, and knew I would not, even "I don't know," which was closest to the truth. He was leaning toward me, his body overflowing into the seat between us. All the old warning lights began to flash. I resisted an urge to adjust my jacket over the money belt, where I'd put my father's letter. Instead, I pulled out my glasses and began to unwrap the slice of carrot cake that came with the lunch.

He was watching me, waiting for an answer, the nosy bugger. I considered telling him, in some configuration of courtesy, that it was none of his business. Or I could just maintain the silence, which is what I did, tearing open the stubborn package with my teeth and biting into the terrible cake. That worked. He excused himself and settled back in his seat for a nap.

I turned to the window and the diminishing light beyond it. By now the plane had dropped through cloud cover and I could see mountains below, an extension of the Sierra Madres, draped in green quilts of vegetation, white mist rising between them so deliberately you'd swear the whole range was on fire. Dusk deepened with the long descent and soon the lights of the capital city spread across what seemed to be a plateau, its edges dropping off sharply here and there into oblivion. I was straining to make that out when we touched down, and the pilot's voice welcomed us in both Spanish and English to La Aurora International Airport. I reset my watch. It was a few minutes before 6:00, Central American time. Pat Crane opened his eyes.

I managed to maneuver away from him as he probed for his luggage in the overhead. But standing in the stalled line waiting to deplane, I felt warm breath in my hair, and when I entered the terminal he was beside me, moving with the crowd. At least he was not talking, both of us wordless as we walked between life-sized blow-ups of black-haired Mayan women lining the walls with *Eight Million Smiles*. A gigantic quetzal bird, made of turquoise and scarlet paper, hung from the ceiling, its preposterous tail feathers waving in the air.

I slipped ahead of him in the line to the caged window where passports and tourist cards were processed, then headed off to the baggage carousel on the lower level. A packed crowd filled a balcony there, shouting and waving at the people they had come to meet. One man at the railing circled a huge bottle of pink Pepto-Bismol over his head. "For the galloping shitskies," said Crane helpfully, over my shoulder.

As I picked my bag off the conveyor belt, he grabbed his, too, riding right behind mine. And so together we joined the line for customs inspection.

Crane's suitcase was given a perfunctory exam by two men, and he stepped several feet aside. My inspector was younger than the others, very young, I thought. He said something to me in Spanish.

"I don't understand," I answered.

He proceeded to explain in English, so muddled I could only shrug in return. "Okay," he said, and as the two older men stood by watching, began to transfer to the counter every single item, first from my suitcase, which contained only clothes, and then from my pack—tapes, books, an apple, granola bars, Walkman, toiletries case. This he unzipped and emptied— toothbrush, deodorant, nail clipper, beard trimmer—all of it looking remarkably mundane. I think that bothered me the most. Nothing interesting here, let alone drugs or contraband. He asked me to empty my pockets. I did. Change, comb, mints. I would be patted down next, I supposed, money belt removed, letter extracted.

But now the kid turned his attention to my books. He placed the four paperbacks side by side on the table, a Spanish-English dictionary (new), *The Red Badge of Courage,* a copy of *Walden* and the Final Harvest edition of Emily Dickinson (all old). After flipping through each, he picked up the novel and brought it over to the other men.

"But why?" I protested. They ignored me. Cover half off, the book was passed from hand to hand among the three of them.

Now Crane, the empty pipe hanging from his mouth, stirred his bulk and walked forward. *"Dispense uds, señores,"* he said. There was a moment of exchange, a question and an answer. The book along with every other item was replaced methodically in the bag and I was signaled to go.

"What the heck was that all about?" I asked, as we passed into the lobby.

"Just an aberration," he said. "They don't usually do it to U.S. tourists."

"Oh, that's comforting."

"The kid's a trainee, I think. Just showing off."

I glanced about for a men's room, saw a sign and headed there. He was waiting when I came out. We walked together toward the exit.

"What did you say to them, anyway?" I asked. "That you're related to the author?"

He guffawed, unoffended. "Lordy, no! I had a hunch the fellow got hung up on the word red, and indeed, that was the case."

It took a couple of seconds for that knot to untangle. Subversive literature? "What bloody nonsense!" I said.

"Oh, indeedy-dee. Ludicrous. But ludicry, if I may coin a word, is often the name of the game around here."

The doors to the exterior, just yards away now, beckoned with wafts of cool air as they opened and closed. Out on the sidewalk the breeze mixed with the exhaust of a fleet of taxis double-parked at the curb. Cabbies whistled and yelled. I turned to Crane to say goodbye. He looked rumpled and tired, his shirt half out. "I appreciate whatever you did," I told him.

"Don't mention it, old chap," he said. Thunder sounded faintly. "Rainy season," he announced.

A taxi pulled into a space in front of us, the rusted hulk of an old Ford Crown Vic. "*Zona Uno?*" called the driver, getting out of the car and opening the trunk. He wore a Mets cap.

"Are you going downtown?" Crane asked me.

I opened the back door without answering. Four people instantly pushed past me into the cab, two in front and two in back. With a squeeze there was room for one more.

"Take it," I said to Crane. "Are you going that way?"

"Yes, to the Centenario." He surveyed the seat skeptically. The cabbie barked something, slamming down the trunk. "It's yours," said Crane.

I got in, both bags on my lap, and reached my hand through the window. He shook it, palming a business card. "Centenario," he repeated. "I'll be there most of the month. Call me if you need another *salvamento.*"

What?

"*Deus ex machina.*"

Oh. A joke? "Sure," I said. I had no intention of ever seeing him again. Then the vehicle was off with a roar, plowing a path through the wet evening haze. In a few minutes we were on a main artery. All the way to the hotel, I watched for landmarks that might have meaning for me, but nothing did—an enormous statue of somebody, a viaduct, wave after wave of plump graffiti. No leaps of sensory memory. On the dark horizon ahead an urban glow edged the sky. Soon buildings closed in on either side, neon lights flashed, and we were locked in a preposterous horn-blaring traffic jam. By the time we reached the hotel, it was raining hard.

TWO

For a long time as a kid I used to think I could make my father re-appear. If I got the equation just right, the right location or the right minute, the right thing to tell or ask him, a door would suddenly open and he would be there, looking just as I remembered him. I hadn't engaged in that fantasy for a long time, and I would never have ad-mitted that I chose the Pan American Hotel with that intention, but it did happen to be the last place I'd seen him in happy circumstances.

He had brought me to the Capital on my seventh birthday for a gift of priority time, just the two of us. The hotel was meant as part of the treat, but the gentility of it, with its glossy terrazzo floors and bowing staff, only befuddled me. I liked things better outdoors. We poked our way through the intersecting streets and avenues, *calles* and *avenidas*, now efficiently numbered, but once with strange names, Street of Solitude, Street of Sorrows.

My father kept asking me what I would like to do most. All I want-ed was to be in his presence, if I'd known how to tell him that. He had been away from home a lot in the previous months. I didn't care what we did, but buy bubble gum was what I finally said, and off we went on the quest. We found it in the underground Central Market, literally under the ground. I studied the word on the colored wrapper: Dubble Bubble. Was that Spanish or English, I wondered, or both, like Chiclets.

We sat on a bench in the public plaza fronting the wide National Palace, while he taught me how to blow bubbles. He had grown a droopy mustache in the time since I'd seen him last, and for the rest of the day it held specks of pink. The mustache was gray, and it made him look older, though his hair was still blond. There was something else. His stature had somehow diminished. He was tall, a towering person, and his clothes had always seemed a little too small for him. Now they looked too big and they were the same clothes I'd seen him in hundreds of times.

"What are you staring at, *raggmunk?*" he asked. That was his Swedish name for me. It meant "potato pancake." In Spanish I was apt to be an *elote*, an ear of corn.

"That dumb mustache," I answered, and then we arm-wrestled, there on a bench in the sunny plaza. He won, of course. He had big hands. Both of mine could have fit into one of his. I never thought he threw a match just to make me feel good, though he hammed up the process, and this time he went into full-bodied contortions that collapsed me in laughter.

That was at the end of January in 1954. This August evening, thirty-three years later, and I now older than he was at the time, the memory surprised me with what it brought to the surface. Maybe I wasn't ready after all. Maybe never.

After registering, I went directly to my room on the second floor. A long night's sleep was what I thought I needed, but the traffic outside my windows was so clamorous I gave that up. I went down to the dining room for a glass of scotch and was informed apologetically by the waiter that there was no scotch, nor any other alcoholic drink, because the hotel owner was a teetotaler himself—"a follower of Riosmont." That's how I heard it, as one word. It sounded like the name of a cult.

"What's that?" I asked.

He spelled it, politely. "M-o-n-t-t. General Efraín Ríos Montt. *Vos?*"

"Oh, sure." I said. Never heard of the man. I settled for a coke and retreated to a divan on the mezzanine. In the lobby below, among the twenty-foot potted palms, a four-man marimba band began vamping with studied lethargy. I listened for a while as they wandered from one song to another. When they launched into a slow rendition of *I'm in the Mood for Love*, I went back to my room.

The traffic noise had not abated, but I slipped gratefully between the sheets, then watched sleep instantly lift away, like an airborne package. So I resorted to an old crutch, the baseball alphabet routine, this time with second basemen as the subheading. I had gotten all the way through G, skipping E, which was usually hard—Roberto Alomar,

Marty Barrett, Pete Coscarart, then Bobby Doerr, Nelly Fox and Joe Gordon—and was groping for an H when I fell asleep.

In what seemed like minutes I sat up, startled out of a dream. Someone had unlocked the door to the room and come in, I was sure. I fumbled for the bedside lamp. No one was there. My surroundings suggested only civility and good will, the slightly worn furnishings, the ceiling fan noiselessly turning, a decanter of *agua pura* on the table covered by a starched white napkin, next to my money belt. I checked the contents. Nothing had been touched, passport, wallet, letter. The French doors that served as a window were shut, as I had left them. It was 4:00 A.M. and still dark outside. Both the rain and the traffic had stopped.

Half-awake in the early morning silence, I returned to the search for an H. And who should appear but Miss Heifferston, like a joke my brain was playing on itself. It had been many years since I had given Miss H a thought. Some of the kids had called her "the heifer," and she was indeed bovine, but her voice was sweet and high, like a little girl's. "Guess what, children," she announced, standing with me at the front of the first grade classroom, her hand tightly clasping my elbow. "A new friend is joining us today. His name is Teddy Peterson, and he comes to us from far, far away in a land where people are very different than we are. So he is going to tell us something about it, aren't you, Teddy?"

I could see myself now, that boy, up there in front of twenty-five staring faces, too tall already, taller than anyone else in the class. He was not supposed to talk about it, where they used to live, and he couldn't talk anyway. It was as if he suddenly had no language at all, though he knew three, and one of them was English. He couldn't even breathe, and something screwy was going on down around his legs. Like a streak, he was out of the room and the school and ran all the way home without his jacket, a good half mile in the frigid Rhode Island air, his pants and socks wet and crappy.

But he didn't cry. In fact, it was as if he discovered that he didn't need to cry at all anymore, about anything, and he didn't. He figured it out, where the boundaries were and how to stay inside them. In a remarkably short time, as I assessed it now, feeling admiration for that skinny, determined boy, he wrested himself from his past. He became a stateside kid. It was like erasing the blackboard, a reward for well-behaved students. For the moment I felt heartened, as if I had looked over the side of the hotel bed and could see my old shoes of self-management waiting to be worn.

Then I shut the boy away, gently but firmly, and took off again in search of an H. Two presented themselves directly, in a bonus of trivia riches: Billy Herman, ancient history with the Chicago Cubs and later manager of the Red Sox, and young Ken Hubbs, his promise cut short by a plane crash in 1964.

It was then that the city's silence was broken, at first with what I heard as faint dull thuds, without resonance. These, as they grew louder, were joined by a chorus of staccato grunts, the bottom note on a hundred bass fiddles, too low to be called music. I got up and opened the French doors. They led to a narrow balcony. I stepped out into the chilly air, half-naked in sweat pants. Street-lights still burned amber through the morning mist. Closed stores lined the sidewalks, their display windows secured by steel roll-down barriers.

It seemed to me the sound was coming from the right. In that next block a dense ceiling of signs stretched across the road, as far as I could see. Some were readable through the shifting fog: *TicTac Relojes, Jordache, Wrangler, Orange Crush.* From under these, out of the fog, a tight rank of figures emerged, a hundred or so of them, wearing identical red shorts and berets, army boots on their feet, chanting off-pitch as they trotted. Some kind of guard, I supposed, maybe from the National Palace, three blocks away. I watched them until they turned a corner and their eerie song faded to a rumble.

I remained outside, gazing at the empty wet street while the damp air enveloped me. The benign silence had returned, the only sound the squeak of the metal signs in the breeze. The air smelled not unpleasantly of wet dust and some kind of smoke. I took note of the sky, its clouds now faintly tinged with pink. A bony dog nosed its way down the gutter. Other than that, I was alone, until my eye caught a single figure on the farther sidewalk, again to my right, a young man, maybe a boy, wearing a straw hat with the brims rolled up on the sides. He was in a hurry, walking quickly, close to the buildings, head down, shoulders heaving, as if he had been running.

I watched him for a second or two, then headed back to the room. I had crossed the threshold of the French doors when I heard the snort of car brakes and a yell and turned in time to see a white van, a Chevy, I thought (snub-nosed), which had apparently stopped in the street, gather speed and swing with a roar around the next corner. The man who had been walking was nowhere in sight.

That was it. You could say I saw nothing, or that there was nothing to see anyway, or nothing ominous. A man was walking, a vehicle came by and stopped, and the man was gone. I knew there were abductions here, everybody knew that. But it seemed hardly likely I'd witness one on my first night, as if the country had arranged it for my orientation. Nevertheless, the effect was total. I felt blind-sided, hit by a board, the sense of control, renewed just moments ago, now knocked askew. The incident had found a match in the molecules of my own inner state and linked up perfectly. I slipped back inside and sat on the bed. My breathing filled the room.

I should report it, shouldn't I? That was the next question, a rational one, I thought. I reached for the phone. But who did I think I would call? The front desk? Police? To tell them what? For all I knew, it was a legitimate arrest. Even if not, any idea that I ought to do something about it, that I had any legitimate role, was naive. I was just an over-reacting tourist, and—I felt with deep visceral conviction—I shouldn't be here anyway. I should leave right now, get a taxi to the airport and stand by for the first empty seat I could get to the States. I took a shower, considering that possibility, to go back. Then toweling off, I acknowledged another question. Back to what?

I dressed and went out again on the balcony. In that last quarter hour the street below had changed, bathed fully now in the rosy light, reflected in the wetness of the pavement. A bus went by, then another. There were people in the windows. They looked normal and composed. Church bells rang somewhere, clunkingly, sounding very much like a pot banged with a spoon, then others, more melodious, at a distance. Something was lying in the gutter that I hadn't noticed before.

On the way to breakfast I detoured out to the street, past two potted fig trees and an armed guard who opened the door and wished me a *buenos días*. The mists had cleared and the temperature was balmy, a glorious day in promise. I crossed over. What I'd noticed from the balcony was a straw hat, upside down. I walked around the corner. Nothing there except a crushed plastic bottle and a sneaker, quite small, but a man's, I thought. I went back to the hat, picked it up and shook it, dispensing moisture and the dirt it had collected. It was an ordinary straw hat, rolled up on the sides, and nothing inside, not even a manufacturer's label. I put it on. It was too small and sat on the top of my head.

I should explain now that I wore that hat often in the following weeks. It was not because I expected to find the owner and return it, and I didn't. I never saw him again and never looked for him. The hat was just a token that something, whatever it was, had actually happened.

THREE

Back in the hotel dining room all was order and decorum, white ta-
blecloths, the subdued voices of early morning patrons. A woman in
native dress was patting out fresh tortillas with a sound as old to me
as my name. "Teddy, Teddy, Teddy," I once thought the sound said.
A sleeping baby was tied to her back by a wide swath of fabric. The
waiter who pulled out my chair was decked in black knee breeches and
an embroidered jacket, a bright scarf with long tassels on his head. I
ordered cornflakes, ignoring the breakfast menu.

I ate slowly, reconsidering my next pre-planned move, to the city of
Antigua, 20 miles or so to the west. I knew one thing about Antigua. It
was home to more than a dozen language schools, and one of these, the
Escuela Méndez, just might be expecting me to make an appearance.
I had chosen that school because it was small and taught only on a
one-to-one basis. For some reason, I had never received final confirmation of enrollment. I could have phoned right now—that might be
sensible—but I decided to just go there instead. Because, where else?

I finished my coffee and stopped at the desk to pay the bill. The
clerk assured me that there were indeed buses to Antigua, even on a
Sunday morning. Would I rather arrange a car rental? No, I predicted
no need for that. He called me a taxi.

The terminal turned out to be the parking lot of a Shell station,
filled with recycled buses, gaily painted in three or four colors. I spotted
one with "Antigua" printed on a card in the windshield, and under
that in black crayon, *Starship La Empresa.* As a one-time trekker, I was
hooked. I paid the fare to the attendant at the door—a kid, really,
maybe fourteen—and climbed aboard with my luggage. It had been
a schoolbus, a U.S. discard probably, with child-sized seats, rows of
three on each side. All were occupied, whole families jammed in, ba-

bies hammocked to their mothers. The windows were shut and several people were smoking.

I turned to retreat. Too late. A line of passengers was boarding behind me, shoving me along, women with baskets of produce on their heads, one with a squawking chicken in a wicker cage. I edged all the way to the back, resigned to standing, my hat brushing the ceiling, backpack behind me against the emergency door. There was no place to store luggage. I stuffed my suitcase on the floor between my feet. Beside me, a very drunk gentleman occupied what amounted to three places, but I decided not to contest it, and no one else did either. The aisle filled quickly, some passengers standing, some squatting on the floor. I stood head and shoulders above everyone in front of me, like an over-grown kid at the back of the bus. Even the men tended to be short. This was not something I recalled. But why would I? All the village adults I had known as a child had been far taller than me.

The horn trumpeted, the boy in charge called out something, and with a lift-off explosion we were on our way. The driver, who wore a head-set, peered through a collection of things hanging from the rear-view mirror, rosaries and small stuffed animals. As I watched, he jumped a red light, pulled into the oncoming lane, then swerved back, just missing a truck. I checked the emergency door behind me, wondering if it would open.

No one else seemed troubled. They chattered sociably, in what sounded to me like an indigenous soup of languages. The men all wore long-sleeved shirts and sports caps. The women wore pastel cardigans over bright hand-woven blouses. For the life of me I couldn't remember what those blouses were called. "Wee-PEEL," prompted a voice in my head, a child's clear, piping voice, rebuking me for the lapse. That was it, how I had once pronounced the word, but not how it was spelled. I had probably never known how to spell it, and I certainly didn't now.

I tried not to stare, remembering a taboo, a hex caused by blue eyes. Did anyone still believe that? There was a word for it, but this time no little voice reminded me. Anyway, I was the object of glances myself. A toddler to my left on an old man's lap, a tiny, black-eyed girl with dusty bare feet, reached out her hand to me. I returned the gesture without touching her. It came back to me, sensually, what it was like when people insisted on touching me as a boy, my skin or my hair, fingers needing to know how a light coloring felt.

Someone tapped me lightly on the arm. It was the drunk. He had moved over to make a place for me on the aisle seat. "Oh. *Gracias*," I said. The offer, I suspected, was one of courtesy to a guest, a habit unblurred even by a night of drinking. I took the space, my shoulder pack and suitcase in my lap and my knees jutting into the aisle.

Very soon I began to get an undeniable olfactory signal. The fruity friend beside me was in trouble. I understood, and wished I knew how to tell him that, but he was staring out the window and seemed unaware of the problem. In a minute the stench became overpowering. An undercurrent of snickers moved up and down the aisle. I heard muttered scatology—*caca, cagadas*—and recalled with a jolt of pleasure that those were words I knew, ones I had been ordered by my mother never to use and like a good boy never did.

The muted hilarity lasted only a minute. The kid in charge up front signaled the driver to pull over, then ordered the people in the aisle to stand as he bumped and squeezed a path to the back. His eyes were on me. I realized that I, the vulnerable gringo, could be considered the source—the curse of Montezuma, the galloping shitskies. "*Levantese!*" the boy barked, his hands in translation. He wanted me to stand. I refused, pretending ignorance. He said something else, something apologetic, and now I got it. "Oh, no," I said. "No, don't!"

He ignored me, reaching across to grab the drunk by the shirt and lift him out of the seat, the man hardly bigger than the boy. I considered intervening—I was bigger than both of them, after all. But I retracted that instantly, picturing a melee, shit flying, maybe literally. I got up and squeezed across the aisle, luggage in my arms, while the kid opened the emergency door with a rasping squeal and shoved the drunk into the street. No one said a word. No cheers, no objections, the driver not so much as turning his head. "Seat, *señor*," the boy said to me, with an elaborate sweep of the hand. I stood where I was, filled with regret, as the bus pulled away.

In another ten minutes we entered a long drop, turned onto a cobblestone street and jiggled to a parking lot. I was the last passenger to dismount and was hardly off the steps when I felt the difference. Not just the relief of breathable air, but the cast of light, the pitch of sound. In fact, I was in an enchanting geographic bowl, all but surrounded by green mountains, still half hidden in morning mist.

I felt received, as if I'd made it successfully through twenty-four hours of some kind of a hazing. Early initiation completed, said the mountains. Admit tall skinny bozo in ill-fitting hat.

FOUR

I had planned to take a taxi to an inn and present myself at the Escuela Méndez early the next day, a sensible Monday morning. But "sensible" had lost a good deal of its meaning, and I needed to walk. I crossed an open-air market, through the smoke of grilling food and shouting hawkers, and entered a business district, where a courteous man gave me directions. That put me on a residential street. Adobe houses in pastels fronted directly on the sidewalk. Heavy flowering vines draped over the walls from inner courtyards. It was suddenly quiet. I smelled coffee.

The school address was a *hacienda* of sorts, a large stucco house surrounded by a flower garden and enclosed by an iron fence. A brass bell hung on a rope, but before I could ring it, a security guard in a brown uniform appeared from under the shadow of a tree. "School?" I asked. "Méndez?"

He eyed me carefully through the gate, without speaking. It occurred to me that there might be another inspection, my paraphernalia spread on the grass, books and all. And if I were to frisk him in turn, would that bulge in his side pocket be a pistol? Like an answer he went for it. I tightened. But it was only a rolled up notebook. He wet his finger. "*Llama?*" he asked. "*Nennen? Nom?*"

I could match that. "*Jag heter* Peterson," I said, with my Scandinavian (third generation) throat. He found me somewhere in the depths of the notebook, then led me through the carved front door into a large treed courtyard set up with tables. Rooms opened off on all four sides, with wall-sized blackboards. In the office the guard gestured me to a seat, mumbled something into an intercom and handed me a phone.

"Professor Peterson!" said a hearty voice. "Carlos Méndez here. Welcome to Guatemala. So glad you made it safe and sound." English.

British schoolboy accent.

I apologized for barging in on a Sunday, and he to me for the country's communication services. "There have been a few strikes, you see, work stoppages, mail and telephone off-kilter." I was enrolled, no question. Everything was "hunky-dory," he said. He had a tutor waiting for me, a very fine tutor, and a place for me to tuck myself in, "a nice middle-class home with a nice Ladino family." He would be around in just a moment to wrap things up and take me to my residence.

He came "around" through a side door into the office. A small trim man, Hispanic in appearance despite the British accent, pulling a large napkin from his neck and running his tongue over his teeth. I had interrupted his breakfast. This estate was apparently his home. He pulled out my file, checked my ID, passport and immunization shots. I paid for three weeks, with a fourth reserved as an option.

Then he bustled me into his car, a clean black late-model Lincoln, which he drove with great care through the narrow streets, his eyes just reaching over the steering wheel.

"Are you a family man, Professor Peterson?" he asked.

I answered with only a split-second delay. "One daughter, in college now. My wife's daughter, that is." Still my wife, at the moment, on paper.

"Good," said Méndez. "Because there are two teenagers in this home. They will also be your instructors, if you let them."

We stopped in front of a house similar to those I had just passed, where we were greeted effusively in Spanish by *Don* Francisco Ávila Espinoza, his wife, *Doña* Rosa, and Marco and Juanita, their kids, all four on the plump side. The smell of roasting meat filled the house. I hadn't smelled a Sunday roast since I lived with my mother in Rhode Island. It made me vaguely uneasy.

"You are in good hands, Professor Peterson," Méndez said, patting me on the arm, and left.

The Ávila parents turned me over to the kids, who gave me a tour of the first floor: a parlor ("*La sala, señor*") with overstuffed furniture and a television set considerably larger than my own, a formal dining room ("*El comedor*"), the table covered with a flowered plastic cloth, and a tiny inner courtyard ("*El patio*") grated overhead but otherwise open to the sky. Cement statues of saints, all with eroded noses, circled a tiled pool. A parrot perched on the head of one of them. "Mandatory parrot," said Marco, without a trace of accent. "What's his name?" I asked. "Polly," he said.

My room was on the second floor. The kids insisted on carrying my bags up the narrow staircase, and I gave in for fear of offending them. They led the way, Marco with the suitcase and Juanita with my pack over her shoulder. Halfway up, out of earshot of their parents, Marco stopped and set the suitcase on a tread. "*Caramba!*" he gasped, wiping his brow with his sleeve. "Excuse my French, *señor*." Juanita was staggering ahead, hamming exhaustion. In the room she collapsed into a chair, her hair over her face. "*Dios mio,*" she gasped. "You see what life ees like in dees contry?"

"*Que sera, sera,*" I said, applauding.

When they were gone, I unpacked, clothes to the hangers on the back of the door and into the one dresser drawer in four that actually slid open. The room was tiny, shared disproportionately with the Holy Family, dolls dressed and bewigged on top of my bureau, Mary holding the baby. I deposited the straw hat over their three heads. A single bed lined the opposite wall, an intrusive piece of furniture with head and footboard. There were two windows, one to the street and one opening into the courtyard. Down there the parrot whistled and called. I could have sworn she said "I'm Elvis Presley."

I was feeling a little better. Or so I thought until I encountered the last item in my suitcase. I had layered a gray sweater across the bottom. As I drew it out, the little room filled with a waft of Rebecca's perfume. The sweater had not been worn for a full year but had retained in its fibers—as it seemed to me now—its last hug, before the hugging ceased. She had come up behind me as I stood at a window. I lifted it with both hands and buried my face in it for a long time, breathing deeply, until the scent negated itself and vanished. Then I returned it to the bottom of the suitcase, which I shoved under the bed.

I considered calling her, finding a phone and just letting her know, a matter of civility, that I had arrived safely, had a room of my own and a pot to piss in. In fact, as the well-heeled owner and director of my classy *escuela* just told me, everything is "hunky-dory." But it was not the time to call, not yet.

FIVE

At eight o'clock the next morning I sat in the courtyard of the school, surrounded by tubs of flowers and the civilized murmur of two dozen voices in assorted languages. The voices belonged to the other students, some of whom were already at work with tutors at tables set up in the sheltered periphery.

Carlos Méndez buzzed about. He had just made a little speech of welcome to all newcomers, explaining the immersion system of language study and emphasizing his "one personal request," that Guatemalan politics and current affairs not be discussed here on "these neutral school grounds," either in class work or personal conversations. Neutral between what and what, I wondered, but didn't ask. No one did. He actually requested a show of hands in promise. I raised mine, not high, a palm up, as others did—everyone, I assumed.

I sat alone with a cup of coffee, waiting for my "very fine tutor" to arrive. The hiatus was welcome. The sun had not yet cut through the morning mist and a moist sweet warmth enveloped the courtyard. In a tree just a few yards from me, two tiny yellow birds flew from branch to branch. The guard who had admitted me yesterday was now gardening, turning the earth under rose bushes. A woman in Mayan clothing made fresh coffee in an urn.

So far I'd met two of the other students, a Peace Corps veteran with a long gray ponytail, back now to polish his Spanish for another project, and a nun from Belgium in a white habit, and one of the teachers, a young man from El Salvador I hoped would turn out to be my own tutor. But he was not. My tutor was delayed by a personal matter, Carlos Méndez told me, but she should be here any moment.

So I knew it would be a woman, and I was thrown off guard when a man entered the courtyard. Nothing else I saw in that first glance told me otherwise—height, shoulders, chinos, white long-sleeved shirt, a black baseball cap with the Yankees logo, and the stride of a lanky guy, a little lift at the top of each step. He was carrying a big multi-colored bag. I rose uncertainly as he approached me. "*Buenos días,*" I said.

"*Señor* Peterson?" The voice was light, clearly feminine.

I nodded.

"*Me llamo Caterina. Yo soy su tutora.*"

"Glad to meet you," I said. I was startled by her height. If she was shorter than me, it was not by much. I surveyed the ground we stood on, to see if it was even. It was, and she was wearing sneakers.

"Six two," she said, following my eyes. "Sorry to keep you waiting." She extended her hand. It was thin, muscular. I released the grip quickly. If it were not for her height I'd have classified her as Guatemalan, or of some Latin American origin, dark eyes, black hair—tucked up into that cap, I saw now.

"Shall I call you *señora?*" I asked. She was wearing a wedding band.

"Oh. No. *Solo* Caterina." Her lips worked, as if she was resisting a smile. "*Don* Teodoro?"

It took me a second. "No," I answered. "*Solo* Ted, please."

"Good. In that case, I'm Catherine."

"North American," I said, feeling a letdown.

"Catherine O'Brien, potato Irish from Milwaukee. I married a Guatemalan." She paused, the little smile returning. "Disappointed? You wanted a *chapín?*"

"A what?"

"A *nacional?*"

"No. Makes no difference."

"Actually, it's unusual for this school to pair male and female anyway, but it seems I was the only available tutor."

"I think I'm lucky to have one at all. Even a Yankee fan."

"Oh, the hat. Actually, I'm not a fan, of anything. Shall we get down to business?" She pulled a notebook out of her bag.

"You're the boss," I said.

She nodded, as if there were no question. "Let's talk English for a while. We'll be immersed in Spanish soon enough. Here's how things go. We'll be working all day, five days, six hours a day, with a two hour noon break, and assignments to do in the evening. We'll speak Spanish almost entirely and we expect you to speak Spanish in your residence, at meals, and as much as possible in all other outside contacts. Spanish TV, radio, newspapers. Does that seem manageable to you?"

"I'll limp along," I said. I was judging her age. She could be younger than she looked. Her face was narrow, bones prominent. A few threads of gray in her hair caught the light where they had escaped the cap. No make-up.

"We usually start with a diagnostic test," she said. "But first I'd like your own estimate of where you stand, with the language, that is."

"I don't know."

"Well, good, that's something to build on." She gave a short laugh. Her laugh, unlike the rest of her, was round and mellow, as if another person lived inside her for that purpose. "Your application doesn't mention language courses, high school or college."

"I took French and Latin. Not that I remember much."

"Not Spanish?"

"No."

"So, then, you've never studied Spanish and you have no proficiency."

I didn't answer, though she gave me several seconds, her eyes on my face. There was an intensity about her that put me on edge, a certain alertness that brought something to her eyes—not a spark, but a further darkening of the irises.

"What brings you here, to language school?" she asked then. "Do you mind telling me?"

Did everybody here ask personal questions? "Well, it's not a passion for the language, if that's what you mean," I said.

"Well, as a matter of fact," she answered dryly, "passion is the furthest thing from my mind. I just think it might help if I have some idea of what you're hoping to get here. You can study Spanish anywhere, of course."

"I have some family business to take care of," I told her.

"All right. Is there any aspect of the language you think might be important, in doing this business?"

There was no way to even contemplate an answer to that.

"Look," she said. "I don't care a rat's patooty about your personal business. All I want is to do the job right. If you can't help me, that's okay. We'll blunder along."

"I'm just a little surprised at the interrogation," I said.

"Interrogation?" She paused. I thought she was going to laugh, but she only produced the reluctant smile. She had nice teeth. In my present mood, they were a little disquieting. "I think this is not your first trip south of the U.S. border," she said.

So she knew. I answered. "I lived here once. As a kid."

Her eyes darkened. "Your accent gave you away."

"My accent?"

"How you said *buenos días,* how you pronounced Guatemala. Yankees work their heads off to get that just right. Why didn't you tell me?"

"I'd rather it didn't raise expectations."

"You can trust me. If you're relearning an early language, it makes a big difference. Were you born here?"

"Yes."

"Oh, then you are actually a Guatemalan?"

"I've never thought of it that way."

"You're a U.S. citizen then, by choice at age eighteen."

"Correct."

"You haven't been back?"

"No."

"And how old were you when you left? May I ask?"

"Seven."

"Seven years old." She stared at me as if I were still a child, a naughty one. "Let me get this straight," she said. "Unless you were hermetically sealed in some Yankee bubble-house for the first seven years of your life, you spoke Guatemalan Spanish—fluently, I expect."

"As fluently as a seven-year-old might, I suppose."

"Did you read it?"

"At an elementary level. A bit of grammar in school, as I recall." With my mother as first classroom teacher, a stickler for grammar, but I didn't say that. Ordered by the same mother to never speak the language again. I didn't say that either. "The truth is, I haven't used it in years and I can't account for what I'll remember," I said. "Isn't that what's important?"

"Have you reviewed it at all?"

"Not really."

"It should come back quickly." She rattled off something in Spanish.

"You've lost me," I told her.

"Old expression. 'Those raised by lions will always know how to growl.' I've been speaking Spanish for twenty years, and if I stopped, I'd get rusty pretty fast. But I'll never forget English. My guess is you'll find your Spanish right where you left it."

"In the lion's den? Then who is to say I won't be eaten?" I thought that was rather funny, but she asked, "Is that why you've never been back?" When I didn't answer, she said, "Well, why don't you ask the questions for a while. You must have some."

And you, Catherine O'Brien from Milwaukee, what brought you to this country? I didn't ask. I didn't really want to know. Three whole weeks in her presence, under her tutelage? "Exactly what are we going to do for six hours a day?" I asked.

"Does that seem like a long time to you?"

"Possibly an eternity."

"I'll try to surprise you."

The diagnostic test took an hour. It was largely a matter of translation, to and from, without a dictionary. I performed as I expected. My original use of the language had been almost completely oral, to say nothing of childlike, and I found little relationship between that and what I saw now on paper.

"How was it?" Catherine asked, as I handed it back to her in the office.

"Well, I'm sure I didn't ace it."

She looked it over. "No. You've got a ways to go, all right."

After lunch she said she wanted to test my ear. She would ask a series of questions and I would do my best to answer. This time I was free to use the dictionary.

I was exhausted in half an hour. It was like a grueling game of singles tennis, even though we were following the most basic dialogue. I dove into the dictionary, my glasses on and off. Hello, how are you? I'm fine, thank you. How do you like the weather? The weather is beautiful. What day is this? Monday. It's Monday, *lunes*. What is today's date?

Date. Ah, give me a minute. August 5th. *El cinco de agosto.* There. What year? Year. Uh. Two minutes, please. —One thousand, *mil.* Nine hundred, *novecientos.* Eighty seven, *ochenta y siete.* There, good for me. She didn't seem impressed. More questions. *"Hable más despacio, por favor,"* I said. Slow down, please. She had offered me that sentence herself, in case I needed it, but it did no good. At last I threw up my hands in frustration. Look, she said, if she spoke any more slowly she would distort the pronunciation. Guatemalan Spanish was slow, anyway, archaic even. That was the Spanish of my childhood, wasn't it, the language of my heart?

"Heart and mind" was the phrase she used, *corazon y mente.* She repeated those words, dragging them out teasingly. To my confusion, I found myself translating them to other sounds. *Tammee. Na-beel.* That's how they echoed phonetically, in Mam, out of the cave of years.

"What section of the country did you live in?" Catherine asked.

"Las montañas," I said.

"Mountains where?"

I shrugged, pretending ignorance. We were strolling in the courtyard by this time, as other teams were doing, the school turned peripatetic. It was almost four o'clock and the sky was beginning to cloud over. I turned to face her. "Listen!" I said, in English.

"Oye!" she corrected. *"Español, por favor. Oye."*

"Listen!" I said again, in English. "We can make this easier. All I'm after is a functional level, just whatever I need for my —." I discarded "purposes," then "search," then "research," and landed on "agenda." That sounded too stuffy, but Catherine said, "Good. That's what we'll do, just get you ready for your agenda."

Did she hit that word a little too hard? Never mind, the day was over. I couldn't have been more thankful. I ran back to my quarters through a gusty, purgative shower.

SIX

The word I'd given Rebecca was even more pretentious. Moratorium. I thought of it later that evening, sitting at my desk in the crowded room, sounds drifting up from below, rain in the patio, television in the parlor.

Rebecca knew very little about my early years here, but she had often asked me why I didn't "go back." My answer was always the same: I had no reason to do so.

"And now you're changing your mind?" she said. "It's a bit risky, isn't it?"

I thought she meant physical risk. "Supposedly it's safe now," I told her.

"Safe, good," she said. "But what's the real reason?"

"Call it a moratorium," I said, and then wished I hadn't. She wanted a definition. Erik Erikson's, for example, a temporary flight from other realities? "But he was referring to adolescents, of course," she said. Rebecca worked with disturbed teens, and her musings sometimes made me feel about age fifteen.

It didn't matter, I told her. I might not actually go, anyway.

"Not go? But why?" she asked.

"There's my mother, for one thing."

"I'll look in on her. You should go. I knew you would some day."

That almost killed it, right there. If I did go, I assured her, the trip would not change anything in our plans. When I got back, right after Labor Day, I would finish moving out. She gave a little shrug. No problem.

There wasn't much left to do. I had already leased a studio apartment in Somerville and had moved over most of my books and personal belongings. We had already taken ourselves through the crazy legal process, filed our "joint complaint" and a sworn affidavit, and all the right papers for this "irretrievable breakdown of marriage." I had contested nothing. There was nothing to fuss about anyway. There was no wrecked home, no devastated children, no name changes, no property distribution. The house was hers, a settlement in her previous marriage. Among "No-fault Agreed Uncontested Divorce Packages" in the whole Commonwealth of Massachusetts, this one had to be a model of simplicity and civility.

I had offered to move out immediately, but she wanted me to stay "until it was really over." That took longer than we'd thought. We continued to live parallel lives, a roommatey unmarriage, in what was, fortunately, a big Cambridge ark of a place. I moved my stuff to her daughter's old room and slept there. We agreed on the rules: No implied guilt, no emotional entrapment, no sexual overtures. We still got dinner together. I did the heavy vacuuming. We even went to the movies and concerts as a couple. I gave her my Eames chair knockoff as a parting gift. She put together an album for me, photographs of our lives together, including Amy. We both skirted the obvious irony to that, since I had never known Amy by much more than pictures anyway, seeing her only on vacations from college, when we tried not to invade each other's space. She had tagged me on first meeting as "seriously uncool," words whispered to Rebecca, who passed them on to me. It became a repeated joke between us.

That had been the nature of our life in that house, always on a kind of high road of civility and good humor, which may be why I didn't catch on earlier. We seldom argued. We "discussed," or Rebecca did. She liked to spread it all out, identify and tag each little part. Some might call this a gender thing. I didn't. I had encountered it in certain male colleagues, notably at faculty meetings. There are people who need to talk, who see their lives best as a journey of words. Rebecca, on the same odyssey, had always gone to a fellow therapist for "annual checkups," and when she began weekly visits I didn't question it. Her privilege. She was "getting to the bottom of things," she said. But when she urged me to do the same, I refused. I had no compulsion to dig around.

But then I lost my job, lopped off in a budget cut. In itself, it was not disastrous. Untenured adjunct English teachers were always in demand in Boston at community colleges and business schools, and in due time I was high on the waiting list of two. But in that process something else "came to light," something Rebecca was seeing now with more clarity, as she had not until lately—the "whole job thing." Not that there was anything wrong with my earning power, she explained, or anything dishonorable about the level of student I taught. It was because I just let things happen, never recognizing my true skills (I was a "good" teacher, she knew that, but I could be "great"), letting myself bounce from school to school, teaching low level lit survey courses, with no sense of—. She stopped, hands up, palms out. No sense of something. Something. She'd been trying to put her finger on it. She couldn't name it but it drove her nuts. That was when she began to cry. I didn't, but a half hour later I lost my entire insides to the bathroom.

There was more to the "job thing" than Rebecca mentioned at that point, because she had promised not to bring it up again. A few years earlier I had backed away from an excellent position when I was at the top of the short list. For all its attractions it opened too many doors of involvement, the necessity of publishing, the expectation of selling myself for tenure and promotion, of selling something to students, in fact. So I turned it down. Rebecca called that "a form of acrophobia," fear of ascending those stairs.

I was not an intellectual, I told her, and I was smart enough to know that. I was a dilettante, a piddler, my head filled with bits and pieces, no grand overview. All I wanted was to make available to whoever might be paying attention the chance of being captured by just one piece of literature by just one worthy author, which just might be a call to a lifetime of reading. That struck me as idealistic enough.

Soon after that she expressed her "wishes," putting it the same way she might have told me she'd rather go to Maine next summer instead of the Cape. It took me several minutes of silent processing to be sure I had gotten it straight, and then I said, "If that's the way you want it." She nodded, as if she'd known what to expect. "Quick release," she said. I said, "That's right," and walked away. I never raised it again. To question, explore, object, protest, defend, maintain, shout, plead, weep, throw, smash—that was a dark pathless forest that led to nowhere.

Now, at my desk in Antigua, Guatemala, on this rainy night, with sounds from the television in the parlor below drifting up to me—some old Western (*High Noon?* Yes. "Do not forsake me, O my darlin'," Tex Ritter's rugged baritone)—I knew what I could have told Rebecca. A moratorium is a place apart, where maybe you can get your head on straight. Thoreau, for instance, went to the woods alone because he "wished to live deliberately," to deal "only with the essential facts of life." I was looking for a few essential facts of my own.

No good. The truth was much more simple. I was here to re-access my Spanish, so I could translate my father's letter, which might or might not contain a single essential fact. But that was no good either, because it embodied its own contradiction. I could study Spanish anywhere, as Catherine noted. In fact, why not just find someone to translate the letter for me there in Boston?

At least I knew the answer to that. I had no idea what it might reveal, and whatever it was I wanted my eyes to see it first. Except, I was not at all sure even I ought to see it. In the two months since I'd found it, I hadn't opened it again, not so much because it was written in Spanish, a language I had been careful to forget, but because of the one fragment in English, the P.S. *Let's keep all this from Teddy. I'll explain it to him myself when he is old enough and ready.* That bit of accidental poetry recorded itself in my brain, in my father's voice.

When I ran home from school that January day, my first day of school in Rhode Island, my mother praised me, not for soiling my clothes, of course, but for refusing to talk. We don't answer questions, she said, even when the teacher asks. We don't talk about our lives "down there." We live "up here" now. This is where we belong. And we don't speak Spanish or Mam. English is our language.

She didn't mention my father, and hadn't since the three months before when she came for me alone, picking me up at the boarding school in Florida where they had enrolled me. Where's Dad? I asked her then. Not coming. Not coming? Why? Because he died, she said, he got very sick and he died, back there in the village. She was not being cruel. She held me tight as she said it and whispered something about being brave and accepting God's will. But *why?* I asked. I asked it over and over, pounding her with the same question—*why, why?*—like small hard fists. Never mind about God and all that stuff. *Why* did *my father—my father—* do that inconceivable thing, get sick and die back home in Guatemala, when I wasn't even *there?*

I'd known he was sick. For months, whenever he was with us in the village, I would wake up in the morning to sounds of vomiting coming from the outside toilet. It happened to everybody now and then. Our name for it was the "both-ends-bends." You got over it sooner or later or you lived with it. I had never heard of it causing a death, and it would certainly not cause his. He would never let that happen.

I convinced myself that my mother was wrong, that he was really alive and well. I sent him telepathic messages. Why not? If God could hear me, why couldn't he? When I faced a problem, I'd ask him to help me. "You're supposed to, you know," I'd say. "You're my father."

In time I dropped all that, confused by my mother's silence. Whenever I mentioned him she grew quiet, in body language as well as speech. If I persisted, she hushed me, her long forefinger tapping her closed lips. If I asked her what was wrong, she shook her head, with a look that ended conversation. There was something I couldn't be told.

I figured it was a grown-up thing, beyond my understanding. I began to fear the unspeakable. My father had done something bad. Was still doing it, back in Guatemala. Like Aladdin, I might find out that he was the leader of a crime ring, or worse. Maybe he'd killed somebody, accidentally of course, and he was hiding from the law. Hiding would be the only reason he didn't contact me, because if he was alive and didn't let me know it, that was worse than being dead.

I stopped asking my mother questions. The answer could be too scary. Anyway, in time life itself, new life, new friends and interests, took over and erased the questions, or wore them down to footnotes. I got used to it, being a person with a secret, one unknown to me and probably better unknown. But whenever the secret seemed jeopardized, as it did by Miss Heifferston's best intentions that day in first grade, it was as if an alarm went off in my brain. Bells rang, lights flashed, red alert, something like a fire alarm in school.

Downstairs in the Ávila parlor the television was silent. The bad guy was dead, and Gary Cooper and Grace Kelly had left on the train, on their way to another life, their love consummated somewhere far off the screen. I got up and paced the little room. Three steps to the bed, five to the bureau, four back to the desk. I didn't really want to know what my father meant in the letter—whatever he thought I was too young to be told. Maybe I still wasn't "old enough," not yet "ready Teddy." Maybe I'd never be. Whatever my father intended to explain, I had become who I was by not knowing it for thirty-three years. Who would I become if I knew?

So what *did* I know, what facts, essential, probable, beyond reasonable doubt? My father was dead. He had died here in this country and was presumably buried here. Then why not find his grave? What could be more concrete and specific, more grown up, if you looked at it that way? Go find it, if it was findable.

Yes, but. I heard it in my head as "*Yah*but," my pronunciation as a kid, like a word from yet another language. *Yes...but,* my parents would say, correcting patiently. Yes, but, if I go looking for his grave what I might find out is that there is no grave. Because that possibility is always there, always returning with the old stab of longing. That's what I really wanted. Of course. To find him alive. Time to say it, in so many words. Say it out loud: *Find him alive.* How old would he be? Mid-sixties. Not old. I pictured him as tall as ever, straight, not stooped, blond hair now gray. *Find him.* How hard would it be?

On the other hand, the very idea made me distinctly uncomfortable—the search for the father, that Freudian cliché. And there was always the other terrible possibility, as well, that he might not want to be found, and I might even endanger him by looking.

So why was I here? I was left with only one essential fact, one beyond any doubt. I said that out loud, too. I *am* here. I had no reason to be, nothing I could defend, but I was *here*, and only one "agenda" was valid right now, to drown myself in Spanish for these next three weeks and do virtually nothing else. I was committed to that, signed in and paid for. It set up its own contract and promised its own brand of sanity.

To start the program immediately (before I could waffle), I studied vocabulary until exactly one A.M., then set the alarm and konked out to the sound of the rain, splashing down on the sorrowful, noseless saints around the patio pool.

SEVEN

I woke at dawn to a splatter of gunfire. That's what I thought, until I remembered (how could I have forgotten?) that birthdays often began with firecrackers, always at break of day, and followed, as they were now, with the frantic barking of half-a-dozen dogs and the crowing of roosters, near and distant. That agitated the parrot, who called "*Hola! Hola!*"

I pulled on clothes and shoes and headed for the central plaza, running in half-light on the cobblestones, fog swirling around my feet and up over the red-tiled roofs. Ancient architecture floated beside me, an amazing lot of it in partial ruins, intricate heaps of rubble toppled in the long series of earthquakes. The plaza was already astir, but quiet, enough to hear the splash of the fountain in the park—water streaming from the breasts of maiden statues—and the swish of somebody's broom outside a store.

The shell of the old cathedral occupied one side of the square. At right angles to that, yellow light warmed the windows of the police station, housed under two-story colonial arches. Three uniformed men stood in the doorway smoking, assault rifles slung over their shoulders. A little spurt of adrenaline. No threat to me, or I to them, but a rifle is a rifle.

At one side of the park a group of Mayan women were already tying their backstrap looms to the trees and spreading their weavings on the grass, a twenty-foot long carpet of color. Several of them carried babies on their backs, secured within a wide strip of fabric. Not far away two long-haired teenagers curled asleep on benches, their packs under their heads, fair-skinned gringos, I noted, as were the half-dozen other runners who approached me out of the mist, like Caucasian ghosts. They panted on by me without a greeting, as if on the last lap of some super-marathon from Stockholm or Chicago. I was panting too, at close to 4,000 feet above sea level.

I stopped to breathe and stare for a moment into the Moorish court-yard of San Carlos University. The name echoed distantly in my head and then up front, with a little ping. My father had worked at San Carlos, at the campus in Guatemala City. I asked him once what he did there. "Talk to the 'stugents,'" he'd said, teasing me with one of my own pronunciations. Another odd memory. Apparently there was more than one kind of forgetting. There were the details that hoped to be found, like a child playing hide and seek, popping out from behind a chair, and there were the ones that hid themselves in earnest.

The run finished, I did a set of push-ups in my room, took a shower and went to breakfast. Alone in the dining room, I ate freshly made tortillas, brought and served by a black-eyed Mayan girl—really a girl, no more than twelve, I thought. A large white apron covered her woven skirt, her long hair tucked under a silly looking maid's cap. I greeted her, "*Buenos días*," but she refused to answer or meet my eyes. Her hand shook as she poured my coffee. Scared witless of the gringo. Her clothes smelled strongly of woodsmoke, and of something else, burnt vegeta-tion. A quick vision presented itself, smouldering cornstalks, carried about the house to get rid of lice and lizards. That triggered another smell, things just in from the rain, wet clothes and hair, wet chickens, wet dogs, all gathered around an open fire in the middle of a room.

Doña Rosa, entering the kitchen in a flowered housecoat, gave the maid instructions in Spanish, her arm around her, patiently repeat-ing, then apologized to me in a whisper, wringing her hands. "*No me comprenda.*"

"What's her name?" I asked.

She shrugged. "No name. Call Maria."

"Where does she live?"

A wide sweep of the arm. I understood that more than *Doña* Rosa knew. The child walked here from a distance, bringing tortillas made before dawn.

At school Catherine and I worked through the morning hours at a table in the courtyard, where the temperature warmed quickly to a sweet seventy degrees, and would, I soon learned, day after day. At noon I joined the Ávila family around the dining room table, Juanita in her green school uniform and Marco (no longer in school for whatever reason) and his father, both in dark business suits, on break from the family *tienda*, one of the downtown stores. While they chattered in Spanish, I struggled to catch a phrase here and there, with my dictionary and glasses beside me on the table.

Back to school then, for an exhausting afternoon of forced dialogue with Catherine, the relentless one. I ended the day at a bar, sipping a lukewarm Gallo while I watched television with the regulars and listened to their sharp consonants and remarkable rolls of the tongue. A soccer game was in progress between the *Rojos* and the *Cremas* and the room was full of cheers and curses. I was not a soccer fan, but I strained to catch the substance within the curses: *Puta! Que imbécil fuiste! Ay, Dios!*

On the way home I bought an English language newspaper, the International Edition of the *Miami Herald*, a couple of days old on the stands. Mostly I was after the baseball scores, with the late season gloom of a Red Sox fan. The Sox, at the end of another losing season, were fourteen and a half games behind the Yankees, fifth place in the AL East. I barely glanced at other news. The front pages were filled with the Iran-Contra hearings, Oliver North pictured repeatedly with his hand raised, swearing in, swearing in.

I studied all evening in my room, wired to my tapes, John Coltrane and Oscar Peterson. Later *Doña* Rosa rustled up the stairs in her slippers with a cup of warm milk and a sugar cookie as big as a saucer. To fatten me up, she said. I was too *flaco*. Besides, she scolded, I would make myself sick if I worked so late. I needed to sleep. "Is why you pipple always sick in Guate, *Señor* Peterson. No slip! Put out light and go slip, like good *niño*." She laughed at herself, allowing me to laugh, too.

In all that, I managed to find a predictable framework for those three weeks. But the mountains were not through with me yet, and they were full of surprises.

EIGHT

Meanwhile, Rebecca seldom left my thoughts entirely. In dreams I often found myself a passenger in her car, my knees pressed against the dashboard, seat stuck in the forward position, as it was in actuality. In these dreams, she was always driving me to Logan Airport, where she was dropping me off, as she did—in actuality—because she was going "right by," on her way to a conference.

I finally called her, only to get my own voice on our answering machine at home. She had not yet changed it. "Please leave us a message," I heard myself say. So I did. "Ted, tell Rebecca everything is fine here. Ask her how she is. How is his Mom?" I left the number and said goodbye to myself. She called back when I was out. Juanita wrote down her message. "All fine here, too. No news. Your mother the same, holding her own." Juanita thought she'd missed a word, whatever it was my mother was holding. It was all right, I told her, nobody knew.

On Saturday, at the end of the first week, I took my run later in the morning while my clothes washed at the local *lavendería*. *Doña* Rosa had been urging me to visit the chapel next to the partially restored Church of San Francisco where a 17th century healer, Hermano Pedro de Betencourt, lay in state. I lingered there maybe five minutes, staring at the mesmerizing display of the wizened corpse in a wall niche surrounded by candles, dead flowers, crutches, and scores of photos of those who claimed to be healed. A woman standing nearby muttered a chatty prayer and crossed herself repeatedly. After leaving the dim recesses my eyes took a while to adjust to the sunlight, and maybe that was part of the problem, because when I got back to the central plaza I saw her.

The plaza was alive with traffic—motor bikes, street hawkers, tourists. She was twenty feet ahead of me, looking in the window of a shop with a sign that read *High Class Tipica.* It was Rebecca for sure. I recognized her from the back as she walked away from me. Same height (just under my chin up close), same solid hips ("broad across the beam" as she'd say), same close-cut auburn hair, and her walk, like a thirteen-year-old boy, I used to tell her, the left foot a little pigeon-toed, arms swinging slightly wide of the body. She was wearing jeans and a T-shirt, as she would be. Sunglasses dangled from her fingertips.

Never mind the odds. I knew it really could be Rebecca, that she could and would fly here if she was so inclined, rather than phoning or writing, to tell me that she had changed her mind. I started after her, shouting her name. Half-a-dozen people turned their heads, and so did she, with a face that was not her own. I spun around and ran in the opposite direction as if I were chased, then studied vocabulary back at the house, finding sanity in words that were nothing but words: Rain: *lluvia.* Rainfall: *cantidad de lluvia.* The language, *imbécil,* just get the language.

But things were not going very well in the language department, either. I heard another student say that success in language study depended on hitting it off with your teacher. Catherine and I were not hitting it off. On the contrary, it's a wonder we didn't come to a blow-up sooner than we did.

I don't know what she saw when she looked at me during those six hours together day after day, but her own appearance never changed—hair skinned back so tight under the visored cap I thought it must hurt, always the chinos and white shirt. Was it always a white shirt? I won't swear to that now. But my sense of her was unchanging. Against the background of astonishing color everywhere around us, and in contrast to the woven tote bag she carried every day, she seemed superimposed in monochrome. She seldom smiled, unless to give me that needling half-way thing. I started a collection of adjectives to pin her down—dour, saturnine, churlish, taciturn. Atribilious. I liked that one.

Not that I was earning medals for charm myself. Often I felt like walking away. Once I did. I got up and left the premises and stayed away long enough to convey a message, which I was pretty sure she got. But otherwise I just fell back on the rules I used in teaching: level voice, never frown, never interrupt. If she disliked me, it was not going to be because I was a mannerless chump. I kept a discreet distance as we sat together at the table. I had no interest in the intrigue of accidental touching. If our legs met, as they were apt to, both of us long-legged, the arousal factor registered below zero.

Mornings were devoted to grammar. In this she was merciless, as she should be, drill, drill, slow and repetitious on her part, clumsy and hesitant on mine. I felt like Heinlein's Martian-man, looking up the code. After the lesson, Catherine would ask me to read something aloud to her in Spanish and translate it to English. These readings were always juvenile, comics with data about the Maya (over fifty percent of the population, identified by twenty-two different languages), and a child's version of the *Popul Vuh*, the K'iché myth of the world's creation. I knew what she was doing, groping for the point where I had left off as a kid. It irked me, but I had no reasonable objection. There's something about learning a language, anyway, that reduces you to babbling childhood.

Afternoons were harder. This is when we were supposed to "dialogue informally," for two whole hours, exhausting as a prospect. But even more tiresome was finding anything to talk *about*, for more than a few minutes, that is. "Anything" is hyperbole, of course, but day after day we faltered and came to an impasse. It was not a minor glitch.

At the beginning, Catherine offered me the choice. What did I want to talk about? I considered sports or music, but quickly backed off those, the language of each too specialized to be practical right now. The same was true of world affairs. I thought I'd get help from news reports, about East Germany or South Africa, say, but that turned out to be more than my low-level skills could take on with savvy.

What about the history of Central America, Catherine asked me one afternoon. What did I know? I assumed she meant short of the big taboo, current politics. Not that I knew anything much about that, or about the history either. I fell back on the old high school ruse, when you're stuck make the teacher laugh. I gave a sniff. "You mean like this is where you get your bananas and stuff?"

"*Divertidísimo,*" she muttered. Not funny, Bozo.

"Okay, here's something I really do know," I said. "This will knock your socks off." I worked it out in Spanish, first in writing, while she waited, then read it aloud. "In 1972, the great Puerto Rican ball player, Roberto Clemente, was killed in the crash of a plane headed for Nicaragua with aid for earthquake victims. I bet even you didn't know that."

"*Puta!*"

"Wowee, that's a dirty word, right?"

I was about to be sent to my room, I could tell. All right, I said, I might be able to describe the Monroe Doctrine, though it was really just a verbal clot from a high school class. Oh, but, I added, Congress abolished it not long ago, right? And hadn't President Reagan resurrected it recently? Wasn't there once something called the Atlantic Charter? Or was that the Alliance for Progress? "And then you've got your Cuba and your Bay of Pigs, right?" She smiled in spite of herself, just a little, so I added the Battle of 1066 and the French Revolution.

All that was in English. Back to Spanish, she said. Let's talk about you. What about my work? What did I teach? What could I say but "Lit Survey," in a full sentence, of course, and list some classics, all of which translated badly. Well, then, how about the subject of my dissertation? I didn't do a dissertation, I told her.

"What? No PhD?" Teasing half-smile. "How come?"

"*Acrofobia academica*," I said. Sarcasm works poorly when you have to put on your glasses and look up the words. What did that mean, she wanted to know. *Nada*, I said.

We had already been through the "Who are you?" exercises in vocabulary. Who are you? *Yo soy el hombre. Americano.* Tourist, teacher, student, husband, son. And the nots. I am not a brother. Not a father, a doctor, a bus driver. I got tired of it and tried to switch the focus. Who are *you?* I am the teacher, not the student, was all she would say.

Once, during a water break, I asked people what they talked about with their tutors. Families, jobs, they said, life in general. Definitely not politics. Most of them joked about the "*mordaza Méndez*"—the Méndez gag, as it got quickly labeled.

The pony-tailed guy, Hank Stenning, the Peace Corps veteran, was adamant. Nobody was going to curb his speech. He'd made that clear to his own tutor.

I liked Stenning. He spoke Spanish far in advance of mine and so I mostly listened, catching what I could. One day he switched to English and I realized he had a speech defect, an articulation disorder, to be proper. It was somewhat charming, just enough trouble with the formation of the phonetic of "L" to require your attention. Did I know, he asked, that I'd been screened for "powiticaw extremism?"

Screened? Yes, prospective students were put through a background check, he claimed. Méndez had friends in the States who did that for him. Stenning said he wasn't sure how he was admitted to the school himself, since his views were no secret. He could understand the caution. The country was a beehive of spywork. But "neutrawity" was naive, a sure vote for the status quo, especially during a war.

"War? What war?" I asked.

"This one."

I tried to report that conversation to Catherine, though I knew it was pushing the envelope. She shut it off, of course, but it led to an idea that worked. Why didn't I keep a log, I suggested, a record of various observations here in Antigua and at the Ávila household? In the evenings I could write some of those out in Spanish and give them to her orally the next afternoon. She agreed, as long as I kept to the rules.

I liked the idea, myself. I had often given journal keeping as a student assignment. I began with the mountains, the surrounding volcanoes, since they were hardly avoidable. In a bookstore I picked up an account of their history. Antigua was nested among three. Of those, Volcán de Agua was the largest, a looming pyramidal presence dominating the city. The tip was long gone, the huge mouth ragged, and therein lay the story. On the night of September 10, 1541, after three days of torrential rain, an earthquake hurled collected water out of the mountain's cone, taking with it a massive portion of the top. The city on the slope below, the new colonial capital, was buried under tons of mud. I wrote it up in my own words (well, a little unavoidable plagiarism) and received Catherine's outright praise.

That led to a discussion of other earthquakes in the country, catastrophic ones, that is, eighteen on record since 1565, three of them in this century. But when we came to the one in 1976 in which over 20,000 people died, she refused to talk about it because the international relief efforts were "highly political." I added a silent "anomalistic" to her list of adjectives and almost walked away again.

Still, the journal strategy was working. My stipulation to students was to log only observations of life outside themselves. The point was to steer them away from the inevitable tendency to moon about their inner lives, which usually led to very bad writing. I liked it now for the same discipline. I found comfort in gathering a list of details—a line of little girls in blue uniforms crossing the street with a nun at each end, a man selling newspapers, piled three feet high on his head. I counted things: the arches on each floor of the Palace of the Captains General (twenty-seven) and the number of women I saw with at least one gold-capped tooth (forty-three).

Then the process itself pulled a couple of tricks. I was walking back from the school to my digs at the end of the day. The sun was still out, rain clouds delayed. The white sidewalk ahead, at right angles to the white building facades, appeared to be part of the architecture, a long geometric shape with sharp shadows and shafts of light. I walked through it, becoming part of it, then in my room described it, put it in an envelope and mailed it to Rebecca. She'd know what it was, another answer to a question she had repeatedly set before me, in her ongoing analysis of what made me tick. What really thrills you? That was how it went. What was I passionate about? Usually I just grunted, but one day I shot back an answer.

"Duke Ellington's *Mood Indigo*. The Adagietto Movement of Mahler's Fifth. *Moby Dick*. Any of the Impressionists. All of Dostoevsky. Emily Dickinson. Pinot Grigio. *The Great Gatsby*. Ted Williams. An inside-the-park home run. Simon and Garfunkel. Bach. *Starry Night*. Did I say Emily D? *Doonesbury*. The quartet from *Rigoletto*. *King Lear*. *The Seventh Veil*. Bob Dylan. Dylan Thomas. *Sergeant Pepper*. The big bang theory. Bucky Fuller. *Lucky Jim*. Hucky Finn. Marshall McLuhan. *Howl!* Franck's D-Minor. Sibelius. The printing press. Arts and Crafts. Gilbert and Sullivan. Fats Waller. Isaac Asimov. The Parthenon. *The Iliad*. Barbra! Aretha! Did I mention John Coltrane? John Cage? Well, maybe not John Cage. John Lennon? Oscar Peterson? Koko Taylor? Lena Horne? *Hammurabi's Code?* How about the theme from *A Love Story*, as sung by Andy Williams?" I took a breath and bellowed: "She fills my *heart!*"

Rebecca laughed, to her credit. I reminded her of Binx in *The Mov-*

iegoer, she said, "Passion by proxy." I told her I was pleased to be associated with any Walker Percy character, especially Binx, who was prone to hearing a great "rumble" in his "descending bowel."

The truth was I could never predict what would "really thrill" me. I actually got a lump in my throat watching the TV retirement ceremony for John Havlicek during half-time at a basketball game at Boston Garden. And once when I was standing in the stadium at Fenway Park before a game began, impatiently waiting out "The Star Spangled Banner," I was knocked for a loop by the words "still there." Not that the flag was still there, not the ramparts, not anything in the song itself, God knows, but the fact that *something* was "still there."

What was happening now was different, but not totally unfamiliar. Thoreau, one moonlit night, fishing from a boat with a sixty-foot line, felt a faint "vibration," a message from another reality far below the water's surface. And Henry James said something once about guessing the unseen from the seen. Though that seemed fatuous to me, I often told students to listen for the faint tap-tap-tap when they read fiction, like a knock on the door in the night, gentle at first, then louder and louder.

I didn't tell them to listen for that in their own experience. But now, for instance, I would be in a *tienda,* say, buying toothpaste from a very cordial clerk—cordial the way almost everyone was, with a little air of old ceremony—and suddenly *tap-tap-tap,* I would know for a just a second that I was living in two worlds, and the one that was visible to me was not the realest reality.

I don't mean by that the seamier aspect of the city. That was here too, like the scorpion that frequented the school bathroom, or the beggars who appeared out of nowhere. Or thieves. Once I watched a pickpocket apply his remarkable skill in plain sight and walk away into traffic, all before I caught on. Or the curious amount of public drunkenness. I learned to be careful to skirt fresh puddles of vomit on my morning runs.

One morning I came upon a young man lying on the sidewalk, head in the gutter, a woman sitting quietly next to him, a baby on her back. Had they been there all night? The guy looked unconscious, but he was breathing, just falling-down drunk. I tried to ask the woman if I could help, move him to safety, at least. But she turned away from me before I could speak, while the baby sucked placidly on the end of her braid.

The new reality I sensed was far less obvious than all that. Of course, I considered Stenning's claim that a war was in progress, right now, all around me. But if so, there was no convincing sign of it. The television news shows I caught in the bars and the Ávila parlor never mentioned war, and the omnipresent camouflage fatigues, the clink of metal and squeak of leather as soldiers passed you on the street, seemed more decorative than anything else.

I inquired. I raised the subject with a couple of fellow drinkers at a bar. "Tell me what's happening here. Is the country at war?"

These were guys I had met here before, always easily sociable, enduring my awkward Spanish. Neither of them answered. One gave me a look that suggested I was nuts, and the other suddenly saw someone he knew across the room, picked up his beer and left.

Then one morning I saw a photo tacked on a tree in the park, a young woman, smiling, a graduation picture on a sheet of cardboard, edges curled by rain, and under it the words *¿DÓNDE ESTÁ?* Where is she? There were more, on another tree and another. Six or more of them, men and women, most of them young, some with that eerie question *¿DÓNDE ESTÁ?* and others with *PRESENTE,* an odd Q and A: Where is she? Where is he? They are *here.*

That day at lunch—it must have been Thursday of the second week—I asked Marco if he ever heard news of the war. I asked it casually, and I didn't ask his father, who sat across from me. That would have lent too much meaning to the question. Marco stopped eating and looked at me in genuine perplexity. "What war do you mean? Cold War?"

"No, here. In this country."

"There is no war here."

"No fighting anywhere?"

"Fighting. Ahhh," he said. "You mean *los guerrilleros?* No, no. They are far away in the hills." He slipped into his goofy accent. "Communeests, *señor.* They are heestory now."

At this point his father jumped in. "*Aquí no tuvo tanta fuerza la violencia,*" he told me, emphatically. "*Verdad?*"

"You hear the man?" said Marco. "He say he doan know nothing about no war."

"But he said *la violencia*. What does that mean?"

"In the mountains. The mountains. It's over. Kaput!"

I said thanks, and went back to eating, but Marco was too far into his act to let it go. He leaned toward me with conspiracy. "Never mine, my fran. You wan a war, we fine one for you. Give me a day, maybe two. A full week at most."

Don Francisco hushed him. "*No hay problema, señor,*" he assured me. He went into a little speech that Marco translated, switching instantly to his father's earnest manner, deepening his voice. "*La guerrilla* has now been defeated, thank God. True, they are still causing trouble in the mountains. Are you planning to travel about the country?" His hands drove a car.

"Maybe," I said.

"Ahh. *Pues, ten cuidado,*" said *Don* Francisco. Be careful. I looked at Marco. He sliced his throat. "*Delincuentes,*" he whispered.

"You see, Mr. Peterson," *Don* Francisco continued, suddenly in English, "many Indian given gun, by *los guerrilleros*, you see, and they use, you know, to rob and kill." He stood to go, then paused behind his chair. "You must not think bad our country. We are democracy now. Our president elected civilian, first civilian fifteen years. *Pero,* your own country, Mr. Peterson, that is also famous for big crime, *verdad?*"

"Bingo," I said.

He looked perplexed but carried on. "Crime, okay, but war, finished, thanks to General Ríos Montt. You know General Ríos Montt former president? He fix things in big hurry, that man. Five years ago. Bring law and order."

It was the most he had ever said to me directly and there was no stopping him now, standing there behind his chair, with me as his only attentive audience. Marco yawned. Juanita asked to be excused, granted by her mother, who picked up our plates and retreated to the kitchen herself. *Don* Francisco sent Marco to get something. It turned out to be a poster, a big blue hand on a white background, two fingers and the thumb held up in a pledge. *I don't steal, I don't lie, I don't abuse,* the lettering said, as I translated it. These posters, *Don* Francisco said, had been distributed all over the country during General Ríos Montt's regime, every store, every business.

He wound up finally with another name, Elizondo, the "next president of the country."

The man's name was faintly familiar and it took a few seconds to realize why. I had heard him speak the previous Sunday. Marco had awakened me early that morning, sent up by his mother with an invitation to join them at mass at the cathedral. I declined groggily, pulling the pillow over my head.

"Okay," said Marco. "But what shall I tell her royal highness?"

"Tell her I'm an unreconstructed post-modern skeptic," I muttered. He said he hadn't heard of a church like that around here.

When he left, I got up anyway, disgruntled and thoroughly awake, and dialed the radio in search of a little music. I got a woman vocalist with a wonderful hot momma style, singing what sounded like a Latinized Negro spiritual. She was followed instantly by this guy Elizondo, who was introduced just as Zondo. I understood little of what he said, and wasn't interested. He was followed by another speaker, a man who seemed to be offering a corrective to the first guy. What got my attention was the one part of his name I caught, López. Coincidentally, my best friend as a kid back in the village was named Luis López, a Mayan boy, nine years old when I saw him last. López was a common name, and I couldn't translate what he was saying, anyway. He had a strong accent. I preferred the torchy singer, but she didn't return.

I put all that down in journal notes and the next afternoon started to convey it to Catherine. She stopped me as soon as she heard the word *guerra*, as I thought she would. "You know we can't talk about the war."

"*The* war. So there is one."

"Change the topic. *Ahora, ya.*"

I obliged, with the subject next on my canary pad, the "*coincidencia*" of bumping into the man named Elizondo twice within a few hours.

"Zondo, huh? *Pues.*" She looked amused. "That was hardly a coincidence. The man is *ubicuo.*"

Ubiquitous? I hadn't noticed. She said we couldn't talk about him either, because that was politics, too.

Fine with me, I said. I'd much rather talk about the difference between Corona and Gallo.

At one point early in the third week, as I was blundering along with a reading, I became aware of a silence across the table. I looked up at Catherine from my notebook, thinking for an instant that she had fallen asleep. She was awake all right, but had drifted off to some other location. "Teacher, teacher," I said, thrusting my hand in the air. She snapped back and apologized, but it happened again, several times. I finally asked her if something was wrong. It was the first hint I had gotten yet, or the first I took, that something *could* be wrong.

She was just tired, she said. She had spent all weekend trying to do an errand in the capital, but had been blocked by detours for a city-wide festival. "A wretched saint's day," she said. "The assumption of our lady into heaven." She winced.

"Big deal," I said. "Today happens to be the anniversary of Elvis Presley's death."

I'm happy to say that changed her mood. She laughed, that fascinating sound from somewhere inside. Then I told her he died on a toilet. It was my turn to wince. She laughed again. In fact, this time she guffawed, then covered her mouth. "Oh, poor Elvis," she whispered.

We went right back to work, but part of my brain was focused on this new piece of her. Maybe, I fancied, like the two Antiguas, there were two Catherines. But how would I know? You'd think you couldn't help get to know someone you spent six hours a day with, five days a week. But I didn't know her, and she didn't know me.

I had enough to occupy my attention. With only a week to go before classes ended, I was facing a jumble of substantives and cognates, and every kind of verb, regular and irregular, present indicative, subjunctive, *pretérito, imperfecto*. Then there was that whole matter of "you" that I couldn't keep straight, when to use *usted*, "you" with a formal distance, and *vos* and *tú*, "you" with shades of familiarity. To use any of them inappropriately could be received as an insult, Catherine insisted. The default position in Guatemala or any Spanish speaking country, was *usted*. Women were careful to use it with men. I'd noticed that Catherine always used *usted* in talking to me. *Tú* was the sticky one, in its various forms, *tú, te, ti*. But actually, *vos* could be even more informal and chummy than *"tú."* Children used it with each other (yes,

I remembered), and guys on athletic teams. To make matters worse, it was also a throwaway word, like "you know," or "yeah, man."

"Just stay clear of *tú*," said Catherine. "Too familiar. Easily misread."

That was a microcosm of a larger subtext, the use of a language that made you a member. It was not a technique you could learn in three weeks, I knew now, or one you could return to quickly after more than thirty years of neglect, in spite of Catherine's assurances. With time and room for error, I could piece together almost anything I wanted to say, and patient speakers could usually make themselves clear to me, but it was all still mechanical and clumsy.

In the parts of the *Popul Vuh* I'd been reading—the sacred stories of the K'iché culture—the gods, the great crafters, sought repeatedly to create beings who could hear and speak, who would talk to the gods and understand who they were. The gods had experimented first with creatures made from clay and then from wood, a gross mistake in each case, for though the carvings managed to reproduce themselves in some way that strained credulity, their hearts were empty. Next the gods tried monkeys. That was disappointing, as well, and at long last they created humans from corn. That worked. Corn connected. But I was not corn.

NINE

On Wednesday afternoon of that third week, Catherine suggested we stroll in the back garden during our *plática*, our informal chit-chat. We were alone, walking slowly side by side on the paths. So far, I'd had only a glimpse of the back garden. It was charming, with beds of flowers and paths laid out among evergreens and palmettos, an overgrown Eden. Behind a fence made of a prickly woven vine I could see green blades of corn, a small *milpa* in the middle of the city. From this point we could look down over the town, and beyond that to Volcán de Agua in its massive rise, gray green this time of day.

"*Dígame lo que está pensando,*" said Catherine, inviting me to present a topic for discussion. I stalled. I was reluctant to talk about the Ávilas again, but my head was full of what had transpired at another noon meal. This time it was today's, just a while ago, and I hadn't had a chance to write it out. I decided to wing it. Here is what happened and how I tried to tell it to Catherine.

In the absence of *Doña* Rosa, who was at a birthday luncheon, Juanita was left in charge of serving the food during her noon break from school. *Don* Francisco had already eaten and gone back to his store, so only Marco was at the table. He was passing me a plate of cold cuts, asking which I preferred, "cat or dog," when Juanita flounced in from the kitchen, muttering, her ponytail bobbing.

"Is something wrong?" I asked.

"*Ella es imposible!*" she said, pointing through the door, where I could see the maid cutting up a melon with a big knife. Her facility with the knife was awesome, but Juanita whirled back into the kitchen, saying, "No, no, no! *Que te dije?* Stop!"

She began scolding the girl so blatantly I wondered if I should intervene. Then it occurred to me it might be more histrionics for the sake of the gringo, with the servant in on the joke. But the acting was too good. Finally, Juanita came back to the table and plopped into a chair. "I don't know is she stupid or *maliciosa!*"

"What on earth did she do wrong?" I asked.

"I keep telling her to wash the fruit first, you know, with the kill germs stuff, before she cuts it up. She never remembers. She's going to make us all sick."

"Sick? *Ay, ay, ay,*" gasped Marco, grabbing himself by the throat.

"Aren't you being too rough on her?" I asked Juanita.

She screwed up her face. "What? Ruff? —Oh. No, no. I must make her listen. It is my job. My mother and I, it is something we do," she said, twisting a corner of the tablecloth. "My mother is very, you know, modern. We train *indio* girls as *muchacha...de servicio. Criadas.* Maids, you know? It is their only chance to—." She searched for a word. "You know, to get out of her village. Otherwise she will just start having babies."

I was pretty sure this was not how her mother would have put it. "But must she be a maid?" I asked. "Can't she learn another trade?"

"She has no education," she said, in a loud whisper. "She doesn't even speak Spanish."

"Why don't you teach her?"

"We are trying. But she is *tonta.* The dumbest one yet. And she smells."

Whoa there! I considered saying that I liked the way she smelled—smoke, tortillas, dogs. I glanced out to the kitchen, wondering still if the girl was a party to a set-up. I couldn't see her face. Only yesterday I'd heard Juanita chatting with her, both of them laughing. "Are you pulling my leg?" I asked, in English.

"What? No, no!" She was flustered. "What are you thinking? This is not—this is serious!"

"Serious? Oh, no, no," moaned Marco, falling to the floor in a spasm.

"And she gets a look in her eye when I talk to her," Juanita said. "Like she is putting a spell on me. She is not real Catholic, you know."

"Heavens to Betsy!"

"*No dobla la rodilla.*"

"*Qué?*"

She genuflected with a little bob. "The other *indigenas* made, you know, *la señal de la cruz*. This one, she never crosses herself. She walks right by our *crucifijos* without even looking. She wears something around her neck, do you see that? To protect from witchcraft. They believe it, you know. *Brujería, mal de ojo.* Evil eye."

At that, Marco escalated his poisoned act to dramatic heights, gargling in his throat as he went into a convulsion. I glanced out to the kitchen again, but all I could see was the girl's solid back in its *huipil* as she stood at the stove. For a second I was taken visually by the dazzle of colors in that woven blouse. I saw nothing on her neck except a zigzag of lightning around the opening.

"My guess is she's a little afraid of you," I said to Juanita.

"That's *loco*. We should be afraid of her." She looked at her watch. "I must go. Do not eat the melon." She gave Marco's limp body a little kick as she left the room.

That was it. When I was done, Catherine said nothing. We just walked, following the paths in the garden.

"What are we waiting for?" I asked.

"*Su reacción.*"

My reaction? I was feeling deeply the need for her reaction, a little teacherly encouragement, maybe even praise, but I answered. "It was too literal, I think. I need more idioms."

"I mean your reaction to what took place," she said. "How did you feel?"

I looked up the word "bemused" and put it into a sentence. *Aturdido*. To that, she gave a barely audible snort. I cleared my throat. "The student would like the evaluation of the teacher."

She stopped in the path. "Wait a second. You tell that story and all you're thinking about is how well you told it?"

"Of course not. But that's sort of what I'm here for, right?"

"And you really don't have anything more to say?"

Why should that surprise me? She wanted me to talk. "This is a language exercise, isn't it?" I said.

"Actually, no," she answered. "At the moment I can't think of anything less important than how you speak Spanish."

She said that in English. Until now I had been struggling—heroically,

I thought—with Spanish. I took the liberty and abandoned it. "I bet there's a message for me in there," I said. I tried to read her face, but she was staring at the ground. "Why don't you actually tell me what's on your mind?" I asked.

"All right." She looked up. "Juanita Ávila Espinosa is becoming a dangerous person."

"Ooh. That seems like an overstatement."

"On the contrary, it's an understatement."

"You're talking about a kid. She acted very badly, but she's just a kid, with her own problems."

"I didn't say it was her fault."

"Something in the water?"

"In the blood. Ladino *ceguera.*"

"I don't know the term."

"Blindness."

"*Qué?*"

"Cultural mindset. Isn't that obvious?"

"It sounds like a stereotype to me."

"Shoe on the wrong foot," she said.

We had stopped in the middle of the path, like two cars just out of gas, and that was how I felt. The mid-afternoon sun was bright and the breeze had died down. My throat was dry and I wanted a drink, anything wet. But Catherine abruptly sat down on a bench and I joined her. We were under a tree, at least, a macadamia, I thought. I peered up into its spiny leaves and let my senses sink into the teeming little society around me, insects, butterflies, birds. A jay on a branch, two shades of heartbreaking blue, warned the world of our presence.

"Look," I said to the bird. "I didn't know this would be so inflammatory, this story. It was fresh on my mind and I wanted to see if I could tell it."

"So you don't think it's important?" Catherine said.

I was wondering if she, too, had been clued in on a joke, a drama of the absurd, all for me. I held up my hands to the bird. "Are you in earnest?"

"Certainly," she said.

The bird flew away. I looked at Catherine. No teasing smile. "Well then, really," I said, "aren't you overreacting?"

"Oh, overreacting, overstating! That's so typical. The North American male academic, reasonable and distanced."

"That's not a bit nice," I said, hoping it only half-masked my irritation. We sat in hot, uncomfortable silence while I thumbed through my dictionary, as if looking for a word that could rescue the moment. "Why don't we go back to the patio and get a drink." It seemed to me a kind and cordial suggestion. I stood.

"Chill out the fervor with a drink?" Catherine said.

"The fervor does seem out of place."

"Fervor often does."

A cloud of insects circled in on me. I batted my hat at them, turning my back to her. It occurred to me to keep on going, walk away, but instead I turned around. Catherine had also stood, behind me. I almost knocked into her, but she held her ground. "I don't know what you're thinking," I said. "But I'm not some racist Yankee lunkhead."

—Dear God, reel that one back in. Too late. She crowed. "Oh, yeah? Well, whoopdefuckindoo!"

I did walk away then, mostly because I'd embarrassed myself. I hadn't gone four steps when she was directly in front of me, facing me and blocking the path. I was beyond exasperation. "What the hell is your problem?" I said.

"Tiny people is my problem, with their teeny, tiny agendas." There was that self-important word, my own, from the first day. Doggone if she didn't remember it. "Can't see beyond their little *miembro*," she said.

I dropped my dictionary in front of my crotch. Play the clown when all else fails. But that failed, too. If anything, her face was disdainful, cold. "Queen Jadis," I muttered.

I said it more to myself than to her, but she heard me and shot back an answer. "Ah yes, the White Witch. What can I say? 'Ours is a high and lonely destiny'."

There we stood on the path, glaring at each other. She was glaring, that is, and I was staring. I was genuinely speechless. First because I'd insulted her outright, and second because she'd just quoted the White Witch herself, with what had been one of my favorite lines from the

Chronicles of Narnia, a phony lament by users of evil magic: Sorry, just can't help it, I've got this mystical power. It didn't help to recall that Queen Jadis was seven feet tall and knock-down beautiful.

"We appear to be at an impasse," I said.

"You give up easy."

"I've been told that before. And right now I'm very thirsty." I edged around her and continued up the path, but she passed me again and paced ahead, all the way to the inner courtyard. There we served ourselves from the glass jug of *agua pura,* gulping down repeated helpings in little paper cups, ignoring each other. At least it was cooler here. We were alone at this spot, though multiple voices drifted out from the peripheral rooms, where ceiling fans whirred. I let those sounds compose me while I watched the color fade on Catherine's cheeks. I thought something should be said about acting like children. I ventured to do it, properly, in Spanish, but what the heck was the word for "childish"?

"I should apologize," she said, beating me to it. "But." She paused at length.

"But you don't know what for," I said. "That makes two of us."

"I know what for, but." She braked again. More silence. "We must stop this right now and get back to Spanish."

But we didn't. We seemed locked into English, albeit in near whispers, and I had no incentive to change that. We sat down across from each other at a nearby table, where she pulled a pad from her bag and began to write. "A few idioms," she said. I watched her, empty of interest in any language lesson, agreeing in some deep organic space that my Spanish was the least important matter in the entire world. Her fingers were long and she held the pen oddly, like chopsticks. Her nails were badly bitten. I suppose I had noticed that before, but it hadn't seemed significant. I wanted to offer her something, a puff on a peace pipe. "I'll make a deal with you," I said. "*Un negocio?*"

"The proper expression is *un trato,*" she said, without looking up.

"*Puta.* I'll tell you something about my teeny, tiny agenda, and then you tell me something about yours."

"Oh, jinkies," she murmured, still writing.

"What happened to whoopdefuckindoo?"

She raised her head, this time with a real smile. Whammo, the sun, just for an instant.

"I'll tell you anyway," I said. "In English."

She glanced around. A couple of tutor and pupil pairs had begun to pace the courtyard, passing by us back and forth as they talked. She handed me her notepad. "Write it."

Write? That suggested something worthy of record. What on earth did I think I would tell her? She was waiting me out, her eyes on my hand, poised with the pen. I printed: *I'm here to find my father's grave.* I looked at my own words. True or not, what else could I say? *If it exists*, I added.

I returned the pad to Catherine. She read what I'd written, looked up at me quizzically, read it again, then scribbled an answer. I watched it go down in a big loopy handwriting, surprisingly girlish. *Along with thousands of other people around here. I wish you luck.* Along the margin she scrawled, *How did your father die?*

The bug, I wrote, my mother's term to the childhood me, and I knew what she meant. In my eyes now it registered as a second class death, a sort of bad joke. *Dysentery*, I added.

Catherine nodded and flipped to a clean page. *How old were you?* *Seven.*

She studied my face again, a long time, as if searching for the child. "Egg?" I asked, swiping my beard.

"Your parents," she whispered. "They were missionaries, right?"

"Huh? Wild guess!"

Had I let something out, absent-mindedly? Bits of Scripture clung to my brain like pocket lint, left over from years of Sunday School and church, and sometimes they slipped into conversations, like "a burning bush" and "through a glass darkly." Those were common parlance, of course. There were others, like "purge me with hyssop," and "the widow's cruse of oil"—and "Balaam's ass," a great story, good for a Sunday School giggle. But I certainly hadn't ever mentioned Balaam's ass to Catherine, or hyssop either, whatever the heck that was.

"All right," I said. "I'm an MK."

"What?"

"Missionary kid. But how did *you* know?"

"Just a guess. Something about you, I think." Teasing smile. "Maybe it's because you don't swear."

"Swear? I do so. —Buggers! There!"

"Hush!"

I grabbed the pad. "What do you want, blasphemy, scatology, or minced oaths?" I began printing. Fuck! Shit! *Caca!* Goddamit! Christ Almighty! It turned out to be a pathetically short list. I added a few from Shakespeare, gadzooks and bodkins. Catherine took over the pad and wrote *vete al carajo, chinga tu madre, hijos de los chingados,* filling another page.

I got the drift. I was beginning to enjoy this junior high stuff, passing dirty notes across the aisle. Then she scribbled another question in her awful handwriting. *What kind of missionaries were your parents?*

Kind?

What did they do?

They were teachers, I think.

Where?

In Mam territory.

You spoke Mam then as well as Spanish?

I suppose so. I don't remember more than a word or two.

So what would you call your first language?

I don't think there was a first. My parents spoke Swedish, too.

They were Swedish?

Second generation American.

Why haven't you mentioned any of this before?

I guard my privacy. It's a Swedish trait. I flipped to a clean page and handed the pad to her with ceremony. "Your turn," I said. "Give me some facts, names, dates."

This time she printed neatly:

BORN: Wisconsin, 1949

EDUCATION: Emory University

MARRIED: Martin Rodriguez Calderon, 1970

SON: Alex, born 1971

OCCUPATION: Read Narnia series to son. There. Are we even?

Not really. You still know more about me than I do about you.

That's because I'm the teacher, silly.

How do you say touché?

Te caché.

Te? Isn't that a form of the highly familiar pronoun tú?

Oh, sure enough. My mistake.

She tore the pages off the pad, balled them up and tossed them into a nearby wastebasket. So much for the story of my life, and hers, as well. She left then and I fished them out, those scribbled pages, smoothed them and saved them in the back of my canary pad. They became part of the journal, which I continued to keep in the days ahead.

TEN

As usual, it had started to rain as I returned to my room. I didn't bother to change. I got out the envelope containing my father's letter and sat at the desk for a long time in my wet clothes, looking at it. I stared at it for so long it began to pulsate with an aura. I held it at arm's length, which was exactly what I'd been doing all along. It seemed totally inexcusable to me now that I hadn't taken it to a library in Cambridge and worked it out myself with a dictionary.

Actually, it was Rebecca who found it, in her new phase of getting to the bottom of things. We had just settled my mother in the nursing home and had turned to the task of dealing with thirty years of accumulation in the house, the tiny, run-down rental my mother and I had moved to in 1955. She had chosen Rhode Island because what remained of her family was there, a couple of cousins, who had helped her find a job in an insurance office.

I had never felt at home in that house. Nothing wrong with the location. It stood in a small cluster of one-time summer cottages in a community the natives called "Rivvahside," a section of East Providence. The river was actually a finger of Narragansett Bay. Our neighborhood was on a peninsula, with salt water lapping against a sea wall not fifty feet away. Single masted sailboats bobbed lazily at the edge of our yard.

The house itself was wrong, mainly because my father was not there. When my mother married again six years later and my stepfather moved in, the place seemed less than ever mine. So I resented Harvey, and everything about him—that he was shorter than my mother, that he parted his hair with a wet comb in front of the living room mirror, that he prayed long, repetitive graces before dinner. I hated him because he sang. I would hear him holding forth lustily, in the kitchen, in the yard, "This world is not my home! I'm just a-passin' through," and

I would think, "Good, keep right on going." I was thirteen, and I'd had no more to say about the entrance of this man into my life than I had about the departure of the other. I retreated to worlds of my own, baseball on my radio, pop and jazz, a few LPs (Duke Ellington and Coleman Hawkins) played softly in my room. Books. Tolkien and C.S. Lewis, reading them over and over.

When my stepfather died, my mother stopped eating. She quickly grew fragile, but refused any alternative to managing alone in that house. She would not even discuss the possibility of moving in with Rebecca and me. Or actually, it would be just me, since she barely recognized Rebecca's existence. Then a neighbor, dropping by, found her prostrate inside the front door, where she had crawled after falling down the stairs. Lying flat in the hospital bed, her broken leg extended, she gave in and allowed a transfer to a local nursing home. Old Harvey, "just a-passin' through," had left enough money behind to pay expenses for years to come.

I wasn't looking for the letter as we cleaned out the Rhode Island house. At that point I didn't know it existed. I wasn't looking for any link to Guatemala. I knew there weren't any. My mother had brought nothing with her from there, none of the weavings and rugs and baskets, no photographs, none of the books that had always been lying about, note paper protruding from their pages. And I'd brought nothing but my fielder's glove that for years I took to bed with me, my "bankie."

The first little surprise turned up in the kitchen. Rebecca was pulling out drawers and turning them upside down on the table, and there among the toothpicks and canning-jar rings was an old can opener I recognized with a rush of saliva, hearing again the sound it made on a can of applesauce, a rare and expensive treat in Guatemala.

Then behind a stack of de-handled cups on a shelf was one I hadn't seen since I was five, with a yellow Teddy bear on one side and the name "Teddy" on the other. This had not lost its handle. There were two handles, and again the physical memory, lifting it with both hands oh-so-carefully, proud to not spill a drop. Goat milk, still pungent and warm from the udder.

"Teddy," Rebecca read, teasing. It was what my mother had called me, however big I got. The one time she called me Ted was my initial visit to her room in the nursing home. She was in a new armchair we'd bought her, with her long hair, always worn in a bun, now cut extremely short. I hesitated at the door as I took this in. "Ted!" she called reproachfully. "It's about time you got here. Let's gather up Teddy this instant and go home." Since then she had called me nothing.

In the bedroom Rebecca and I boxed up blankets and sheets, tied up ten years of *The Reader's Digest* towering in a corner, and cleaned out the closet. That's where we found the sewing basket, stuffed full. Rebecca (getting to the bottom of things) turned it upside down on the bed. Out tumbled a dozen spools of half-gone thread, needles, crochet hooks, and a collection of sewing machine attachments resembling medical instruments. These were followed by a final plop—a false bottom to the basket and an airmail postal envelope, *Correo Aéreo* in the top left corner. The stamped date was blurred and faded. There was no return address. In the envelope were two onionskin pages folded together, inked handwriting showing through the back of the thin paper. I'd know it anywhere, my father's slanted penmanship.

My mother had gone to lengths to prepare this hiding place, making the false bottom from a piece of cardboard. Maybe she hid the letter so well she couldn't find it herself. I pictured her as I had often discovered her on the nights I stayed with her in the past year, a gaunt figure in her nightgown, standing before the bureau or the desk, opening and shutting drawers.

I put the pages back into the envelope and shoved that into the pocket of my jeans. I didn't look at it again until I was alone an hour later, sitting at a weathered picnic table behind the house while Rebecca prepared a snack in the kitchen. It was late afternoon, April, a time when a kind of recycled light often reflected off the bay, turning the old house into a romantic seaside watercolor.

I sat there in the yard a long time, postponing what could be a sudden shift in the tectonic plates of my life. When I finally opened it, I saw that the writing was mostly in Spanish. I recognized a word here and there, nothing suggestive. Otherwise it was beyond me. Good. I felt becalmed, like the Sunfish out there in the cove, waiting for a breeze, its sail slackened.

The letter ended with a Swedish phrase familiar to me, *Jag alskar dig,* I love you, and a Scripture reference in Song of Solomon. Nothing unusual about that. He often added a Scripture reference to his letters. Then at the bottom the P.S., in English, and my own name. *Let's keep all this from Teddy. I'll explain it to him myself when he is old enough and ready.*

Looking at it with new eyes now (as "Ready Teddy"?), I saw that he had dated it September 10 at the top. No year was added, but I thought I could make out 1954 in the faded postal stamp on the envelope. That was the year my father was away so much in Guatemala City, while my mother and I remained in the hills. It was in the previous January that I spent a few days with him in the Capital, as my seven-year-old birthday treat.

He came and went in his old Buick from January to July, and in between we had watched, my mother and I, for those envelopes with *Correo Aéreo* in the corner. That was a joke, since they were carried close to the ground. They would start out in a truck from the Capital to the nearest repository of mail five winding miles away from our village, then be delivered in person by someone doing errands in the village pick-up, walking the last undriveable distance.

But this letter would have been just to my mother. I was not there in September. Near the end of July we had left for a month in the States, the three of us, to get medical help for my father. We left in the middle of the night. I remembered almost walking in my sleep, stumbling over the bumpy lane to the pickup truck. Someone drove us to the airport. We stayed with a couple of my father's sisters and by the end of August I had been tucked into the boarding school in Florida, while my parents returned to Guatemala.

I didn't dwell on that now. I'd long ago learned to circle it, like a murky pool. The point now was that I didn't know where in the country my father would have been when he wrote and mailed this letter.

Querida, it began. Dear, darling. I scanned the first page quickly for anything that looked easily translatable. *Please take care of yourself and don't worry about me. I have what I need. No appetite anyway.* In the next line, he sent his greetings to the village, and "encouragement" to F. *Tell him to carry on.* F, I assumed, was Felipe López. He was a leader in the village, and father to my own friend, Luis. Luis's mother had been my "nanny" when my mother was teaching in the village school before I was old enough to attend. For the life of me I couldn't resurrect her name now, but Felipe and Luis I had never forgotten.

I have been trying to reach TG. We need to talk. TG would be Tomás Garcia, I was quite sure, a man from Guatemala City who used to visit our village often in a green station wagon. A small person, urbane and bright-eyed, he appeared in my memory whole, presenting himself as important, as he had always seemed to be. He came bearing gifts, books and supplies for adults, and candy for all the kids in the village.

The following sentence expressed regret for how *tú* (my mother, that would be) had been *wounded*. I braked here, red alert. *But, as much as you wish I would, I will never —*. The word he used was a form of *retractar*. Recant? Change his mind? He was seeing J in a new light, he said. Who the heck was J? It could be Jesus, referred to often in our house like a favorite cousin, very much alive. But there were other J's in our village, four Juans, as well as a guy actually named Jesus— *heySOOCE*, we pronounced it—who was known to have fathered children with more than one woman. I played with his kids, like all the others, only vaguely aware that something was a little strange.

Second page. *Where do we go next?* That was clear. Then lines I couldn't decipher. He seemed to be saying that he was supposed to own no land (*sin tierra*, landless, a term also meaning peasants), but that he owned two pieces of land, and he loved them both and intended to keep them. He carried them on his back as if they were part of him.

That hardly made sense. And I didn't know he owned land. I supposed it was metaphorical, ground to stand on, or ground he would hold up or defend. It was a big linguistic stretch.

Then the love sign-off in Swedish (*Jag alskar dig*), and Song of Solomon 4:6, and the P.S. in English.

There was something stiff about the whole letter, an awkward whisper, as if someone was listening in, not like the mail we used to get from him, full of teasing and jokes. He had hurt my mother somehow, that much was clear, or he thought he had. But it occurred to me that could be just the follow-up to an argument, the kind my parents often had, tiresome adult wrangling over some theological point, and then apologies with embarrassing affection, words that sounded "mushy" to my ears, even in Swedish.

Except that was hardly a reason for my mother to keep it, let alone hide it, and that hinted at something beyond an ordinary argument. He had *done* something, I felt more than ever sure, maybe as serious as shacking up with another woman, like *heySOOCE,* maybe with a village girl. He had the opportunity, no doubt, maybe the desire, how would I know? Had mixed-breed children grown up back at our village, blond, a little taller than the others? Had he refused to give up the other woman, though he still loved my mother? It was too predictable and corny. I didn't want him to be predictable and corny.

So now what did I know? Nothing. I'd learned nothing. This mysterious, portentous fragment of my father had not told me anything I could build on, maybe nothing important at all. Reading it had not changed a thing.

It was after 1:00 A.M. I removed my shoes and lay down on the bed in my clothes, still not quite dry. Grow up, Teddy, I thought. I should get out of here, now, tomorrow, go home, back to Boston. I needed to nail down a job, move into my apartment, learn to live life without Rebecca.

But I'd told Catherine I would be looking for my father's grave—the grave or its absence—and telling her that, telling someone, writing it, made it more than ever a real "agenda." Surely there was someone who could help me. I could at least check on that. Tomás Garcia, for instance, the T. G. in the letter. If he was still living and available. If I was prepared to hold the conversation it would require. Whatever, I had only one week left to do it.

I found myself curled into a fetal position. Disgusted, I stretched out full length, pressing my feet against the cumbersome footboard. I was a bad fit everywhere I put my body, even in a bed.

ELEVEN

The very next day, Catherine claimed to notice a change, a new freedom in my speech, she said. I denied it. The lesson we'd just finished had been the same as all the others, like pushing a freight train up a hill.

I suggested taking another week, though I didn't intend to. She wiggled her shoulders, noncommittal. "That's up to you. But I won't be available next week. Not that it should matter. Méndez will find someone to take my place." Obviously she entertained no regret at our parting. Why should she? The twinge that brought was entirely unjustified.

When school was over at four, I took off for my run and a beer. The TV in the bar was full of news of a soccer tournament, an important event, judging by the clamor of the men around me. A game was about to begin and a reporter was thrusting a mike in the faces of players. One after the other they gave their spiels in rapid-fire monotone sentences, exactly as I'd heard it scores of times by football players back home. They were saying the same things, too. Just gotta get out there and show 'em who we are. Just gotta play both ends of the field. It might have been three minutes before I realized how I was listening, which was not by conscious translating. The language entered my head not as words and phrases, but as meaning. Skeptical, I left my beer and wandered around in the plaza, deliberately eavesdropping on bits of conversation. I listened to a couple arguing, about money, of course. I got it. He had been suckered, according to her, into buying warranty insurance on a television set.

I headed for a *tienda* and bought a Guatemalan newspaper and began to read as I stood there on the sidewalk. I remember even now the story my eye fell on and that I read with no trouble. Charles Glass, ABC news chief and Mideast correspondent, had escaped from Hezbollah kidnappers in Beirut. I tested out an inside page with "further details" of an earlier story about Rudolf Hess, who had hung himself in prison three days before. I didn't know that. Further in, the Order of the Garter had opened up to women, an odd item for a Central American paper.

On every page I was really reading, not getting every phrase, certainly, but getting the meaning with ease. It occurred to me with wonder that I was reading the way a kid does, maneuvering around the "big words," but getting the larger sense of things. All right, I thought, be a kid, be seven years old. That was fine, poetically just. I had found my private functioning level, ready for my "agenda." I was even willing to admit that Catherine's approach had been right, be a child again.

I went a little *loco*, buying earrings (for no one), haggling over the price. Then I stopped at another bar and ordered another beer and sat there exulting. By the third beer I was indeed envisioning myself as a boy, trudging the hills of the country, alone on a winding road, stalwart and unafraid. Starting a fourth, I realized that was a scene I'd read over and over years ago, when Frodo climbs alone to the Seat of Seeing, the lookout tower atop the hill called Amon Hen. But Frodo was no child, by Hobbit chronology. A little guy, to be sure, but out of his "irresponsible tweens," maybe even age forty. Clearly I'd had enough to drink.

On the way home I bought a big bouquet for the Ávila family, and that night I called Rebecca, just to tell her the news. It was after 11:00 P.M. my time, after 1:00 A.M. in hers. I knew she hated the portent of a late night ring, but I thought I'd better do it while the impetus was strong, while I was still in the Frodo buzz. I had to find my way in the dark to the house telephone. It sat on a table next to a wall niche where a candle in a red glass burned before the virgin. It was enough light to dial all the numbers on my phone credit card, and I did it before better judgment caught up to me. I was lucky, or Frodo was. Rebecca was awake.

"It's you," she said. "Well, hi."

"I hope I didn't startle you."

"Well, yes, you did. Is something wrong? Why are you speaking softly."

"Nothing is wrong. I don't want to wake anyone here in the house."

"Where are you?" she asked.

"Antigua. Where are you?"

"You should know. You called here."

"Where in the house? Tell me exactly."

"In the kitchen, getting a snack. In the center of the room, exactly four feet from the sink. In fact, my left foot is on the black linoleum square that's, let's see, the eighth one in from the east wall, and my right foot has just landed on the white square which meets the black one kitty-korner."

"Okay, yank my chain."

"And now I'm walking to the counter and I am sitting down on a stool."

"What are you wearing?" A tiresome cliché, but never mind. I wanted to know.

"You're cheating," said Rebecca.

"I know. But tell me."

"My UMass jersey, what else?"

Good. I could picture her, which was what I wanted to do, for just a minute. I had loved that big old shirt, faded and laundered out of shape. I had loved it on her, that is, as it settled on her comfortable roundness.

"How's the Mom?" I asked.

"The same. But I have something to tell you. Are you ready? Your mother spoke to me today. First time ever."

"You're kidding. Did she know who you are?"

"I'm sure. She looked me right in the eye and addressed me clearly."

"What did she say?"

"She called me an asshole."

I managed to hold down a shout. I had never heard anything approaching a "dirty word" from my mother's lips. "Oh fudge!" was her standby expletive.

"I was thrilled," said Rebecca. "It's the most attention she's ever paid to me.

There was a little awkward silence, then she said: "There's something else I want to tell you, as long as you've called."

"I'm listening."

"This is cheating, too. Sorry. It's just that I'm concerned."

"What is it? Amy?"

"No, no. She's fine. She's visiting her Dad right now. This is about you."

I answered with a grunt, emphasis up, a question.

"Well, first of all, I heard from the attorney yesterday. Everything is going along on schedule."

I had nothing to say to that. She paused and swallowed. "I suppose it's not unusual to, well, wonder," she said. "I mean, I just wonder if we've gone about things the right way. I think of you down there and I wonder if—. I mean, did I do the wrong thing?"

Was that a real question? I stopped breathing altogether.

"Or did I do it the wrong way? I mean, did I send you down there? In effect, that is?"

I mumbled a negative.

"There was a story in the paper this week," she went on, "a personal account by someone who just returned from Guatemala, and he said it was extremely dangerous."

"Dangerous how?"

"Robberies and murders, in the cities at night and even daytimes in the mountains. He said the guerrillas are poor and hungry and they kill people for money. Have you heard that?"

"No."

"You'll be going up into the mountains, won't you."

"Possibly, yes."

"Then I'm really concerned. I would feel so terrible if. Oh nuts. Now I'm embarrassed."

Her voice wandered off into a familiar little sniff. She'd always cried easily, not real tears, but what her daughter called "Mom's melt-down," rushes of brightness in response to anything that moved her. But this was more than a habitual reaction. I knew her well enough to recognize it—second thoughts by the decision maker. She needed my reassurance. Not just that I was safe; that was a route to the high road. What she really wanted to hear me say was that she, the decision maker, the initiator of our breakup, had done the right thing.

"Please answer me, Ted. Say something." An old complaint, my failure to return a quick response. I found my voice, but not my sanity.

There was no time to grab that essential by the tail as it flew out of reach. "Becka, no," I said. I repeated that several times before I went on. "Look, don't be embarrassed. It's understandable. It's just like you to——. Look, first of all, first, well, second, whatever, what's done is done, right?" Good God, did I mean that? "And it doesn't make any difference where I am. Really. Does it? The lion can eat you anywhere."

"What?"

"I'm not in any danger, if that's what you mean."

"What lion?"

"It's just a metaphor. Skip it. Listen to me. Are you listening? Move in closer."

"What metaphor?"

My mouth was operating on its own. "Never mind that. Move in close to me. Are you close?"

"Okay, yes, short of 2000 miles."

"Good. Now listen. I know two things. Two things. Or rather, I don't know two things. I don't know anything. I certainly don't know why I should be in any danger. That's two things, right? Two things I don't know. Do you understand that?"

"I think so."

"Good, because I don't."

She made a noise, a sniffly chuckle.

"Hug me," I said.

"Oh, no. Ted!"

"Hug me."

"All right, but it won't make any difference."

"Of course not, but do it anyway."

"All right. I am."

"Good."

"Well, as long as we're doing this madhouse thing, you could hug me back. I need it too, you know."

"You bet. Gosh, what an armload you are. I'd almost forgotten."

"No cracks, wise guy. I'll break your effing head."

"Rebecca."

Silence.

"Rebecca."

"Yes?"

"Listen."

"Speak. I'm listening."

"I'm sorry."

"I know. We're both sorry."

"I'm very sorry." I was very, very sorry. I had failed to be the person she needed me to be. I knew that now. And I couldn't, not then or now—be that person. I knew that too. I knew those two things. Did I have to come all the way here to find them out?

"Steady on, old chap," I said.

"Right. Steady on," she answered.

I could feel her withdrawing from me then, leaving my arms, the miles of space between us restoring themselves unquestionably.

"Goodbye, Rebecca."

"Goodbye, Ted."

"Goodbye."

"Goodbye."

"*Q'onk tipeya.*"

"What's that? Is it Spanish?"

"No. It's Mam." It had slipped out of its hiding place, glottal stop and all, which I was never good at. "It means 'Strength to you.' I think."

"Oh. Thank you."

Then we said goodbye again, about four times each, and hung up. It was a real goodbye. Hers and mine, too. It was over, with a finality that all the legal papers and signatures in the world could not produce. Not *adiós*, and not *hasta la vista*, not "See you later." More like "You may leave now, if you like." Go, in safety and health. *Vaya con Dios, my darling*.

Why hadn't I said *that*, I wondered, finding the way back to my room in the dark. I'd also forgotten to tell her why I called.

TWELVE

The next morning at the school, before meeting Catherine, I made it a point to connect with Carlos Méndez. We conversed in Spanish in the office, while he beamed at my progress like a proud parent.

"I must show you off tonight at a little party I am giving," he said. Friends of his from the States were staying at the Buen Viaje, a local inn, and were joining him in entertaining some other U.S. visitors. He was inviting students. I promised to be there, politely.

I told Catherine about the language breakthrough next, expecting her to come up with some kind of an I-told-you-so. Instead, she gave me a high-five. But that was the extent of the celebration. We reviewed verbs most of the day. She had listed them on a pack of three-by-five cards. She shuffled these over and over and fanned them out in her hand. I was to pick one, blindly, and use it in a sentence. I had two minutes only for each sentence, completed and corrected. We did this all morning and again after lunch, until I couldn't stand any more. I reached over and gathered the cards together in a swoop, lifting them out of her hands. "I'm tired," I said.

She didn't seem to mind. "Good. I'm tired, too. I've got to turn in your progress report to the office." She wrapped the cards in a stretchy blue headband, then began packing up her bag. "You're getting an A plus, in case you're wondering. Hey, we're done here. Finished."

She stood and so did I. "You mean this is it?" I said.

She said *sí*, then "done" again in several Spanish versions, clearly amused. It was turning out to be much too abrupt. I was caught off-guard by a sense of incompleteness, that we still owed each other something. Not sex, nothing so recognizable. "Well, then, can I buy you a drink?" I asked, not very smoothly. "A parting glass—like?"

She hesitated, then said "No, I shouldn't," and I remembered her husband. "You're not going to the party?" she asked.

"Oh yeah. I forgot. I don't want to."

"I don't either, but I must."

"I promised Méndez. But just in case I don't, well—." I held out my hand. She took it in a quick firm shake, then shouldered her big tote bag and walked toward the office door.

"Listen," I said, catching up to her. "*Escuche!* You've been a good teacher. I'm grateful. I hope you know that."

"Well, you've been a rather unusual student," she answered. "Which, of course, is what I predicted, isn't it?"

"Must you always be such an insufferable know-it-all?"

"To the bitter end," she said, and turned into the office with a wave.

The Buen Viaje was an upscale inn, sprawling across a couple of acres of land at the southwestern end of the city. I walked there in a watery blue twilight, aiming directly toward Volcán de Fuego, watching a final finger of the sun as it caught the bottom of a cloud circling the mountain. It had rained briefly and stopped, and the air was full of the sweet-sour smell of ripe vegetation. On a muddy side road a dozen kids played pick-up soccer with a half-deflated ball, shouting curses as it splatted into the puddles. I observed them with a little pang—barefoot, filthy, falling, every man for himself.

I was arriving late, a reluctant guest. The parking lot of the inn was full of cars and the lobby was crowded and thick with smoke. I found a door leading to the exterior, a large grassy courtyard and two illuminated swimming pools. A marimba band played near a lighted fountain.

I looked for familiar faces and spied them, students and tutors, standing near the sliding doors of a first-floor suite, along with a dozen others I didn't know. Carlos Méndez came to meet me and introduced me to the co-hosts, his friends Angela and Norman Harris from Long Island, a couple perhaps in their fifties. He was wearing Bermuda shorts and she a long skirt in the same plaid. They were owners of an international import company, Méndez told me. "And *Señor* Peterson is one of our star pupils, an English professor from Massachusetts," he added.

"Oh-oh. I'd better watch my language," said Harris, laughing as if he'd coined the joke.

In the suite another two dozen people had gathered around a long table packed with party food. Little U.S. and Guatemalan flags had been stuck on all the platters. I poured myself a scotch and ambled back outdoors. I saw Catherine on the other side of the patio, in conversation with a couple. I recognized her first only by her height. Her Yankees cap was gone, her hair down, hanging in waves around her face, abundantly. How had she managed to get all that tucked into the cap? She was wearing an ankle-length skirt of blue woven cloth tied at her waist around a lacy blouse cut low on her shoulders. She had excellent shoulders, I noticed, now that she had tossed the white shirt. I saw no one near her who might be her husband. It was all gringos.

I slipped through the crowd, stopping at the edge of one cluster after another. Everyone was speaking English, and in nearly every case the topic of conversation was some aspect of tourist life in the country—the exchange rate, when to pay a bribe, the safety and danger of travel. I gravitated to a couple of guys standing apart. One was Hank Stenning, the pony-tailed student I saw every day. The other, stocky and hot-looking in a tightly buttoned shirt, introduced himself as somebody Tornquist. He was "with coffee," he told me. Who was I with, he wanted to know.

"Myself, I guess," I said. He seemed puzzled. He was more than a little oiled already. I switched attention to Stenning. He didn't look like he was "with" anybody either. He picked up on the conversation I had interrupted, telling Tornquist about a water project in the western hills, where he was headed next. "We find ways to connect remote communities with the nearest water suppwy," he explained.

"Suppwy?" echoed Tornquist. Then he caught on. "Well, who pays you for that?"

Stenning was amused. "No one."

I backed away and eased myself around the guests, headed for Catherine, curious to observe the transformation up close. "*Hola,*" she said, when I reached her.

"Are you *with* someone?" I asked.

She laughed. "How about do I come here often?"

"How about what are you drinking?"

"Papaya juice."

"Right."

"It really is."

We raised glasses to each other. "You look very nice," I told her, hoping I didn't sound surprised.

"Thank you. I thought I'd better clean up for the *fufurufus.*"

"The what?"

"The *nouveau riche.*"

We drifted to the edge of a group of about a dozen people dominated by the couple Catherine had been talking with earlier. "Who are they?" I asked. She shrugged. "Cindy and Bob. They're from Ohio. He sells fertilizer here. Shall we be nice and listen in on the conversation?"

"You be nice. I'm always nice," I said.

Bob and Cindy were telling the story of a couple who had been recently robbed as they were climbing Volcán de Pacaya. "By two masked gunmen muttering something about the gods of the volcano," said Cindy.

"It was stupid to go climbing alone," someone inserted. That raised the question of who was responsible for crime in the country, and everyone had an answer: guerrillas, local police, Indians, and jealous wives. Laughter.

"We're okay as long as we stick close to the touristy places," said Cindy. "That's what the State Department says."

"Well, if you want my theory," said Bob, "statistically there's no more danger of being robbed or killed here than in any city in the United States. But the Tourist Commission wants us, and they know one way to get us is to convey just the right sense of danger."

Tornquist, who had moved to the group along with Stenning, had a theory too. Since he was "literally from Missouri," in the ten years he had been coming to Guatemala he had made it a practice never to take at face value anything he heard. "So help me, I swear to God the country operates on rumor and hearsay. Take away rumor and everything comes to a halt. Rumor is the machinery that powers the whole country, okay? It brings international loans, cancels foreign debt, builds hospitals." He paused, and took a sip of his drink. A wave of cognizance passed over his face, as if he'd just realized he was onto something. He was standing on a rise of ground and it appeared to give him a podium.

"You see what that means?" he said. "It means there's no war. Not here. It's just a rumor. Okay?"

"True," said someone. "The war is over."

"No, I mean there never *was* a war." Tornquist said. "I myself have personally never seen a single sign of actual war. Ten years and twenty visits and I never have, I swear it."

An uncertain chuckle passed through the group, not sure how to read him.

"So," said the guy named Bob, "All those M-16s we're seeing are just toys?"

"Excellent observation," Tornquist said. "Ever see one fired? Ever see anyone shot?"

He was even drunker than I'd thought. Catherine, standing on my left, made a gesture with her hand that I took to be a dismissal and turned to walk away. I was more than ready to go myself.

"Speaking personally," said Tornquist, "I have never seen a dead body in this country. Personally, I have not."

Now Catherine turned back, and drew in her breath as if to speak. "Be nice," I whispered. She did the suppressed smile thing and elbowed me gently. And she *was* nice. "Oh, you know, you are so right," she said to Tornquist, in a warm voice I hadn't heard her use. "Mister—? I didn't catch your name. Never mind. You're right. That's exactly what a lot of people here believe. There is no war." She smiled, one that was also new to me, light and girlish. "But then, of course, it depends on what you want for a war. I mean, we aren't talking about two armies meeting with bayonets in a peach orchard, are we?"

"We certainly are not," said Tornquist. "There never was a war here. It's all fantasy and rumor, like I say."

"Or maybe it's the socio-economic condition of things," said Cindy. Stenning, on my right, choked noisily.

"Except, oh wait a minute." That was Catherine's new voice again. She had struck a thoughtful pose, fingertip on her chin. "If it's fantasy, we do have a little problem. I mean, four hundred villages destroyed, a hundred thousand people murdered. And the disappearances, so many. We do need to account for those somehow, don't you think?"

"Oh, something happened to them all right," said Tornquist. "Runaways, unfaithful husbands, unpaid debts, all the reasons people usually disappear. That's my theory."

That drew another run of laughter, but with distinctly less spirit, and a couple of people slipped away. "Let's go," I said to Catherine. Not that she should go anywhere with me, even across the lawn, but I think she might have, until Hank Stenning spoke.

"That's not a new theory, in case you want to know. It's what an Army officer here said to some women who asked what happened to their husbands. And he wasn't kidding."

"So, who's kidding?" said Tornquist. "I'm serious. A non-war has been propagated with American tax money. We paid for a war and didn't get one, and you can bet our money is lining somebody's pocket."

"Oh, we've got a war, for sure," Stenning answered. "A war by different means, so they say. One body at a time."

"Except in a Mayan village," said Catherine. "Then you don't count."

I looked at the sky. A sudden cloudburst struck me as a really good idea, the kind that sends everybody flying in different directions. It didn't rain, but two other things happened right at that point. The marimba band—this is the truth—began to play "God Bless America," and Angela Harris, the hostess, arrived with a tray of miniature tacos.

"Just off the *comal*, everybody!" she announced brightly. "Get them while they're hot!" She thrust the tray in front of Catherine, who waved it away. And now she wasn't nice any more. Maybe it was Angela's cheeriness that did it, or even her plaid skirt, for all I know, or maybe the music. Or the papaya juice. When Catherine addressed Tornquist again, her voice was steely.

"You know what, mister-what's-your-name?" she said. "Rumor is too easy. Let's talk about lies instead. *Tonterias.* "

"What?" said somebody.

"Intentional misinformation," said Catherine.

"Bullshit," said Stenning, with a big grin. It came out as "boo-shit."

"Such as," said Catherine, "there is no war in this country."

"Or this country is now a democracy," said Stenning.

"No longer a military state," said Catherine.

"Reports of human rights viowations are greatwy exaggerated," said

Stenning.

"And there is no pursuable evidence of genocide," said Catherine.

"Genocide! What genocide?" That was Bob, I thought, who stood somewhere behind us.

"Check it out in your travels," said Catherine. "Try Agua Fria. You might find a mass grave. Or a well, stuffed with murdered people. Or Rio Negro. Over four hundred residents assassinated there, mostly children."

"Oh!" interrupted Angela. "Oh, but! Isn't this a wonderful place? There's so much to see. What about the hot springs in Zunil? Has anyone been there? Or the ruins of Tikal in Petén?"

"And if you go to Petén," said Catherine, her voice rising, "search for the village called Dos Erres." She rolled the R's with a flair. "You won't find it. It was wiped off the map by the Guatemalan army."

"Not the army. Guerrillas did that," said Bob.

"Is that so. What's your source?" asked Catherine.

"My boss, the U.S. of A. We stand behind the army here. That's good enough for me."

"Which means you are sanctioning murder."

"Murder? Watch your tongue, lady. I call that remark criminally libelous."

"Well, at least I'm not criminally naive."

Now a couple of the women began to sing loudly, along with the marimbas—*From the mountains, to the valleys*—. Others joined in, and over that racket Bob and Catherine began shouting at each other. I stood there like a silent partner, "with" her but not wanting to be, and not wanting to forsake her either.

I could barely hear them. Bob called her a babbling bitch and she told him he was nothing but a puppet, without brains or balls, like most American tourists. I got that much. After that, their words were lost to me. They went at it, back and forth, until the marimbas suddenly cut off, the singing stopped, and into the interstice sailed Catherine's elevated voice, mid-sentence, all by itself, loud and clear: "—And by the bloody Guatemalan butchers and their fucking U.S. money!"

Across the green terraces heads whirled our way. She looked down. I looked up, at the sky.

The marimbas instantly began to play once more, this time—I swear again—the Guatemalan national anthem, a melody my bones identified. There was a flurry of action at the door of the suite and all eyes turned to where Carlos Méndez were emerging with a party of several men. Méndez looked short next to the person beside him, a large, slightly balding man in a green silk shirt.

"It's Zondo!" said Tornquist, and he and Bob hurried over to greet him. Méndez held up his hand for silence. The band came to a ragged halt, and now it was his voice that projected across the yard, beckoning everyone to come meet his "long-time matey, leader of the *Buenas Nuevas* party, Elizondo the great!"

Well, well, here he was before me, the "ubiquitous" politician. He was a remarkably handsome man, I noted, if quite a lot too chesty. His smile looked genuine, a little abashed, as he waved aside the flattery. "And what a lovely looking bunch you all are," he said, holding out his hands to us one by one, working his way through our group, greeting several people by name. I recognized that voice, the good baritone I had heard on the radio. He spoke English with a flat American accent. Someone commented on it. Oh, sure, he had learned English at Notre Dame not so long ago, he replied. He got an A in English, but failed miserably at U.S. football.

Later I wasn't sure I witnessed what I thought I did. He was standing in the group just four feet away from Catherine and me. He turned as he finished speaking, saw her and did a second take, or so I perceived it. "Cat?" I thought he said, in surprise. Just that. If he was speaking to her, she didn't answer. She was walking away. It was over in an instant. Stenning was asking Elizondo a question. "What's the Good News party? Is that the same as the New Jerusawem of Ríos Montt?"

"Well, since you asked," said Elizondo. He laughed. "If, with all due respect to our former president, you refer to national unity and high moral values, then yes, I believe Guatemala can certainly be the New Jerusalem of the modern world. But there is much more to that, of course."

"Never mind the much more, *amigo*," prompted Méndez. "Multitudes are waiting to greet you."

"He knows me too well," said Elizondo. "So I will just say this, quickly. There is now a fragmented Guatemala, as you know. There is the land of the tourist. There is the land of the campesino, the Indian. Of which I am one, by the way. Yes, part Kaqchikel. Proudly. And there is the land the world sees from a distance, the one of internal conflict." He was using his hands, gracefully. "But there is another Guatemala, made up of people like you, who work hard and strive to live with honesty and human kindness, pursue art and music and intelligent conversation. I want that to be the whole new Guatemala. There is no excuse for poverty and illiteracy. I want to see every citizen in this country enjoy the wealth and well-being God intends for us all. That's our best strategy in the battle against evil. We can become a mecca of peace and prosperity, the Switzerland of the southern hemisphere. We've got the mountains, haven't we?"

He chuckled, as if embarrassed by his own largess. Méndez said, "Hear, hear," giving him a good-natured sock on the arm and hustling him away. The group followed and Stenning and I were left standing together. "What did you think?" he asked.

"Political stump."

"We've been snookered," Stenning said. "By Méndez. He denies us the right to tawk powitics on his turf, then he springs this guy on us at a party."

"Is he important?" I asked.

"Did you notice the bodyguards? He's rich as heck, I've heard. He owns a bunch of businesses and runs a big charity. A favorite of the business crowd."

"That's where Méndez comes in?" I didn't want to talk, I wanted to go. I was scanning the lighted areas for Catherine. I should say goodbye.

"It's the churchy stuff that bothers me," said Stenning.

Had I missed something? "Méndez?"

"No. Zondo. And his mentor, former President Ríos Montt."

That name again. "I heard Ríos Montt was a good guy."

"Depends on the source."

I was tired of Stenning. We were moving back toward the suite. I thought Catherine might have gone inside but she wasn't there either. Maybe she had already left. So be it. Stenning poured wine at the drink table and handed me a glass.

"Hey, that's your tutor, isn't it?" he asked.

"Where?" I asked, glancing around.

"I mean the one who took on the powers-that-be out there. She's right on target. You know that peace agreement cooked up here two weeks ago?" He didn't wait for me to answer. "Endorsed by the UN, but President Reagan rejected it." He raised his glass. "Here's to your great country and mine."

"*Skoal*," I said.

THIRTEEN

I escaped, left the party without paying respects to the hosts and headed into the lobby. I decided to stop at a bathroom and almost bumped into Catherine, who was emerging from the women's. She looked unwell.

"Are you all right?" I asked.

"Not really." She could hardly speak, breathing hard.

"Do you need to sit down?"

"Anything but that. I need to get out of here."

"Then let's go."

I started in the direction of the courtyard. "Please, not the scenic route," she said. So we pushed our way through the lobby to the front entrance. Outside she stopped and leaned against the doorway.

"Let me get help," I said.

"No, no. It's nothing. Just a little panic attack." She took a pack of cigarettes from her purse and knocked one out. Her hands trembled as she lit it. I didn't know she smoked.

"Racing heart?" I asked.

She nodded.

"Sweating? Dizzy? Hyperventilation?"

"Yes. My parents used to think I was having a tantrum."

"Stomach in turmoil?"

"How come you know?"

"I'm a veteran."

"You! I can't believe it. What happens?"

"Abdominal distress, as they say. I learned how to spell diarrhea really early."

"Now?"

"I can still spell it."

She choked a little as she drew on the cigarette. "Have you been treated?" she asked.

"Gosh no. No clinical diagnosis. Mostly I've learned to control it."

"Didn't you say your father had dysentery?"

"No connection, I'm sure." I didn't want to talk about it. "Are you headed home?" I asked. "Did you come in a car?"

"I walked. It's a short way."

"Shall I walk with you?" Always a gentleman.

"Thanks. I'd appreciate that."

As we reached the road she looked back for a second at the inn, as if she'd forgotten something, then to the right and the left. Irrational fear, I thought. I felt it, too, a sympathetic reaction, breathing it in with her smoke. The road was dark, no street lights. The mountains were invisible against the black sky, but I could feel their presence.

"What causes it in your case?" I asked.

"Who knows? Suppressed anger, I've been told."

"You suppressed it? Oops, sorry."

"Oh, Lord, I've got to apologize to Méndez. Did I make a complete fool of myself?"

"I wouldn't say that, but you sure kicked ass."

"Really bad, wasn't it?"

"Well, next time you could try being forthright."

"I shouldn't have done it."

"Why did you?" I asked.

"I had to break through all that nonsense."

A car passed us from behind, going slowly, its light shining on the puddles between cobblestones. Catherine dropped her head until it went by.

"I only do it in English, by the way—get bitchy, I mean," she said, as we walked on. "There's something about English that gives me permission to mouth off."

"There's an idea."

"They say speaking another language allows you to be someone else," she added, after another minute. "Have you noticed that yourself?"

"When I speak Spanish?" I thought about it. "I feel very young, with a child's bravado."

She laughed, the good one. We got chatty, a little hyper. She began talking about people she would like to be if she were not herself. The list was long, ending with Sojourner Truth. And who, she asked finally, would I like to be?

I mumbled about and finally said I'd settle for Oscar Peterson, since we at least had a name in common. Though, actually, I explained, come to think of it there was only one particular moment when I would like to be Oscar Peterson. It was when he was at the piano doing that thing skilled jazz artists do, letting out a line little by little, eight, twelve, twenty-four bars, more—and just when you think they are hopelessly lost, swept out to sea, crazy, absolutely suicidal and taking the whole world with them, back they come, slowly and certainly and not even out of breath.

There was nothing original in those remarks. I wasn't sure Catherine even heard me. We may have been talking at the same time, in fact. But then she said something that stopped me short. "Maybe Oscar Peterson has your *nahual*." It was a Mayan term, an old acquaintance appearing out of nowhere on this dark road, a funny word with a gulp in the middle. "How do you know that?" I asked.

"I think I got it first from *Men of Maize*. Miguel Asturias. It's your shadow self, isn't it, the *nahual*? It protects you. But it wanders. You can lose it. Sort of like losing your soul."

"There's another word for that," I said. "For losing your soul. But I can't remember it."

"*Susto.*"

"That's it!"

"A Spanish word for a Mayan idea."

"Trauma can do it, right? Cause your soul to fly out of your body."

"And if you know where it happened, you can go back and retrieve it. You stomp hard on the ground where you lost it, and maybe it will return."

"Or you lure it back, with music, or a drum, or the smell of tortillas, or maybe food in a bowl by the creek. Or is that your *nahual*?"

My throat tightened and I stopped. Not that she noticed. She was smoking furiously, staring straight ahead of her. Who was she now? And who was I? Whatever, we were a pair, she puffing away at her cigarette with shaky hands, and me so blurred up I could hardly see where I was going.

We walked without speaking for a few minutes. There were no other pedestrians, and only one other car, but still she was fidgety, glancing frequently over her shoulder.

"Do you know that guy Méndez brought?" I said. "We've talked about him before. Elizondo."

"Oh, Zondo, you mean. Our paths have crossed, years ago."

"I thought he spoke to you. Would he recognize you?"

"I doubt it. My hair was very short back then. I didn't look the same." She dropped her cigarette in the road and ground it out on a cobblestone. "The house is off here to the right."

We crossed and turned onto a street I had run down on numerous mornings, the house fronts joined and similar, cousins in pastels. People were gathered sociably in groups, enjoying the cool evening air. Someone was playing a *chirimía*, a hornpipe, and I heard the bright snaps of the *claves*, two sticks hit in rhythm. The music followed us and when it faded it played on in my head.

We stopped soon at a door in a wall, hard on the street, fronted by an iron grating, a typical Antigua home. "Thank you for being decent," Catherine said, pulling a ring of keys out of her bag.

"Anything for a fellow panicker."

"This is my aunt's place," she explained, sorting through the keys. "My husband's aunt, that is."

"Not your home?"

"Oh no. She willed it to the Cathedral. She died three weeks ago."

Three weeks ago was when I'd arrived. I didn't know what to say. "Were you close to her?"

"Quite. She was our favorite of my husband's whole tribe. She had emphysema and I came last month to be with her. That's why I'm here."

"I," not "we." And "here" as opposed to "where"?

"She was an old friend of the Méndez family. That's how I got the job." She opened the grating. There were three locks on the door. She inserted the keys and it swung inside with a squeak. The house was dark. If she had a husband, he wasn't here. Nor the son either, I assumed. She snapped on an overhead light. "I've been helping to wrap things up for her this month, lawyers and so forth. But I'm through with it now." She waved away a big moth, instantly drawn to the light.

"Are you all right now?" I asked.

"Yes. Thank you." A phone rang inside. "I'd better get that," she said.

"Right. *Adiós.*"

"*Sí.*" Another brief wave, at me or the moth, and she went in. A second light went on. I could still hear the phone. I stood there until it stopped, waited a moment more, then walked away, filled with that odd sense of incompletion. But some things just come to an end. Wasn't I learning that?

I had gone only two dozen steps when I heard the gate squeak, and her voice, calling softly. I walked back, unduly relieved.

"Are you leaving Antigua tomorrow, by chance?" she asked.

"That's the plan," I said.

"Well, so am I. That phone call. I just found out. How are you traveling?"

"I'll be going by bus. ...Oh. *Lo siento.* Do you need a ride? I'd gladly offer one if I could."

"I'm offering one to you. If you can stand it to ride in an ancient jeep."

"I'm not fussy."

"To be honest with you, I'd like the company. I may still be a little shaky."

"What time?"

"Morning. No later than 6:00. All right?"

"I'll be here."

"*Bueno. —Hasta mañana.*"

"*Mañana, sí. Bueno. Sí.*"

Sometime during the night Antigua treated me to a farewell surprise, my first earthquake. Not an important one, very low on the Richter scale. But it woke me up. My jacket swayed gently on its hanger on the back of the door and the Holy Family trembled on the bureau. Outside it was pouring, with occasional flashes of lightning. Downstairs the parrot gave a sleepy squawk and swore. I sat up, with a new sense of anxiety, as if the quake had spilled negative energy into the night air. I connected it to Catherine, a delayed distrust of that momentary rapport. Or more likely, it was just the obscurity of tomorrow's agenda.

I wrote for a while and read here and there in Thoreau and Dickinson. Usually they both offered composure. But that didn't work this time, so out came the baseball game, which I hadn't called on since my night at the Pan American Hotel. Batting order. I labored into the W's, regardless of team or position. Honus Wagner, Bucky Walters, Bill White. I stopped at Ted Williams. It occurred to me with sleepy amusement that maybe he, another namesake, was actually the guy who was harboring my soul. If so, he could have it. It seemed safe enough in his hands.

FOURTEEN

When my alarm went off at 5 A.M., the foreboding was still there. I had to deal with it, and did, under the tepid stream of the shower. Facts were still the answer, I told myself. I pictured them as a little collection of hard objects I could pack in my suitcase or bury in the ground and leave behind. Then back to Boston, like it or not. I made that a mental contract, with the date: Saturday, August 22, 1987. Signed it.

I helped myself to a quick breakfast in the quiet kitchen, the family still asleep. I wrote them a note of thanks and put it on the table under the saltshaker. The maid arrived while I was there. I gave her a tip, a little wad of *quetzales,* which she accepted shyly, slipping it into the band of her skirt, still refusing to look me in the eye. On the way out I whispered *adiós* to the parrot, who lifted her head from under her clipped wing and hoarsely reminded me of who she really was.

Outdoors I could hardly see for the fog. It was not raining; it was as if the air had turned to water. It settled in a layer on my head and face, and the soles of my shoes squeaked on the wet street. Catherine was waiting for me in her jeep at the curb, the motor running and the windshield wipers carving an arc in the collected dew. She hadn't exaggerated its age—an old Willys that had seen many moons, its once red body now a nasty brown. The passenger door was jammed shut. She signaled me to stand back, then gave it a hard kick. It popped open. I dropped my luggage and hat in the back beside a suitcase and her familiar woven tote bag.

It wouldn't have surprised me to see her as her old self, the usual chinos and long-sleeved cotton shirt, or as she had appeared last night, carefully groomed. Instead she was wearing a pair of jeans with holes in the knees, western boots, and a gray T-shirt with some kind of a logo on it in Spanish. Her hair was in a ponytail, caught up in a blue hairband, maybe the same one that had enclosed the verb cards.

"How are you this morning?" I asked.

A shrug for an answer, a glum teenager.

I tried again. "Is it something I said?"

My voice was lost in the growl of the jeep's motor as we pulled out into the street. I found the mechanism for moving the seat back to make room for my knees, but it was stuck, as it was in Rebecca's Honda. Was I spooked? On the road again, a poor fit in my passenger space, and an enigmatic woman at the wheel. Maybe she was entertaining an uneasiness like my own: Keep a distance. But we had at best another hour together. That was all, forevermore. Why should it be unpleasant? I would try again, I thought, magnanimously. "How long have you owned this jalopy?" The words jiggled as the jeep bumped over cobblestones.

"Three weeks." Ah, success.

I let a few minutes pass, then hit it again. "I have an idea," I said. "Let's make conversation in English, so you can mouth off and I can be a grownup."

"Whatever. What do you want me to say?"

"You could elaborate on your last reply."

"Oh, the jeep. It was Mag's, Magdalena's."

"Who's Magdalena?"

"The aunt I've been living with. The one who just died."

"I see. —So where are you headed now?"

"Home. Eventually. To Costa Rica. Where I live."

Home is Costa Rica. I let that sink in. We had begun to climb the long hill out of the city, the link leading up to the Pan-American Highway, the only civilized route back and forth between Antigua and Guate City. The wind had picked up and puffs of fog blew against the yellow headlights. Catherine shifted into second and the jeep strained, climbing slowly and painfully. Cars passed us, impatient, spraying us with last night's puddles.

"I can't see out the back," she said.

"I'll get it."

"There's a rag in the compartment there in front of you."

I found it and wiped all the windows I could reach. We were still in second. It was driving me nuts. Catherine's eyes lit repeatedly on the rear view mirrors. At the top of the hill she shifted into third and relaxed, visibly. "My son and I moved to Costa Rica after my husband died," she said.

You could have told me that, I thought.

"I should have told you that," she said.

Things were improving. I hesitated to ask her how her husband had died, but she answered as if I had. "A car accident."

"How terrible for you," I mumbled. How much did this explain about her? It was like reading through a book and finding you had skipped a crucial chapter.

"Martin," she said. She pronounced it with its Hispanic emphasis—MarTEEN. I imagined him in a flash: confident, urbane, Ladino. Statuesque. "How old was your son?" I asked, after a moment. "When this happened?"

"Nine."

I grunted.

"He'll be enrolling soon at the university in San José."

I started to ask more, but we had entered the Pan-American Highway, joining the stream of early morning rush into the city. There was an insanity to the traffic now, the same mindless aggression I'd witnessed on the bus coming in. Catherine, too, began passing cars unnecessarily, including two motor bikes riding in tandem, carrying an upholstered sofa between them. My incentive for conversation died. Getting through this alive was all that mattered. I checked for a seat belt. None.

The wind came up, bringing real rain. Water poured down our windshield. Then the shower stopped and the windows fogged up again.

"Do you have an air conditioner?" I asked. "Just kidding."

"Broken." A very small smile.

I mopped once more with the rag and cracked open my window. We were passing a strip of ramshackle houses with doors opening right on the highway. Then a fruit stand, melons, bananas, roses, then a *finca* spreading lushly into the mist. A cluster of pedestrians huddled along on the shoulder of the road, a whole family, it seemed, two half-grown children, a woman with a baby, walking behind the man who was bent at a 45-degree angle under a load of wood. Branches with leaves still on them waved from the top. *Mecapal.* The word slid neatly into home plate. It meant tumpline, the leather strap across the forehead, tied to a rope under the wood. It steadied the load, made it a part of you. The hips and thighs did the hard work, the way a pitcher's fastball depended on strength in the lower part of the body. That was how my father had explained it to me once. I watched in my mirror until the family was out of sight, hoping they didn't have too far to go.

We entered the city and merged with a new influx of traffic, a yet more intense and greedy battle for space. Whenever we stopped at lights, vendors walked perilously between vehicles, selling newspapers and flowers at car windows.

"Where should I drop you?" Catherine asked.

"Wherever it's convenient. Where are you headed yourself?"

"I have an errand in the city. It's your call."

"I'm going to need to rent a car. Know a good place?"

"*Sí, por supuesto.*" Of course.

So it appeared that our inevitable goodbye might be postponed for yet another few minutes. I found myself caught again in the tangled sense of unfinished business, as if we owed each other something we had overlooked.

She drove me to zone nine, a slick area full of modern architecture and up-scale shops. The rental business, an office with a small car lot, was framed in flowering bushes. Outside the office door a guard in fatigues slouched against the wall, his rifle at arm's width, stock on the ground. He looked damp and bored.

I invited Catherine into the office with me, in case there were any language hitches. As it turned out, the clerk, a patient young man, and I did fine together, quickly deciding on a black Plymouth midsize sedan, cheap and on the lot ready to go. I was about to sign for it when Catherine interrupted. "Where are you driving it?" she asked.

How could I answer that? My intention was to try to locate Tomás Garcia here in the city (if indeed he was still alive), call him and make an appointment (if indeed he had a phone), then maybe take off for the highlands to see if my old village still existed. "Into the western hills," I said.

The clerk took notice and politely suggested a four-wheel drive. Catherine agreed, less politely: "God, yes." Anyone with half a brain would know that. But there had been no four-wheel drives when and where I was a kid. The vehicle in most common use was the ancient Ford pick-up that did all our errands.

"What have you got available?" I asked the clerk.

"Only one on the lot."

That was true, a Toyota Land Cruiser, bright red, no choice in color. If I wanted to wait half an hour he might come up with a beige Montero from another lot. I settled for the Land Cruiser. I rented it for one week, the maximum amount of time I expected to still be here. The insurance premium was onerous, with a standard deductible of $1800 American money. There was a spare in the back, the clerk made it a point to tell me, and a jack and a lug wrench. I bought maps and a tour guide.

Outside, I asked Catherine for a little orientation, like directions to the best public telephones. I spread the city street map over the hood of my red golden goose and marked the streets with a pen, following her finger. As we stood there, the sun broke through, blindingly. Even this car lot was suddenly gorgeous, light bouncing off the wet surfaces of the vehicles.

"Wow. Cue in the music," I said. I was answered by a bark from across the lot as a dog entered stage right, limping, a small gray mongrel, a bitch. She began to sniff at some garbage, the crust of a pizza on the open space just behind my car. I made a comment about the critter's pathetic condition, and Catherine remarked, in return, "They say hell is a dog's life in Guatemala." At that, the mutt turned her bloodshot eyes on us and gave a bark, not a healthy "woof," but a sharp, hoarse wheeze, like "hawf."

"That's spelled *g-u-a-u*, in case you want to know," Catherine said. "It's what dogs say when they bark in Guatemala."

I answered with something about my final lesson. It was lost in what happened next. Catherine saw it coming before I did and let out a short scream as she jumped out of the way, yanking me by the sleeve. Four other dogs bounded toward us from between two cars, clearly on the scent, and circled the bitch in a snarly stand-off. Then one of them sprang onto her back and humped her, to a chorus of frantic yaps and howls, a regular open-air gangbang. Into this cut a rat-a-tat-tat, like drum sticks on the rim of the snare, and all five dogs convulsed into the air one by one and collapsed on the pavement. They lay there, thrashing and twitching.

I whirled to face the guard, still at his post outside the office door. He was resuming his earlier posture, body and rifle at ease, his face expressionless. "You could at least finish them off!" I shouted.

Catherine made a shushing noise. She stood frozen, studying her fingernails. The clerk appeared at the door of the office, then walked over, hands raised in a question. "Oh," he said, eyeing the dogs. He apologized profusely. He would get that cleaned up right away, he said, and walked back into the building, with no word to the guard. The dogs were still twitching. They had landed in a rough circle. Circle of hell, I thought. It struck me as an obvious truth, unquestionable, like a flash of reefer wisdom.

"Let's get out of here," Catherine whispered.

I walked her to the jeep. She hesitated as if she wanted to say something. Instead, she just held out her hand. "Goodbye, Ted. Have a safe and successful trip."

"Wait. Wait a minute," I stammered, ignoring her hand. "Wait. I'm thinking. About hell."

"I don't wonder. We may be lucky to be alive."

"And since we are, could we, is there a chance—suppose we meet again sometime later? Later today? For a tour, maybe, of the city's circles of—?" I stopped, I'm glad to say, short of that egregious analogy. The dark logic of seconds ago was quickly losing its force, like coming down off a high. I expected her to say no, as she had to the "parting glass" yesterday. But she agreed. "I think I can manage that," she said.

If she was teasing, I didn't detect it, not in the teen-aged persona standing before me. Later on I would have reason to understand her readiness, but now I was just relieved. We made arrangements. She needed a few hours to do her errand, after which she would know if she had time to spare. She described a particular parking place a few blocks behind the National Cathedral. She would either meet me there at 2:00 or leave a message with the owner if she couldn't make it. Then we got into our separate vehicles and she drove away.

I sat and surveyed my dashboard. My own car back in Cambridge was a ten-year-old Volkswagon bug, well-used when I bought it. Gray. It got me where I needed to go. But the *machismo* of this big red vehicle actually felt good. There were two gear shifts. There were also three horns. What for? I was not a horn blower, often could not even find the horn when I needed it, but I blew all three with gusto now as I ventured into city traffic.

FIFTEEN

The nearest Guatel office was exactly where Catherine said it would be. There I was assigned a nook and handed a phone book by a woman who sat behind a caged window. And there, sure enough, was Tomás Garcia Castillo in readable print, the TG in my father's letter, the person he had been trying to reach, "to talk," the guy who used to come to our village in a green station wagon. Actually there were two of them in the phone book, but only one was a *Reverendo*. I took a guess. The woman assistant dialed the number for me, and when my light blinked on I picked up the phone. What I heard next was a series of breaths and clicks, as if someone was eating, then a male voice, faint and slurred: "*Buenos días.*"

I answered, "*Buenos días. Reverendo Garcia, por favor?*"

More clicks, more breathing. The voice asked for my name.

"*Por favor, me llamo* Ted Peterson."

"*Qué?*"

"*Yo soy* Ted Peterson," I repeated. Silence. I tried again. "*Señor* Garcia? *Me llamo* Ted...."

The line went cold, then a dial tone. But I was pretty sure it was he. There was a quality to his voice that had intrigued me as a kid, a kind of papery crackle, as if he produced his own static, and that was what I had heard now, I thought, only more pronounced, the voice of a very old man. No protocol seemed right. Calling again could be cruel, and appearing in person might be ungracious. Still, back in the car I explored the city map for the address I had copied from the phone book. He was in zone nine, not far from where I'd rented the car. I decided to take a look.

After a scramble through traffic, I found the address, a square stucco apartment building in what I judged to be an upper middle-class neighborhood. There were trees, sidewalks, curbside parking places. I was sitting in the car, deciding what to do, when a boy appeared at my window.

"Watch car, *señor*," he announced, pointing to himself with a winsome bow, Guatemalan courtesy.

"Watch car? *Por qué?*"

"Ooh, danger, *señor*," said the kid. "Bad *hombre* steal."

Well, well, a protection racket. I got out and glanced up and down the street for the not so winsome big brother or uncle. No one was in sight. How did this work? Did refusal make vandalism a certainty? Politely?

"*Cincuenta centavos.* One hour. Pay now."

"Half now, " I said, digging into my pocket for coins. "*Cómo se llamo?*"

"Sergio."

"Okay, Sergio," I said, locking the door. "Car safe!" I put on a monster face. He laughed, spreading his arms over the hood.

Halfway down the block I looked back at him. He was leaning against the passenger door smoking a cigarette.

There were two apartments in the two-story building, two solid doors, two bells. The name Garcia was over one, for the second floor. I pressed that bell and in a moment heard someone descending stairs, very slowly and noisily, then clumpety-clump inside the door, followed by silence. The door was equipped with an eye viewer and I supposed I was being examined. I stepped back and tried to look unthreatening. Still no action, but the distinct sense of a presence on the other side of the door. I spoke, raising my voice. "*Hola! Me llamo* Ted Peterson. Son of Hulda and Ted."

Now I heard locks unfastening, and the door opened, just a crack at first, then wider. The person before me was bent almost double on a cane, a slight man with a prim white mustache, in a business suit and tie. He wore thick glasses and was staring up at me intently.

"*Señor* Garcia," I said.

He acknowledged with the merest gesture, staring hard at me.

"I am sorry if I startled you." I used the word for "frightened," the only one that came to mind, but it seemed not far-fetched.

He let out his breath, with something like a smile. Half his face was paralyzed, I saw now. The cheek on the left side sagged, the corner of the mouth drooping. "Ah! Ah! Ah! *Tú—? Teddy pequeño?*" he said, in a shocked whisper.

I have to admit, I melted. "Yes, I am. Little Teddy."

"*Sí, sí, sí!*" He reached out his hand with the cane and almost toppled. I grabbed his arm.

There was a garble of Spanish. "You sound and look so much like your father." I thought that was what he said, in that slurred, crackly speech. How could I have been so stupid? He was seeing a ghost of the other Ted he had known more than thirty years ago.

He smiled again with half his face and said something I had to ask him to repeat. "Stroke, stroke," he said in English. He turned toward the stairs, then stopped, indicating that I should go first. "*Pase, mi hijo.*"

I mounted slowly, but by the time I'd reached the top, he was still below, relocking the door before he began the climb. I feared for him, every step an obvious challenge to his strength and dignity, but I knew better than to ask if he wanted help. My mother had taught me that. I waited at the edge of a dim parlor, crowded with furniture. The shades were drawn and it was airless. A finger of odor reached me from another part of the apartment, sour, like an unwashed hand towel.

Garcia paused, breathless, at the top of the stairs. "*Perdone,*" he said, as if he had read my observations, then something about his wife. Dead three years? I mumbled sympathy, wondering what kind of linguistic chaos we were entering. But I was determined to make this work, without a dictionary, my first solo flight outside the safe boundaries of Antigua.

He led the way now, into a small study, and pointed me to an armchair covered with a crocheted afghan. He positioned himself behind the desk, as formally as his body allowed. The desk was neat—a marble pen holder, a cup of yellow pencils, all sharp. Two framed diplomas hung on the wall behind his head, one from the *Seminario Biblico Latinoamericano* in Costa Rica.

His posture made it necessary for him to gaze at me from the top of his glasses, giving him a slightly sinister air. He went on to ask a question I couldn't understand. He repeated it twice. Did I remember that he had baptized me, as an infant? He was still using *tú*, as if I were a child.

"Oh. I didn't know," I faltered. "Shall I thank you belatedly?"

It came out as "too late." This amused him. It was a mistake to make him laugh, I realized. I held my breath until he recovered, dabbing his mouth with a white folded handkerchief. "Theodore Cavalier Peterson," he announced then, with ceremony, hands open and lifted, as if presenting the baby before a congregation.

I bit back a smile. I seldom heard my middle name spoken. When Rebecca heard it for the first time, actually during our wedding ceremony, it almost broke her up. It was the part of my name a village leader had given me, an ancient custom. It sounded best as Garcia pronounced it, with the stress on the second syllable. Ca-VAL-yay.

He was asking a question. I leaned forward to get it. "Are you your father's spiritual son?" Before I had time to fudge an answer, he had rephrased it. Had I followed in my father's footsteps?

"I'm a teacher."

"As was your father," he said, "*esplendido.*" He asked about my mother.

"Her body is well, thank you, but her mind is——." I touched my forehead. He nodded, kept nodding. I cut in. "I need information. I am hoping you can help me understand some mysteries." Nuts. The word I came up with, *misterios,* suggested the occult. It was too soon for me to get so frank, anyway.

"What can you tell me about my father?" I asked, carefully.

Much too generalized. His voice slid into a long monotone hum, and for the next minute he straightened things on his desk, lining up at right angles a book and the pen holder, his face inches away from them in his bent posture. I thought he was contemplating an answer, but suddenly he looked up, past me, to the ceiling, as if he had heard something up there, hearing it before I did, like a dog. It was only the high whine of a jet, but in a matter of seconds the windows began to vibrate, the pencils chattered in their cup, and it was as if the air above us splintered and fell into shards. I grabbed my ears, but it was gone.

"Take-off pattern," Garcia said in English.

I re-launched. "My father. *Mi padre.* What did he do here?"

Pues, he said, he could answer that. He knew all about what my father did, my mother, too. My parents had been put under his *tutela* when they arrived, his supervision. He was the one who found them a home in a village and introduced them to the work of other missionaries. He went into an aside then, about himself. He explained that his own *patrimonio* was pure Spanish, and something about his family being among the first in the country, back in the 19th century, to become Protestant. I sensed an odd pride, as if this were some kind of aristocracy.

"But your father, *sí,*" he said. He made a few more right-angle adjustments on the desk, cleared his throat, and swallowed several times. "What he did."

I listened intently, reluctant to interrupt, though he was not telling me any more than I had vaguely understood as a child. My parents were here under the I.F.F. As a kid learning to spell, I thought it meant just "if." It stood for Independent Faith Fellowship. "*No affiliación,*" said Garcia. Its purpose was to assist other work already established, and so my father "taught and preached and helped out in various ways wherever he was needed, for the Presbyterians, Methodists, Central American Mission, even some Roman Catholics."

He dropped his voice to a whisper at that and glanced out the window, as if someone out there could hear, then turned back to me with an apologetic gesture.

"Your father," he said again.

He reached up with his good hand, pulling resistant words out of the air. "*Un hombre de talento excepcional.*" He continued with something undecipherable, about the University of San Carlos and a group of students, "that last year, the last year he was here."

"1954?" I said, in English.

"*Sí.*" He paused to deal with saliva. When he spoke again it was just one word, "*Pero*"—but. He was wiping his mouth at the same time. I waited for him, then asked: "*Pero?*" He looked confused. "Did you say *pero?*" I asked again. "Did I?" he said. At that point he folded his hands on the desk, the right one over the limp left, and raised his eyes toward the ceiling, as if giving thanks, and sure enough, we were instantly shaken to the teeth by the take-off of another jet. His voice slid again into that low nasal hum, like a bee hovering over the desk. "He changed."

The verb he used was the predictable one, *cambió,* with no implication intended, good or bad. Now he said, "*Se torció,*" meaning "He turned," or more precisely, "twisted." It was a strange word to apply to a person. Before I could chase it down, he switched back to *cambió,* with a flick of the wrist. It was either damage control, or just a bilingual adjustment for the gringo.

"Changed how?" I asked.

His answer came through as a puddle of disconnected sounds. We entered a kind of slapstick together. I pressed the question every way I could manage, feeling like Moe taking jabs at Larry, and he kept answering with slush. It occurred to me he could drop dead at the desk. Still I persisted. "What happened?" I asked. He answered. I didn't get it. I longed to use a dictionary. It was in my pocket but looking things up seemed too awkward. I reached for my father's letter instead. "There are people," I said, "people my father mentioned to my mother."

He shut his eyes and put his hand to his head. "I hope you will forgive me now. I tire rather easily." With that, he made an effort to straighten his body, pushing himself away from the desk.

I felt wrung out myself. I stood and begged him not to get up, but he insisted, gathering himself out of his chair, brushing me off. I followed him back through the parlor, anxious for fresh air, and slowly, slowly down the stairs. At the front door, as he began to unlock his three bolts, I made one last sortie into the man's mind. "Felipe," I said.

He turned instantly, part way around. "*Sí? Felipe López?*"

"That's it."

"*Muerto.*" Dead.

"His son. Luis?"

"Luis. Oh, *sí, vive! Realmente!*" Alive indeed.

"Do you know how I can reach him?" I asked.

In the phone book, of course, he said.

"He's here, here in the city?" I felt like a hound just given a scent and probably looked like that. But Garcia ignored me and went back to the business of the locks. He opened the door, then shut it again and positioned himself to look up into my face. "Teddy! Teddy, *mi hijo!*" he said, his voice projecting as it had not before, his Spanish more distinct and deliberate. I understood it all, without question. "Let me give you some advice. In this country it is best to choose your company with the greatest of care. Do not ask questions. Questions are dangerous. They endanger us all. Be a tourist, enjoy this beautiful place, and then go home. Go home, go home to your own country! *Regresa a tu patria!*"

Then he opened the door once more and, in effect, swept me through it.

SIXTEEN

I found Sergio sitting contentedly on my right front fender. He alighted with a smile and held out his hand, palm up. "*Cincuenta centavos*," he said, cheerfully.

"I paid you half," I said.

"Oh no, *señor*. Still owe big."

His brazen deceit was actually a relief. He stood his ground, waiting. The car seemed fine, hub caps, antenna, license plates, all there. I flipped him more change. "*Hasta la vista, bandido*," I said, and the kid was off.

I drove back to the center of the city to look for the parking lot Catherine had designated. It turned out to be a muddy alley between two houses with room for half a dozen cars. A hulk of a man appeared from the rear door of one of the buildings and gestured me to stop. This was no Sergio. He peered in through my open window and told me to get out of the car, and I did.

"ID," he said. "Show."

I pulled out my passport picture and held it up to him. He took longer to look at it than I thought necessary. "Who sent?" he asked. Catherine O'Brien Rodriguez, I told him. "Okay," he said. "She call."

With a message for me? "What did she say?"

"She say red." He stepped back and studied the car with an exaggerated frown. "Ah *sí*, red!" He smiled broadly. He had three gold teeth.

"What do I owe you?" I asked.

"Pay later."

I pulled into the slot he indicated, next to a dusty black Ford Escort. When I got out of the car he was gone.

It was still only noon and I had two hours to kill before meeting Catherine, so I walked to the public plaza, the Parque Central. It was bigger than I remembered it, the size of a couple of football fields, paved in large black and white squares and sectioned off into areas of neglected grass. At the one where my father and I had arm-wrestled, an old man was cutting weeds with a small machete. The palace, of greenish stone three stories high, stretched along the far side.

Under the warmth of the late morning sun, people had gathered lazily around a three-tiered fountain, while a brisk trade was taking place in a row of stores along the sidewalk. In front of these, other merchants had spread their wares—cassette tapes, sunglasses, black velvet paintings of Marilyn Monroe and the Virgin. At one booth a child held a live rooster, cuddled in a blanket. A smoky cart sold roasted corn.

The noise around me was all-encompassing. I stood still and listened. It broke down into the shouts of hawkers, bus horns, backfires, brakes, radios, dogs barking, somewhere a siren and somewhere the wail of a reed pipe, but it rose together like a great concert of expectancy and alertness, as if a terribly important event was about to break upon us all.

The immediate event was the arrival of an ice cream truck, playing a Scott Joplin rag as it pulled up at the curb. Instantly, a half-dozen children appeared, with a swoop, like the flock of pigeons that fluttered out of their way—half-grown kids, eight or ten years old, boys and girls both. They alit together beside the truck, hands extended with a chorus of demands, and were quickly shooed away, retreating in a body. They darted here, there, finally to the gutter, where they hovered, nibbling discarded corn cobs

Then they spotted me, the undisguised gringo, and were upon me in seconds. They gave off a smell, a great waft of dirty kid odor, as if that were communal, too. What are you doing here, I wanted to ask. Where are your mommas? They were all hands, growing more hands as they stood there. The ice cream vendor was still at the curb. I beckoned them over and bought them all popsicles, acutely aware that this pink and green ice was not what they needed.

While they were distracted by slurping these, I hurried away across the tiles in the direction of the palace. In a moment I became aware of a female voice behind me calling softly, "*Por favor, por favor.*" I peered over my shoulder, and that was all it took to bring a girl to my side.

She was carrying a tray of trinkets. Young, a child herself, maybe fifteen. Her clothes were modest, but her real commodity was expertly advertised, pressing against a silky top. Not bad. "*Buenos días, señor*," she said, catching my eye with purpose. "Chip. Ver chip."

"Ver nice, but no thanks," I said, smiling, and walked away.

She closed in behind me, cheeky. "Full service, *señor*," she said. "Chip and clean. I give you address. *Chupar? Frotar?*" I kept walking and still she followed. "I like funny hat, *señor*." I waved a thank you over my head.

Now above the din I heard again the piping chorus of the children, who were finding their way back to the rich gringo. They were remarkably fast, surrounding me like a runny-nosed army. I shook my head: "*Nada, nada.*" But they knew better. "Bye-bye!" I crowed, turning my back. One of them echoed it, "Bye-bye!" Then they sang it together. "Bye-bye, bye-bye!" They began to giggle, calling out that hilarious sound over and over. What did they hear in it? Not a verbal construct, I was sure, just an infant's babble. One clown threw himself on the ground, helpless with laughter. I stood and watched the show, laughing too, then did the gringo thing, doled out *quetzales* into their hands, uncounted, ashamed of myself, sure they would spend it on glue, or something worse.

Still they followed me, across the plaza toward the sanctuary of the palace. And behind them the girl, with her enticing merchandise. She had not given up. "Ver nice!" she called. I was running away from a bunch of children and a teen-aged prostitute.

To the left on the next corner I saw the sign of the Hotel Centenario atop a square building, and remembered that George Patton Crane, my verbose airplane companion, had said he would be staying there most of the month. The notion of a talkative academic hobo seemed very appealing at the moment. I crossed the street, and entered the lobby. When I looked back, the children and the girl were gone.

And Crane was there. "Oh yes, he is expecting you," said the clerk at the front desk. "You can go right up." Right up? Had he been watching my little parade from a window? "That can't be," I said. "I didn't know myself."

"*Señor* Crane said that when *norteamericano* comes I should send him up, to the terrace on the third floor. Only you are early, so perhaps you can catch him in his room. Shall I ring?"

"Yes, please."

Crane also expressed no surprise. "*Amigo!* Come up, come up! I'm happy to hear from you."

He was at his door on the second floor when I got there. "You must be waiting for someone else," I said, as we shook hands. He was dressed in the same crumpled suit he had worn on the plane, only now he had added a broad-brimmed cowboy hat. His empty pipe hung in its s-curve from his lips.

"I am," he said. "But no matter. What can I do for you? Another *deus ex machina?*"

"I'm escaping from a *puta*," I said.

"Hooker! Fate worse than death."

"And I could use a phone book, if you don't mind."

"Help yourself. The switchboard downstairs will forward calls. I'd better go up to the terrace in case my party arrives. Join us, please. There's food. I ordered out." He gesticulated to the ceiling with his finger, then put it aside of his nose, like a red-bearded Saint Nick on his way up the chimney.

The room was littered with papers, a whole filing system it seemed, spread out on the bed, the floor, the small desk—his dissertation, I assumed. I hopscotched between the piles to the telephone and dug into his phone book. I looked up López, found many, three of them Luises. I gave the switchboard the first number.

A woman answered in Spanish, a young clear voice. No, she said, Luis was not here just now. This was Carmen speaking. Might she tell him who was calling? There was a lot of noise in the background, children laughing, a dog barking.

"Tell him Teddy Peterson," I said.

"Oh!" she exclaimed. "Oh, Peterson? Really? *Teddy* Peterson? Old friend Teddy? Is it that one?"

"Yes. That one. Turkey-call Peterson."

"I know you, yes! I know about the turkey call. I am Luis's wife. So many times I have heard that name Peterson. You are in the country?"

"I'm here in the capital now."

"Oh, he will be so glad to see you." He was away for a couple of days, she said, but tomorrow he would be in Quetzaltenango, at the "branch office." Could I go there, she wanted to know. Yes, I said, tomorrow, in fact. I repeated "Quetzaltenango." It was familiar to my tongue. All right, she said, he was speaking somewhere in the morning but he planned to be at the office early afternoon. She knew how to reach him and let him know I was coming.

Branch office, speaking somewhere. I sat for a minute, pondering all that, then scouted my way to the terrace, up an exterior stairway to an open stretch of concrete set up with plastic tables and chairs. Crane waited there alone, seated in a far corner under a deep overhang. Spread out before him was a paper platter of sandwiches and bottles of beer. He was drinking from one. He shoved out a chair for me with his foot.

"I had a hunch I might see you again," he said. "I hope you came for more than one's phone book."

"Just tracking down a few facts," I told him.

"Facts? That's a laugh. What did Hegel say? If facts run counter to what you believe, so much the worse for the facts." Same old talking machine, but this time I didn't mind. "Most facts around here have something to do with trouble," he said. "Have you noticed? As if everything else is hearsay, undependable information. Don't trust good news."

He handed me a beer and an opener. I flipped the top off my bottle and a flume of vapor shot out. I sipped, half-listening as he chattered on. "What did Tolstoy say? What's the difference between reactionary violence and revolutionary violence?"

"Cat shit and dog shit?" I said, not sure how we got to Tolstoy.

"I think it was the other way around."

I laughed but he was in earnest. He mopped his forehead with a paper napkin. "It's just possible you may know the chap I'm waiting for," he said. "Name is Luke Treadwell. He's an MK. Ring any bells?"

"No. Why should it?"

"Because you're an MK yourself. Missionary kid."

I sighed. "Apparently it sticks out all over me."

"Oh, not at all," he said. "I've been getting into the *Archivo General de Centro America,* under the Ministry of Foreign Relations, etcetera, and I've gathered a list of just about every foreign family that came and went in the country for a hundred years. Smoking out my subjects, you see. I found record of a Theodore Peterson and his wife Hilda, or Hulda, here between '44 and '54, with one son, Theodore something, born 1947. I added two and one. That's you, isn't it?"

I was astounded. There was actually such a record? "What else did it tell you about us?" I asked.

He laughed. "Let's see. This son Theodore was an uncontrollable brat. Something like that."

"Hey, I was a good boy." I thought of asking other questions, real ones, but hesitated to make Crane too much of a confidante. He was pushing ahead on his own course, anyway. "Surely you knew the Tread- wells," he said. "They've been here a long time. Central American Mission. Remember that family?"

I didn't. I could see a thunderhead building over the city rooftops, obscuring the mountains. I watched it as Crane gave me the Treadwell history. Five kids in the family, all "well-adjusted grownups," the oldest, a woman, a doctor, general practitioner in Minnesota, a sister getting her Ph.D at Stanford, one brother a teacher in Syria and another in foreign service in Japan. "All happily married to their first spouses and producing another generation of well-adjusted children. Scary, isn't it? You're about to meet one of them."

"The guy you're really expecting?"

"Yes, and he's the exception that proves the rule, which is why I'm trying to pick his brain. He doesn't fit the family model. Quit college, for instance. Vietnam vet. Married three times. A bit of a roué, I'd guess. What interests me is that he's chosen to stay in this country, a real expat. He runs a big bird service, owns a Huey. Transports all kinds of people—tourists, anthropologists, missionaries. No bells yet?"

"None."

Crane's eyes shot to the other end of the terrace. "And what do you know, here is our man in person, Luke Treadwell."

I turned, half-expecting to see a swashbuckling soldier of fortune. Instead, the guy who stood there looked like he needed a good program in sit-ups. He had stopped at the top of the stairs, grinning, his hands on his knees as he caught his breath after the climb. He was wearing jeans and sandals and a Rolling Stones T-shirt that looked its age. We stood to greet him.

"Ted Peterson is a Guatemalan MK, too," said Crane.

"No kidding. Doesn't that make you feel about ten years old?" said Luke, shaking my hand.

"It certainly sets the agenda," I said.

"*Carpe diem,* gentlemen," Crane said. "I have questions for the two of you."

Luke laughed, a high cackle. I studied him as we sat down. The only other missionary kids I had known here were the ones I played with when the parents held conferences, and nothing about him sent a signal. Traces of the young boy he'd have been were surely gone. His face was scarred by acne, and his hair, brown, looked like a slipped toupee, hanging down to his collar at the back. An eagle was tattooed along his right forearm, wings spread between his elbow and wrist.

He lit a cigarette and eyed me over the flame of his match. "Negative," he said. He had not known any other missionary kids except the ones here in the city. "Maybe our parents knew each other."

At that point the torrent slammed into the terrace. We watched from our dry corner under the eave. Lots of water, not much of a lightning display. In a minute the surface of the floor had turned into a shallow pool. We propped our feet up on the chair rungs. It passed over quickly. Roof drains gurgled and gulped and the sun emerged. As we dove into the sandwiches, Luke gave his cackle laugh again, and now I knew where I might have heard it.

"Where did you go to college?" I asked.

"Norton," he said.

"Indiana."

"That's it! Mid-sixties, right? "

"But you weren't called Luke."

"No. I was Bucky."

"I remember a guy named Bucky."

"Do you? How come I don't remember you?"

"I made it a point not to attract attention," I answered.

"Wish I could say the same. I left early in my sophomore year."

"I dropped out as a freshman."

Crane was gleeful. "Excuse me for interrupting, gentlemen, but shall we call this a corking coincidence?"

"Nah," said Luke. "Lots of MKs went to Norton."

"We got in free," I added. "A small college, defunct now, I think."

"Were you happy there?" Crane asked us.

"Not especially," said Luke. "But my siblings loved it."

"Where do you come in the family?" I asked, hoping to keep him the center of things. Crane was opening a pen.

"The middle," Luke said. "Hemmed in on all sides." He was squinting at me. "Ever play the you-know-you're-an-MK-if game?" I hadn't. "Here's one for starters, the most obvious," he said. "You know you're an MK if they ask where you're from and you don't know."

"Corking!" said Crane.

Luke stuck his finger at me. "It's your turn."

"I'm not ready."

"I've got one," said Crane. "Army brats can play, too. You know you're an MK if you speak two languages but can't spell in either."

"Okay," I said. "You know you're an MK if you never ask questions about what you're eating."

"Where He leads me I will follow, what He feeds me I will swallow," Luke recited.

It was wearing thin, but Crane was into it. "You know you're an MK if you find yourself seeking some kind of an interstitial culture."

"You got that from a book," Luke said.

"Not entirely. Hang on just a minute." He began flipping through the pages of a notebook.

Luke was squinting at me again. "Take off the beard," he said. I covered my chin. "By criminy, you *did* attract attention."

"Afraid so. And so did you." The Bucky of twenty some years ago had restored himself wholly, as the "missionary brat," the noisy show-off on campus, and I knew exactly what he was remembering about me.

"What are you guys talking about?" asked Crane.

"I was an arrogant son of a bitch," Luke told him. "You can write that down, but it's all you get."

Crane turned to me, pen poised. "And what were you?" he asked.

"Nothing worth mentioning," I answered.

"*Amigos*," he said, "you cause me great suffering. Help me out. I'm trying to nail down a thesis. Where's the common ground among MKs? Those I've interviewed seem to fall into two categories. Some have become productive world citizens. Others don't seem to belong anywhere. They live forever off shore, one might say—emotionally, *id est*." He seemed to like that, almost smacked his lips. "What about you? Not to get too personal, of course. You first, Ted. What do you have to say about that?"

I opened my arms, empty. "You want a yes or a no?"

"And what about you?" Crane asked Luke.

"Me? Hey, I'm just making a living." He brushed a little puddle of water off the table. "Remember that song, 'Accentuate the positive, eliminate the negative?'"

"'But don't mess with Mr. In-Between,'" Crane obligingly added.

Luke handed us each a business card, whipped from his shirt pocket: *Mr. In-Between Transport Services.* He scraped back his chair and stood, and so did I. It was 1:30, almost time to meet Catherine.

"Oh shucks," Crane said. "Am I losing you? Can we meet again? Where are you going next, Ted?"

"I think I'm heading into the highlands."

"Whereabouts?" asked Luke.

"Quetzaltenango."

"Xela," he said.

That's what we had called it, the Mayan name, pronounced SHAY-la, the closest metropolis to our village.

"What takes you there?" Luke asked.

I gazed at him for a second, his sweaty, pock-marked face. "Have you ever given a ride to a guy named Luis López?"

"Luis López. I know who you mean. But I haven't ever flown him."

"What do you know about him?" I asked.

"Not much. He's an organizer. Hob-nobs with the peaceniks and NGOs. Pushes the envelope, what I hear. An outspoken Indian, not a good combination. You know him?"

"As a kid. I'm hoping to find him."

"I don't think he'll be hard to find," Luke said. "He makes himself pretty visible. I'd be careful."

Crane had stopped writing and was glancing back and forth between us. "Is our friend here playing with fire?" he asked Luke.

"Probably not. He looks like he just got off that guy's boat—Erik the Red. He'll be safe."

"And what does not safe mean?" I asked, but he was backing away across the steamy wet terrace, holding out his hand in a "heil."

Crane began talking fast. "Please, boys. Before you go, allow me to make a suggestion. I leave for El Salvador tonight, but I'll be back Sunday. If Lukas here can fly me to Chichi on Monday for an interview I've lined up there, I'll buy you both breakfast at the Santo Tomás, best hotel in the highlands. How does that sound?"

"I can't promise anything," Luke said. "I'm obliged to register all flights with the military, you know. I comply. I couldn't even own a bird without their okay."

"Do you ever fly for them?" Crane asked.

"Sometimes." He was still backing away. "I made a drop on a remote village a while back. Hope I didn't hurt anyone. It was hard candy. Well, I'm off. *Carpe diem.*"

"Wait a second," I said, with a last minute hunch. "If you think of it, ask your folks if they knew mine."

"Sure thing, I will. It's been corking, fellows." He was gone.

"And you, Ted," Crane said. "About Monday. Can you make it by 9:00 A.M.?"

I was trying to picture a map, pinpoint the location of Chichi. I told him I couldn't promise, either. I'd check it out with the military. He didn't laugh.

SEVENTEEN

Catherine was nowhere in sight at the alley parking lot. I got into the car to wait for her and she popped into my rear view mirror, as if she'd been hiding somewhere. I reached over and opened the door for her. The teenager had been into her mother's make-up. She had added black eye-liner, quite a lot. It changed her face, not for the better.

"Can we do this tour in your wagon?" she asked.

"Sure, but where's your own?"

"Died on me."

No wonder there.

"The battery. Maybe other stuff. It's at a garage. I can get it later."

"What about your errand?"

A gesture of dismissal.

"I'll pay the parking guy," I said.

"No charge."

"Do you still want to do this?" I asked that reluctantly, sure the answer would be no. She said, "Why not?" which was worse than no, a teen-ager with nothing better in view. Either I had misunderstood her earlier willingness, or something had changed in the hours since we parted. But as we climbed in she asked me where I wanted to go first, and I said with barely a thought, "San Carlos University."

"Really? Why there?"

"I don't know."

"Whatever." She began navigation as soon as I'd maneuvered out of the alley. "You've got a left turn coming up." I took it and had to brake with a screech as a car cut in front of me. "Jackass!" I yelled, not finding even one of the three horns.

Not a good beginning. And what can I say about the next two hours? They were as unpredictable as the meandering course we took through the city. I might have found the way to San Carlos a lot faster by myself. Her directions, which she seemed to be reading off the rear-view mirror, were so circuitous I wondered if we were trying to shake somebody. We drove south in start-and-stop traffic through a sea of smoggy emissions, past landmarks—a zoo and a park, a couple of statues, and a puzzling pint-sized replica of the Eiffel Tower. She pointed out embassies, U.S. and Spanish, "the scene of that terrible fire seven years ago." Fire? Yes, she said. Surely I knew about Rigoberta Somebody's book. I didn't answer.

We reached the airport, then turned and reversed our steps, for no reason I could fathom, and crossed into a maze of side streets known only to a veteran, I was sure, and onto a road that led us at last to the university. What we entered then was not an elmed and ivied quad. It was more like a little city in itself, gray concrete filling its boundaries, as ugly as sin. Or it would be, except for a display of brightly painted murals on the walls of the campus buildings, and the vibrant presence of students, on foot and bikes. We had driven into an energy field that, as it felt to me, electrified the car with its force. I pulled over into what appeared to be a legitimate parking area, and turned off the motor.

"Why are we here?" asked Catherine.

I was staring at the murals. All of them were supersized, in Stalin-esque art style. In one, the American flag covered the sky behind a field of barefoot men bent over their hoes. In another, a farmer worked alone in a brown garden, his back to a drop-off in the land, where the tips of a dozen bayonets peeked just over the brow, like a crop of unlikely plants. It was terrible art, and wonderful, like the art of children.

Catherine was watching me with the witchy penciled eyes.

"What was happening here in 1954?" I asked.

"Before or after the coup?"

A noisy cluster of students passed our car, running, book bags swinging on their backs. She asked the question again after they had gone by. "Do you mean during the revolutionary period? Or after the coup?—Do you know the difference?" She knew I didn't. She sighed. "The revolution came first, in 1944. That was a peaceful uprising. It was as if everybody had gotten sick and tired of everything and just stopped. The whole place shut down. There's a joke that even the whores stopped working. The dictator, Ubico, quit and a democratic government was voted in."

"And the coup?"

"Ten years later the coup changed everything back to the way it was, every new freedom reversed."

"Who was behind that? Guerrillas?" It seemed like a logical question, but no, it was stupid, and once again I got the witchy look. "There were no guerrillas here in 1954," she said. "Can we move, by the way? I don't think this is a public parking place."

I drove on, slowly, watching for an exit.

"Did your parents have any idea what was happening during the coup?" she asked.

"I don't know. —Didn't I tell you that before?"

"Never mind. They wouldn't have the facts, anyway. It took twenty-eight years for the truth to be published. Not that they'd believe it. The truth can't make you free if you don't accept it."

So now she was quoting Scripture, sort of. And here I was at another moment when the direction of everything changed. It was not the import of whatever Catherine meant. I wasn't picking up on that at all. What rose to the surface was a long-lost piece of data. Somewhere, in some class years before, I'd been given a stray bit of Greek exegesis that had traced itself on my brain. The word "truth" in "the truth shall make you free" actually meant the "revealed," or the "unhidden."

We had left San Carlos behind us and were back in traffic before I was ready to speak. I said, "You know what? I don't know. I don't bloody know anything. I don't know the difference between a revolution and a coup and I don't know which side my parents were on, and I don't know about a bloody fire in the Spanish Embassy or a book by bloody somebody or other. I don't know if the war is over and I don't know who is fighting who, and I don't know any of that stuff you were ranting about at the party last night. I don't even bloody know why I'm bloody here at all."

I was peering out the front, driving as I talked, but I saw her head swing around to me, the ponytail following, I think at the first bloody. She said, "I thought you told me—. You mean you're not looking for—?"

"My father's grave? I don't know that either." It was several minutes before either of us said anything else, other than her navigational directions. She didn't ask me to explain, though I knew she was waiting.

"There's a possibility that my father did something here," I said finally. "Something he shouldn't have, I mean. Done, that is. Or not. Done. Something he should have done that he didn't, or shouldn't."

Our eyes met and I realized hers were reflecting mine, my own bumbling candor. It diverted me. I covered my tracks. "It's hard for me to believe it was anything scandalous. Not—what's the word for family shame?"

"*Verguenza.*"

"Not that there weren't a great many ways a missionary could get into hot water. But I don't think he deflowered an Indian girl or took to drink."

"When did you start to suspect this?"

"After we moved to the States when I was a kid." I was beginning to be sorry now that I'd told her. It seemed like too much truthfulness, a betrayal of my father, more so because I had no solid basis for it. *Aletheia.* There, that was it, the Greek word for "unhidden." I felt unprotected, my long secret flapping in the wind.

"What about siblings?" she asked. "Would they know?"

"I was an only child." Time to move the searchlight: "What about you?"

"An only child? God, no. I come from a rollicking, foul-mouthed bunch. Secrets were impossible in our house."

It sounded good to me. "Do you go home often now?"

"To the bosom of my family? Never. I've been *persona non grata* there for a long time."

"*Por verguenza,* by chance?"

"As effective as that. My Dad was an Irish Catholic conservative of the old school. He stumped the streets for Senator Joe McCarthy when he ran for the Senate."

"Wisconsin, sure. You couldn't have been more than a baby then."

"I wasn't even born. But my father was a hidebound ideologue all the years I knew him."

"Let me guess. The day came when you faced each other down."

"Over and over. Every visit back after I'd left home for college. One day he called me a fucking Communist and I called him a fucking fascist. Something like that. Probably worse. A lot worse. I was disowned by the whole family and I haven't been back since. My father recently died."

She returned to the job of watching our back in the mirrors. "I'm running out of time," she said. "What would you like to see next?"

I said I'd like to ride by the Pan American Hotel. She didn't ask me why. It was fine with her, on the way to her jeep. So we continued north to zone one and drove under the canopy of signs on 6 Avenida. There it was, right where I left it, the stranded ocean liner. There was the balcony, where I'd stood half-naked that early morning. Pedestrians now filled the sidewalk. The stores were open. The air was full of the din of traffic. What did I expect? I felt nothing. We drove on by.

"What was that about?" asked Catherine.

"I think I was mistaken. I thought I saw something here, three weeks ago. A guy abducted. What's the word?"

"For abduction? You mean *desaparecido?*"

"As in Chili? Argentina?"

"As here. We did it first. You saw that happen?"

"I thought I did. How likely would it be? My first day here? It seemed almost staged."

"What kind of a car was it?"

"A white van, a Chevy, I thought."

"Believe it or not, one like that has been cruising the city a lot this year, kidnapping people, especially in the early morning."

"So I didn't imagine it." I felt no relief. "Who drives it?"

"No one knows. One of the paramilitary death squads. There are several. They have lovely names, like the *Mano Blanca*. They leave a drawing of a white hand near the body. *Avenging Jaguars* is another. That one's a smoke screen for the police. Then there are auxiliary groups, vigilantes. They feed info into the military computer system. That's one way people get fingered."

"For what? What could my guy have done, exactly?"

"Done, huh. Let's see, maybe he got on a bus one day and sat down next to the wrong person. He said good morning in the wrong tone of voice. After that it was just a matter of time. It's not what he did. It's what he *could* do. You can drop me off at the parking lot."

We were back at the plaza. I stopped while pedestrians crossed. "But we haven't finished, we haven't seen half the city," I said, grasping after anything. "Where is the old Street of Solitude, and that other one, the Street of Forgetting?"

"Just numbers now."

"Show me."

"I shouldn't. I should go. Really. —However."

"I've always liked that word."

"There is something I could show you. Just quickly. If you wish."

I didn't ask why she'd changed her mind or where we were going. In a few minutes we were on Avenida la Reforma, a business strip. From there we turned right around a park, down another major highway, passing the tarmac of the airport and a park and the zoo and soon angling off onto another highway (all I caught was the name "Bolivar" on a sign) then another turn and another, into a block of shacks, built like a wall along the street, remarkably constructed of anything that would enclose, strips of corrugated metal and blue plastic tarp. The street was busy, workmanlike, people carrying stuff in both directions, all kinds of stuff, furniture, car parts, building material. Then the houses stopped but the pedestrian traffic continued.

"Here we are," said Catherine. "*El basurero.*"

She'd brought me to the city dump, a spectacle that would have piqued Dante's creativity, acre after acre of raw garbage, and more being dumped into little mountains from the backs of trucks, as if the city were throwing away half of itself. People, dozens of them, were digging around in this, some with shovels. I watched a woman in rubber boots wade into a pile of garbage and pull out something she gave to a child, who proceeded to eat it.

The whole set-up was a huge preternatural beast, breathing spurts of fire here and there. Steam and smoke and dust rose together, gray, yellow, green. Over it vultures hovered like pieces of trash caught in a draft. There was something fiendishly beautiful about it. The smell was exotic.

"Hades," I said.

"You can call it Exhibit A," said Catherine. "B is half a mile up that street."

"Up that street" we passed the morgue on our right and crossed another street to an elaborate gate between two stone pillars. There we paid a guard three *quetzales* and parked.

"This is La Verbena, "said Catherine, as she opened her door. "Are you coming?"

A cemetery. It was enormous. I followed her on a walkway between walls of niches, three and four vaults high in places, some of them with names, some without an ID of any kind. I was attacked by another smell, an ominous one that made the dump odors merely fruity by comparison. At the end of that corridor we stepped out onto what was apparently a potter's field, here and there a flat stone, a wooden cross, a rock, or just a slight mound in rough weedy grass.

We walked through this, meandered, answering some directional guide of Catherine's own. I had the sense that this was a place familiar to her, one she visited often. We walked until we came to the edge of a ravine, a *barranco*, deep and wide and empty. It was windy here, a stiff breeze that watered my eyes and almost took my hat. We stood there for several minutes.

"One more stop," said Catherine. Her eyes were watering, too. She wiped them with a tissue, smearing the black make-up. She removed the rest of that in the car as she gave me directions. I found the traffic a relief, filled as it was with live human haste and anger. Back we went, retracing again, finally onto Avenue of the Americas, where we stayed a good while until Catherine said, "Quick! Left lane, left lane!" I squealed us into a turn-off, risking life and limb. I was getting better at this.

We made two more turns, and suddenly it was quiet, as if a big door had slammed shut behind us. We were on a narrow boulevard, totally arched by palms and shade trees. I slowed to a creep and rolled down my window. Sweet grassy air washed in, replacing the stenches that had found a home in my sinuses.

"Exhibit C," I whispered. "Paradise."

"Take a good look," Catherine said. "What do you see?"

I looked, as we poked along under the foliage. I saw well-kept lawns stretching back behind high iron fences to whitewashed mansions. I saw bougainvillaea, magenta-colored, climbing the walls of a house, entwined in something shiny along the eaves. Razor wire, that's what it was, glinting sharply in the sun. I saw, above that, in one corner of a red-tiled roof, a small dark structure, a kind of bristling, like the nest of a stork. "What the hell is that?" I blurted.

"Don't point. It's not nice."

"But look at it! We're in its sights, for Pete's sake!"

"Hush."

I saw, could see, now that I was really seeing, the same installation on one house after another as we inched down the boulevard. Several of them were manned—that is, I mean, real live men stood on the roofs beside them. They were watching us.

"Some families hire private police guards around the clock," said Catherine.

"Who lives here?" I asked. The rich and famous, I expected, but that's not how she answered.

"You could say the descendants of Spanish conquerors. Or *mestizos,* the great-great grandchildren of knocked-up Mayan maids."

She began pointing out houses, a surgeon there, a legislator, an army general, the owner of a coffee finca. So-and-so also had a home in Paris, as well as a beach house in Maui. There was an olympic-size pool behind that place over there. "We all used it."

Light dawned. "This was your home," I said.

She gestured past me to a private winding lane, paved in stone. At the far end I could just see a *hacienda* behind the trees. "Once owned by my in-laws. We lived with them."

"Good Lord. Catherine O'Brien from Milwaukee."

"*Fufurufa.*"

"You've used the word before."

"Yacht cruises, polo events, shopping trips in Paris. Once upon a time."

"Not now?"

"No. The family business went belly up about five years ago. No one is left. The aunt in Antigua was the last in the family. Some good people lived in this neighborhood. I have to say that. *Caballerosa.* Do you know the word?"

"Genteel?"

"And generous. A lot too *noblesse oblige*, but not phonies. The Exploradores originated here."

"Explorers?"

"Scouts. Martin and I used to call it the Boy Scouts. It's a big charity. Every rich person in the country belongs, I think."

I saluted her, palm out, little finger under the thumb.

"You were a Boy Scout?" she said.

"Just a Tenderfoot for a while. I failed knots, I think."

A dog, an oversized mastiff behind an iron fence, had picked up our scent and begun to bark with significance. It was not a hoarse *hauf-hauf.* "Let's go," said Catherine, and in less than a minute we were back in traffic, heading north.

"Tell me about Martin," I said. "What did he do?"

"He worked for the family. They owned a line of clothing factories. He ran one."

"How did you meet him?"

"College. Rich boys are sent to U.S. schools. He wanted to teach. But he felt an obligation to his parents."

"He never taught?"

"No. But he was writing a book, doing research every chance he got."

"What about?" I asked, postponing the closure I saw coming up next. I considered faking a motor failure, or running out of gas, but she could see as well as I that the tank was more than half full.

"There," she said. "Let me off at that corner. I can pick up a taxi there."

"What was he writing about?" I asked again, not stopping.

"It was an investigation, I guess you'd call it, into social and political power here."

We were approaching the plaza. Questions, any questions. Costa Rica. "Do you have a house there in Costa Rica?"

"I live with friends. What about you? Are you going home now?"

"Later. Into the hills tomorrow. I've promised to meet a couple of guys for breakfast on Monday, at the Santo Tomás Hotel in Chichi. Where next for you?"

"West. To the highlands. I'm making a delivery for a store."

"Well, why didn't you say so? Can I drive you there?"

She thought it over. "No. But thank you."

We'd arrived at the Plaza and I began to circle it, searching for a place to pull over. Except you can't circle it, you have to "square" it, following the one-way streets. West on 6 Calle to 6 Avenida and the corner of 5 Avenida. North on 5 Avenida to 5 Calle, right on 5 Calle to 8 Avenida, right on 8 Avenida to 6 Calle.

"Just let me out anywhere," she told me. "I'll be fine."

"You'll get out of the car and we'll never see each other again," I said, embarrassing myself, and her probably, though she replied without losing a beat.

"Right. I'll go my way and you'll go yours."

The reality of that hung in the car between us. I yanked myself back to sanity. When her errand was completed she would go to Costa Rica, to a life that had never had anything to do with me and never would again.

We stopped for a ragged flow of pedestrians, walking against the light, preposterously. She could have gotten out, but didn't. She was fishing around in her bag, peering into its depths. I moved on.

"My husband was not killed in an accident, " she said. "He was murdered."

I stepped on the brake. The car behind me blew its horn, not politely, then other horns, blasting, lots of horns. Somebody yelled "*Cerdo rojo!*" Red pig. I shot ahead and we began the circumference of the Plaza again.

She was still talking into the bag, poking around in there for something, then raised her head and reached for the door handle. "Here. Stop here. Please."

"Don't you dare open that door," I said. "You think you're going to tell me something like that and just leave it hanging in the air?" I picked up speed, past the Cathedral, past the palace, past the Hotel Centenario.

"He was disappeared for three days," she said. "He had witnessed a shooting. A guy was killed right in front of our house, a labor organizer in Martin's factory. Martin was permitting that, unions, which was dangerous enough in itself. Let me out here, please. Right here."

"I can't stop. I'm not stopping."

"Then his body was found."

"When did it happen?"

"In the summer of 1980. Right after the big Coca Cola strike. Forty-four union advocates were kidnapped that summer. Never seen again. We were luckier. We had a body, or did until his parents refused to claim him." She turned her face away from me, toward her window.

"Why?"

"He was found in compromising circumstances, as they put it. His parents were scandalized. So they just let him be buried there at *Verbena*, in an unmarked grave, with the other unidentified victims, and I agreed. For them it was saving face, but for me it was what I knew Martin himself would choose, anyway."

I stopped at a light. She could have gotten out of the car here, too, but didn't. She'd begun poking around in the bag again. We were approaching the Cathedral. "Soon after that I moved to Costa Rica with Alex. Martin's parents went bankrupt and moved to Honduras. They've both since died."

There was a barricade in front of the Cathedral. No parking. "Why Costa Rica?" I asked.

"Why not Scotland or Switzerland? Because I wanted my son to stay close to the life that had been important to his father." She'd left off looking in her bag but was still not returning my glances.

"Who killed Martin?"

"It may never be known," she said. "Go to the parking lot. Please."

"Why are you telling me all this now?"

"Maybe because we're never going to see each other again. Maybe it's a farewell gift. How incredibly generous of me."

"It is, yes," I said. "I wish I had something to give you in return. I can't say how much I wish that."

We'd reached the parking lot. I pulled up, in front of the entrance to the alley.

"*Adiós, compañero*." She turned to go.

I took her by the arm, pulling her toward me. "I'm not a good hugger," I said, reaching awkwardly over the emergency brake and two gear shifts. It was a neck and head hug. I won't claim she melted in my embrace, but she didn't resist. She gave me a pat on the shoulder, like an aunt or a sister. "Feels okay to me," she said, lightly, in my ear. "Feels Presbyterian or Methodist, whatever the hell you are." The old needling self. But her face softened as we separated and for an instant I thought I was seeing her as other people had known her, really known her, how her husband and her son had known her, defenses at rest, nothing to mask, what you see is what you got. Then she opened the door and climbed out. Too late I thought of suggesting a Presbyterian kiss.

"*Me acordaré de ti*," she said, through the window. I will remember you.

Ti. A form of the pronoun *tú.* "I heard that!" I yelled. "*Tú!* You just said *tú! Tú, te, ti.*"

Like a maniac I started to sing, aping Perry Como. "*Eres tú, eres tú!* Like a promise, yes, that's you." She stood at the window, rolling her eyes, then actually smiled, tenderly—my gosh, tenderly. "*Asi, asi, eres tú,*" I sang. A bus pulled up behind us, blasting its horn, sounding not much worse than I did. Catherine gave me a silly wave I'd seen other women here do, hand up next to the face, palm inward, fingers waggling, then she turned that into a Boy Scout salute. I returned it and she was off into the alley with her bouncy long-legged stride. I worked my way into the traffic, wondering what she had been groping for in her bag, and regretting, of all the things in the world there were to regret at the end of this incredible day, that I would never know.

EIGHTEEN

The next morning, Sunday, I was on the Pan-American Highway half-way to the city of Quetzaltenango before it occurred to me that I was being followed. Not that I believed it. I understood instantly that the suspicion itself was the real issue. Being followed was something I had no way of proving. It was only a guess, while suspicion, its sudden appearance on the stage of my imagination, was an undeniable phenomenon. It pulled my eyes, like Catherine's, to the world of the rear view mirror.

If I was being followed, it was not by a white Chevy van, but by a very ordinary, rather ratty black Ford Escort. Did people in Guatemala get followed by black Fords? If so, what was the implication? Not a warning, not to frighten me, surely, with a presence so unthreatening. But if not to warn or frighten, then to truly follow me, to shadow and survey? And what for?

It hung behind me at a distance and I didn't see the driver until I had to suddenly stop. A clump of branches had been piled in the middle of the road. The Ford, then, pulled up behind me and filled my mirrors. The driver was a man, a gringo—stocky, bald, big sunglasses, the lone occupant in the car. I signaled an apology and he waved back.

After rounding the curve ahead, I caught on to what the branches were for, a heads-up to motorists of danger ahead, in this case a stalled bus halfway out into my lane. It was one of the recycled school buses, a beast of a thing, its hood up like a giant maw and a handmade sign across the top of the windshield: "Jesus, my Pilot." A barechested man waved me around it with his T-shirt. The Ford and I continued on. It seemed to make no effort to keep up with me. Now and then I saw it among the hills and curves of the road behind. There were plenty of other vehicles. It was hardly unsafe. Suspicion was unwarranted.

I was feeling a little insecure anyway, cautious about meeting Luis, about him meeting me. And I had just said two final goodbyes in twenty-four hours. Goodbye to Rebecca, goodbye to Catherine. The vacuums they left behind were different, not equal in size or quality, but just as empty. I thought of a Sunday School story about an evil spirit that got cast out of a man and decided to go back when he saw the nice empty space he'd left behind, inviting seven other demons to join him. It was one of the few Bible stories that had interested me as a kid, a kind of science fiction, but right now I found it a little unnerving.

So I turned to the unquestionable reality of the world outside the car, positioning myself on the map I had studied this morning. To the south, on my left as I drove, I knew rivers dropped off the mountains and crossed a plain to the Pacific. On my right, the land sloped gradually northeast into the jungle of the Petén. Behind me were the borders of Salvador and Honduras, and if I continued west beyond Quetzaltenango, before long I would cross over into Mexico. Solid geography.

Quetzaltenango, or Xela, as Luke called it, was the second largest city in the country. I'd been brought there on occasional day trips with the school children of the village. Xela was short for Xelaju, pronounced "Shay-la-HOO." It meant, we were told, "under ten mountain-lords," spirits who live in the spent volcanoes surrounding the high valley.

The mountain sides that surrounded me now were occupied and gardened, with *milpas* climbing up their sides. Cluster after cluster of corn fields, some on sixty degree slopes that hardly seemed tillable, lay over the hills in a textile of stripes, as if the farmers had created a painting with a hoe. That was a romantic view, I knew. My father had told me so once, and he had used that word, "romantic." You just planted where you could when you got "bumped off your land," he said, using those words, too.

If I could remember that, why the heck couldn't I remember the name of our own village? My sense of it was lush and expansive, not struggling farms on a mountainside. It was tucked into a valley, where the corn at maturity was almost as high as the roofs of the houses. You could hide in it, disappear, play games among its stalks, until someone called you out for dinner.

Maybe that was romantic, too, but I dwelt there now, feeling the warmth, getting the right smells, until the reverie ended in a shout. My own, that is. I had rounded a curve and driven straight into zero visibility. I slowed to a crawl, fumbling for the fog lights. I'd forgotten about this, how the sky expanded as you climbed and clouds could suddenly surround you in a misty blindness.

It was over quickly, but that was it for comforting thoughts. As the cloud disintegrated and as I emerged into sun and clear air, there on the passenger seat beside me was a demon—an honest-to-goodness spirit, not demonic, mind you, but daemonic, for sure. To put it differently would detract from the reality of the memory, and that's what it was, of course, another memory, and not one I wanted. Its name was Fern, *her* name. Had word gotten around? *Empty seat in red Cruiser on Pan-American Highway.* Or was she conjured by yesterday's encounter with Luke Treadwell? Not Luke, Bucky. Because he was here, too, squeezing in between us in the front, minus the girth and the tattoo.

Good. I would think about Bucky instead of Fern. I knew what he meant when he called himself an "arrogant son of a bitch," a recollection I found refreshing at the moment. He'd been a defiant rule-breaker at Norton College. Drinking and smoking were forbidden on campus and it was an open secret that Bucky often sneaked into the next town to do both. Apparently he had a need to shock, and he did that one day at the school's October revival meetings, an annual affair calculated to reach those students whose souls had slipped through the cracks of their churchy upbringing. He "went forward." Going forward, walking the aisle to the front of the chapel, was serious business with that particular cloud of witnesses, peers and mentors whose opinion you cared about. I didn't do it, "go forward," at college or ever, not at any of the evangelistic rallies my mother had brought me to, where the altar call could be all but overpowering. Neither the threat of hell or the tug of a mighty love pushed my body to the front.

As I discovered in time, our little Swedish Covenant Church in Rhode Island provided an escape. At Covenant you were "confirmed" at the "age of accountability," a ritual with the same theological intent but with far less emotional drama. It was a simple declaration that made you a legitimate part of the church family. I participated in that rite of passage not out of a religious impulse, but because the other kids my age (twelve, thirteen) were doing it, and because the cookies in that church were superb and the people immensely kind. I liked it there, a small society in the heart of the city. Whenever the place stole back into my thoughts it was with the smell of coffee, always just down a hall. Sometimes the memory was auditory, a gabble of voices, a half-dozen Sunday School classes in session, laughter, kids cutting up, which you could do, shamefully, and never be scolded. And there were no revival meetings, no embarrassing invitations to the front.

But when Bucky walked down the aisle in the Norton College chapel, it was not with the intention of turning his life around, as anyone might be excused for thinking. Instead he faced the student body and barreled out the poem "Invictus." *Out of the night that covers me, Black as the pit from pole to pole, I thank whatever gods that be, For my unconquerable soul.* By the close of the next day the poem had been memorized by every maverick on campus. It was all largely ignored by school officials. The only word of criticism I heard was the lament of an English professor who wished Bucky had chosen a better piece of literature. Soon after that, he dropped out of college and I hadn't given him a thought until yesterday.

Fern was another matter. I hadn't forgotten her, just tuned her out whenever she entered my mind. Now she refused to leave. She was still there on the seat beside me, quietly waiting her turn. When I saw an overlook ahead of me with a cluster of parked cars, I drove in, hoping that would dispel her. A little market was in progress there, fabrics spread on the grass, vendors with trays, and an armed guard at watch. I walked to the edge of the cliff and scanned the horizon. The ravine dropped off steeply and the floor of a valley, a forest of evergreens, swept for miles. It was hazy, but I could see a spot of turquoise, as if a gem had been dropped between the shoulders of the mountains.

A boy approached me with a tray of jewelry.

"Lago de Atitlán?" I asked, pointing into the distance.

"*Sí, señor*," said the kid. "You buy?" He meant his jewelry, but I wouldn't have put it past him to try to sell me the lake. A pounded and carved silver bracelet nestled in the middle of his tray, shaped into a snake. A classic Mayan symbol, I knew, though I didn't know what it represented. Its tail was in its mouth and halfway into the circle the body looped in a knot. The workmanship was excellent. I bought it, paying his first price and a little more. Another child approached, with a bunch of carved wooden masks hanging around his neck, a heavy load. I bought one, polished mahogany, big-nosed. By this time a signal had gone out. I bought something from everyone, a straw basket, a clay pot, a small woven rug from a woman who raised her price even as I paid her.

I barged to the car with my arms full and dumped everything on the rear seat. As I backed out of my space I saw that another car had pulled off the road and was waiting to get in, the black Ford Escort, driven by the stocky bald gringo. I remembered then where I'd seen the car first, or one like it, next to mine in the parking lot behind the Cathedral.

I found that chilling, justified or not. I made a point of getting a start on him, driving faster than was wise on the winding upgrade, hoping the child merchants would hold him captive for a good long time. At least I'd lost Fern, or thought I had. As soon as I relaxed and moderated my speed she was back and I knew she would stay until we had seen it through together.

It seemed all wrong. I was in the lush mountains of Central America and the space was being invaded—pirated—by something that happened on the cold flat ground of Indiana twenty years ago. It was remote and foreign and I didn't want to go there, any more than I had wanted to go to Norton College in the first place.

It was the only school my mother would approve. She and my father had both gone to North Park College in Chicago, a school founded by the Swedish Covenant, but she was sure it had since become too liberal. She was also sure that was true of Barrington, a Christian liberal arts college across the Bay from our house. She had "heard things" about a couple of English teachers there with "funny ideas." Norton was the place for me. No liberal hanky-panky there, no drugs or drinking, no rock-and-roll. "Pray about it," she kept saying. "Ask for the Lord's leading."

Leading or not, it turned out to be a good choice in many ways. At least it was far from Rhode Island, and all that really mattered to me was to be away from home. But I found things I liked there, a sports program that let me in (intramural basketball), a kind of level-ground friendliness among the students, and attentive teachers—one in particular, a woman with butchy body language who drew me to her side with a love for the books I loved myself, the Narnia Chronicles and Tolkien's Trilogy, and science fiction—Bradbury and Asimov and Heinlein—then led me on to the "adult novels" of C. S. Lewis and from there into the wide open sea, Tolstoy and Camus. "Keep this to yourself," she told me in a whisper, handing me her own worn paperback of *The Stranger*.

But I made no close friends, and there were no dates until Fern. She sat across the aisle from me in Basic Math, second semester, a tiny person, quiet, and pretty in a precarious way I couldn't explain to myself, except to note that she looked best when her face was completely blank.

Our first date consisted of walking into town for ice cream at the local drugstore. In the weeks that followed we fell into a pattern more passive than otherwise, sitting together at school affairs and weekend meals in the dining hall. Now and then we held hands or indulged in a dry kiss at the dormitory door. Neither of us proposed that it be more than that, until one bitterly cold night in February, when virtually everyone else on campus was at an evening piano recital. We were in the library, and it was Fern who suggested it, that we go to her room, and I thought it was an excellent idea. It was a stupid idea. Visiting a girl's room was breaking a hard-bound rule.

I knew where this memory was headed. Some things are better forgotten. I said that to Fern, on the passenger seat beside me. No, she answered, keep going. Then how about a little rhetorical distance, I suggested, a simple switch in pronouns, to her, him and they? No, she said. First person, I, me, we. Do it right. Balanced sentences, correct punctuation, no dangling modifiers.

Not that anything much happened that evening, just fully clothed bodies rubbing awkwardly together, some uneducated kissing. We were both virgins and simply assumed that about each other, as most Norton students did. We weren't familiar with the term "technical virginity" or conscious of preserving anything. We were just indulging in what we could. It went on for about half an hour, then we heard footsteps, and I decided to dig out. Too late. Mrs. MacDonald, the housemother, stood on the other side of the door.

At two o'clock the next afternoon we faced a hastily called session of the Student Affairs Committee: three students, two faculty members, and the Dean of Women. Mrs. MacDonald solemnly submitted her testimony, managing to imply the worst, though she had seen nothing. Then we were asked to speak for ourselves.

Fern began to cry, maintaining that "we didn't do anything," and was let off the hook. Not me. I was pressed to be more explicit, both as to what we did and what we did not.

"What did we *not* do?" I repeated, honestly baffled. How much was I supposed to list?

"Did you take your clothes off?" asked one of the students, helpfully. The question scandalized me. "Of course not," I said.

"Did you touch her intimately?" asked the Dean of Women. That gave me pause. I remembered my hand, hovering over her breast, and feeling the heat of her body rising through her blouse, and I remembered the scent she was wearing, which she had told me was called "April Showers" and which I feared I was throwing off this minute from my own body as incriminating evidence. I wasn't trying to lie, but I felt ignorant. Answering their questions with some kind of sophistication was apparently more important than the event. That made me angry, as if I hadn't been given a chance to study before the exam.

Another student spoke up, a senior, his point that there was only one important issue anyway, our intentions. He quoted Jesus, that if a man "looks at a woman to lust after her he has already committed adultery with her in his heart." Those words were familiar. They were the subject of bull sessions in the boys dormitory. How far could you go in your observations before it was actually a sin? I held my tongue, because I had to admit to myself that of course I had lusted, not just with my eyes but every inch of my body. I had wanted to go "all the way," in dormitory lingo. The words of a hymn had popped into my head, "All the way my Saviour leads me." I was ready to go for it, but at a critical instance Fern pushed me off, and we scaled back to just kissing.

Finally a moderating voice intervened, a teacher in the history department. He was an older man who tended to ramble in class, but he didn't ramble now. If lust was the key, he said, the college would have to expel most of the student body and fire the entire faculty. If these kids had broken a rule, discipline them accordingly. Otherwise leave them alone. The session ended.

Late that afternoon Fern and I received official notification of the committee's decision. A first offense warning. We were put on a kind of probation and were to discontinue dating. There was something demeaning in the lightness of the sentence. I realized I had hoped to be expelled. Fern, mortified beyond endurance, also wanted to leave. So we pooled our meager personal funds, packed our clothes and took a bus to Indianapolis, where we rented a room in a motel. There, bonded by our disgrace, for two full days we undertook (there is no better word for it) what the committee had assumed.

And then what, after that? I was determined not to go back to Rhode Island, so we both continued by bus to Fern's home near Rochester, New York, to convey the news to her horrified parents. "It's all right. We're going to get married," Fern told them. We had decided no such thing, but her parents consented readily, as if there was no alternative. Her father, a Baptist minister, married us, in a private ceremony my mother and Harvey refused to attend. We stayed in Rochester, found jobs clerking in stores and rented someone's mother-in-law apartment, a room with a bath and a hot plate.

It suited me fine. In college my future had been hanging before me as an ambitionless gray void. Marriage to Fern was settling something. All I really wanted to do was what I'd liked doing for ten years, read, listen to jazz and follow sports. Now I could throw in legitimate sex as well. Everything in a box, securely tied. For that I was willing to hold down an entry level job eight hours a day. I actually felt lucky.

The little paradise lasted less then a year. Soon Fern gave birth to a five-month fetus who lived outside the womb for two days, and after that it seemed of paramount importance to her family that we return to Norton, redeem ourselves, and finish school. Fern was willing to go, but not I. It was the only gesture of decisiveness I made in the whole affair. Until then everything else had been a path of least resistance. But I was not going back to Norton. So we split up, went separate ways. Her father arranged the divorce, the undoing of the sacred vows he had administered, and paid all the bills it entailed. An "annulment," we were told. The word was new to me. I had to look it up. It meant, as I got it, "unhappening" what has happened, a sort of magic or miracle, the antithesis (it occurred to me now) of *aletheia*, a lie that shall set you free.

We lost track of each other totally, Fern and I. I moved to Boston, found a full-time job nights in a supermarket while I finished my undergrad studies at Boston University. Don't ask where the incentive came from. I just knew it was a second chance and I'd better not blow it.

It took five years to get a B.A., a class or two at a time, evenings, summer school, part-time jobs, shared apartments, food hand-to-mouth. In another three years, I got an M.A. in lit, with a teaching fellowship, taking on the swollen classes in English 101 that nobody else wanted.

That was the last half of the sixties. I evaded the hazards of the decade, including Vietnam (in college before the lottery), like a person walking through a room full of frenzied dancers. I watched it all with interest, applauded the sit-ins and the protests (but didn't participate), loved the music, made "Howl" and *On the Road* required reading. I was not "uncool" in my eyes, and not judgmental of anyone else's choices. I just wanted to keep myself free of unpleasant surprises. So I never got into trouble—drunk on occasion, and stoned, but never out of my mind. I never got arrested, never made anyone mad enough to hit me, never got anyone pregnant—not again, probably through sheer dumb luck.

I heard a noise beside me in the car, something like a faint clearing of the throat. Fern, still there. I was avoiding something. She didn't need to remind me, I knew what it was. All right, I said, but how about an impersonal fly-on-the-wall point of view for this part? No, she said, firmly, as firm as she could get. No evasion. See it through.

It's about the baby. That's easy to guess. I felt no grief, but Fern was devastated. This I failed to understand. As the doctor explained to us in the hospital room, finding a euphemism he probably thought would spare us, the fetus had "never completed itself." There was hardly any brain. It was a wonder it had stayed in the uterus so long, he said. It was a boy, a mere fragment of human life, but at five months clearly a boy.

I opted for a quick burial, but Fern wanted it (him) baptized, and her father, a capital B Baptist (baptism not efficacious for infants, and surely not after death) got a free-spirited clergy friend to do it. I thought it was pointless. If you had no brain, did you have a soul? Did you have a soul anyway? But what knocked me speechless, at the little family ceremony in the hospital morgue, was that Fern, without my knowledge, had actually named the baby. There stood the minister, wearing a clerical collar, bending over that tiny unfurred kitten, touching its head three times with drops of water: "Theodore Cavalier Peterson, Junior, I baptize thee...."

Fern had no capacity for dark irony. What she meant, what I had never allowed myself to even entertain until this moment, was simply that the baby was mine as well as hers. I received that realization now, like a long, bright spear from the god of one of the volcanoes rising before me in the distance. I thought I might have to pull over, as if I were bleeding from the wound. I had a son. I had a son and I had all but disowned him. He was very much my child, this uncompleted being.

Fern was still on the passenger seat, watching me. "You were right," I told her. "He's mine. He's my *hijo*."

With that she left, as quietly as she came. The seat was empty. I actually looked over to be sure.

Goodbye, Fern. *Q'onk tipena*. Strength to you, wherever you are.

Now I did pull over, not because I was bleeding, but because I was shaking too hard to drive.

It was several minutes before I dared to move on. When I did, I found the landscape changing yet again, opening up, not unlike the English moors, wind sweeping through tall grass, mountains lost in clouds that piled into the sky. The air was thin and crisp. I passed a boy herding six sheep with a long stick, a woman behind on a horse. A few more miles and the highway began a descent from that rarified plateau, dropping gradually into green valleys and richer foliage. Soon I could see in the distance what appeared to be a major intersection, and guessed it was the four corners, *Cuatro Caminos,* my turn-off from the highway. I stopped there to get my bearings. The coast looked clear. At least no Ford Escort in my mirror. The main road continued northwest to Huehuetenango. The road to the left was the one I wanted.

NINETEEN

Quetzaltenango had always seemed a forbidding place to me, cold at 8,000 feet, with lots of gray stone buildings, and it seemed unfriendly to me now. I found a hotel first, then set about to look for Luis's office. I was quickly lost. The search took me past a massive military complex. It filled more than a block, fronted with cement barricades and posted with half-a-dozen armed guards at the entrance, a statement that spurred me on by without a second curious glance.

I found the right address several blocks south, and thought it must be wrong. I parked across the street and sat in the car, staring. The building was a light blue double-story, tightly packed in a row of small adobe houses. Every structure on the block was badly in need of paint and repair, but this one was in shocking condition. The front wall was pitted with holes. A piece of plywood had been nailed over one part of the door. I got out of the car for a closer inspection. A sign on the wall had been broken and hung in two pieces. I put it together, bending almost double to see it. *Los Rebozos.* In a lower corner was a drawing of two stick figures, both with loads on their backs, a woman with a baby and a man with firewood. I backed away to look for a sign of life in the upper windows, and the door opened.

A man stood there. It was Luis. No question. It was his nose I recognized first, what anybody would see first, prominent and heavyboned, too big for the face, like the mahogany mask I'd just bought. His jaw was clean shaven, his hair a bushy mop of black, some of it caught in a ponytail. Then his eyes, with long lashes—like a girl's, I used to tell him—now framed in silver-rimmed spectacles.

"Hello, old friend," he said in English, without hesitation. "I knew you would come back some day."

I stood there in the doorway, just bobbing my head for several seconds, unable to speak. I noted with gratitude that he was fighting for composure as well. As we reached out our hands, my muscles remembered what I had watched adults in our village do repeatedly, the traditional gesture of respect and affection, left hands on right shoulders, right hands firmly clasping, forming a geometric design. That's what we did.

"I am so enormously glad to see you, Teddy," he said. He spoke English with a rich accent, the throaty undertones of Mam. I was still unable to reply, not more than a mumble, knocked off-guard by that moment of Mayan body language. I followed him inside, both the boy and the man. The boy I had held in my mind for three decades had been taller than me; now he was shorter by more than six inches. His torso was that of a taller person, but his legs were short, the physique of an Indian farmer under western clothes. In fact, he was wearing a suit, with a necktie hanging out of his jacket pocket. His wife had said he would be speaking somewhere this morning and I understood now that it was probably in a church, a possibility that seemed totally discordant with the person I knew.

He led the way through a central hall—limping slightly, I noted—as he talked over his shoulder. "I'm sorry you have discovered us in this appalling condition," was what he said. We stopped at a doorway, hung with a red-and- yellow weaving. Luis pushed that aside and I looked in.

It appeared to have been an office. A desk, its surface gouged, slanted to the floor, two legs broken off, the contents of drawers spilling out. A couple of wooden chairs had been whacked in two, a sofa sliced open repeatedly, a bulletin board splintered. A green metal file stood upright, but with gaps where there had been drawers. The pieces of what must have been a gorgeous hand-woven rug were scattered everywhere in the mess, like bright flowers popping up in a trash heap. It was as if someone had stood in the middle of the room and swung a long-handled ax. Not just an ax. The walls, I realized, were riddled with bullet holes, like the front of the house.

"Wh...?" I mouthed, the breathy start to a series of unfinished questions: who, when, why?

"Military," said Luis. "People across the way saw them drive up. Last night. No one was in here, thankfully." He was speaking softly and an answer was not required. I was still expelling whispers of shock. There was a quality of excess in this scene, a beating that couldn't stop once it got started. One bulletin board had somehow been spared. On it were tacked a dozen children's drawings—crayons, magic markers—and some of them, I saw in a glance, were brightly violent, red streaks of gunfire, huge spurts of blood, as primitive as the murals at San Carlos.

Some effort had been made to clean up. Glass from a sliding door to a hall was swept into a corner, papers and file folders gathered into rough piles. I wondered, vapidly, if I could help. As yet I'd said nothing intelligible.

"Can I offer you a drink?" Luis asked. "Sorry. Only water available right now."

With our feet crunching on bits of debris, we stepped across a tiled patio to a small kitchen: a sink, fridge and hot plate, two plastic chairs and a chrome-legged table. This room had been ravaged as well, though I could see it had been swept, with a pile of broken dishes in a corner. Luis took down two spared glasses from a shelf. "Tell me what you are doing here."

Something else about his eyes had not changed. They had often looked as if he was about to say something funny, as they did now. "Talk to me. You haven't uttered two words yet and you used to talk constantly. What do you say these days? Still speak bird?"

I answered with an excellent wild turkey ulalu, rather astounding myself.

He returned that with the dove, not a human coo-coo, but the soft throaty tremolo, an oboe of a sound. He had been better at this than me. I'd envied a space between his front teeth that accommodated the piercing calls of other birds. It had been part of our secret code. The dove was an invitation to come outside and play. The turkey meant you were grounded. That was usually because of some adventure Luis devised, like pissing into a newly built cooking fire. "You got me into a lot of trouble," I said, my first real words since arriving.

"Hey, stick around."

"We invented a call for the *quetzal* bird, right?"

"Yes, and if I had found you in the States I was going to ring you up and do our *quetzal* on the telephone."

I paused, half-way down into a chair. "Found me?"

"Yes. I tried several times."

"Wait a minute. You mean you were in the States? When?"

"Oh, I go pretty often, all over, for fund-raising mostly. Where do you live?"

"Boston."

"I was in Boston for two years. Cambridge. Harvard Div."

I sat all the way down. "My God! You were in Cambridge?"

"Sure, just a few years ago. Aren't you in the phone book?"

I shook my head no, locked up again. My phone was unlisted; I liked that privacy. But that wasn't the point, or the fact that he had been at Harvard Divinity. It was how many times we might have just missed each other, in a library, say, or holding straps in the same car on the "T."

"Let's catch up," he said, as he poured the water. "You start."

"Wait," I said, collecting my senses. "Have you eaten anything? Can I take you to lunch somewhere?"

"That's a great idea, but we're due home this afternoon for a, well, a little feast. I hope that's okay. We should leave pretty soon."

"Home?"

"My old home and yours, *amigo,* where else?"

Las Cavernas—The Caves, the name for our village, returning to me under its own speed. How could I forget? The caves on the hills above the settlement had been a constant source of dark fascination, especially for children. "They know I'm coming?" I asked.

"Of course. I got word to them yesterday afternoon, when Carmen called me."

We clinked glasses. "*Mucha felicidad,*" Luis said. I said, "*Buena suerte,*" good luck, which struck him funny.

He asked me what I'd been doing with my life.

"Teaching English."

"English! Here I been sufferin' for Jesus and you been putterin' with English?"

"You've been putterin' with it yourself, obviously."

"For forty years. You were my first teacher, you know, when you were a baby. Goo-goo, gah-gah. It went uphill from there. That last year you were here, you read to me from your books, just about every day.

I thought all pale-skinned kids could read English at age six."

"I was probably making it up."

"But you weren't, because when your parents left, I was given those books and learned to read myself. Jeeze, don't look so stunned. Your Mom gave them to me before she left, everything you'd grown out of. Your comics, too."

"So that's what happened to my Captain Marvel. My C.S. Lewis, too? Who grows out of those?"

"Losers, weepers." He laughed, a sudden rush of glee, the tell-tale sound that had so often gotten us caught when we were doing something wrong. "Superman, Batman. I loved that English word 'kapow.' And your Narnia Chronicles. I loved those, too, though I wish the bad guys hadn't been so dark skinned."

"Or the women so icy. So much for Oxford dons."

"And your father's books. I've still got them. They're yours, if you want them."

Then again he was asking about my life. I gave him an abridged biography, a series of dry items ending with the divorce. He didn't hint for more, just gave me his own quick story. He'd spent most of his life getting an education, he said. Before seminary he finished college at San Carlos (that took a decade, part time), and before that public school in town, where we'd gone together for a year, whenever the pick-up was running and there was someone to drive us, whenever there was gas in the tank, or the mud was not too deep.

He did a bit of teaching, he said, with a flick of the wrist, and lectures here and there on Mayan rights and identity. He and Carmen were the parents of twin boys, both now starting at university in Mexico. And our mothers? Mine—*Doña* Hulda, he called her—had been his first school teacher. His mother had been my "*madrina,*" as he reminded me, my godmother.

"Alicia," I said. Her name spoke itself, answering a roll call just in time. But that was her Latinate name and I had called her something else, something in Mam, a word still hiding.

"She's eager to see you," said Luis.

"And your father?" I asked.

"Died when I was eighteen."

Felipe's face came back to me in Luis's craggy features. "He still talks to me," he said, "and I talk back. Is that crazy?"

"Maybe not. Hamlet talked to his father's ghost."

"Well, he really was crazy. I've got the Mayan tradition, at least. We keep our ancestors close by, so we can have little chats. Do you talk to your father?"

"Not lately," I said. I sipped water.

"By the way, what did happen to you? Let's clear that up right now. Your parents went to the States and took you with them. But then they came back without you. I remember thinking, how can this be? How could you be in another country all by yourself? I had never been more than twenty miles from home. I kept asking them, where is he? In school, they said. A school where students also live, in Florida. I'd never heard of a school like that."

"Neither had I."

"But I couldn't fathom how they could leave you there. Or maybe you wanted to be, I thought, maybe you liked it in that school and didn't want to come back."

"Not so! I gave them a hard time." That put it mildly. "When they left I ran after their car until the principal caught me." A giant of a man who got me from behind in an arm lock. Now, now, he said, no tears! Here we are all little soldiers.

"I kept thinking you would just show up," Luis said. "Even after your parents were gone I still thought you'd come back. It was as if there had been some kind of an oversight, and it would surely be corrected."

I reached into my pack for something, a bit of business that gave me a chance to look away.

Luis lifted the water bottle again, his own bit of business. "But now you are here. And for what reason? Besides looking up old pals?" He asked that without eye contact as he topped off our glasses. Mayan courtesy. If I didn't care to answer, it would be my privilege, and it would be as if no one had asked. "To find out more about my father," I said.

"I'd be delighted to talk about him," Luis said, "about both of our fathers. I think a lot about what they must have faced with this organization. Their logo for it then was the *mecapal*. You know, that strap across the forehead, with a load of wood on the shoulders. We've added the *rebozo*, the shawl that holds a baby on the back, to give it gender balance."

"You said *their* name."

"Yes. Hold the horses. You don't know our fathers started this work?"

"I don't know a lot."

"Actually, it was started before we were born, with that priest, Luis Cavalier."

Accent on the second syllable again. The man we were both named for, though by that time he'd left the village. "He got booted out of the country, didn't he?" I said.

"He was working for Mayan rights. It was in the thirties, the day of dictators. Then your father moved here in the forties and things got rolling again. Power from the bottom up, that was the idea, even then. —Hey, bottoms up!" He drank his water.

"And now?" I slipped Luke Treadwell's assessment down over Luis's head like a garment—an outspoken Indian who pushes the envelope.

"We do anything to promote the legitimacy of the Maya," he said. "Start schools and clinics, make the aristocracy nervous, confuse the military."

He smiled, but my neck prickled. And right at that instant someone began pounding on the front door. I leaped out of my chair. Luis stood too, losing his balance as he suddenly straightened. My hand shot out instinctively, but he caught himself. "Ignore me," he said, waving me away. "Crazy knee." He was on his way to the front hall and I followed, feeling irrationally protective. A male voice called through the door. "Luis! It's Win!"

Luis answered with a shout. "Hey, Win! What a great surprise."

I paused in the patio. There were noisy exchanges in English, then appalled exclamations by the visitor as they entered the smashed office. I could see who it was now, a stocky gringo, my shadow, the driver of the black Ford Escort, sunglasses pushed up on his head. He saw me too and waved, as if we'd already met, then turned back to the chaos in the office. I returned to the kitchen, where in a minute they joined me. Luis introduced us.

His name was Winston Hall, from San Antonio, here in Guatemala as a volunteer. We shook hands. I guessed him to be about sixty. "I think we have been following each other," I said.

"Something of the sort," he answered.

"Ted Peterson is my oldest *hermano* in the world," Luis told him. "And Win," he told me, "is a regular rescue squad. Always shows up just when we need him most." The guy actually blushed. Probably I did, too. His face, on finding me here, had not reflected my own surprise, but he struck me as someone not apt to display surprise, or any tell-tale reaction.

"I tried to call you," he said to Luis.

"The phone line is cut. I've scheduled a board meeting for tomorrow to talk about all the repairs."

"Where do you want me to start now?"

"Anywhere you like. Supplies are in here." Luis pulled a broom out of a closet. "Ted and I are taking off for home. Can you manage?"

Hall said he would manage very well, with the air of a long-time manager. He was dressed in western boots and jeans and an old leather jacket. I pictured him on a Texas ranch, out hunting rabbits with a good dog, rifle bent over his arm. But he only carried the broom as he headed for the kitchen.

I offered my Cruiser for the trip to the village, but Luis wanted to show me his "chariot" first. We walked three blocks to a parking place behind a house and a well-kept garden. "We rent the use of this lot," he explained. "I can't leave it on the street." I understood perfectly the second I saw it.

It was a Chevy, a white Chevy. But this was not a side-doored van, it was a panel truck, painted in multiple colors, like a 60s love bus. I walked around it. There was a lot of red. On one side a machine gun held by a soldier in a red beret blasted red flames, and on the other, red blood flowed from a child on the ground.

Luis patted the grille affectionately. "Tells the truth, everywhere it goes."

"But doesn't it invite trouble?" I asked. It was hard to stop staring.

"It's a fine line, admittedly. Very unMayan." He gave the grille another pat. "Shall we go back to your safe, respectable, middle-class car?"

"Let's go in this," I said.

"Are you sure? Please don't feel obliged. It can be like riding inside a bullseye."

I was not sure, but it seemed downright insulting, if not cowardly, to choose otherwise. We cleaned off the front passenger seat for me, tossing books and papers into the back, which was already full of gear. I saw a net of soccer balls, a box of books, a carton overflowing with children's clothes, supplies he often delivered to schools, he explained.

I settled once again into a passenger seat. The mechanism for moving it back worked just fine, lots of room for the legs.

"Before this, we had a pick-up truck," Luis said, starting the motor. "That met disaster six months ago. Run off the road, totaled. But the cap wasn't on the back at the time. I saved it. It's on top of our house."

"But doesn't all that make you feel—?"

"Scared?" He slipped the word in quickly while I was groping for a more dignified one. "Yes," he said. "Scared half out of my pants every day of my life. Best thing I never learned in seminary." He backed into the street and we took off into traffic. "Did you know there are over twenty synonyms for fear in English and Spanish? But the one I like best is in Mam." He spelled it: *Xob'il.* "Sho-*beel*," he pronounced it, with a little startled gasp of air in the middle. It meant a panicked state that affects your thinking, he said. "Look in the glove compartment."

I pulled out an owner's manual, registration, a torn map, the moldy remains of a tortilla, and a plastic bag containing several pieces of paper. They appeared to be notes. One was scrawled on the back of an envelope.

"Try that," Luis said. "See if you can read it."

It was in thick pencil, with bad spelling, all except certain words in English. I read it out loud, translating slowly. "Greetings, fucking pinko bastard watch your back you piece of Indian shit it won't be long now." There was a crusty brown smear across the bottom.

"That's typical. Low-class intimidation from some hired thug," Luis said. "Almost everyone on our board has gotten something similar."

"What keeps them from actually—?"

He came to my rescue again. "Wiping us out? We have a lot of international interaction. That gives them pause. And our openness,

I think. Indians have learned to be secretive, which makes them all the more suspicious. There's that old idea that we harbor an on-going threat. You know, some day we'll rise up? So I stay as visible as possible. Everything out front."

Like now. People were staring at us, pointing. A horn honked, a long blast. A man on a corner waved, or did he give us the finger? Luis waved back with a big grin.

"I brought you this way on purpose," he said.

We were passing a park, slowly. A crowd had gathered around a huge marimba band. The sound was great. The musicians wore uniforms and red berets. Soldiers. "*Kaibiles*," said Luis. "They play here almost every Sunday."

"And on Saturdays they wreck your office."

"No. They hire people to do that. Their job is bigger."

Red berets. Their facsimile was painted on the side of this truck. I was relieved that we didn't linger.

"So what would you like to see next?" Luis asked.

"Tecún Umán." I knew there was no way we could avoid him, anyway, the Quiché warrior king. His oversized statue stood at the exit we always took from the city. Every time we came to Xela on school trips the story was repeated.

"Still there," said Luis, slowing down.

Still in the fighting pose that had intrigued me as a kid, his legs astride, body bare except for a very long cod piece and a cloak of feathers, *quetzal* feathers, none of it a protection from the weapons of the Spanish. As he died, the *quetzal* lost its voice, never to sing again as long as captivity lasted. Just a myth, my mother, our teacher, would always make it a point to tell us. And who would question her, my sure-mannered Mom with her bun of soft, blond hair?

Luis pointed off to the hills beyond. "You can begin to see the caves now from here."

I couldn't see anything but rocky cliffs against the rise of mountains, green into misty purple, but I knew the caves were up there. They had also figured large in local legend. Some were famous show places, with stalactites, others reputed to be the sites of Mayan rituals with animal sacrifices, where *brujos* cast spells and killed people by proxy.

"I'm remembering something," Luis said.

I was, too. Once he and I, in rash disobedience, had climbed a steep hill to a particular cave. It was exciting. We got as far as the opening, close enough to catch a waft of damp air and stale smoke. Luis wanted to go in and listen for the voices of people who had died there. I agreed, doing my best to be brave. But we were called home anyway and grounded for two days.

I thought he meant that, but no, he said, it was something else. "It was while you were in the States at that school. Your father had been gone from the village for a long time, and when he came back he was so sick he couldn't walk. They brought him up to that same cave on the hill. Arturo carried him on his back. I saw it. —That's not a good mental image, is it?"

Wrenching. "Why the cave?" I asked.

"For a healing ceremony, I suppose. That's where they held them."

"My father permitted that?"

"Maybe he wanted it. You know what the ancients say, when you're ill, your body is out of sorts with the cosmos. It all happens in your stomach, your *t'uj.*" T-oo-ush was how the word sounded. "Like the Hebrews and their bowels of mercy."

"I don't think my mother could have approved."

"For good reason. It was illegal, like all Mayan ceremonies. It had to be done in secret. There were lots of secrets, you know. We kids were warned never to tell anyone your parents were among us in those days."

"Among you! They lived there."

"Well, sure, but they'd moved out of your house by then and given everything away. They were staying with us, in our house."

"But why was it such a secret?"

"Oh, that crazy Communist business, of course, after the coup. You know the village was searched."

"No. I was never told that."

"No kidding? They were looking for our fathers, *amigo.* Mine was in the cornfield and yours was somewhere in his old Buick. They were lucky."

Why was my father out in the car if he was so sick? We were talking around each other, Luis and I, but I wouldn't know that for days ahead.

"There are things I've got to get straight," I said. "Was there another secret, too? About my father?"

"Another one? Like what?"

"Something personal. Dishonorable, maybe. Unprincipled, inglorious, I don't know."

His eyes shot back and forth between the road and me. "A *personal* secret? Inglorious? Not in my view. He was a good man. If more people had listened to him we'd all be better off."

"Would anyone in the village know?"

"A secret? If so, they'll keep it that way," Luis said. "I'll ask my mother. She might tell me."

We were almost there. He was taking a route my t-oo-ush was remembering very well, what we used to call the shortcut but was really longer, a dirt road that avoided the traffic to town on Sunday market day and brought us in view of one little hamlet after another. Technically, that's what Las Cavernas was, a hamlet, though we referred to it as the village. It was another school lesson, a chart of our tiny world. Hamlets were the smallest of the settlements, mostly extended families, a lot smaller than an *aldea*, which was a more widespread community with a Catholic church and a store. There were four *aldeas* in our area, three of them up by old ruins, one down among the *fincas*, and perhaps half a dozen hamlets. Ours was due north, in the valley of a narrow river.

"The electric lines are new," I noted. Tall steel poles marched ahead of us supported by guy lines, preposterous anomalies on the landscape. I was glad for them. They cut through the possibility of overwhelming nostalgia.

Luis pointed to the west, to a structure snuggled between two rises. "Sentry post. We're watched. Good visibility from up there. Now and then soldiers make an appearance, just to keep us on our toes."

He was interrupted. I thought the car stereo had come on by itself, at high volume, but the source was outside the car, the sound riding over the hills, not marimbas this time, a full orchestra and a chorus of voices. Luis waved at the sky. "They've come for us at last, *amigo*." It happened every Sunday right at this time, he said. "Tapes broadcast from that little church right down there."

I didn't see anything that looked like a church. "House church," he said. "Evangelical." He used the English pronunciation. He was distinguishing it, I supposed, from "evan-*hel*-i-co," the Spanish pronunciation, that as a child I'd been taught meant Protestant, or just "not Catholic." During the next couple of miles, he pointed out one location after another tucked into the hollows of the hills. A new little church there, and there. "An outgrowth of Ríos Montt's presidency, and other influences. Pat Robertson, Jimmy Swaggart. You know all about that, I'm sure."

The music faded behind us. The road got very bumpy and the net of soccer balls bounced in the back. I wasn't much interested in the turn of subject. I was listening badly, with no premonition of how important it was going to be.

"It comes down over and over to what keeps you from getting killed," Luis said.

Now I was listening.

"At the moment, it's mostly safe to be an evangelical. But there's a whole new movement that alarms me. Its members walk hand-in-glove with the military, and that reflects badly on the rest of us."

"Who's that?"

"Who what?"

"Who is the rest of us?" I asked. "You too?"

"Me what?"

"Are you an evangelical?" I was inquiring about his safety, not his theology.

"Who me? Which kind? Like Jerry Falwell or Bishop Tutu? Ríos Montt or Martin Luther King? Tammie Fay or Dorothy Day?" He laughed, that rush of glee. "Hey, I'm on a roll here."

He was thoughtful for a minute, his hand on the shift as we entered a long hill. I noticed that the fingernail on his middle finger was missing altogether. I had to look twice.

"I'm a hopeless case," he said. "I'm a Presbyterian, Presby*serious*— as your Dad used to say—but not very serious. I married a Roman Catholic, but I hate the dogma. I'm not a Marxist, but I distrust the bourgeoisie. I'm still just a peasant. Every morning when I wake up that's who I am. I doff my hat to the dawn and blow on my hands before eating my tortilla. So I figure the old folks have it right. There's always *Ajaw.*"

That last word came out sounding like a snag in the throat, a breathy cough: Ah-h-haw. He had to spell for me. It was the Mam word for the heart of the universe, the god above all others, he said. "Male, but the old Mayan drawings look like a bossy mother. The female component. —Seminary lingo."

We had dropped into a valley and now we rose again, a sudden steep thrust. The cliffs had turned to limestone, wide white streaks of it, filled with hollows where it had been dug out to use in soaking corn for tortillas. We were on top, looking down at a group of adobe houses, sheds, dimpled green spaces, a brook. Then that was gone. The car hung on the side of the road, hit a rock, the steering wheel almost yanked from Luis's hands.

"What about your father?" he asked. "Would you call him an evangelical?"

"I don't know." I'd never thought of him in those terms.

We stopped. It was as far as a vehicle could go. From this point we would walk, as we always had.

"And what about you?" Luis asked. He looked at me, turning off the motor, this time expecting an answer, no Mayan choice to evade. "Are you a hopeless case, too?"

"Probably."

"Not going to save the world?"

"I'm counting on baseball to do that."

TWENTY

We stepped out of the truck together, straight into mud, a long stretch of it where rocks had been placed as dry islands for walking. These led into a field of maize, a gauntlet of half-grown corn. Though my head was well above it, I saw nothing but corn, a huge garden.

"The corn has not done well for years," Luis said. Oh? It looked wonderful to me. I knew this place, as I knew it when the corn was over my head. I smelled moist earth, animals, wood smoke. My feet knew we would walk down, and down we went, walking into the world's navel, as it had always seemed. Dogs barked somewhere nearby, a rooster crowed. I heard voices in the distance ahead of us. A boy appeared between the corn stalks, barefoot and grinning. "*Hola!*" he called, and ran ahead of us, shouting.

Our path leveled out as a cluster of houses came into view. In another minute we stepped inside a courtyard half the size of a baseball field. Children jumped out from behind clothes on a line, setting off a sputter of firecrackers. We were here and announced.

Two men took the place of the children, elders, gray-haired, one wearing a Chicago Bulls jacket. They greeted me formally, with something like a bow, an elaborate courtesy. I returned it, feeling tall and awkward. "*Bienvenido a casa,*" they said, repeatedly. Welcome home. *Gracias, gracias,* I said, my voice in a squeak.

The children darted into a house, calling excitedly. Luis followed them to a low door where he leaned into a smoky interior. He beckoned me. I ducked my head inside. A dim space, no furniture, other than what appeared to be sacks of grain. Stuff hung from rafters, corn husks, tools. The floor was dirt, with a low fire burning in the center, open. Pots of food sat around it.

Now a figure took shape in the smoke, moving toward us. We

stepped back to let her exit the door. A woman, most definitely, though not much more than four feet tall. She stood very straight before me in the courtyard, as if making the most of her vertical powers. She was dressed in a blue striped skirt wrapped around a red *huipil* woven with yellow tongues of flame. I knew who she was, in spite of a thousand wrinkles. She addressed me, saying something in Mam. "She says she is very glad to see you," said Luis. "She welcomes you home."

She reached out her hands and I took them, looking down at her. Her smile showed a loss of half her teeth, but her eyes were young, Luis's eyes, deeply lashed and ready for humor. "*Doña* Alicia," I said.

That was not the name I once called her. My tongue sought it desperately, but she was still speaking herself, with little explosions of air in the glottalized words. I looked at Luis, who translated with a straight face. "She says the last time she saw you, you were a lot shorter than she is."

I laughed. Would it be disrespectful to hug her? Her head would come just above my solar plexus, and once she had carried me around on her back. I resorted to the honorable greeting and placed my left hand on her right shoulder. She passed questions through Luis. Did I have a wife? Yes. (Liar.) Children? No. She made a long sympathetic sound. How is your mother? Fine, I said. She remembers you fondly and sends greetings. (Liar, liar.) Another comment, Luis interpreting. "She says your mother never cried, not once."

By now others were gathering around. Luis identified them, his older sisters, cousins, aunts, uncles, a niece, a dozen children, the school teacher. They greeted me shyly, some in Spanish, the older women in Mam. Luis funneled it all. I remember you. Do you remember me? You look so much like your father. How is your mother? She taught me to read. Your father saved my life—drove me to the clinic in the middle of the night. Do you remember that?

Did I remember the measles, the year of the drought, the run-away pig, the pinata that wouldn't open? Did I remember somebody's brother, uncle, sister, father, husband? Yes, I said, yes. I said yes to it all.

Then others came, climbing up out of the cornfield, Antonio, Rosa, Chepe, Lucas, Maria, Pablito, Rubén, Hulda. *Hulda?* A woman named for her mother's first teacher, my mother. I had no idea who any of them were, including several men whose names began with J. No sign of old Jesus—heySOOCE—the village adulterer.

When the others moved away, a white-haired man with a young face came forward and offered me that regal bow. "*Buenas tardes, buenas tardes, mi hermano,*" he repeated. He grinned widely, with teeth that seemed to have exploded in his mouth (no tooth loss for him), then continued to tell me something in Mam.

Luis stepped in. "This is Arturo Diaz." His tone suggested importance. "He says he had the honor of serving your father when he was ill."

"He did?" I grabbed the man's hand. "Thank you, thank you," I said, in the Mam word that lit on my tongue. He looked surprised.

"Off by a hair, chum," Luis told me. "You just called the police."

Arturo gave me a pat on the shoulder. I wanted to talk with him more but there was no chance. People were still coming. When they stopped, I looked around. The courtyard seemed smaller and more disordered than I recalled it. It was enclosed by a woven reed fence, cluttered with a rain barrel, feeding trough, woodpile, grinding pallets, a sawhorse, a bicycle missing a wheel, a sink with a cloudy mirror hanging above it. The faucet was new. Our water had come from the river, carried daily, up the hill to our house. And where *was* the house, my home? Trees obscured it, if it was actually still there.

I smelled tortillas and was suddenly assaulted by hunger. A makeshift table, consisting of an old door and a slab of plywood, had been set up in the center of the compound, and women were covering it with lengths of woven cloth. "I hope you don't mind being a guest of honor," Luis said.

"I don't think I know how. What should I do?"

"Just be merry, like the prodigal son."

We helped pull up an assortment of seating to the table, anything able to hold a body. Then two dozen men, young and old, sat down while the women and older children brought the food. At either end of the table a pot was placed, and in the middle the lid of a metal trash can filled with steaming tortillas, separated by banana leaves. The yellow feet of chickens stuck out of the stew. It was *piola* (names for things were popping in my head now like firecrackers), chicken boiled with corn meal and chili peppers. And the dishes were—ah, help me, heavy plastic, pink, yellow and aqua, my mother's own set, unbreakable stuff. I had eaten a thousand meals off these plates. Alicia, with Luis's eyes, said something to me in Mam, then laughed and whacked a plate on the table. "Your mother gave her these dishes," said Luis, "and she wants you to know she has not broken a single one."

When the food had been set out, the children were hushed and the cooks retreated to Alicia's house, hovering in the doorway, rocking on their feet. One of the older men cleared his throat and prayed in Mam and Spanish. I heard my first name repeatedly. I was being blessed along with the food. Then a silence fell as the tortillas were passed and we began to eat. I was thankful for the diversion. People had stopped staring at me and were talking to each other, though Arturo continued to regard me from across the table, smiling broadly with his unbelievable teeth.

A drink was poured, fresh apple cider, pieces of fruit bobbing at the top. "Sorry, no booze," said Luis in my ear. "No homemade brew." Food was passed. The men blew on their hands and reached for the tortillas. I ate like a half-starved kid. The stew was chili hot and the drink cool and sweet. Children were everywhere, eating on the run. A dog under the table curled up on top of my feet. More tortillas were brought from the outdoor oven.

I suspected food was not always this plentiful. They may not have killed the fatted calf but certainly a couple of chickens. I glanced around with new eyes. Nobody looked over-fed, maybe not fed enough. I looked again at the children. What was I seeing? Not enough of something, not enough luster and shine.

Now two of the older women, setting a pink plastic dishpan full of boiled plantains on the table, whispered something to Luis as they eyed me significantly. "They're midwives," he told me. "They say they delivered you when you were born, after your mother fell." Yes, he said, to my raised eyebrows, that was what happened. "You were supposed to be born in the clinic at Xela, but you came too quickly."

"I didn't know that. Where exactly did I enter the world?"

"In that house right up there, second from the left. They couldn't get to your own house in time."

The two women were still standing there, smiling. I stood up and bowed to them. "*Gracias,*" I said. "Good job."

Luis rubbed his chin. "Here's a new thought. You know, if you are a citizen of the place of your birth, then you are not only Guatemalan but Mam. What do you make of that?"

"I don't think I qualify," I said.

"It's all a matter of identity. For instance, do you remember when you had the tapeworm?"

"I had a tapeworm?"

"*Sí. Solitaria.* That's what it's called. One big long single—worm."

"That's a myth," I said.

"Let's check it out. Where is my mother?" He turned to Alicia, standing in the doorway. "*Solitaria?*" he called to her, and something in Mam. She shook her head vigorously.

"She doesn't think it's a suitable topic for the dinner table."

"I'm on her side."

"I'll tell it in Spanish, so the ladies won't suffer."

"What about me?"

"It proves you are one of us, see? All Indian kids get worms." Luis stood up and raised his voice again, addressing the men. "Listen, one and all."

Someone hit a glass with a spoon.

He went on in Spanish, slowly, for my benefit, I suspected. "As you all know, my mother is famous for her *nab'al.*" He poked me. "Ancient wisdom, to you." He was enjoying this. "When our Teddy here was little my mother helped take care of him. But he was a very skinny little guy. Just like now." Laughter. "He was so light I used to carry him around on my back. I was six and he was three." Was he making that up, too? His eyes challenged any doubt. "You ate a lot, and yet you got more and more skinny. And as we have learned from centuries of experience, that's a sure sign of you-know-what."

Vocal assents up and down the table, groans, *sí, sí,* a good audience. I was being roasted. The women were poking their heads out of Alicia's door, laughing behind their hands. Maybe they knew more Spanish than Luis thought.

"So my mother resorted to an old Mayan remedy," he continued.

"She sat him on a pot of milk and told him to stay there until the worm stuck its head out to get the milk. Then she would, uh, well, she would do the rest."

Ah, *sí!* Vigorous nods. Alicia stalked over and slapped Luis on the back of his head. She had to reach up to do it, but it was a good sound smack. It didn't deter him.

"But Teddy," he continued, "being only three years old and unappreciative of Mayan lore, thought the whole thing was a very bad idea. He got up and ran, and three weeks later we found him hiding in a cave."

Ohs and ahs, Greek chorus.

"But how did you finally get rid of it, that *solitaria?*" asked someone at the other end of the table. He was addressing me.

"To tell the truth, *no se,*" I said. "I guess it must still be in there."

"Still in there?" Luis consulted his mother. She examined me for a moment with the eye of an expert, then offered an estimate.

"No problem," he reported cheerfully. "You are no longer the host of the Loch Ness monster. My mother says you have grown too big for that."

"So I don't belong here after all?" I said.

Arturo reached across the table to me. "Nev' you mind there, you Teddy boy *tú*. We get you a worm."

Luis roared. His mother hit him again.

Then, as if following a well-used script, Alicia and the women began to clear the dishes and the men picked up the seats and carried them off through the trees. Someone was rapping on a pot with a stick. Luis cornered his mother at the sink and returned to me.

"They're going to hold a little service. It's part of the celebration. They expect you to preach. Are you ready for that?"

"How do they feel about baseball?"

"Tell you what, I'll preach. You can offer a word of greeting."

We picked up our chairs and followed the others up the hill. A soft dewy rain had started to fall, but no one hurried. We passed the sweat bath and the basket factory, a shelter with baskets of all sizes hanging from the ceiling. And here was the house, at the top of the hill. It took a few seconds to recognize it. I'd always thought of it as big, because it was the biggest house in the village. Now it had shrunk. Gray mold crept half way up the walls.

"This building held up well during the '76 earthquake," Luis said, "though a lot of the others were destroyed. And it was high enough up to be spared in the flood, so we think of it as a kind of sanctuary." Flood? "Effect of a hurricane, '55, I think. After you left. The river overflowed."

"You've had trouble here since I left," I said.

"No more than any other village around here."

We were entering the house now. Luis said something about looking for notes he had dropped. "Make yourself at home," he said. I had a hunch he was offering me a moment's privacy, which in truth I needed. I found a shadowy spot near the door, where a pile of firewood gave me something to lean against while I got my bearings.

It was half the size of Rebecca's living room back in Cambridge. A brick stove with a chimney filled one corner—a missionary luxury, I had known even then, no open fire in the middle of a dirt floor. The floor was concrete. A single incandescent bulb hung from the ceiling. That had been added since we lived here. We had used kerosene lamps.

I replaced our furniture. The table had been under the only window, not just for eating but for everything that required a surface, school work, sermon writing, chess and checkers. My parents' double bed, with an incongruous maple headboard, had filled the space to my left. My bed was up in the loft. The ladder was still there. A wiry boy was climbing the rungs from the underside, as I used to do. I felt it now the length of my torso. Half way up he hung from his hands and dropped to the floor.

The place was already filling with people, shaking off sheets of wet plastic as they entered and dispersing themselves on the variety of seats. One of the men lit a piece of *ocote* in a bowl and set it on the altar—my mother's old sewing machine. The wheel and the treadle were gone, lost to rust, no doubt, and what remained was the wooden surface with its fancy wrought iron legs. It had always been the altar. When church services took place inside the house, my father would roll it to exactly that spot and put a Bible on it and some flowers.

So far I hadn't allowed myself to project the presence of my parents.

Now I let my imagination play the old game. If I shut my eyes and opened them again, he would be there, doing that little job, his presence giving off energy, as it always did.

Over to one side, I could see just the corner of another piece of furniture, but I knew what it was, the pump organ my mother had played for services, a wheezy old thing. She had given me lessons on it. It looked unused now. A rug had been thrown over it.

Children roamed at will. One toddler was stretched out on a sack of meal, asleep. Another, a tiny boy, wandered to the altar, where he took his little pecker out of his pants and examined it with great interest. A man with a guitar squatted beside him and strummed spooky bass notes until the kid toddled to his mother.

The guitarist remained up front, vamping. Luis still had not appeared when the meeting crossed from chatter into singing. Voices fell in with the instrument, growing in volume in an old hymn I finally recognized, "Showers of Blessing." The tune, as it emerged now, was not even a reasonable facsimile. There were no hymnals and the first verse was sung again and again. That was followed by *"Grande gozo, en me alma hay,"* a sporty tune, totally familiar—"There is sunshine, sunshine in my soul today," the words sounding a good deal better in Spanish. Voices filled every inch of the low-ceilinged room, volume the substitute for pitch, hands clapping. The guitar could hardly be heard. In an impulse that felt perfectly natural at the moment, I walked to the organ, removed the rug, pulled out a couple of stops and joined in, fingering out the tune. There was no bench. I had to stand up, one foot pushing away on the pedals.

When we were done and I started back to my perch, abashed at my nerviness, the leader waved at me, calling, *"Hermano! Cántanos algo!"* I started to beg off, then saw their faces and knew I had no choice. Luis was among them now, nodding vigorously. I went back to the instrument and let my fingers slip into one of my mother's favorites, a tune written by a Swede. She had sung it in Swedish. The lyrics referred to the grandeur of creation, stars and mountains and thunder. I had heard it in English too on occasion. But it was the Swedish that came to my lips—with the rolling r's: *"Ooo stor-r-r-eh-Gy-uud* (take a breath) *nar-r-r-yog-war-r-r-ld-beeskader ...."* I didn't really sing those words. I spoke them on pitch, sort of like Rex Harrison in *My Fair Lady*. The second line trotted right after the first, though I had to fake the next two, mumbling along with similar Nordic sounds.

At the chorus I was in trouble. Here, the music soared suddenly, leaping up the major scale. There was nothing to do but let it rip, full voice, in English—not Rex Harrison now, more like Louis Armstrong: "Then sings my soul, my Saviour God to Thee! How great Thou art! How great Thou art!"

For a second I felt like the biggest phony in the world. Then someone coughed, loudly. Or no, it was Luis, I was sure it was, calling out "A-h-h-h-aw!"—that cough of a word for the heart of the universe, or a bossy mother. I accepted it as permission and finished the chorus, which meant soaring even higher on the scale. Then I started the chorus again, this time with a sweep of the arm, inviting everyone else to join in, which they did, making up their own words and their own tune. It sounded wonderful to me, atonal, polyphonic. Stravinsky would have been thrilled. It all ended in a cheer as I sought refuge again at the back of the room.

More people were arriving, squeezing into what spaces they could find. An ancient woman, led along, held up really, by a younger one, hobbled to the front. One of the men got up and brought over his chair. The old woman sat and the younger crouched on the floor beside her.

The leader called for prayers now, and several men responded. Off the cuff. That had always been the way. Just talk. *Señor*, some began, and some in Mam, *K'man*, Father. The prayers were interspersed with the little uncomfortable silences that used to make me squirm, panicking at the possibility that the missionary's son might be expected to pray, because he should know how, however young. At the last amen, Luis gestured to me and we walked to the front.

I had been trying not to feel uneasy about my "word of greeting." I was determined to keep it short, to say thank you to all who had welcomed me so warmly, and to those who had once treated us as family. I got through all that without a hitch. I ventured out a bit farther, telling them that I understood my own parents better now since I had met some of those who knew them. That sounded more sentimental than

I liked, but it didn't matter. I felt their uncritical acceptance.

Throughout that muddle another voice was also speaking—close to me, actually at my feet. It seemed to be saying one word, over and over, in a loud whisper. At first I paid no attention. It was the kind of disturbance I was used to in a room full of students. But as I finished, it came again, this time in a full croaking voice, flung out, up, a knot of sound. I looked down. The old woman who had come in late was glaring at me from her seat, her face full of astounded recognition. She pointed at me, locking her black eyes to mine, then staggered to her feet, jabbing her finger at me. At me, clearly, not Luis, who stood beside me.

"Kom kom!" she cried, hoarsely. Then a hiss. That's how it sounded to my ears. She croaked it again, took a step forward and spat at my feet. The gathered group was stone silent for two seconds, then a baby burst into wails. The young woman tugged at the older woman's skirt. Still she stood, she and I, facing each other, she looking up, I down, frozen together in some misbegotten tableau. "Kom kom!" Then that hiss between two teeth, two only that I could see, one upper and one lower, meeting each other. Luis stepped over and spoke to her softly in Mam, and in a moment she sat down.

I said "*Gracias*" to the congregation and walked to the back of the room to my spot by the lumber. Luis was still up front, taking over. He was not going to speak, he said, just read a little Scripture and then they would sing. He began to read the story of the Good Samaritan in both languages. Not anxious to be brought to the organ again, I slipped out the door.

The rain had stopped. I stood for a moment in the damp wind, raising my sweaty palms and breathing deeply before I began to walk, carefully, feeling with my feet. There was no moon and it was very dark. I heard animal voices, sleepy, goats somewhere in a pen, settling in for the night. Something flapped past my head, a hen, from a roost on a branch. At the crest of a hill I paused. I knew what might be down below. If I was right, it would be a tree, a particular one, standing alone, and the river would be not far below it, where the women did their laundry on the rocks.

My feet knew the way. The path down the hill was the same one, shaped by rough steps, here a stone, there a root. They were singing now back in my old house. The sound muted as I descended, mixing with the rising chorus of insects, night birds, a dog barking. I was listening for another sound—and there it was, the rush of running water, rapids plunging over the rocks. By the time I reached the tree I was sure it was the right one. It was an avocado, almost as tall as a New England oak. I placed my hands high on the trunk and moved them down. Nothing. Its lower branches, I knew, had been chopped off for firewood long ago, like all the local trees. I was feeling for the pieces of wood we had nailed on for climbing. They were gone, too, and I could see nothing, peering up, that resembled a treehouse. Maybe I had gotten it wrong. I reached down to about three feet from the ground and around the other side of the trunk. Nothing. I reached lower and fingered my initials. The tree was mature thirty years ago; I was the one who had grown. My shins were pressing hard against something, the remains of a small bench, near the base. I sat down, knees jutting almost to my chin. "The children's *lugar santo*," my father had called this spot, the sacred retreat. He had helped us build the treehouse.

I heard footsteps on the path and stood up. For a moment I thought I saw the shadowy figure of a child. Then I recognized the shape as Alicia's. She continued on down, nimbly, and stood at a distance, six or eight feet from me, without speaking. I beckoned to her. She moved in closer and stopped before me. For a minute we simply looked at each other. I was waiting for her to speak first as a woman and elder, and she me as a male and the guest. I took the privilege and asked her in English, "Is this the right tree?" I patted the trunk. I asked it again in Spanish. Whatever she thought I said, she answered, softly. She kept speaking, then, an extended reply. The words were Mam, but beneath the drawn out vowels and glottal stops, those punctuations of air, I heard something new begin. She was speaking, to be sure, but in a voice that was somehow like a song, a soft crooning. I knew this sound. I resisted it. I wanted to tell her to stop.

"I'm sorry," I said to her in English. She fell silent. "I'm sorry," I said again. She said something more, an apology of her own, I thought. She was backing away. "Oh," I said. "Don't go." I reached out my hand again and she moved closer and took it. She turned her face up at me and said something else, I had no idea what. She said it again, the same words, briskly this time, pointing to the bench. A maternal order.

"Sit? Okay." I lowered myself to the bench, leaving room, thinking she would join me, but I should have known better. She would not take that liberty. She stood where she was, looking down at me now, our roles reversed in terms of altitude. She was assuming charge, my nursemaid. Then she began the singing again, very softly, her voice rising and falling, the Mam words blending. The scene struck me funny. I laughed, though I didn't mean to, and then realized I was weeping out loud. She gave no sign that she heard me. She continued with her keening, lost in it, not looking at me. She was singing to the sky, rather than me, to the river and the corn. Together we made a strange duet, with the noise of the rapids behind us.

When she stopped, I spoke, in a mixture of Spanish and English. "I never said goodbye," I said. "Not to anyone." Out of the hundred reasons I might give for my outburst, this was the one that made the best sense to me at the moment. Goodbyes were not far from my mind, after all. She stopped singing and nodded, unperturbed by that babble. "Not to my father," I said. "Not to Luis. Not to you."

From this angle, from below her in the half-light, her face took on another familiarity. This is how I had viewed her as a child, looking up. "You were my—." What was it I used to call her? "*Mi comadre*," I said instead. Co-mother.

"*Ent-shu-u-yeh*," said Luis. He stepped out of the shadows of the path and stood several feet from us. "Baby talk for love and honor."

"*Ent-shu-u-yeh*." It fit my tongue, the last syllable a puff of breath. I repeated it, to Alicia. She broke into a wide smile and grasped both of my hands. "*Chi-hoe-on-te en-cual-eh.*"

"What did she say?" I asked Luis.

"Thank you, my little boy."

She turned and left then, quickly, murmuring something to Luis as she scrambled up the path. The voices of the departing people carried down to us. I stood. "I'm afraid I've confounded your mother utterly," I said.

"Apparently not," Luis answered. "She just told me she understood everything you said."

"Then she's a wizard."

"She said you told her you had found your father's grave."

"She thought that? But I didn't."

"We are standing on it, Teddy. It's where he asked to be buried."

I looked down. There was nothing there. It was just dirt, grass, weeds. I stamped and felt it under my feet, solid plain ground. It felt good. Just dirt. As real as any reality could be.

"She came to help you mourn, like the women do," he said.

I stamped again, as if sending down a message, a kind of greeting. Hey, Dad, it's Teddy. I'm here. I've found you.

"You're supposed to exhale hard with every stamp," said Luis. "It cools the stomach."

"Join me."

We stood there stamping together, with great serious huffs and puffs, Luis with his one good leg and me with my two until we were both out of breath. I sat down on the ground to get closer, then I stretched out on my back, covering the space he would occupy down there. I had reached his height, maybe taller. Luis stood above me, watching and murmuring approval.

TWENTY-ONE

Arturo escorted us back to the truck with a flashlight. He and Luis conversed at length in Mam the entire mile, Arturo doing most of the talking. I followed their shadows and the utility lines against the sky. The mud was slippery and night vapors, gathering between the furrows, curled around our legs. I was carrying a boxy package wrapped in a grocery bag. Alicia had insisted I take it, contents unidentified.

Once at the truck, Arturo climbed in, sitting in back among the soccer balls. I offered him the front seat but he refused. Luis explained. He was just going a little way with us.

We drove another mile along a lane full of puddles and stopped at a small house I could barely see in the dark. I caught a glimpse of what looked like children's play equipment, a swing set.

"This is a school for women, self-run," said Luis. "He stays here nights as a watchman." Arturo got out, then spoke to me through my window, in his brand of English. "No worry." He touched his forehead. I realized he was talking about the old lady. "Anna *loca*," he said, and then something else. Pops of air. "She's from a village over the hill," said Luis. "She's one of the confused, he says."

Arturo was struggling to tell me something else. I looked at Luis, who was also puzzled. "I don't quite get what he's saying. Your father did not intend to die, if that makes sense. He intended to see you again."

I shook Arturo's hand through the window. "Ask him," I said to Luis.

"You mean that other secret?"

"Ask him to please tell me if he knows."

"I'll try."

Clicks and huffs. I watched Arturo's face, lit by the dashboard. Bewilderment, then clarity, and a long negative swivel of the head with a long "No-o-o." I thanked him, and he went off with his flashlight across the grass.

We drove on slowly in the dark, avoiding potholes picked up by the headlights. "I asked my mother too, by the way," Luis said. "Know what she said?" He recited a word that I thought would choke him. "Know what that means? Where in God's name did you get such a looney, crackbrained idea? She said she would swear on the bones of her ancestors that your father did nothing wrong."

"Thanks for asking," I said.

"Where *did* you get such a looney, crackbrained idea, by the way?"

"Just a hunch." A misreading of my own, growing with the years, feeding on silence. Or something blown out of proportion, by my mother, by Tomas Garcia, whatever he was trying to tell me by "He changed." My father had not *done* something unspeakable. He had gotten sick and died. I had found his grave. I had said goodbye, again, this time the ultimate one.

Yes. But. *Yah*but. No, no buts. It was time to close the book, the thirty-three-year-old story, and I did, at that moment. I shut it, in all deliberation, with a whump that resounded in my head.

Luis was rubbing his knee as he drove. Where was I staying tonight, he wanted to know. In the hotel, I said. What about him? I offered to spring for a room, or share mine, but he said he'd better "bunk down at headquarters." Win Hall would be there and probably others. He wanted me to go home with him to Guate City, meet Carmen, but he was tied up tomorrow with the board meeting, then he was coming back here (thumb over his shoulder) to confer with some of the women at that school. "They're worried about a couple of guys from the next village. They've been snooping around for a month now, *orejas*. Ears for the military." Thumb toward the hill where a light flicked on and off through the trees, the sentry.

I said I had people to meet in Chichi in the morning and after that I might fly back to the States. Really? he said. Carmen would be disappointed. He hoped I would not take off until I'd met her. He'd be home himself in two days, on Tuesday. So I agreed to join him then at his house in Guatemala City. Two days from now.

I've thought back a hundred times to that exchange, wondering if

I missed something in Luis's voice, or some detail that would have compelled me to stick around here with him. Would it have made any difference if I had?

Whatever he was thinking himself, the subject was dropped. He began to sing, loudly, a familiar old ditty that was part of a game we used to play, a kind of blind man's bluff. He sang it in Spanish and in a minute I joined in. "I am a little Indio, and I am made of corn." That diminutive was the worst kind of insult, and even as kids we understood the joke, the reversal. The yous were *tús*. "Catch me, catch me, if you can, and I will be your slave!" Luis and I sang it over and over again now, at the tops of our voices. Then we sang the Guatemalan national anthem, all its tedious six verses, as we had morning after morning at the public school.

We left Luis's truck in its secluded spot behind somebody's garden and walked to the office. Win Hall's car was still parked on the street, behind mine, and there were lights on in the building, both floors. I waited until the Texan appeared at the door, then tooted one of my horns and drove away.

In the hotel room I opened Alicia's package. The grocery bag was tied up with a strip of weaving. Inside that was an old Wheaties box, on its front a faded photo of Jackie Robinson, an old friend, urging me to eat the "Breakfast of Champions," as he had on a few privileged mornings. We seldom ate Wheaties. This box had come in a missionary donation from friends in the States and when the cereal was gone I had saved the box. It had survived all these years in Alicia's house, amazing enough. Whatever was in it now fit snugly, solid yet soft. I opened it and the moldy box fell apart at its seams into two pieces.

I yelled as if bitten and dropped the contents on the bed. Or rather, it sprang from my hands like a black cat. When I picked it up, I held it at arm's length for a moment, as if it really could bite me, then pulled it to my chest, eyes shut, then held it away again, mildew powdering on my fingers. Nothing in the world could have seemed more familiar, a good 7 by 9 in size, two inches thick, a black leather case with a zipper around three sides. The back of this case, I knew, was fitted with a pocket on the inside, where my father had often kept paper and a couple of crayons he would give me before church services, and sometimes a surprise, a piece of wrapped candy.

The zipper was stuck, green with mold. It didn't matter. I knew what the interior looked like, columns of print with wide margins for notes. It was a study Bible, a "Thompson," as my father called it. I had seen him make notes in its wide margins. He mislaid it a lot. He'd rush about, late to somewhere, yelling, "Where's my Thompson?" It was so big, I could never figure out how he lost track of it, but he did lose things and he was often in a hurry.

He must have given it to Felipe, or maybe my mother had, when she packed up to leave, and Alicia had kept it after Felipe died. Because who throws away a Bible, even in a language you can't read? Now it fell to me to decide. It was like receiving a pet you don't want but belongs to you by heritage, with an undeniable family resemblance in its face. Throwing it away may not be an act of sacrilege, but it seemed profligate as well as heartless, full of his notes as I knew it was, as underlined and arrowed as my own textbooks.

I'm not eager to explain this. I told myself it was just leather, paper, print, ink. But it wasn't. It was a force, pulling into it my childhood, my history, and all the old questions about my father. It was all still there.

Maybe I could mislay it myself, accidentally leave it here in the hotel, along with the Spanish Gideon Bible in the bed-table drawer. But I couldn't do that, abandon it. I wrapped it again in the sections of the Wheaties box, tied on the grocery sack and placed it in the bottom of my suitcase, along with the letter. I wrote for a long, long time in my canary pad journal before I slept.

TWENTY-TWO

The tour book described Chichicastenango, forty-some miles northeast of Xela, as a place of "old world magic," notorious for market days and festivals. The hotel Santo Tomás, Crane's choice for our meeting place, was a white-washed, two-story structure, its inner patio a rainforest exhibit with flagstone paths among tropical trees, a waterfall, and live free-flying macaws.

It was still early, so I registered for the night and took my suitcase up to the room. A haven of comfort, high plump bed, soft towels, my own balcony. I yielded, called the desk and registered for one more night, before I drove back to Guatemala City.

As soon as I entered the dining room at 9:00, I heard Crane call my name. He and Bucky Treadwell were at a table together, with an elaborate breakfast spread out before them, fruit and tortillas and sausages. "This is just a start," said Bucky, as I sat down. I poured a cup of coffee from a pot and studied the menu.

"We must try to get a lot done this morning," said Crane, busily slicing through a sausage. "It could be our last chance, so I hope you will both be truly nice and cooperative." He was leaving this afternoon for Venezuela. Then he would be back in Guate City, and after that who knows.

As I opened my mouth to comply, a waiter approached the table. Did there happen to be a *Señor* Peterson among us, he wanted to know.

"Yes," I said in surprise.

"*Alguien le espera en el vestíbulo.*"

"Someone in the lobby?" *Alguien,* someone, not gender-specific. But it had to be Luis. There was trouble. I scrambled to my feet and followed the waiter past the registration desk to a gift shop just off the foyer. A woman stood there with her back to me, inspecting a display of jewelry, a tall woman.

"It's you!" I said.

The teenaged expat disguise was gone. She was wearing a long denim skirt and a blue jersey with daisies embroidered around the neck, a big sun hat, a shoulder purse, sneakers. The familiar woven bag and a suitcase were on the floor at her feet.

I was glad to see her, glad enough to surprise myself. "Don't tell me!" I said, covering my eyes and my pleasure. "You've done something to your hair."

"I'm sorry to intrude on your life this way," said this new Catherine. "I remembered that you'd be here this morning. I've been waiting for you. It's the jeep."

"Ah. Broke down again, I'll bet."

"Stalled not far from here. I've called three mechanics, but no one has time to fix it. Not right away, and I've got to do this thing today. The delivery for the store."

I saw what she wanted. "I'll drive you there, of course," I said, without hesitation.

"It's apt to be a rough ride," she said. "Unpredictable roads. Mountains. You need to know that."

"I hear you. I'll be free in a while. I'm eating breakfast with a couple of friends. Come join us."

"No, no. I can't wait. It's another three hours of driving and I'm overdue. It—there's a woman. I'm bringing money to her. She's needed it for weeks now."

"Just come with me while I explain to these guys."

"Who are they?"

"Acquaintances. *Norteamericanos.*"

She held back. "I'd rather you didn't tell them anything about what I'm doing."

"No problem. I'll just say you have an appointment and can't be late."

I picked up her suitcase and bag. At the table the two men stood to meet her. She apologized for interrupting. Bucky (as I introduced him) pulled up a chair, but she refused to sit. I explained, expressing regrets to Crane, who looked crestfallen. This will only take a day, I told him. Could we try again later?

"I'll be back at the Centenario in a couple of days," he said.

I promised solemnly to call him there.

"Is your jeep in a safe place?" Bucky asked Catherine.

"I don't know," she answered. "I had no choice."

"If you don't get back before dark it could be stripped," he warned.

Catherine smiled. "It hardly matters."

"Registration?"

"I've got it. In my suitcase."

"Where are you going?" he asked.

I thought he had no business asking, but Catherine named a place, a shushy word that slid right out of my head. Bucky's eyes came to attention. "West of Nebaj," he said. Nebaj meant nothing to me as well, but it stuck, and I remembered it later. "Triangle?" he asked. She nodded. He made no effort to cover his curiosity. Why on earth was she going *there*, he wanted to know.

"An errand," Catherine said. "Picking up weavings."

"You've driven it before?"

"Oh yes. 7W off 116."

Bucky hesitated, opened his mouth and shut it. He looked at me, with a question on his face.

"He's a pilot," I told Catherine. "He owns a chopper." I had what I thought was a bright idea. "Is there any possibility of flying her?" I asked him. "She's facing a time factor."

Catherine instantly shook her head no and so did he. "I can't," he said. "I don't fly up there. Too easy to intrude on the wrong air space." Then he added, "But if you need me later I might be of service." He pulled out his wallet and handed Catherine a business card. Then he gave one to the waiter who had come to fill our water glasses, and with a flourish poked one into the beak of a parrot who had perched on a nearby plant. "You never know who may need a ride," he said.

Crane, who had been fussing with the food like a housewife, gave me a paper napkin-wrapped package. He had just made sandwiches out of tortillas and sausage. "You could get hungry," he said.

Catherine waited in the lobby while I went upstairs to get my pack. There was nothing much in it—my sweater, Rebecca's perfume still wafting off it, the Spanish dictionary, tour guide, a couple of granola bars. I found my Red Sox cap squashed at the bottom of my suitcase. I hadn't worn it at all yet. I stuck it in the pack, along with my Red Sox windbreaker. The last second I added my overnight case and the old sweat pants that served as pajamas. A Boy Scout is prepared, right? I was wearing my money belt, as always, inside the waist of my jeans.

I left my suitcase in the room, assuming I'd be back tonight. Then I stuck the straw hat on top of my head, and went downstairs.

We were in the car with everything stowed away and ready to go, me in the driver's seat, when Catherine said, "Wait."

"Now what?"

"I've got to be sure you want to do this. You can back out right now. I'll understand."

Not a chance, I told her, and what did she take me for?

"Then we should top off your gas tank and get extra water." We did that quickly enough. She wanted to pay. I said no and won. It was just after ten o'clock when we left the city.

So here I was again, on the move, going somewhere, the roving hero of literature. But I was no hero, and no anti-hero, not even a *pícaro*. Just a guy in an oversized gas guzzler, doing somebody a favor.

To this day I can't say with certainty where we went or how we got there. You are supposed to be able to tell where you are in Guatemala by geographical differences. You are supposed to be able to tell by the temperature, by the birds, and by women's clothing patterns, deliberately planned as a form of area identity. But I was unschooled in all those details. I knew where I was yesterday, all right. I knew where I was earlier this morning. But not where Catherine and I were throughout this wandering day. Did I watch the car compass and the position of the sun? Yes. But very soon our twists and turns robbed those of any long-range meaning.

I know where we could have been if we had stayed on a real road. Yet when I try to put it together, with maps and memory and subsequently gathered knowledge, I find myself viewing it from high in the sky, our Cruiser crawling along between the hills, in the sights of a helicopter or the telescopic vision of the hawks and vultures and buzzards, *zopilotes,* soaring above on some lofty airstream.

I'm making this sound as if we were alone. That was hardly true for the first several miles of the journey. We were on a paved road, Route 15, headed north, accompanied with regularity by buses and trucks and vans. The driving was not much different than it had been the day before, though now the road cut through pine forests among the ravines.

Catherine fell asleep almost as soon as we left Chichi, her face lost under the big hat and wrap-around sun glasses. Prior to that our conversation consisted of one brief exchange. I asked her where we were going and if I would need a map. She said no, a map would not help and to just stay on this road until she instructed me otherwise. She said one more thing. "By the way, we are tourists, just tourists, in case anyone should ask. It's simpler."

I had thought we might talk again, pick up where we left off on Saturday afternoon. But she was curled in the corner, her breathing deep, her hands in her lap. She was not wearing her wedding ring. Maybe that was true yesterday and I hadn't noticed. The textile bag was at her feet. "I know your tote bag better than I know you," I muttered.

She heard me. She opened her eyes and sat up. "It was made in Quiché. The men there crochet them. Watch out now. We'll be turning off to the right here pretty soon. You'll see it."

"Right" was east, and I had west in my head, "west of Nebaj." We had even been passed by a bus a while back with "Nebaj" displayed as its destination, and I had thought we might follow it. When we didn't, I decided there must be more than one way to Nebaj.

"Now," she said. "Turn here."

I saw no road, only what could, with blind faith, be called a passable track. We nosed instantly downhill, way, way downhill, steeper than yesterday's descent in Luis's truck. I slid on mud, changed gears, changed again, then fought to keep the steering wheel in my hands until the path leveled off in a valley. Catherine consulted her side mirror, said "*Bueno*," and "Keep going." We were on a lane under dense pine trees. Looking hard you could imagine a tire pattern or two in the mud ahead of us and a little black grease on the grass between the ruts. It was even a bit trafficked, a man on a burro and a boy with three pigs on a leash.

In a matter of minutes we moved out of the glade into sunlight. I opened my window. Smoke from somewhere, wood smoke, blew in on a cool breeze. We were moving through a populated area—children playing, babies tied to their backs, children carrying children. Three little girls in beautiful clothes were doing the laundry at a *pila* in the middle of the road, chatting and giggling. The department of tourism would have been proud.

Catherine had shut her eyes again. When she opened them, I ventured conversation. "How much farther to Nebaj?"

"We're not going to Nebaj."

"I thought you told Bucky we'd be headed to a place west of Nebaj."

"I wouldn't go near Nebaj. The whole town is an army garrison."

"Then why did you tell Bucky___?"

"I lied. And he got the message. He knows you don't take 7W off 116 to ___." The shushy name again. "In fact, nobody around here refers to highways by their numbers."

I considered this bit of intrigue, Luke and Catherine, who had never met before, for all I knew, in an odd codal interchange: Where are you going? None of your business. Oh, righto.

"Tell me about this woman we are going to meet." I hadn't the slightest interest, but it might make decent talk. "How do you know her?"

"I'm an agent for the store. They look for superior handwork around the country. Isabel embroiders *huipils*. I bring her money and supplies and leave orders."

We'd come to a narrow stream covered by a crude bridge made of logs. I bumped across it. If an ogre had popped up and asked for a toll it wouldn't have been out of place. "And is this the only way to get to this Isabel person?"

"No, actually, it's not. But it's the safest and easiest. The maintained roads are monitored. We're avoiding military checkpoints."

"Why should we do that? We're tourists."

"Checkpoints are a time-consuming nuisance. Slow down. We're approaching a road. Beyond that next hill. We should turn right there again."

The road (another weak distinction, but at least not a track) was unpaved. I could see, as we pulled up onto its gravelly surface, that it might be a half-decent dry-weather route. Right now it stretched before us in an obstacle course of potholes, many filled with muddy water. Before long the landscape changed. Ahead in the distance mountains took on a snaggle-toothed look. According to the car compass we were going north and east. We were also climbing. The road wrapped itself around this barren terrain without guard rails at even the most precipitous plunges. Washed-out shoulders at the edge of ravines, one marked by half a dozen white crosses, began showing up with disturbing frequency. As we left a small village, we passed a graveyard of smashed cars and trucks, stacked up ghoulishly, close to the edge of the road.

Catherine seemed unconcerned about any of this. Maybe she had seen it before too many times. Another few miles of it and I abruptly stopped the car. That at least got her instant attention. I pointed helplessly. On our right was a drop of hundreds of feet, on the left a wall of forest, ahead a blind curve with hardly enough room for two cars.

"The vehicle on the way up has the right of way," Catherine offered.

"Oh, I know that. But I don't trust the guy on the way down to know."

I tooted twice, and poked my way around the curve. On the other side a pick-up truck headed toward us had pulled over onto a wider spot to let us through. The driver must have seen us coming from some vantage point above. I waved my thanks, then came quickly to a steep little rise with no visibility beyond the summit. I slowed to a creep, the car growling in low gear, smelling of hot metal. It occurred to me that the real goodbye to Catherine might be the death of us both.

"Wasn't it enough for you to almost kill me with Spanish?" I said.

"Which I notice we haven't been speaking."

"Maybe we both get mad better in English."

"I warned you it would be rough."

"You failed to mention suicide."

We passed a *tiendita* with an Orange Crush sign, set off from the road. That meant there were people nearby, surely, but that truck back there was the only sign of humanity we'd encountered for miles. Helicopters had been more and more frequent, off on the horizon, between the mountains farther north of us.

"Where are they?" I said, mostly to myself, but she answered. "In and out of Nebaj."

We'd been driving for over two hours by now. It was getting cold. We rolled up our windows and the pungent aroma of the sausage in the compartment between our seats filled the car. I suggested we share it, but Catherine was uninterested and I was not going to eat in front of her. It was right about then that I caught a glimpse of another Orange Crush sign. I made motions to stop, but Catherine gestured me on. She opened a couple of bottles of water instead. I slugged mine down as I drove, dealing now with the return of that flitting bird, suspicion. It circled my head, casting its shadow, soaring away and returning in a dive.

It dropped straight into the middle distance. Something had happened on the mountainside, blackened ground for acres and acres, blackened tree stumps sticking up out of a lower green growth.

"Scorched earth," said Catherine.

I mouthed that. A term borrowed from Vietnam? "This is part of the old red area," she said. "The military often burned out what they thought were guerrilla hiding places. Hot spots. —Quick! Over there!"

"Where? What?" Hot spot? No, to the right, an actual town, a little metropolis, spreading out far below us in an expansive valley, a white church, terraced gardens on the slopes, human movement, maybe even human kindness. I could see what looked like an honest-to-goodness road winding down into it. That was surely our destination, where we could stop for awhile, stretch our legs, get something to eat, get gas, take a legitimate piss in something like a toilet.

But I was wrong. "There" meant a turn that was almost a U-ey, onto another "road," away from the town.

I protested. "Why not go down there first?"

No, said Catherine. "It's occupied, taken over by the army."

"So what? We're U.S. tourists."

We don't have time to answer their questions, she said, and something else about civil defense patrols, "spies, really," who reported there, "ratting on their relatives," and something about a stockade, "just beyond, see, that's a model village, so-called, where the Maya can go to live if they give up their heritage and their language and their freedom of movement and—."

"Okay, okay," I said. "We won't go there."

I took the U-ey. Now, according to the car compass, we were going directly south. We splashed across a small gully, a stream of water pouring off the side of a cliff. Now the road had angled us north again. The sun was obscured by a milky haze, preparation for the inevitable afternoon rain. On we went, for another hour, turning east, then north again. I sighed dramatically. "I'm hungry. Are we there yet?"

"Actually, we are."

And we were—at a crossroads of sorts, with a small outdoor market similar to the one where I'd bought the bracelet and other things the day before. I stood outside, wolfing down a few bites out of the sausage sandwich while Catherine spoke to a robust woman frying something over a bucket of fire. I assumed this was Isabel and we would surely buy whatever she was cooking. Their conversation was in low tones, but I could hear enough of it to know it was a mixture of Spanish and something else. Catherine had carried over her bag, but returned with it, having added or deposited nothing. She was in a hurry and not at all happy.

"Isabel has left already. I've got to find her."

I stifled a groan. "All right. Do you know how to do that?" I held out a share of the sandwich to her, but she refused it.

"The woman there thinks she may have gone to her old village. She'd be walking, so we might catch her."

Maybe she said "her old village," or maybe "her ancestral village." Whatever, I heard it as Isabel's home and had no reason to question it. It was only the first confusion of the next several hours. In my memory, ensuing events have fallen into definable stages, a way of making the chaos manageable, I suppose, forcing a linearity onto the dimension we now entered, whatever that was.

TWENTY-THREE

You could call the first stage the "Dead-end Road." We got to that by retracing our steps a couple of miles and, as I'd come to expect, began traveling upward, on another route without maintenance, the worst one yet. We were not on this long before it suddenly ended, just plain ended, at the edge of the forest, thick trees and vines on three sides, rising into hills. There was no passage forward, or in any direction I could see.

"This is it," said Catherine. "In there." She pointed to the woods on the right.

"In there? A village?"

"A tiny one, yes."

I cut the motor, assuming we would walk. "How far is it?"

"Not so far."

That was not the right answer, but a little walking was a good idea. "Okay, then. Let's get going," I said, opening the door.

She did not open hers. "Ted, listen. You can't go with me from this point. People in there are nervous about strangers and they don't trust blonds. You can wait for me here. I won't be long."

"You intend to walk in there alone?"

"I was hoping to drive, by myself."

"I see."

She restrained a smile. "You could sit on those rocks there in the shade and finish the sausages while you wait."

"Very funny. You drive this vehicle into the forest primeval, to hell and back for all I know, while I wait here, eating sausages? You must be really *loco*."

"That's possible. But I can't stop to decide right now."

"And what if I say no?"

"I'll walk." She opened the door and got out, tote bag in hand. "See you later, Ted," she said through the window.

I scanned the woods again for some faint semblance of a road. I saw nothing but dense, shadowy growth. " 'Oh, that way madness lies,' " I mumbled.

She walked off with a pained face.

"All right," I called after her. "I'll drive. You're not the only person around here who's gone completely wacko."

She stood still, her back to me, staring into the woods, fighting her own battle, whatever it was.

"Don't worry," I told her. "I'll stay out of sight."

She got back in and sat there, one foot out the half-open door.

"Catherine O'Brien Rodriguez," I said. "Look at me." She did, the old straight-on gaze. "I want to do this," I said. She pulled in her foot and shut the door.

"So where do I go?" I asked.

"*Ve todo recto.*"

Straight ahead? That had to be a joke, and thankfully, it was. She allowed a smile. A change had occurred. She had settled something, I thought. And so had I. The truth is, I was invested. In spite of my complaints, I was where I wanted to be, with Catherine. I wanted to stick with her, hold at bay the impending goodbye, which right now just meant finding a person named Isabel. A sense of destiny? Much too high flown. One step at a time. Just find Isabel, that's next.

"If you back up a little," Catherine told me, "you'll see an opening in the trees on our right, less traveled, as you might say, but passable."

And so began Stage Two. Call it "Something is Wrong." There was indeed an opening, a space between two hemlocks just big enough to allow the car to enter, hardly an inch to spare on either side. Once in, I recognized an indication of human activity—trees stripped of lower branches for the fire, though all the stumps were gray, meaning no fresh cuts—and just the semblance of a track, more likely for an animal drawn cart. Then that ended in a hundred feet or so, in an impasse of forest growth. I was totally dependent on Catherine's directions—to the left up that slope, around that rock, under that vine—all the while climbing in low gear. Over and over what I saw as only dense forest opened to a pre-traveled way, a ghost of its former self, but clear.

Even so, the width of the Cruiser was a problem. We snapped off young saplings. Twice Catherine got out to hold back a larger branch, and once we had to hang together on one to break it off. I had a rotten feeling that I was squashing rare flora, the kind that grow in high, secluded places. I almost hit a small animal waddling across our path. Question (not asked): If this road has not been recently used, how do the occupants of the village get in and out?

We went maybe half a mile this way, until we splashed across a shallow brook into a grassy clearing. A large delegation awaited us there. There were easily two dozen of them, brown and white, billies, nannies and a passel of kids, a matted, uncombed bunch, comical with their flapping ears and long sad overbite. "Goats," I said, oh so unnecessarily.

"Can we get around them?" Catherine asked.

I blew one of my horns, a good loud trumpet. She grabbed my arm. "Not that. It could scare people."

Really? Never mind, it did no good anyway. The animals were unimpressed. I began moving into them slowly, nudging them, but stopped, concerned about bumping the little ones. An old guy, bearded, straight out of *The Billy Goats Gruff*, stood in the middle of the flock, the patriarch, no doubt, of this extended family. I knew nothing about wild goats, but I had a hunch my red car was a territorial challenge. We needed to defuse that. With a flash of crystal clear inspiration, I grabbed what remained of the sausage sandwich from the napkin and flung it into the bushes ten feet to the side. The godfather raised his head. I could actually see his nostrils flare as he caught the scent. Then he went for it and the whole gang began to follow. "Gee-haw!" I yodeled. "Let's roll, Minnie-Lou!" Catherine shushed me, hitting my arm.

I edged on as the animals scattered, but before we were half into the clearing they came trotting back again, with the master in the lead, his droopy face full of disdain. The sausage had been rejected. I thought goats ate everything.

We decided to walk. Out we got, moving quickly around the back of the car, skirting the flock with an ample margin. I carried Catherine's bag. It was not a long walk, but hardly pleasant, an obstacle course of vines and briars and slippery moss. We stopped, scratched and bug-bitten, at the base of a short hill. On our right the thick woods continued, and to our left I could see a treeless area, what I thought at first glance was a corn field. We stood in silence for a minute while Catherine looked around, up at the hill, off to either side, listening. All I could hear were birds and insects, a million instruments tuning up before a concert. "Where do we go from here?" I asked.

"I go. Stay here, please, out of sight."

I made a face.

"Try to be brave," she said.

"No problem. My middle name is Cavalier."

"What?"

"CavaLEE-er."

"You're joking."

She headed up the hill with her bag. I caught glimpses of her all the way to the top, where she paused, pushing aside some bushes and looking down. In a minute she descended the hill again, partway, and disappeared behind a large rock.

Stage Three. I have no accurate title. By my watch it was approaching two o'clock, but it was getting uncomfortably colder, the sun in and out. I had tied on my sweater as we got out of the car, a choice I was glad about now but would soon regret. I pulled it over my head and did some calisthenics, as much as I could in my hiding place. Other than insects and birds, it was quiet, until a dog barked, not far away. A rooster answered. I took that as assurance that Catherine had arrived at the village and was being greeted.

I decided to take a leak while I had the chance. My aim disturbed a snake. I jumped as it slithered away, a tawny brown. I'd seen a lot of them once and knew it was not poisonous, but still, "zero at the bone." As I got on with my business, a dog appeared (the one that had been barking, I assumed), sniffed my foot and raised his leg. I jumped out of the way again as he let out his own stream. He was mangy, with a mongrelized history beyond identity, and he stank. I relocated once more. This brought me closer to the edge of what I had guessed was a maize field, and it was, a *milpa*, though badly neglected, I saw now, one that had once filled a quarter of an acre. What I'd noticed before was green growth that had reseeded in the soil, old squash plants and tall weeds, a garden untouched for years. Maybe the villagers had found a better location. But this was a little plateau, a boon at this height, good level ground, not likely to be abandoned.

It was too quiet. I was paying better attention. The dog and the rooster had fooled me. Too much was missing, children yelling, voices echoing in the hills, the hubbub I had heard as Luis and I approached Las Cavernas yesterday. And something else, the right smoke. I was smelling an old fire, and if this little village was nearby, fresh wood smoke should be wafting sweetly through the trees.

I suppose only half an hour went by, though it seemed much longer. I was sick of the mystery. I found my way up the side of the hill, searching for a path at the rock where Catherine had slipped out of sight. But there was no path. A flowering vine, orange and red, hung in a thick drape from a tree branch to the ground, impassable. I continued on up to the top of the rise. Before me was a wide open valley, covered with a gray haze. Mountains layered themselves in mist on the far side, while dark clouds worked around the closest tier.

I pushed aside the branch of a bush, as Catherine had done. Below me I could see a road, switchbacking through the hills, wide enough for two lanes. I thought I heard a motor, a rough sound, a truck, not far away. That road was certainly the commonly used one to this area. I knew now for sure that we had come here by an abandoned route.

The dog trotted up behind me and sniffed my shoes again. I stooped to give him a pat but he dodged away down the hill, stopped and looked back at me, then disappeared under the flowering vine. Follow the dog, bozo. The vine opened up from the bottom, and there indeed was a path, leading into the deep shade of the foliage. I took it, slowly, pausing often to listen, while the smell of old burning grew steadily stronger. I got a sense of open space ahead. I expected to see another charred hillside, "scorched earth." Instead, I stood at the edge of what must have once been a community, a hamlet or whatever, flattened and blackened by fire. New saplings spiked green in the remnant of a courtyard. I could see faint outlines of the surrounding houses in foundation stones and within them the ringed stones of the central fires. But the buildings were gone. They must have been made of sticks and wattle to burn so completely. Only the *pila*, the community sink, remained standing in the center, filled with tall weeds—and the adobe cookhouse, I saw now, with a young tree growing out of the opening in its conical roof.

I moved a little closer, still (I thought) concealed by bushes. Here and there, among black puddles of the season's rain, I could make out parts of what had once been the classic tools of a village, the unburnable parts, a metal wheelbarrow, a hoe with a charred handle—the wide-bladed Mayan hoe—and the grinding stone, indestructible. Not far from me lay a pile of matted feathers and bones, a dead chicken, not burned, probably eaten by the dog, and just ahead a much larger pile of bones with patches of fur, attached to a charred rope. A tied burro, was my guess, unable to break free.

Nothing I could see from this vantage point suggested incinerated human bodies. And no living ones either, no person called Isabel, no residents to be nervous about my strange presence, and no Catherine.

The dog scooted ahead of me. I followed him with my eyes, out through young trees at the far end of the courtyard. Another structure stood beyond that, apparently untouched by fire, a large shed of some kind, a good twenty feet long, with half-walls of sticks. A pig sty or a chicken house. No, a pen for goats. The goats had escaped this conflagration, formed their own community and increased their tribe. A rooster, speckled black and white, stood on the roof of the shed, like a guard. He and the dog and the goats. They owned this whole eerie place, and they had managed somehow not to kill each other.

Still no Catherine. My eyes searched for sight of her beyond the goat shed. The word *engaño* spoke itself, intentional deception. I fought it off. I told myself that she must not have known about this, or maybe that the community had rebuilt itself somewhere else nearby, out of sight, and that was where she had gone.

But she *was* here. She emerged from one side of the shed, bending over in what must be a doorway. As she straightened she saw me and sent a frantic signal with her hands. Back up and be quiet. I stepped into the trees behind me and watched as she chose steps through the rubble of the courtyard. She was not carrying her bag, I noticed. She passed me without speaking, her finger still on her lips, and I joined her without a word, back along the path, under the bower and down the hill, where we turned to face each other.

"You shouldn't have followed me," she whispered.

I bristled. "And did you know all along about this—that—there?"

"Yes, of course."

So she did know, which would simply mean, in a less charged context, that something was going on that I was not privy to, that she felt the need to camouflage. So why should that bother me? It did. I was more offended than angry, more rueful than offended. My "investment" was looking more whimsical by the second.

"You couldn't have told me?" I said. "Where is everyone?"

"Who?"

"All those nervous village people. What was all the hush about?"

"For Isabel." She rubbed her face with both hands. Her hat was askew and her sneakers were filthy with soot. "I thought she was there, somewhere on the grounds. I don't know what to think now. I left my bag and the money, just in case."

A rustle in the bushes whirled us both around. A woman was standing twenty feet from us, half-hidden in the foliage. Catherine said, "Oh!" and darted across to her. They disappeared together into the shadows while I processed the photograph still in my eyes. It was the face of any number of women I had seen in the last three weeks, high cheekbones, round cheeks, not just Mayan but Minoan, Inuit, Algonquin. Then I caught sight of another figure, a boy, I thought, before he slipped out of sight like a forest animal.

Catherine returned in just a moment, alone. "I'm so relieved," she said. "She's been hiding, she and her son. She heard the horn and your yell and didn't know who it was."

"And now she knows I'm harmless, right?"

"I told her you're from the store. It's run by Norwegians."

"Cute."

"You could do worse. Anyway, we can go now. I told her where to find the bag. My job here is done."

"Hunky-dory. So is mine." We had found Isabel. "Let's go."

"I wish you could trust me," Catherine said.

"What the heck do you think I've been doing all day? How about trusting me?"

"Oh, God," she said, "you haven't got a clue."

Maybe Stage Four begins here. We started back, retracing our steps. I walked ahead of her, eager to get to the car, to something reliable, like a motor that would go "whoom" when you turned a little key. Catherine was right behind me. "Ted! Isabel has her own problems. It's not my place to——." I felt some satisfaction in the need for her to speak to my back. Walking in tandem was difficult, or she'd have been beside me, I knew, or would have whipped past me to take the lead. I kept on going without answering. "I just bring money and supplies and pick up the finished *huipiles*," she said. Except she hadn't picked up anything. She was empty handed. I put that on hold and asked another question, over my shoulder. "What happened to that village?"

"Surely you can guess," she said. "It was an army massacre, of course. Four years ago. Isabel's husband and children were killed. Three children. She saw this. She saw them murdered, shot. And her parents, a sister, grandparents, aunts, uncles, cousins. It was the usual ghastly raid."

A left hook to the jaw. I should be getting used to this, I thought, these blows of information.

"She escaped with one child, Manuel. He was a toddler then."

"All right. I should have known," I said.

"The survivors scattered. At first a few of them managed to sneak back to bury the dead. Isabel visits the graves whenever she thinks it's safe."

That was believable. If you are Mayan, that's what you do. "And you usually meet her here," I said.

"No. That would be risky. I came with her just once. She wanted to show me the place. We've always met at that market. That's where

I'd find her."

We had reached the grassy domain of the goats. They were still there, the whole ratty family, all of them lying down now. We circled them and got into the car, I in the driver's seat, no discussion. I put on the headlights, high beams shooting into the pack. The old billy, hunkered in the middle of the group, turned his head to gaze at us, his pale eyes shining in the lights. I needed that space, the one they occupied, to turn the car around.

"I'm so sorry," Catherine said. "About you, too. I've been treating you badly."

It was hard to buck against that. I put my hand on her arm, finding inordinate reassurance in the fact that she didn't pull away. I was looking at her and she was looking out the window. We sat like that for several seconds, until she said, "Uh-oh."

The patriarch had risen and was facing the car in what I took to be an unmistakable attack position, head down. He gave a snort and began stamping on the ground. Maybe it was an empty threat from one so arthritic, but it sent a message. Others were scrambling to their feet. By quick estimation six were males, all with head-pieces big enough to dent a fender or smash a head light. Backing up was not an option. A preemptive strike was called for, something to put the fear of God in the old fart. I picked up a half empty water bottle and pressed the window button as Catherine grabbed a hairbrush from her purse. I lobbed southpaw out my side while she threw a right-handed zinger from hers. My bottle hit the billy on a horn. Her hairbrush landed squarely on his nose.

For a mindless two seconds I thought the sound I heard came from the goats. They were laughing at us. But it was coming from somewhere else, somewhere in the forest. There, again. I heard it this time as a bunch of people in a coughing fit. But Catherine and the goats knew otherwise. The goats dove splay-legged into the brush and before I could gather my wits Catherine opened her door and ran—or plunged, not away from the sound but directly toward it, which was back the way we had just come. I jumped out and ran after her. One thing only was obvious at that minute: Catherine was heading straight into some unpredictable chaos, and she must not go alone. What is crazier yet is that we could have driven. The goats were gone.

There's a replay of this scene I like better than the way it happened. In that version, I do stay in the car. I drive after Catherine. When I reach her, she jumps in and we hurtle like demons over the floor of the forest, half airborne, me leaning on all three horns, blowing them again and again with long bellowing trumpets of protest. I can't stop. If I stop, back up, back out, she will jump from the car and take off on her own. I know that, so I keep going, crashing through the underbrush, blowing the horns like we're some kind of cavalry arriving with trumpets and blood-curdling banners. And all the while I am thinking that whatever we do, any choice we make—to be noisy or quiet, to hide or pursue, retreat or charge ahead in an act of self-destructive heroism—either could be exactly right or exactly wrong, and there is no way at this moment, this one that counts above all, that I can possibly know.

But that's not what happened. We went on foot, running in and out of the trees, tripping over stones and stumps. The ground was spongy, bad enough when we were walking, far worse running. We both fell down twice. Catherine's hat was knocked off and the blue headband under it snagged in a branch along with a strand of her hair. I untangled her as she winced in pain. During that eternity, the guns coughed once more, a quick volley, and when our race ended at the path leading up the hill to the burnt village, everything was quiet, even the dog and the rooster.

We stood still and listened, getting our breath. My better instincts were working now, and maybe hers, too. At least we seemed to be in some kind of accord. When nothing reached our ears, no voices, no crunch of feet in the bushes, we climbed the hill and entered the viney curtain. We moved ahead with caution, two steps and pause, listen and look, repeat. My legs were so heavy I could hardly move them. Fear. Hello. I hadn't felt it while we were running, but now it took over, shooting me up with another hormone, a wipe-out. Everything disappeared but the immediate instant, all sense of time, all history, the hope of a future.

Now a motor, a quick roar starting up at some location beyond us, the same rough-throated truck sound I'd heard earlier, a shift, then another, and the slowly fading hum of a departing vehicle.

"They're gone," said Catherine.

We waited, our breathing shaky, long enough for the earlier spurt of adrenalin to ebb away, then crossed to the goat shelter. There, at the side, where I'd seen Catherine emerge before, a gate of sorts stood open. She peered in, crouched in the little doorway, and I joined her. Stage five begins here.

TWENTY-FOUR

What met me first was the smell, barnlike, warm, meaty, deeply private. Narrow strips of light pierced the interior through the cracks in the walls, falling across a floor of old straw. No one awaited us there behind a semi-automatic, but something *was* there, lying in a far corner, some*one*, sprawled awkwardly in the hay. We rushed in together, knocking into each other, bumping our heads on the low roof, and dropped down on the ground beside a bloody heap. Now we had really found Isabel.

She had been shot in the face and chest. The face was all but gone. Her hands were on her chest, fingers spread, her arms crossed, as a woman might try to cover exposed breasts. She was wearing a *huipil*, an awesome thing, the woven cloth heavy with a thick overlay of embroidered flowers and vines and birds. I could see the wonder of it, even as blood was flooding into it, pouring not just from her wounds but as if from some secret source where blood is kept, spreading into the brilliant colors, the artistry, and down into the striped weave of her *traje*, those wonderful joyful clothes. That's what she was protecting with her hands. Her work. That's how I saw it.

Catherine was muttering, swearing, rocking back and forth like a keening woman, bending to embrace the body, over and over. Finally, I put my hand on her shoulder, lightly, not sure she wanted to be touched. She got to her feet, covered with gore. Flies were gathering, dozens, scores, with the buzz of lunacy. We crept backward out of the building. Outside I stepped on what I hadn't noticed before, spent shells, dozens of them in the grass.

Catherine whispered, "The boy, Manuel. Where is he!"

He wasn't far. I got to him first. He was on his back in the grass, his head resting on a small backpack, which had flipped up from under him, askew. His hair was over his eyes. I brushed it away. His eyes were partly open, dark eyes, a handsome child, seven or eight. He was wearing a red sweatshirt. The bullets had cut a line through the *Rojos* logo. Catherine was beside me. We felt his wrists and got no pulse, but his skin was not cold, not to my touch. I began to yell into Catherine's face. "That road! Down there! Quick! Let's go!" We could hail a passing car, get help. I started to lift him. Catherine yelled back. "No, no, Ted! It's too late! He's bled out." I put my hands over the wounds, and breathed into his mouth as he lay on the ground, hideously mindful of my ineptitude.

"Ted, there's no use. He's dead," Catherine said in my ear.

"Maybe not, maybe not!"

I was furious with her but I knew she was right. The boy's face had grayed. There was no pulse anywhere we probed, no feather of breath. I lifted him into my lap, reluctant to send him off by himself. He was light and limp. Something else had left his body besides breath and blood, an energy or will, the part of him that was running to his mother. I had never seen a person die, never witnessed that deflating loss of spirit.

Catherine stood, glancing about, distracted by something. She went back to the shed, returning quickly. "My bag is gone," she said. "I'll take a look around."

I lowered the boy to the ground and rose. "You're not going anywhere alone."

"She was meeting her brother," she said. "He could be hiding. He knows me but not you."

"I'll introduce myself."

We walked the edge of the woods, slowly, scanning for signs of human life, easy targets ourselves, for a brother or anyone. I saw a flash of red in the bushes. A red beret, for sure. Before I could react, it took flight, flapping high and out of sight with a coarse cry. I thought of Luke's assurance, safety in my Nordic appearance. It crossed my mind to make myself more noticeably so, but I couldn't think of anything except to shout out the few Swedish expressions I knew. *God yule! Jag alskar dig! Valkommen til var stuga!* Merry Christmas! I love you! Welcome to our house! —No, I didn't do it.

We walked as far as the cemetery. It ran across the top of a low hill on the other side of a short section of woods. It was large, bigger than the village, a hundred graves, mounds of all sizes, adult and child, visible in spite of the overgrowth of weeds. Here we saw something. We both pointed. A hat. Not straw this time, a beat-up felt fedora. "It's her brother's," Catherine whispered.

There had been a struggle. The short trail of blood was easy to follow. He was curled under a tree, a slight man with bushy gray hair. He also had been shot in the face as well as the chest. I saw a leather holster under what was left of his jacket. If it had held a gun, it was gone. Not far from him lay the dog, on his back, legs in the air, still twitching.

Catherine's bag was on the ground nearby, its contents dumped out. She began to replace things and I helped, with great concentration, as if this bit of housekeeping might be the only thing on earth that could rescue my sanity. We picked it all up, a box of salt, dried corn and beans half-tumbled out of their packages, a pound of coffee, and an odd collection of other items—candles, toothbrushes, a kid's stuffed elephant, a bottle of aspirin. Two paperbacks. One was Hemingway, *Adiós A Las Armas.* Catherine picked up another book, a large slim one with a hard cover, green and white. *Yertle the Turtle,* of all things, English version, so familiar looking it could have once been mine. She opened it. I saw the page, the one where Yertle, at the top of the heap of other turtles, king of all he can see, takes a dive off his throne. On that page something had been drawn in ink over the illustration, a map, I thought. Catherine snapped the book shut and thrust it into the bag.

"The money," she said. "It was tied up in a piece of fabric. Do you see it anywhere?"

We searched the grass, the moss, among leaves. She felt in the brother's pockets, with more stamina than I could have mustered. "Nothing here," she said. She picked up the bag. "I'll leave this stuff in the goat shed. Someone else may come."

I answered "Of course," not meaning to be sarcastic, just not caring any more if the moon was made of green cheese. I had enough courtesy left to carry the bag. Back at the goat shed she emptied it onto a shelf inside the door, along with Manuel's pack. Except *Yertle the Turtle*. That stayed in her bag.

Thunder sighed faintly in the distance. I looked over at the boy lying in the grass and wondered if we should bring him into the shed with his mother. The idea of leaving him out there in a certain rain seemed intolerable. I glanced up, looking for clouds, and saw vultures, hang-gliding slowly, just waiting for us to leave. I said, "We should bury them, now." I was sure it was right. I never considered the audacity. "The shovels are here in the goat barn," Catherine said, without hesitation. There they were, leaning in a corner, two of them. She picked these up while I got the Mayan hoe with the charred handle I had seen in the burned patio. We carried those back to the graveyard. Yes, the graveyard. We could have buried them where they were. That might have been easier. We didn't discuss it. The cemetery was where they belonged.

You might think that this, above all, must be another fantasy of how it could have gone, but it sure isn't. We agreed that our first task was to bring over the bodies, to protect them from animal predators while we dug. I got the wheelbarrow. We lifted Isabel and Manuel into that and pushed them the fifty-foot distance. The brother we dragged together by his feet. I begged his pardon, silently.

Then we dug. The ground was soft and damp, easy to enter but full of roots and stones. The space we excavated was not a nice neat cavity by any stretch: a rough five feet long, three wide, four deep. It was barely big enough for a trio of small people. "By tradition it's supposed to be two *vara* down," Catherine said. "About a yard." As we stopped to breathe, she told me something else. During some raids, women were forced to dig their own graves, then dance around them naked before being raped and shot.

We lowered the brother in first, then Isabel, then the boy on top of them, after I had checked for breath and pulse once more, and then again, until I was sure that all signs of life were gone. All were wearing several layers of clothes, Isabel three *huipils*, I noted. Why? "Beats a suitcase," Catherine said. More green cheese.

We buried them according to custom, the little we knew, with their heads pointing west, toward the reclining sun. The last step was to kiss a handful of dirt and throw it into the grave. We each did that, then shoveled in what we had dug out, tamped it, stamped on it, mounded it, and covered it with branches to deter the animals.

By the time we finished, the sun had paled and the thunder, though still distant, had become a sustained growl. A wind had come up. We stood by the hole, filthy and stinking, blowing on our blistered hands. "I know a little K'ché," Catherine said.

"You're on."

She spoke a sentence directly to the grave. "What does it mean?" I asked.

"May the ground seem level under your feet wherever you are walking. It's what Isabel used to tell me when we said goodbye."

It was my turn. I spoke to Manuel. I told him that I hoped there was a good soccer ball wherever he was going and a good enough space to kick it around with other kids. I had no idea what to say to his uncle.

Following that we walked away, dutifully returning the wheelbarrow and tools to their places, like responsible adults. Catherine carried her bag, empty now except for the book. When we got to the *pila* we stopped and poked through the weeds, looking in vain for a working faucet or pump. No luck. The *pila* was a dry sink. There were poolings of rain water all around us, but they were muddy and filled with dead bugs. We walked on through the burnt-out courtyard, down the hill and through the stretch of woods to the car.

The goats had not come back, but there perched the speckled rooster on the roof of the car, pruning his feathers. I whacked him off with a stick, not gently. I hated him for being alive. Catherine's purse was still on the front seat, and her suitcase and my pack were still unopened in the back, along with the mask and other stuff I had bought at the roadside market on Sunday morning. She looked through her purse. "They weren't here," she said.

"How can you be sure?"

"They'd have taken my cigarettes."

We drank from our remaining bottles of water, then splashed the rest on our hands and heads. It was nowhere near enough. I was still thirsty and my beard was sticky, my jeans and sweater stiff with coagulating blood, as was the entire front of Catherine's top and skirt. Her hair hung about her face, matted. She'd lost her sunglasses somewhere. We'd both left our hats in the cemetery. They'd have blown away by now. It didn't matter. I didn't need mine any longer to assure me that something had actually happened.

The car clock said 4:00 but it was getting dark with the pending rain. I put on the headlights, turned around in the goat pasture and followed the trail the car had mowed coming in. Crossing the stream I resisted the urge to get out and roll in the water, maybe forever.

TWENTY-FIVE

It wasn't until we reached the dirt road that I began to imagine a world ahead, the one of civilized expectations. "We've got to report this, haven't we," I said.

"Report? Who to?"

"Local authorities. A priest. Hell, somebody."

"The only priest I knew about locally was assassinated five years ago."

"But surely the police?"

"Oh, yeah? That's the same as going to the army to tell it what it just did. You want to go to the army? There's a garrison about five miles from here."

"You're so sure it was the army."

"Nobody else owns those guns. Army-issued Galils, made in Israel. They make that distinctive sound."

"Guerrillas could have stolen them."

"Yes, they've done that plenty of times. And killed to do it. But believe me, this was not guerrillas."

Other questions were inserting themselves, as if they had climbed into the back and were hissing over the top of the seat. Why not pop off Isabel on the street somewhere? Or at the market? Why dispatch the storm troops to do it? I asked that.

"I don't know," she said. "Maybe they were expecting a fight."

"Why did the army raid that village in the first place, four years ago?"

"The village was feeding guerrillas. That much I know. They had a big community garden and they had always shared with other people. Even after the guerrillas explained who they were, they still fed them."

"Then where were the guerrillas when the village was raided?"

"Good question. No angels in this story."

We were at a fork. Where next? Hang a left, she said. To where? I asked. Straight back to Chichi.

A three or four hour drive. If we were lucky we might get on to a decent route before darkness hit, or the storm. The thunder was much louder and in the mirrors I could see a black cloud gathering heft behind us. I glanced at the gas gauge. Enough maybe, but filling up would be a good idea. Above all, we needed a place to wash. Even Orange Crush would do for that. The idea was heavenly. "We've got to stop somewhere," I said.

She refused. Absolutely not. It was dangerous to stop.

"Time for a pow-wow, Catherine." I was determined to win this one.

But, *pero, pero,* before either of us could speak again, what little was left of the light of day switched off. The thunderhead was upon us in all its anger, and with it a whipping wind. The car rocked. I saw a grassy verge ahead and pulled over into it, shutting off the motor. Rain followed instantly, roaring down on the roof.

"Car wash," said Catherine.

"Wash," I repeated.

I was already removing my money belt and Catherine did the same, pulling it from under her top. We stumbled out our doors and were soaked to the skin by the time we met in front of the car. As fast as we could we stripped off everything, the wind snatching our clothes out of our hands as we removed them. In seconds we were both naked to the shoes. I watched with dismay as my sweater and jeans sailed off forever into the darkness, but Catherine laughed and flung her skirt into the air, where it danced away over the trees, a fat ghost, illuminated by lightning.

What kind of a crazy hiatus was this? I won't try to defend it. It seemed all wrong and completely right, like the reveling of an Irish wake, as inevitable as the rain itself. And it was over in a flash, the cloud speeding on ahead and an amber light filling the sky, the final phase of the setting sun. We splashed back to the car and turned on the heater, children hosed down by the gods at the end of a day.

Well, not quite children. Catherine's long strong legs were no child's, or the small hard breasts. I made it a point, with admirable will power, not to stare. But she did. She stared.

"What are you looking at, nosey?" I said.

"Nothing, poopy-face."

She was right. Boney, freckled shoulders, blond chest hair descending to the private parts—the *parte péndula,* so shriveled with the cold it was not much larger than a misplaced thumb. But growing apace, I noticed, and so did she. Never mind. It was the wrong time for prurient impulses.

She thought so, too. At least, she turned and knelt to reach her suitcase on the back seat and began busily pulling out garments, slacks, a jersey, a pair of sandals. "My aunt's," she said. "We weren't quite the same size. She was heavier than me and shorter."

She drew out a small towel, a gift from heaven we shared. Probing in my pack, I found the old sweatpants I had stuffed in at the last minute. I envied her as she yanked on the slacks and dropped her aunt's shirt over her head.

"Anything in a guy's medium long?" I asked.

She tossed me a jersey, pink with lace bordering the neck.

"Nothing in blue?"

"Not in your size."

It was tight but warmer than bare skin. She surveyed me with amusement. I paid her with one of the granola bars from my pack.

"Now we'll go find some safe little town, won't we," I said, as we munched. "Now that we look so spiffy."

"Not a chance." She began fluffing her hair in front of the heater vent.

"Well, guess what," I said. "Me, I'm gonna stop somewhere and get something to eat and drink. You can wait for me on that rock in the shade there and I'll come back and get you when I'm done."

"All right." She straightened up, hair over her face. "That *tienda* we saw earlier. I'm uneasy about it, but let's go."

Progress was slow. The storm had raced ahead of us, doing considerable damage to the road. We rounded a scary washout on the cliff side. Here and there stones had rolled down from the hill, one so big I had to get out and move it. It was getting dark again, this time with nightfall.

"It's dangerous," I said, back into the car. "It will be better to pull over somewhere and sit it out until morning."

I expected a fight, but she sighed and agreed. "There's an alternate way to get there. Longer but easier. We should come to it in about a mile."

A slippery lane and a grinding climb brought us to another dirt road, but so different, graded, with graveled-in potholes and telephone lines running beside it. A car passed us going the other way and there was actually room for us both.

"Who maintains this?" I asked.

"The army, of course."

An actual sign, its fluorescent graphic glowing in my headlights, warned us of a switchback ahead. That took us down the side of a hill. Around the last curve we were brought to a dead stop by flares. In a flood-lit scene just ahead of us, an army truck was positioned horizontally across the road, and beyond that rose a heap of mud and rocks ten feet high. Men moved about in the dark, a lot of them. One, dressed in camouflage rain gear and pointing a rifle, stepped into our headlights.

"*Atrás, atrás!*" he yelled, waving us back.

I reversed, then opened the window and called, "*Qué pasa?*"

"*Derrumbe!*" he answered, with a long role of the "r's."

"Rock fall," said Catherine.

I peered into the darkness behind me, looking for a way to turn, when the car interior filled with light. The guy was at the window with the mother of all flashlights. I shielded my eyes. He beamed the light from my face to Catherine's, then around the interior of the car, on all the stuff on the back seats. Was the blood still visible? Could he smell it? The light returned to my face.

"*Hola, señor,*" I said.

"*Cómo se llama?*" His Spanish was heavily accented.

I answered slowly. "*Me llamo* Ted Peterson. I am from the United States. *Turista.*"

He looked me over. What was he making of my lacy pink jersey? The light switched back to Catherine, who smiled into it brightly, her wet hair in a tousle, half over her face. I put my hand on her shoulder. "*Está es mi amiga. Elle llama—.*"

She interrupted me. "*Novia,*" she said. "Girlfran." She giggled.

The light swung back to me. "ID, mistah."

It was in my money belt on the dashboard. I pulled out the passport and handed it to him. He looked at it with the flashlight, then at me again and gave it back. "*Vos?*" he said to Catherine, but she was already reaching across me with a booklet I supposed was her passport. I opened it and positioned it for him in the beam of the flashlight. The photo was of a serious, dark-eyed woman, with long black hair tucked behind one ear and covering half of the other cheek. The name was Magdalena Rodriguez Adrela. My heart jumped, but Catherine was leaning forward, squarely into the guy's light, still smiling, her hair down over one side of her face, raking her fingers through it, comically. "*Caught in rain!*" she said, with an accent. "*La lluvia, la lluvia! Ay, ay, ay!*" The guy actually laughed.

"*Qué pasa, por favor?*" I asked again, to divert him. What happened?

He paused a moment, then leaned his face into my window, water running off his rain hood onto my arm. He was not much more than a kid, his cheeks round and smooth. He pointed ahead of us, in the direction of the landslide and spoke in a lowered voice.

"*Pues, señor,* is them turds, them shit-ass commie pinkos." So, he knew some English. "*Es* fuckin' *sabotaje.*"

"I see."

"*Hijos de putas!*"

"Right on," I said, agreeably.

"*Cogeremos los* cocksuckers!"

"*Va! Bueno!*" I said.

"Assholes! Them *hijos de las chingadas!*"

"*Sí, sí,* them poopy-faces!"

He gave a guffaw and thumped me on the shoulder with his fist. I asked him to help me turn around. He directed me with his light, forward, backward, until I was facing the other direction. "*Cuidado!*" he called, waving me off. "*Gracias,*" I called back and began to climb the height we had just come down. I didn't care where we went. Magdalena and I could drive until the gas was gone and then sit down somewhere and die of hunger and thirst. Before we passed out, maybe she would tell me who she really was.

"Conscripted Indian," she said, on her own track.

"And the *groséria,* the display of vulgarities?" I asked that, but I knew.

Fellowship in *machismo*, one real guy to another.

She gave me a motherly pat on the shoulder. "You did pretty well yourself."

"I've had a good teacher," I said. And now? "Now what do we expats do, Magdalena?"

"That was my aunt's passport. My husband's aunt."

"It sure as hell wasn't yours. Why did you give the guy a false ID?"

"A precaution."

"You stole an ID?"

"Borrowed. I borrowed one of the fakes. She had three."

"You stole it."

"Sure. Look, we can't go on. At that *tienda*, there's also a *posada*. They may have available rooms."

"And this time you know exactly how to get there, right?"

"Pretty much, yes. I stayed there once a few years ago. Just follow the wires."

TWENTY-SIX

We arrived in fifteen minutes, guided by an electric line along a side road. All I could see through the rain were the open shelves of the store built into the front of an adobe house. A large van was parked next to it. We dashed for the store's overhang.

I shouted for attention and in a moment a man appeared, looking as wet as we were and a bit harried. He shook his head no when I asked for rooms. We were too late. That van had brought twelve people and they had already moved in. *Los Franceses,* he said. *Turistas.* There was nothing left, he was very sorry. All right then, I said, could we sleep outside here in our own car? That was all right, he supposed. And how about some food? Only what you see here (a nod to the shelves). I bought bottles of Orange Crush and bags of chips and other stuff. We stood there under the canopy, guzzling down our drinks in gulps. He watched us. Finally he sighed. There was one room, a storeroom. No furniture. We would have to sleep on the floor.

"We'll take it," Catherine said. Did he have any folding cots? No cots. Blankets? Yes. Towels? In luck. Two towels. A *colchon,* mattress. She asked him if she could use his telephone. He refused. It was not for the *público.* She asked him to reconsider. It was important. She needed to call her son. He said no again.

We waited there, pigging out on junk food, until the room was ready and we followed the owner through a courtyard paved with stone. Brown hens flapped out of our way. We passed the customary *pila* in the middle and three lighted rooms on either side. I heard chatter in French as we walked by. Our room was at the far end, a building standing alone. It was not much bigger than a prison cell, with one high window. Supplies had been stacked along a wall. A cockroach the size of a mouse shot between boxes.

The space had been hastily furnished with a narrow mattress on the floor, a wooden chair and a bed table holding an outsized lamp, an ugly ceramic thing with a twisted green shade, like the old picture window lamps. But there was no electricity. Our light was a small candle burning under the lamp. "*El baño?*" I asked. He pointed. Bathroom next door. Well, that was a plus.

Catherine went there first, then I took a turn. Standing near it was the plumbing—several pails of water, that is, to pour down the hole—and the usual bucket for chucking toilet paper. The *pila* in the courtyard was the community wash room.

I was conscious of how naturally I was acting, a marionette still on its feet, strings taut. Back in the shed I found my toothbrush and tube of paste in my pack and stared at them thankfully, remnants of life before this day. "Gleam." What a lovely name. My beard trimmer and nail clipper were items of beauty, symbols of order and decency in the larger universe.

Catherine was staring at a bottle of shampoo as if she didn't know what to do with it. "Want first dibs in the shower?" I said.

"You go. Maybe you could bring me back some water, in a bucket or something. I'll wash up here."

I removed my pink top and went out to the courtyard. The rain had stopped. Two of *les hommes Français* and one of the women were sitting in front of their doors, smoking and batting at bugs. I said "Good evening" and they nodded. I don't remember now what they looked like, except that I wanted to stand there and admire them, ambassadors of civilization. It seemed incredible to me that they knew nothing of what I had just witnessed.

Cooking pots were stacked upside down at one end of the *pila*. I filled a pot with water and brought it back to Catherine, then returned to the sink. As I washed, ducking my head and shoulders under a stream of ice cold water, I let myself get lost in the sheer relief it would be to walk over to the tourists and pour out the whole story. I reached for my high school French. "*Ecoutez, ecoutez, s'il vous plait.*" Instead, I toweled off and brushed my teeth with a splash from the bottle of *agua pura* provided there. Why die of bacterial flora when you've just eluded gunfire?

"Were you also turned back by the landslide?" What? One of the men had spoken to me, in English. I nodded yes, in the middle of rinsing my mouth. "Where are we?" he asked. "Can you tell us? We're lost." I went over and joined them in their cloud of smoke. "Where are you headed?" I asked. They were on their way to Chichicastenango. Did I know how to get to the Pan-American Highway from here? My "companion" would know, I said. I would ask her. All that still as if nothing had happened.

In the room, Catherine was rubbing her hair with the towel, filling the little space with the scent of shampoo. She was wearing a terrycloth robe, too short, obviously her aunt's, and a pair of knee socks.

I began to spread the blankets over the mattress. It was hardly wide enough for one of us. "This is silly," I said. "I'll go sleep in the car."

She answered quickly. "Oh no. You'll freeze."

"I'll borrow a blanket from the French."

"But I'd rather you didn't leave me alone."

"Oh. All right then. I'd rather not be alone either."

She looked forlorn there in the candlelight, like an oversized girl in a garment she had grown out of. "Why don't you go have a smoke with the French tourists," I suggested. She had not smoked at all the whole trip, I was realizing, had not displayed the shakes that had overtaken her after the party three nights ago. Neither of us had shown any of the familiar signs of our panic attacks. It was as if we were beyond all that.

"They want to go to Chichi," I told her. "They don't know how to find the highway."

"I'm too tired now. I'll catch them in the morning. They can follow us."

It was 7:30 and it felt like midnight. Outside in the courtyard laughter rose and fell, a bottle clinked on the stone paving, a door slammed.

"It could be a noisy evening," I said.

Catherine dropped to one side of the mattress and curled up with her back to me, blanket over her head. "I don't care if they sing the fucking *Marseillaise*."

I took off my shoes, blew out the candle and lowered myself to what space was left for me. You might have slipped a piece of paper between us. My feet, still in their socks, stuck out of the blanket. The sounds of genteel festivity continued. The French had brought their own bar, I figured. I fantasized about it, one of those little leather cases you'd see in European movies, outfitted with cocktail glasses and a shaker. I could have used a drink and considered going out there and asking for one. That possibility was the last thing that passed through my mind before I awoke, my eyes wide open.

Maybe I hadn't been asleep very long, because I was not disoriented. I knew where I was, though the room was very dark. Rain splattered on the zinc roof. Otherwise it was quiet. The partying had stopped. A nightbird called, the screech fading as it flew away. I was willing myself back to sleep when I heard the sound that must have woke me. It was Catherine's muffled weeping. I listened for a minute or two, reluctant to intrude. Her tears were her own affair. When it didn't stop I reached over. Her head was under the blanket. I gave it a rub.

"Are you all right?"

She began to sob, hard. I pulled the blanket off her face. She fought. In a minute she yielded. "It's my fault," she said.

"What is? Never mind, I know. You're a shit-ass commie pinko girl guerrilla and you caused that landslide."

"How simple that sounds."

I listened while she took several more breaths, the kind that prepare intended speech. "She gave up on me. Isabel."

"What do you mean?"

"Never mind. It's too complicated."

"Why were you doing this hellish errand anyway? Tell me that."

She raised on her elbow and faced me. I couldn't see much more than a shape, it was so dark. "I did stop. That's the point. I begged them to find someone else. But I was the only one Isabel trusted. Twice the store sent other people, and she wouldn't even acknowledge them. All she dared to go on was a physical appearance, me, the really tall lady with the hair. When I didn't come that was a signal to her. I couldn't let her know I really was coming. I couldn't call her. When I didn't come she thought something was wrong and decided to go to the mountains with her brother. That's what she told me back there when we saw her in the forest. And something *was* wrong. Oh nuts, I'm babbling." She dropped down again, her back to me.

Some basic truth had jumped out of her closet and dodged back in again, its tail flick catching in the corner of my eye. I thought if I could just re-open that door a crack, everything would thunder out in a great *derrumbe* of facts.

"Whatever, it's over now," I said, haplessly. "Done. *Marchito.*"

"No. You mean *se acabó*. Finished." She was actually correcting me.

"Teacher, teacher," I murmured. I gathered her up against me. She didn't resist. I felt her heart beating, the pulse in her neck that I had not felt in those others, back there. I heard my own heart beating. Her long legs against mine were warm and tightly muscled. "How can we be so alive?" I whispered. "Don't ask," she said. "Better not to know." I kissed her wet cheek, held my lips there. "Is this okay?" I asked. Was I taking advantage of her? Or rather, of *them?* Was it still not the right time?

"It's okay." She turned around to me. "I'm not presuming anything," she said.

"Presume? Oh, God, me neither."

The next kiss was hers. I let it be hers for the lovely long minute it lasted, thankful to receive it. The kiss I returned was not Presbyterian. Further presumptions followed in rapid succession, my lips finding the way down, taking their time, and she with her hands in my hair, guiding. Once I entered the nest she offered, we both sighed, deeply, from the core, and lay still for a moment, as if gathering the strength to go on.

Then the scene lit up in my head, the whole thing rushing back, the destroyed bodies, the smell of spilled life, the weight of the boy in my lap, the incredible blood, the flies. The marionette collapsed. I groaned, "God Almighty."

"It doesn't matter," said Catherine, rubbing my back. "It's okay."

But it was not. Like a shot I was off the mattress and out the door to the *baño*. I considered staying there for the rest of the night, in the company of spiders and whatever else. When it was all over, I returned humbly to the room.

"I hope that was a panic attack," her voice said in the dark.

"You could call it that."

"Good. Now we're even."

"And how are you doing yourself?" I asked.

"Not very well. In fact, awful. Terrible."

"How can I help?"

"I just want to go home."

"Home?"

"I just want my Dad, that's what I mean."

"I understand." I was still standing in the cold.

"When I was little," she said, "really little, and couldn't get to sleep, sometimes he would lie down beside me in bed." She patted the mattress. "That's a hint."

"Then shove over." I hate to use the word "snuggle," but that's what we did, kids at a frigid summer camp.

"Sometimes he would sing," she said. "He had a lovely tenor voice. He sang *Bendemeer's Stream* and *Danny Boy.* Honest."

"I'm not going to sing to you," I said. "I've already done that."

"But then we would talk, until I fell asleep. He used to ask me what I wanted most in life, and then he'd tell me what he wanted most, as if I were a grown-up."

"That sounds good. We'll talk. Mostly. You first."

She took a breath. "I shouldn't get started."

"Start or I'll sing."

"I just want to go home," she said again. "To my son." To Costa Rica this time. Her heart was pounding.

"Tell me about him, your son," I said. I thought it might calm her.

"His name is Alex. He wants to be a priest. He's a good Catholic boy like his father. And he'll never be a priest, like his father never was."

"Martin." I pronounced his name as she did, Marteen. "What was he like?"

"He was six inches shorter than me."

"That's not what I mean."

"But it's what I mean. We looked ridiculous together. I was what was known as a big girl. Not just tall, big. Not reedy, like I am now, and not fat, just big. I played basketball and field hockey. A jock. He was five six. And I'd have killed him if he'd worn elevators."

"I believe you."

"He taught me so much, everything I know about the world. He loved the world. He loved Guatemala. He'd have died for it. He did."

I skirted that one. "He was Ladino, right?"

"Oh no. He was K'iché Maya, adopted as an infant and raised as a rich kid. I was always astonished at how he accepted his wealth. I mean, he accepted it but never needed it. I didn't even know he was rich until he brought me home to his family."

"Was he a Marxist?" I asked. I thought she'd told me that before.

"No, though some people thought so. He despised the aristocracy. That was enough to make him an outright Commie in the eyes of his parents. They were *criollo.*"

"What?"

"Old Spanish elite. Hispanic old-fashioned. They couldn't accept me either."

"Too tall?"

"Among other things. They'd have liked me to be more docile. I was too—feral. I didn't look down enough, at my feet, that is. There's this social taboo here about looking somebody directly in the eye. It suggests a challenge."

"Who'da thought it?"

"It's your turn. Why don't you tell me about your wife. Something is wrong."

"What makes you think that?" I had never said a word to her about Rebecca, I was sure.

"Come on, when an *hombre* doesn't mention his wife even once in the course of three weeks of conversation, something is screwy."

"I don't think I want to talk about this," I said.

"Jayzuz Christ, Ted! After I just emptied my heart at your feet!"

"Hush! You'll wake the Frenchies."

"What does she see in you?"

"I'm a wild and crazy guy."

"I never doubted."

"We were totally comfortable in each other's company. That was what we both wanted. I hadn't felt that way with anyone else."

I heard myself say that cornball thing and I couldn't believe I was doing this, lying in bed with another woman, talking about my broken marriage. What was worse, I didn't stop. "Her first husband was a brute. They married very young, a sixties marriage, and he left her cold when she got pregnant. After that she had a couple of other really bad jaunts. One guy was an addict. Then me. She said I offered her gentleness and space. I think she got more of both than she bargained for. Then she changed, or her expectations did, of herself, and me, about a year ago. She wanted us to open up to adventure, get off dead center. That's how she put it. It seemed phony to me, precarious."

"What did she want to do?"

"Make something of our lives, that sort of thing. I was supposed to make some radical changes in my psyche."

"And you refused?"

"No." *Aletheia, aletheia.* "I wouldn't even discuss it."

"You walked away, didn't you?"

"Yes."

"More than once."

"Often."

"I hope she knocked your ass right through the ceiling."

"No. She divorced me."

Neither of us said anything for a while. I thought Catherine was asleep or had determined never to speak to me again. But she had not left my side and her presence was still awake, her heartbeat still unslowed. I scratched an insect bite on my arm. Something rustled over in the storage boxes, a mouse or that giant cockroach. I mumbled on. "She could see me now for what I really was. That's what she said."

"Stubborn Swede?"

"Don't be mean. Trapped. That was Rebecca's word."

"And yours?"

"Careful. Just careful." Another word slid off my tongue: "Contained."

"Packaged? Tied up?"

"Safe. —Fucking tight-assed safe."

We both laughed, but I was shaky, standing on the edge of a cliff. "So is that a sin?"

"Maybe," said Catherine. "Once I had to memorize the seven deadly sins. You know, as over against venial, the less important ones."

"That's R.C. talk. We Prots lump them all together."

"There's that one called sloth, which mostly means you don't do anything. You don't engage. It's the deadliest of the sins because you might as well be dead."

"Bless me, fahtha."

"*Absolvo*, my son." She turned over and drew the sign of the cross on my forehead. "And what has made you guilty of such dereliction?" I thought she was still mocking me, but she said it quietly, kindly, in fact.

"*Susto,*" I said.

"Oh, right, d-i-a-r-h-i-a."

"You left out an R."

"Humph."

"And what about you? Do you need to be absolved of anything?"

"Blurred focus. Caught between hubris and sloth. Too much and too little."

"Forgiven," I said, drawing a cross on her heart, a location I much preferred to her forehead.

"Do you have anything else to tell me?" she asked. "I think I might go to sleep."

"I found my father's grave," I said. "Yesterday, in my old village. He was ill and died and was buried there, as he wished. So I was told."

"No *verguenza*?" She was processing things. I could feel it in the tension of her muscles.

"No ugly secret," I said.

"I think that's not the only reason you came back." She pulled the blanket up over her head, turning her back to me again. "Maybe you just wanted to come home. Oh, God help you." Her voice was muffled. She was falling asleep, really this time, her breathing deepening and her heartbeat slowed at last. Outside an animal called, a pathetic cry, some poor creature looking to get lucky.

I dreamed that night, but not of Catherine. At first there was no visual aspect to it, just sound, mostly clear-noted bird calls. Then the black screen lit up and there was the *quetzal*, with colors so stunningly bright I had to shade my eyes: bronzy green and berry-rich vermillion, a blue eye and a sharp yellow beak. It was in profile, as every drawing I had ever seen of it had been, the tail feathers trailing on and on out of human sight. In the dream I knew it was Luis, playing a trick. He was the one making those calls so skillfully. The joke was double pronged, because the call of the *quetzal* in real life is actually an unpleasant "awk-awk" expressing territorial warnings and macho mating demands. Later I would remember that I had dreamed of Luis, early on Tuesday morning, August 25.

When I woke the music was still in my head. I thought it was from Beethoven's *Pastorale*, the nightingale, quail and cuckoo. But it wasn't Beethoven. It was the cries of birds in a wild morning clamor, and voices, wonderful chatter in French, and the busy tap of heels on the patio. Catherine was gone from the room, but in a moment I heard someone outside the door singing *Frère Jacques*. She came through, bearing a tray of Guatemalan breakfast from the *tienda*, coffee and fruit and freshly made tortillas.

I took stock as she set the tray in front of me.

"Who are you this morning?" I asked. She was dressed in more of her aunt's clothes, gray slacks, baggy on her and too short, and another T-shirt, this one with an appliqué of gamboling lambs around the neck. Her hair was down, and she was wearing the stretchy blue hairband, with a couple of blood stains, I noticed, not quite washed out.

She inquired after my health. I allowed as how I was badly in need of a little TLC, and got a rub between the shoulders.

"Heaven can wait," I said.

"It will have to," she told me. It was 6:15 and we had to get going soon. She had been talking with the Frenchies. We would be leading them *en caravan* to Chichi as soon as everyone was ready. The trip was likely to take several hours because we had to skirt the landslide.

"Where are we headed ultimately? You and I?" I asked.

"The airport."

"We?"

"I am. I'll be doing a standby for a plane to Costa Rica. What are your plans?"

"Visit my friend Luis in Guate City. That's all I know." Unless maybe, I thought, but didn't say.

I turned to groping for clean socks in my backpack. Down in a corner my hand found the silver bracelet I'd bought at the highway market on Sunday. I held it out to Catherine. She looked at it. "The snake," she said.

"'Zero at the bone?'"

"No, this is a good snake. It represents the seasons, renewal. It's lovely."

It was even nicer than I remembered, and smaller, to my chagrin. Perhaps it was a child's. I reached for her left hand and tried to put it on. She took over and finally forced it down around her wrist, where it just fit. "I think it's on forever," she said, lightly. I approved.

I went out to put gas in the car. I'd seen gallon cans of it at the back of the store. The inside of the car still smelled. I wiped off the vinyl seats as best I could. The French were in high spirits as they loaded their luggage, bantering over who was going to have to sit on which lap. I paid for the gas and we were ready to go. Catherine wanted to drive. That was fine with me. Driver designation had lost all meaning.

The day was clear, almost cloudless, with a breeze. Mists were lifting from around the hills in active swirls. We traveled back roads all the way to Chichi, but real roads, not bushwhacking, the French van bumping along behind us.

We arrived at Chichi late morning. The room at the Santa Tomás hotel was mine for another hour, the beautiful room where my suitcase had spent the night alone. Catherine came up with me, to use the phone, the call to her son. She did that while I showered. When I came out of the bathroom she was still talking, in Spanish, but it made absolutely no sense. Maybe she and her son spoke in code, like twins. She was dead serious, somber, after she hung up. "How is your son?" I asked. She said he was fine.

I changed to my own clothes, dug my Red Sox windbreaker out of the suitcase, and we were off again, *sans* the French, Catherine still driving. I suggested a quick detour to the place where she had left the jeep. It was there, just around the corner from the hotel. As Bucky had predicted, it was stripped, a skeleton of itself. "Let it rot," said Catherine. "Airport. Airport next. Let's go."

To get from Chichi to Guatemala City, you first descend into a canyon, then S-curve steeply up a series of switchbacks. Once back on level terrain, there's a stretch of straight road for a few miles to Los Encuentros, the junction with the Pan-American Highway, where you turn left, southeast. I must have fallen asleep, and woke when my head whacked against the window. We were going over forty where you ought to go twenty, if you expect to stay on the road. Catherine was doing her mirror thing again while I watched the edges of the road and the plunges into eternity. At the intersection with the Pan-American, she paused for a split second, then turned right, accelerating. After a zany two miles we crossed the highway to another road, zipping in front of a convoy of traffic headed in the direction of the city. Which *we* were certainly not. In a few minutes she reduced the speed. I refrained from obvious comments. She asked me if I'd ever seen Lake Atitlán.

"Only from a distance."

"You can't leave the country without seeing it up close."

"At this rate we could end up inside it," I said.

"There's a restaurant there I like, at a hotel on the shore, a little beyond Panajachel. I thought we could stop there for dinner. My treat, please. I owe."

My end of the see-saw went up. I congratulated her for the initiative, to say nothing of masterful driving. "And why are we in such a hurry?" I asked.

"To watch the sun set, of course."

"But I'm due at my friend's house in the city."

"Can you call?"

I could, of course. I could visit Luis later. Getting to the city also meant separating from Catherine, a reality I wanted to postpone. So that's why we went to Lake Atitlán.

TWENTY-SEVEN

Panajachel, on the shore of the lake, is a town that swallows you up, its narrow streets lined with boutiques and tiny outdoor bars, noisy with the beeping of three-wheeled cabs. "*Gringotenango*," said Catherine, as we poked our car through the crowds of white-faced pedestrians. I was one of them, I reminded her, another tourist, on my way to yet another hotel, hungry for a little excellent cuisine, my undisputed entitlement.

I was not disappointed. Catherine's restaurant choice turned out to be a resort on the north shore. There the lake spread itself out before us in alternating shades of blue and green. We observed it first from a deep expanse of lawn, where we walked among terraced gardens with fountains. I could feel stress and weariness dropping off of me in chunks.

We reserved a table inside for dinner but decided to stay outside for drinks. First, I found a pay phone in the lobby and called Luis's house, to tell him I was still coming, though a day late. The line was busy. I tried twice, figured I'd try again later.

Our wicker chairs on the lawn were halfway down to the water. Behind us the two-story white hotel reflected the amber of the western sun. Civilized conversation surrounded us. It couldn't have been more benign. No guards with conspicuous rifles anywhere in sight. Waiters moved about from terrace to terrace. We ordered papaya juice, Catherine's choice. No *vino verace,* to be sure, but who needed it?

In all my *cosecha*—harvesting—of the next ten hours, the lake holds as a backdrop. More than fifty square miles in total, said my tour guide, which I dug out of my pack as we sat there. The depth in the middle was over a thousand feet, though it had never been accurately sounded. Across from our location, volcano heights doubled themselves in the rippling water, their cones streaked with magma. The tallest was Atitlán, the smaller one San Pedro, and Toliman, which was still occasionally active.

"But you have to understand the secrets of the lake," Catherine said, "to appreciate it fully." A goddess was in charge of it, an evil lady, a wicked tease. Strange winds could kick up without warning, little whirlwinds, called *Xocomil* (Sho-ko-MEEL). There were stories of mysterious drownings. Little villages not far from the shore had fared badly during periods of violence, with many bodies buried in the water. She named locations. Sololá. I played with it on my tongue. Could anything bad happen at a place called Sololá? Yes, it can and did, said Catherine, and across the lake, too, in Santiago Atitlán. That's where Father Stan Rother was assassinated, a priest from Oklahoma. He was thought to be aiding guerrillas.

But for rich people the lake was different, she said. They could swim and boat and play here without danger. The goddess held them up, so the rumor went, safe and sound. I nodded, feeling rich at the moment, held aloft, fucking safe. A water skier streamed by, far out, behind a white motor boat, and farther on a small ferry chugged toward the land, trailing smoke.

We sat there a good long time, Catherine talking, dreamily, and I perfectly content to listen. As dusk approached, the amber light began to fade. Mountains and sky blended together, a Japanese watercolor, the paper still wet with colors running. Green slid into gray, and pinks and golds appeared, staining the mists as they rose out of the valleys. Somebody was playing a double-reed pan pipe, making human sounds, its high notes cries of joy and lower ones the hoarse voice of a woman who had been weeping too long.

Then it got cooler, all at once, and the sky began to darken. Lightning flashed around the peaks of the volcanoes. They were making their own weather over there. Catherine began to shiver. "There's something else I want to tell you," she said. But she wanted to do it inside. "The restaurant," I said. We climbed the lawn, following ground lights, edging our way between the clusters of guests. I reached for her arm, at the same instant that she reached for mine. A quick breeze blew her hair across her face and she left it there. Inside the lobby, she stopped. "I don't want to eat. Can we try to get a room?"

"My preference exactly," I said.

The lobby was full, the sound of chatter and laughter echoing off a tiled floor. A small parcel of people had come in behind us. Out of the muddle of voices someone said "Cat!" I turned instantly, but Catherine stiffened, her fingers tightening on my arm. There it was again, two voices this time, male and female, right behind us, a sort of shouted whisper: "Caterina!" And now they were in front of us, a man and a woman, reaching for Catherine's hands, all smiles, both talking at once in Spanish. It *is* you! *Vos!* How wonderful to see you. It's been ages. How have you been? Catherine responded politely, but without enthusiasm, which didn't deter theirs in the least. They went on non-stop with their chatter, in a style that annoyed me deeply, the woman taking the lead in a chirping voice, the man adding a kind of chorus of chuckles and nods. They were both middle-aged. The woman had a serious overbite and a small chin. The man, a bantam, no bigger than she, wore silver chains at the neck of a dark sport shirt. The woman kept touching Catherine as she talked, then gripping her arm to tell her something else. I lingered at a safe distance, and Catherine made no effort to introduce me. Finally they turned into the bar.

"Old friends," Catherine explained. "I haven't seen them in ages."

We went to the desk and once again took pickings in a full establishment. This time it was no storage shed. The only thing available was a suite on the second floor overlooking the water, the most expensive space (I had to conclude) in the entire hotel. "*Ambiente muy tranquilo,*" the gentleman at the desk assured us. Oh, the evil goddess of the lake is good to us rich folk, I thought, handing over a credit card. Theodore C. Peterson, on tour with his Guatemalan *novia*.

A valet was waiting to take us up to the second floor. I suggested Catherine go ahead with him while I got our suitcases from the car. "Oh, not now," she said, quickly. "Get them later. Just stay with me."

The suite we found ourselves in was my room at the Santo Tomás tripled in comfort and beauty, an ample sitting area all in white, a terracotta fireplace, a bathroom with a shower the size of a small room. As soon as we entered, Catherine hung out the "Do Not Disturb" sign, turned the two locks on the door and fastened the burglar chain. She asked me to draw the drapes. I did, reluctantly, though by now the mountains were almost invisible anyway, across the darkening lake.

"Please don't answer if someone knocks," she said.

"Not a chance." But banter was not what she needed. She looked stricken. She dropped onto an upholstered two-seater, and sat there biting the nail of her right forefinger. I sat down beside her. She was breathing hard.

"I've been using you," she said.

"Using me?" Well, I knew that, didn't I?

"I'm so sorry."

"You've already apologized."

"It's worse now. I shouldn't have dragged you into this."

"This," I echoed. This was not that, as I heard it. That was what had already occurred. This was something new, something I was bound to not much like.

"I told you once before that you should feel free to leave, and I'm saying it now. Please release yourself, while you can."

Leave? We just got here. I looked around at the elegance of the suite. Too carefully perfect, I saw now, the upholstery on this sofa too impossibly white. A full-length mirror had been laminated to a closet door opposite us. We were reflected in it together on the sofa, in a kind of mockery. "Then why have we gotten a room?" I asked.

"To get out of sight and sound while I explain. I might not have another chance."

"But then you want me to go."

"Yes, I do. We should separate. For your sake," she said. "I didn't realize I'd be putting you in so much danger. I needed someone to come with me."

"I think I'd rather not hear this."

"I want to tell you. Let's start over, with last Saturday. The tour of the city. No, before that. Friday night, after the party. The phone call when we got to my house, remember? It was from the store, the one I work for. The delivery was ready to take to Isabel. But I was told to be extra careful. Something was in the works. That's why I offered you a ride to the city. That's all I intended right then, your presence as protection, just to the city. But when you suggested the tour—of the city—it seemed like a way to stay in contact, in case I needed you for this trip. Yes, that's true. In case I needed you. I hated myself the whole time we were together last Saturday. It was so deceptive. You must have realized something was screwy."

Last Saturday was four screwy days ago. Or four thousand screwy years. "Screwy how?" I asked.

"I changed my mind about you every five minutes," she said. "But then it seemed so providential that you might be in Chichi on Monday morning and possibly able to drive me. And by that time you'd gotten a seal of approval."

"Good Housekeeping?"

"You were followed on Sunday, on your way to Xela."

"Followed! Ah, the Ford. The volunteer from Texas? What's his name? Win Hall. How do you know that, for God's sake? You know him?"

"No, I don't. Not at all. A friend of mine, the parking lot owner, arranged it. He knows Hall."

I pictured the dusty black Escort in the slot beside mine in the alley.

"He followed you to your friend Luis López. Yours and his. Luis told him what he needed to know."

"*Luis* knew he was following me?"

"No, no. Not unless Hall told him."

"Wait a second. Are you saying *you* know Luis?"

"Not personally. But I know about him. Lots of people know about Luis."

"How did you know he's my friend?"

"I didn't, until I got the report from Hall. Look, all that matters now is that you get out of this while you can. This is about you. Don't fight me, please. Just go."

"You mean drive away? Just like that? In my nice red Cruiser?"

"No, not that. It was fine at first. Nobody rides around in a bright red car if they've got something to hide. But now it's like a red flag. Leave it here and take care of it later. Call a taxi. No, not a taxi. Go in the hotel van. They make regular trips. And wear some kind of a disguise."

"Disguise!" The word sat in my mouth like something that had gone bad. I got up and went to the window, thinking I'd give anything right now for another raging storm, a *xocomil*, or a tidal wave on the lake, not big enough to hurt anyone, just enough to wipe out the necessity of scaling this new wall. I even parted the curtains to look out, just in case. All was black out there, not even the flashes of lightning around the mountains. The euphoria was completely gone now, those dreamy moments on the lawn.

I can't say I prayed, or if I did who it was to. The plotting goddess, for all I knew, or Ajaw, Luis's Mayan god. I make no case. What slipped into my head was a line my father often quoted, "By my God have I leaped over a wall." I had once drawn a picture of it with crayons. I meant it to be his own long-legged body in full jump, but it turned out to look more like a big colorful insect, sailing over a high fence.

I closed the curtains and returned to the sofa, where Catherine still sat, watching me. I sat down. "Monday," I said. "Monday morning. Just yesterday." I stopped to control my voice. "In Chichi, at the Santo Tomás hotel, when I was called from the restaurant to the lobby and saw you standing there, I had one overwhelming notion, that you had come back to find me. And when you asked me to drive you to—wherever—I thought to myself that I would go with you to another planet, just not to lose sight of you again. Nothing has changed that. Nothing is changing it now. Do you understand?"

She was still for a moment, then reached out with her sneakered foot and touched my shin. I might as well have been torched.

"And I really did come back to find you," she said, in just above a whisper. "And not just because I needed your help. Nothing has changed that. Do *you* understand?"

"I do now." For a moment I let that build a bright little fire between us on the white sofa. Then I asked the inevitable. "So how can I possibly leave you now?" I said.

"Because I want you to be all right. I would never knowingly have led you into danger."

"And if I go, what will *you* do?"

"I don't know. Time may still be on your side. It's different for me. I'm old quarry, and I've run out of options. I've tried everything. Foolish disguises. And hiding behind people. In Antigua Méndez was protection, the school, and *Tía* Magdalena. Then you. And the French tourists. *Acompañamiento.* But even that can take you just so far."

"Tell me," I said. "Are we safe *here*, right now? There's no one in the closet or under the bed. No one is going to barge through the door with an assault rifle and shoot us up?"

"Not in this place."

"So I assume we can stay here long enough for you to convince me. And if you do, if you convince me it will be better for both of us if I dig out, I will."

How reasonable that sounded, and how patiently she answered. "Except the more I tell you the more you know and the more vulnerable that makes you."

There could be wisdom in that. I considered giving a little ground, but it was like stepping backwards into a big hole. "Just give me one solid clue to what's going on."

"We are being tailed."

It had to be that, of course. It was almost a let-down. "That couple in the lobby?"

"The Melanos? Gracious, no."

"But you tried to elude them, I thought."

"I don't much like them. They're such bores. No, it's two others. Men. They've been following us since Chichi. Maybe before. You didn't see them?"

"I didn't see anyone else. Not in particular. What kind of a car?"

"I don't know. Green, I think. Dark green, a van. I tried to shake them. I thought I had when I turned off the Pan-American to come down here. But I saw them just now on the lawn."

"You're sure?"

"As sure as I ought to be."

"What do they look like?"

"Like a thousand other guys you see around here."

"It couldn't be a coincidence? I'm sorry. I need to ask that."

"It would be extremely reckless to suppose so. I can't deny what I saw."

"But why now?" Not many hours ago we were running straight into possible gunfire. At the rockslide we were a couple of strands of her hair from who knows what. And *now* we were in trouble? "Why haven't they come after us sooner? Like last night at the *posada?*"

"They might have there, except for the presence of the French. I think the owner is a link. A *comisionado militar*. You don't own a telephone in that area unless you've got intelligence connections."

"Spy?"

"He may have recognized me from an earlier trip."

"All right. The Frenchies saved us. So what are these guys waiting for *now?*"

"They have certain proprieties. They won't cause havoc in a place like this."

"Aw, come on!"

"You're not convinced."

"Convinced of what? I'm convinced that you're convinced of something. I'm convinced that something malicious happened back there at that village. It appears we're in some kind of deep doo-doo. But I'm not convinced I should leave."

"Try to take me at face value."

"That's what I've been doing, for God's sake. I've been fighting questions for two days now!"

"Don't shout." She took off the headband and ran her hands through her hair, tossing it wildly, then smoothing it down, pushing it back. "You're right. Ask your questions. This is about you. So ask."

"Good. I will." But in fact I was totally disarmed. I began three questions and cut myself off. What she had said was true, I saw clearly. The answer to any question could draw me into the inner circle of those who know too much, an odd mixture of privilege and incrimination. What is the right body language for that? I got up from the sofa, and sat back down again. I leaned forward, started to speak, leaned back. My arms were folded, the posture of resistance or denial. I unfolded my arms, dropped my hands to my lap, saw that they were clenched, unclenched them, clasped them together. I didn't know what to do with my damn hands.

"I can help you," said Catherine. She spoke quietly, not with the old edge of mockery, but a kind of tired concession. She was still in her aunt's garb, in the jersey with the gamboling lambs around the neckline and the sneakers stained with the graveyard mud, and she was wearing the bracelet I'd given her, maybe only because she couldn't get it off.

None of it went together. She was a picture of contradiction. I knew what to do with my hands. I took hers. They were cold. I held them between mine, not at all sure I was offering warmth. "Go ahead," I said.

"There's only one question that matters. Why are we being followed? It's because of what we know. What I know, and presumably you do too."

"What do *we* know?"

She removed her hands and sat on them. "We know about the CPRs. In English that's Communities of the Population in Resistance. There are a bunch of these groups, people who have fled to the mountains to escape army assaults. They're under the aegis of the EGP. Guerrilla Army of the Poor. It's one facet of the guerrillas. Isabel's brother was an officer in the EGP. Are you getting the picture?"

"Yes. What else do we know?"

"We know, you and I, that after the army raid on the village some of the survivors escaped. They were led by Isabel's brother into the mountains, where they joined a CPR. But Isabel didn't go. She had a toddler to protect, so she found a new home in another local village. Now and then she went back to the old village, to be close to her dead children. Pretty soon she began to meet her brother there. He'd come down from the mountains to pick up supplies. So they set up a plan. She would deposit supplies in the goat shed for him to find whenever he could make the trip. You know what's coming next."

"You."

"Yes, but ultimately you. That's the only reason I'm telling you this. Two years ago I discovered her handwork and started ordering from her for the store. I began to bring supplies, too, for the mountain people, a few things I could carry without raising suspicion. I also brought messages. I brought pertinent information, to be picked up by the brother."

"You were a carrier pigeon."

"Yes, *mensajería.*"

"And this information, where do you get it?"

"The store, Ted. The store sent it. The store is part of an underground network, a cell group, a big one, international. It helps support these mountain communities and the EGP. For a long time I've been part of this urban cell."

"—A subversive. I see."

"An enemy of the state. Now you know that, too. I don't expect you're very surprised."

"No." No, I wasn't surprised, but the fact came to me wearing an air of fiction, and I wanted to reject it, not just because it was fiction but because it wasn't good enough fiction. A carrier of secret messages. Juvenile posturing, a Hardy Boys mystery, *The Secret of Skull Mountain*.

"What are you thinking?" she said.

"It seems just so convoluted and—old. You travel all this way with hidden messages? There must be better ways to convey intelligence these days."

"Of course. Everything is used, but the army's detecting system is powerful. Nothing is secure. So here I am, a middle class North American woman, an agent for a classy store in the capital, and there's Isabel, a poor single mother who sells embroidery at a roadside market. What we do has been the safest way."

Something bumped our door and we both jumped. I heard the wheels of a room service cart. We sat still, unbreathing, until it passed. I felt silly, angry with myself. In a few seconds Catherine continued.

"All these past weeks, all the time you've known me, I've wanted to get out of it. But then I decided I had to, I had to do it, for Isabel's sake, because I was the only one she would trust. She needed the money. And those people, up there in the mountains, families, and some people sick. But when I got to the store last Saturday morning to pick up the money and things, the store was closed. Something had happened overnight. Nobody was there. That's always been the signal. The store will be closed and locked if something is wrong. —Oh, God, there's so much to explain."

Hands in the hair again. I didn't know how to help her. "I'm listening," I said.

"We've always had contingency plans. If the store was closed, we could go to certain other parties for information. I followed that trail on Saturday morning, after you rented the car. I found out that one guy in our network had turned himself in to the government. There's been a general amnesty in operation this year. Guerrillas who recant will be forgiven by the government. That's the wording, forgiven, especially if they're willing to rat on collaborators. So everyone was in hiding. But the errand to Isabel was still on, with the message for her brother waiting for me to pick up at that parking lot in the city. Messages are always hidden somewhere in the supplies, in a bag of coffee, or enclosed in cigarettes. I think you know where this one was."

"Inside *Yertle the Turtle.*"

"I know you saw it."

"I saw a map, that's all."

"You already saw the helicopters. The military is involved in a new campaign to liquidate guerrillas in the mountains by the end of this year. It's supposed to start soon. Nebaj is the launching center. The U.S. has been helping, a lot, with helicopters and money. Another badly kept secret."

And one I now know. "The map?" I prompted.

"Safe route to new locations for CPRs, avoiding land mines and surveillance."

"So now I'm a collaborator? Dr. Seuss and I."

"Don't make light of it, please."

I wasn't, not at all, though it seemed more fictive than ever and full of holes. "If that message is so urgent why would it be put in a goat shed to be picked up whenever?"

"It wouldn't be whenever. He'd be already there, her brother. He'd be hiding in the area, waiting for this information. Waiting for me. And this time it got too risky for him to wait any longer."

"And she was meeting him there, to go with him, into the mountains?"

"They were saying goodbye one last time to their ancestors and dead family members before they took off."

That at least rang true.

"But apparently word got out. That the brother was there. That's why if I had come when I was supposed to—. Look, when I first started out in this, back when Martin was alive, it just was a movement to end oppression—doctors, lawyers. The guns came later, a bad idea, and that failed, and it will keep on failing, because the army outnumbers armed guerrillas by the thousands, and everybody is talking peace, talk,

talk, talk, but there's still this persistent belief on both sides that only an armed hold-out is going to get what you want, so the killing goes on and on. —Are you still with me?"

"Never left."

"I want you to know that I've never kidded myself. I've been part of armed insurrection, even though I've never touched a gun. But you can't just quit. Quitting makes you a liability. You can't cut yourself off from what you know. So you look for excuses to just be out of commission. *Tía* Mag offered me one for months. But as soon as she died one of the store owners came to Antigua to beg me, *coerce* me, into making this trip. And I poured coffee in his lap. It was hot."

Ooh.

"It was a rotten thing to do, but he insulted me. He said I was a loose cannon and can't be trusted. And he was right. You saw that at the party. I get mad and shoot off my mouth."

She stopped, to take several deep breaths. "That phone call I made this morning, from your room at the Santo Tomás? I made two calls. One was to Alex and the other to my contact in the city. To report what happened. I found out then that one of the Norwegian owners of the store was arrested last night. The other owner escaped. No one knows where he is. He's at large."

"I see," I said, maybe for the hundredth time. This time I did see. This part was "about me," where she'd been headed all along. "A Norwegian," I said. "The hunk I could pass for?"

"Yes. But when I told you that yesterday, back in the forest, I didn't know about this latest thing, the store and the arrest. I would have warned you."

"Hush. I understand."

I looked back at myself in the closet door mirror. I'd never felt so Scandinavian, trapped inside this Nordic skin. I'd always liked being a Swede. It had been a secure, dependable fact. As appearances go, I could be Danish, German, Dutch, an Anglo, or "angel" as the blue-eyed blonds of the north were once ludicrously called. But I was a Norwegian, not the safe one Luke referred to, just off Erik the Red's boat. I was "at large." I'd been transmuted twice, from a protector to a collaborator and a collaborator to a fugitive. "And by chance is he the one you poured coffee on that time?" I said.

She nodded, yes. "The thing is, you really do look alike. Tall, blond, forty."

With a stain on my pants? I actually looked down, at the clean chinos I'd pulled on back at the Santo Tomás hotel. "This is too weird," I said. "I'm not believing it."

"You should. The army has a sophisticated computer system, remember."

As yet during this disclosure, I hadn't felt real fear. Vertigo of the spirit, yes, but not the white-out as I'd felt it yesterday. What came now was a sharp needle of indignation, nothing as honorable as fear, just a kind of high umbrage at the impertinence of it all. "If I look like him," I said, "what about the dozen others who also do?"

"They haven't been with *me*. But it's logical that *he* might be with me. We're in the same network."

"Okay. And when I'm arrested, how long will it take them to find out that I'm not who they think I am? Does our Norwegian speak Yankee English? Is he carrying my passport?"

"He speaks perfect English and three other languages, and none of them are likely to do him any good. And they don't care if there's a mistake. Once you're picked up for questioning, even if it's a mistake, that alone makes you too dangerous to release. Or they release you, and you get into a deadly accident. It's so easy." Her voice was hoarse.

"So we're in it together," I said. "Whatever happens, we stay together." Bravado maybe, but I saw it as responsibility. Even though she had lied to me, lived a lie in my presence, *used* me, from the beginning a large ratio of my ignorance was due to my own evasion of what the truth might be. I tried to look at her piercingly, the way she so often looked at me, the way polite Guatemalans are careful not look at each other. She turned away, quick tears in her eyes. "We'll find a way out," I said.

I believed that. It had snapped back in, the entitlement to safety. I got up and walked to the telephone by the bed. If we were safe in this haven of expensive hospitality, with the rights of North Americans, with advice and rescue surely out there somewhere, why not just stay here until we got help? "I'm going to call someone," I said.

"Who?" Catherine asked, alarmed.

"The police."

"Ted, no. I told you. That's a bad idea."

"The U.S. Embassy, then. Citizens in trouble. I bet they're in the phone book." I looked for a phone book. There was none. "I'll call the desk and get the number."

"Do that for yourself, not me," Catherine said. "All they have to do is look up my record."

"They can't ignore us. What are embassies for?"

"You think they're going to send a posse for us on the basis of a phone call?"

Surely there was somebody here they could ask to check us out. It didn't seem so hard. I ran that through my head. Hello, I'm a U.S. citizen. I'm in a hotel with my girlfriend and we're being tailed by two guys from a death squad. Can you help us?

Well, maybe there was a better way. I suggested calling Méndez for advice.

"Never!" said Catherine. "He doesn't know about me and I don't want him to know."

"What about your parking lot friend?" I asked. Her eyes said I was mad, and with a wallop I knew why. She'd lost her support group. She was a "liability." She couldn't be trusted. The fiction was taking on an adult rationality. This whole thing, after all, was far less about me than about her, who was really who she was and who really knew too much. "You're being sought by both sides, aren't you?" I said.

"Among others," she answered.

So, all she had was me, and I was hardly a fortress of help.

But no, there had to be someone else, a third party, fourth, someone on neither side. What about all those international entities, the huge network she supposedly belonged to? I asked that, pressing: "Who do you know?" She just shook her head.

I ran through my own list, the scant number of people I'd met here. Pat Crane. He might be aware of someone here in this town. But he was out of the country. Still, I found his card in my wallet, got an outside line and dialed the Centenario Hotel. Sorry, no forwarding number.

Who else, who else? Luke Treadwell, Bucky. I pulled out his card next and dialed again. *Please leave a message for Mr. In-Between Transport Services.* I didn't.

Win Hall. He was exactly the right contact. He could still be in the office at Xela, where Luis and I had left him, cleaning up. The phone had been cut there and I didn't have a number anyway, but Luis would have it, of course. In fact, I should have called Luis first of all. I dialed his home number in the Capital and got a busy signal, as I had earlier. I tried again in two minutes. Line still busy. Then again. The same. And again.

Catherine sat watching me through all of this. She looked as worn out as I was beginning to feel.

"What about that couple in the lobby?" I said. "I bet they're in the dining room."

"The Melanos? Definitely not. I won't involve them."

That seemed foolish to me, but she had every right to decide. "I'm going to dial Bucky again," I told her. She shrugged. This time he answered. I was very careful. I assured him I was not asking for transportation, just some advice. I told him where we were. I said it appeared (word carefully chosen) that Catherine and I were being followed. What would he do in such a case himself?

"Who is Catherine?" he asked.

"The woman you met at the Santo Tomás."

"Oh, yeah." He hesitated a long time. "*Who* is being followed? You or Catherine?" I said both of us. Then he asked why. I said I couldn't explain that now. Another long pause. "All right," he said. "If it were me, I would get the desk to call the local police station in Panajachel. You don't have to tell the hotel why. Just say it's personal. The police there will help you. They're used to dealing with tourists. They could get you out of town or to a safe place."

"One problem," I said. "Catherine is reluctant to contact the police."

"Oh, is that so?" he said. "Then you do it. Maybe you'll have to split up."

"There's no way I'm going to do that," I told him.

"Not even to save your own neck."

"No."

He sighed. "Then I don't know what to say, man. Good luck. Call me later and let me know how things are." I hung up in an angry sweat.

"There have got to be U.S. expats in this town," I said. "Tourists, business people. Missionaries. Somebody willing to come get us."

"Us?"

"Yes, that's the answer. Expats, missionaries. A church pastor. Where's the damn phone book? I'll call the desk."

"Ted, stop!" Catherine pleaded. "Please stop. Or do it for yourself. Just for yourself. Leave me out of it."

"You're crazy. How can I do that? I won't."

"I can't endanger anyone else. And neither should you. We're a danger to anyone who might try to help us. Can't you see that?"

Did I give up too easily? All I can say is that this was the point when my feet dropped to the ground, or what felt like ground. It didn't feel like giving in or giving up. It felt sane. It went like this: Wait until morning, get a good sleep, as any sensible parent might say, and then just go. Go. Walk out of the goddamn room and down the stairs, no hiding, no sneaking, no glancing around, get in the big red Cruiser that is costing you your life savings, and drive to the airport. The idea was enormously emancipating. I proposed it to Catherine.

She surprised me. "We'll do it," she said, after just a moment's thought. She sounded relieved, as if all she needed was someone to voice what she knew we had to do. "Just not in the red car," she said.

I buzzed the front desk. Was there a hotel vehicle that made runs to the airport? Indeed. When was the next departure? One was scheduled for 5 A.M. There were two seats left. I reserved them. That was it. We'd scaled the wall.

Catherine was still sitting on the sofa. I reached for her hands and pulled her to her feet. "Have you told me everything?" I asked. Yes, she said, there's nothing more. I said, "So now I know you better than your tote bag." She said she certainly hoped so.

There she stood, at her full height in front of me, eyes all but level with mine, everything she was and had been, all her disguises. She was still wearing the silly looking borrowed clothes, the slacks that were too short and loose, and the jersey with the gamboling lambs around the neck.

"I'm sorry," I said. "I can't make love to your aunt."

It was easily remedied. She undressed, *we* undressed, down to what was now familiar territory. After all, we'd already done our naked rain dance and observed each other like curious children, and snuggled in bed with our darkest secrets, giggled and wept. Like children, we'd already experimented, and failed.

I held her off at arm's length for a long adult observation, then drew her back and down, onto the white carpet. Her skin was wonderfully warm now, smooth, tan next to my sun-bruised and bug-bitten body. Gauguin did only half the job. All those lovely Tahitian girls were not a true "other" unless he included himself in the paintings, a sly-looking Frenchman, pink or yellow. But I was not making love to a Tahitian or a Guatemalteca. This was Catherine O'Brien from Milwaukee, my torn and divided friend, weary and maybe defeated, but—I'm happy to say—fully engaged in the activities of the moment.

"What, no quotes?" she said.

" 'My love is like a—.' "

"Not that one."

" 'Shall I compare thee to a summer day?' "

"No."

" 'Who is she that looketh forth as the morning, fair as the moon, clear as the sun, and scary as an army with banners?' "

"I like that one. Who wrote it?"

"God. You can look it up."

That was about as elegant as anything else we said to each other. Mostly it was the same old primitive language of gasps and whispers, cries and laughs. Youthful color returned to her cheeks, and to my soul, but this was not young love. That's what made it remarkable, lack of youthful haste, stepping over the threshold of our ragged needs into a generosity that was timeless, a deep underground river. She had a lot to give. Every touch of her fingers, her tongue, her teeth, those long strong legs tight around me was a new and bounteous gift. Did I give as much back? I don't know. I only know I gave her everything I had. Perhaps for the first time in my life, that's what I did.

"*Pues,*" she said, when we lay exhausted on the white carpet, "you're a good hugger, after all."

TWENTY-EIGHT

We slept for an hour, then made plans, like grown-ups, those get-a-good-sleep-and-be-careful kind, talking it out, like arranging our next jaunt as tourists. The bottom line was that we would stick together long enough to get Catherine on a plane to Costa Rica. If possible I'd get a seat on the same flight. My passport would qualify me for a limited time ticket. Then I would come back to visit Luis and Carmen in Guatemala City, as planned. From that point we would make future decisions.

It was now 4:00 A.M. At 5:00 there would be activity in the lobby, people loading into the hotel van. "Whatever happens, we stay together," I said again. She was not to leave my sight. She agreed. Again.

We showered and dressed in the clothes we'd removed. To ease her mind, I shaved off my beard. In the mirror I hardly knew myself but smiled to think how pleased my mother would be. She associated beards with sixties sin, no matter that Jesus himself probably wore one.

"What about you?" I asked Catherine. "Cut your hair?" I said it with great hesitancy. It struck me as prodigal, to lay waste that bounty. But she refused, anyway. She might need her hair again for camouflage. It was down around her face right now, with part of it caught on top in the blue band. I persuaded her to wear my Red Sox windbreaker. I zipped it for her, slowly, to the top, over the lambs on her jersey.

"This will protect you," I said. "It's magic."

It was not an authentic Red Sox jacket. That was what I had wanted when I was fifteen, but my mother couldn't afford it. So I sewed a big red B I got at a yard sale on the back of my white nylon windbreaker. It was now more than thirty years old and looking a bit ragged. Catherine shoved her hands into the side pockets and waggled a finger at me out of a hole.

I offered her my cap as well, just a loan, of course. She refused. I put it on my own head, visor lowered, and then sunglasses. Wrong. "That's the look of the urban guerrilla," Catherine said. "Wear your cap tilted up. Show your forehead."

We checked our money belts, counting our cash. She handed me a squashed up piece of paper from hers. "In case we get separated." I smoothed it out. It was a phone number in San José, Costa Rica.

"It looks like something you threw away," I said.

"I meant to give it to you before, when we said goodbye last Saturday, and I changed my mind." So that was what she was looking for in her bag. "If you call," she said, "let the phone ring exactly nine times. And if I'm not the one who answers, expect to be quizzed."

I wrote out Luis's home number for her. She put it in her money belt and adjusted that under her skirt band.

"And who are you anyway on this leg of the trip?" I asked. "It might be good for me to know."

"Between here and the airport I'm Magdalena, *tu novia*."

"But can you fool them at the airport with that photo?"

At the airport she would need her own ID, she said. She took it out of her bag, a U.S. passport, and opened it to her photo. There she was, much younger, hair short, cheeks fresh and full. She looked happy. "If you smile you could pass," I said.

"Then I'll smile. Whatever gets me on a plane."

"Shouldn't we phone in for reservations now?"

Absolutely not, she said. That would connect with data in the computer. "The military knows seven hours ahead who will board a plane. We just take whatever seat is available. TACA does commuter flights."

"Who?"

"Capitol letters, TACA. Known as Take-A-Chance-Airline."

It seemed chancy to me indeed. Any airline. Too many ways things could go wrong. But it was 4:45 and time to start. Down we went into the bright lights of the lobby, me and my Guatemalan "girlfran," both of us disguised and felonious. I settled up at the desk. Outside it was still dark. A lot was going on. A taxi was pulling up and staff people were arriving in cars and on foot. The hotel van was parked at the main entrance, motor running. It was almost full already. Three of the passengers were large people, taking up extra space. There was scarcely room for one more person. I told the driver I'd reserved two seats. He shrugged. I asked about the passenger seat up front. He said a second driver would be taking it. Could a third squeeze in up there? No. Against regulations.

"We'll get that taxi," I said to Catherine. I signaled the driver, who was standing outside it. I could feel Catherine resisting. "Taxis are vulnerable," she whispered. But she climbed with me into the empty back seat, her bag on her lap. Then I remembered our luggage, still in my car. I got out and jogged over to where I had parked it, about thirty steps away. I unlocked the rear door and lifted out the two suitcases. How long did it take to do that? No more than half a minute.

As I shut up the car I heard Catherine's voice. She was out of the taxi and hurrying toward me, walking with another woman. It was the over-bite lady. What the hell could she want? I went to meet them, but Catherine was calling, "Quick, Ted!" She was pointing to the hotel van. "Quick, get that empty seat!"

Picture this scene now, from a fair distance away, but within hearing. The three of us stand in a little cluster, there in the parking lot in the morning mist, Catherine and I like two long sticks beside this short plump woman. "There's been a change in plans," Catherine says, "You take the van seat or the taxi. I'll go with the Melanos. Meet me there." I open my mouth in disbelief. "It's for the best, Ted," she says. She's a little breathless but her voice is steady. "The Melanos are flying to San José. To visit her family. I'll try to get on the same plane. TACA. Really."

When I open my mouth again, she says, "This is best, for everyone." I protest. "No. We agreed. Stay together."

She says, "But this is best." Then again that word, this time in Spanish. *Lo mejor.*

At that moment a car drives up alongside us, a black Mercedes, the woman's husband at the wheel.

I pick up Catherine's suitcase and hold it out to her. She shakes her head. "I don't want it now. Hurry." She glances back at the van, parked at the hotel door. "Get that seat."

The scene shifts a bit now. *Señor* stays behind the wheel, motor running, watching us. Panic floods me, all the old alarm lights flashing, bells going off, the fear of losing Catherine again, and I say, in English, without question, "I'm riding with you," and walk toward the car.

All three of them say no at once. "*Lo siento*," says the woman, firmly. "*No espacio*." No room. I see that. Two bucket seats in the front, a big cooler and a carton in back on the seat, suitcases. "Never mind," I say. "I can hold things on my lap." The woman shakes her head, apologetically. She nudges Catherine into the front and shuts that door, then scrambles into the back, next to the cooler. I drop the suitcases and aim my body for the back seat. I'll sit on top of the silly woman if I must. She shuts her door too, just missing my fingers. Catherine waves at me through her window, that sideways wave next to her ear, smiles (a real one), brings her hand to her forehead in a Boy Scout salute, a comical snap to attention, then slides it quickly down to her lips. She throws a kiss and with the other hand gestures emphatically toward the hotel van. I wave back, standing there like the ass I've just made of myself, no salute, no kiss, my heart a cold stone. They drive away. I start for the hotel van, but that too has just taken off, as does the taxi, with a plume of black exhaust.

I run back to my own car, throw in the suitcases and jump into the driver's seat, where I instantly calm down. What am I so upset about? She has chosen to travel with her old *fufurufu* friends, in the protection of the elite. That makes sense. She knows what she's doing and I don't.

I could call for another taxi, but that seems pointless now. This is the natural, adult thing to do, drive my own car to the airport, Norwegian at large or not. Satisfy myself that she is safely on a plane, that it really is "best," and catch a flight for myself.

I start the motor and begin to move. I have a flat tire. And why not? It's a wonder it hasn't happened before on a mountain road. All right, I can handle it. There's the spare and a jack and a lug wrench. Just a little sweat and ordinary know-how.

The tire is flat all right, but I can't see anything wrong with it. It's out of air. Of course it crosses my mind that someone might have done it, but it seems like too much of a kid trick for any serious intent. Why not cut my brakes instead? It doesn't take long to make the change, anyway. When I'm done it is still only 5:45. The sun has begun to burn off the mist and a shimmer hits the lake. The whole body of water turns gold. I take off my Red Sox cap and wave goodbye to the lady demon somewhere in the depths, and to anyone else who might be watching.

Two hours later, at 7:45, I drove into the parking lot of the Aurora International Airport in Guatemala City. Catherine was not in the main lobby. I found the TACA waiting room. Not there. I checked the lines to the ticket counters—TACA first, then Pan American, Iberia, Mexicana, others. Where would they be with a little time to kill? The food concession, of course. Yes, there sat the couple, the Melanos. They were eating at a small table, their carry-on bags at their feet. They waved, as if expecting me. I went over.

"*Dónde está?*" I asked.

"*Elle está aquí,*" said *Señora*, wiping her fingers on a paper napkin. Her mouth was full.

"Where?"

She shrugged, glancing around. Oh, she went into the bathroom, she said, as if just remembering.

"Has she found a seat on your plane?" I asked.

The husband answered this time. Yes. No problem.

"What time is your flight?"

He looked at his watch. "8:55."

"What airline?"

"TACA."

"I'll wait for Catherine," I said. I needed to see her for myself, just to be absolutely sure. Of what? Everything.

The restrooms were in a marble structure in the middle of the room. I sat on a bench outside it where I could watch the entrance. A dozen women entered and emerged, but no Catherine, not in any guise. I wondered if she could be sick, a panic attack. I asked an older woman on the way out if she had seen a tall woman in there. She shrugged, embarrassed by the question.

I should get my own ticket while I could. I scanned the schedule board. There was indeed a TACA 8:55 flight to San José and it was on time. I got into the queue at the TACA counter. The flight was full. All right then, give me a seat on the next one scheduled. No seat until 3:50 that afternoon. Down the row of desks all the other lines looked long. I secured the 3:50 and went back to the food concession.

The Melanos were no longer there. It was 8:20. They had gone to the gate, I supposed, which was where Catherine herself should be. All the gates opened off one corridor. My ticket and passport admitted me to this area with no trouble. But Catherine was not at the TACA gate, nor were the Melanos. I stayed there in plain sight by the desk through the first, second, third boarding calls, until the access door to the plane closed and the waiting area was empty, even the desk.

Back to the schedule board, to check other flights to Costa Rica. Two were posted for within the hour. I went to those gates, though I knew it was early. I checked all the gate waiting rooms, one by one. I went back to the TACA desk where I paged. The message blared three times through the PA system, in Spanish and English: "Queen Jadis, meet Ted at the TACA gate."

I waited there fifteen minutes, then walked through the whole airport again, food concession, main lobby, balcony, and out into the parking lots for rental cars, looking for a black Mercedes. Who rents Mercedes? Hertz, Avis, Alamo. I found none. Of course not, fool. The Melanos owned their own luxury car and they were gone.

You can drive to Costa Rica on the Pan American Highway. Then why had they come here to the airport at all? To put Catherine on a plane, an earlier one? To wait for me, to lie to me, keep me occupied? None of it made any sense, and none of it had anything to do with me. Unless, of course, it did. Obviously, it was me she was hiding from, along with all the others, because if she was right, about everything, we were a danger to each other.

I got a cup of coffee and sat down to think. Two armed guards walked by my table, scanning the crowd. I hadn't been giving a thought to my own security. Now I felt obvious and vulnerable, desperately alone, with an overwhelming need to make contact with somebody, any version of normalcy and sanity. I thought of trying Rebecca again, just to ask if my mother was still cussing people out, a possibility that struck me as fundamentally sane and safe. The call I finally made, at a bank of phones, was to Luis's home, to let him know I would be postponing my visit again.

After one ring a voice I recognized as Carmen's answered. Before I'd half-identified myself, she said, "Teddy," and my heart stopped. I heard it in her voice. Something was wrong. "Luis has been arrested," she said. "I can't talk now. Please come. Come if you can."

"Tell me how to get there," I answered.

TWENTY-NINE

In the car I wrestled with the city map. By the time I'd finished unfolding it, swearing at it, shaking it viciously into place over the steering wheel, ripping it in half, then quarters, whacking it into a ragged ball and tossing it out the window, I was thinking with a fair degree of everyday half-brained intelligence.

It was shortly after 10:00. There was time. Leaving the airport felt like cutting my only physical link to Catherine, but I could do both, split myself in two, find my way to Luis's home, find out what was going on, and find my way back here to board the plane for Costa Rica.

First I had to ditch this red machine. It was like sitting in the middle of a shout. I ought not to drive it to Luis's anyway, if there was the slightest chance it was being watched. I was tempted to leave it here in the airport parking lot and take a taxi back and forth, but that simply introduced another unknown. I'd rather be the driver.

I found my way to the car rental in zone 9, where the guard in fatigues still lounged with his rifle and the same desk attendant welcomed me back. We examined the condition of the car together. He wrote it all down, every little scratch and dent. If he noticed any trace of blood or smell, he didn't say so.

There was a Volkswagon Bug on the lot, beige. It looked like my own, except lots cleaner. Beetle, said the clerk, *escarabajo*. I claimed it, for what I thought would be no more than a few hours. In traffic it felt like a kiddy-car, a silly mistake.

My destination was northeast of the city, easy enough to follow. I drove to Calle Marti, a commercial boulevard, crossed a bridge over a ravine and chugged up a steep rise, counting. Seven streets on the right, without names or numbers, Carmen said. Streets? Muddy lanes with streams of water running down them, zinc and plywood shelters jammed together, blue tarp billowing in the breeze, a *tiendita*, and poking above it all like an absent-minded mistake, a little white steeple.

At the seventh street, things changed. Cement block took over as the architectural preference. Electric lines now, water pipes and half-covered sewer lines in place of open gutters. I passed another church, so claimed its sign, *Templo del Espíritu Santo*, no steeple on this one. Then, as Carmen had assured me, there was Community Garden, *Jardín de la Comunidad* in black spray paint on the side of a house, and the number, 100, with no obvious numerical basis, and no garden that I could see.

It was a tall, narrow structure, maybe twenty feet wide, concrete block, three stories, each level a different color, blue, yellow, terracotta. Curtains blew out at open upstairs windows. At the top, on the flat roof, perhaps thirty feet up, something flashed in the sun—glass and metal. Definitely not a machine gun nest.

I glanced around, decided I had not been followed (though how would I know and what would I do if I were?), parked as instructed next to a couple of other cars in a weedy lot across the way, and entered a vine-shaded front patio. I could hear voices inside the house, a lot of them, and a frantic announcement by a dog. The door opened a crack.

"Ted Peterson," I said.

"Come right on in." A tall, dark-haired guy stepped aside, holding back an Irish Setter with his foot. "I'm Sam Matthews," he said, in English with a deep south accent, then announced my name to the house. He had to shout to be heard.

I took three steps inside and stopped. It was like walking accidentally onto the set of a theatre project, a noisy play in progress. Several multi-staged scenes were developing at once, all of them bordering around an interior atrium, the source of light. An iron staircase spiraled up one side of that. On the other side, in an open kitchen, three women worked at the stove and sink. I smelled hot cooking oil. Two other women sat at a table directly under the overhead light, one taking notes, the other—short and square with red hair—spoke on the phone in rolling Spanish, her voice loud enough to blow out the windows. Behind me in a parlor of sorts, where Sam lingered, a television set played without audio.

I was almost ready to believe it really was theatre, and I a befuddled participant, dragged out of the audience. None of the people before me did more than glance up from whatever they were doing, except one, a woman who walked quickly from the kitchen, reaching out with both hands. "Teddy," she said. "I am Carmen." She was small, with Latin coloring and green eyes, straight light brown hair, tucked behind her ears. She invited me to sit down. I followed her a few steps to a wicker divan. "Tell me," I said.

"It happened yesterday morning," she answered, her voice almost lost in the noise around us. "Yesterday," she repeated. "Tuesday, early morning. He was staying with Arturo at the women's school. Arturo, you know? He's the watchman there." She spoke in English with the familiar Hispanic beat, her consonants hard. "In the morning, Tuesday morning, a couple of women came in early and they saw what happened. An army truck drove up and Arturo went out to keep them from going inside and they began to rough him up and Luis went out and said "I'm the guy you're looking for," and they put him in the army truck and drove off with him, like that."

Her voice and face showed no emotion, but she was rocking back and forth as she talked. I found myself doing the same. "Have you heard anything since?" I asked.

"Nothing. No one has heard anything."

The phone rang and she was beckoned. "*Llamada de Mexico!*"

"*Perdone*," Carmen said, jumping up. "Our sons calling from University."

While she was gone, the red-haired woman came over to meet me. I stood. "Dina!" she shouted, though she was two feet away from me. Her breath smelled of cigarettes. "*Abogada.*"

I shook my head, not getting it.

"Lawyair, lawyair," she said. She looked anything but professional. She wore high heels, too high, and a short tight skirt. Up close, her hair was more violet than red. I greeted her automatically, one ear hearing Carmen's voice in a rush of affectionate Spanish: "No, no, don't come! It won't help."

"Why are you here?" Dina asked me, emphasis on the you, *usted*, strange male. "What can you do for us?"

"I don't know." I couldn't have felt more useless. "What do you need me to do?"

"Contact anyone you know with influence." She pointed to a pile of newspapers on the floor. "We've called papers and TV and radio stations. And embassies, US and Canada." She listed other groups: Americas Watch, Amnesty International. "We've sent messages to President Cerezo. Not that he will do anything. Who do you know with influence?"

It felt like a bad joke. I told her I'd give it some thought.

Carmen returned, with a faint smile now, her appearance an extreme contrast to Dina's as they stood side by side. She was not beautiful, or pretty, but she didn't need to be, I thought, with whatever part of my brain was noticing. Something classy in her carriage. "It's so hard for them," she said, sitting down. "Our boys. They left just a week ago, for the start of, what do you call it, the semester."

The phone rang again and Dina went back to her shouting post. Sam adjusted the TV. Dishes clattered in the kitchen area. Someone climbed the iron staircase with a mop, pong, pong on the treads. Everyone here was worried, I knew that. But they were worried about one person; I was worried about two. One at a time, please, I begged the air around me. I wanted to ask if among all these calls there had been one for me, maybe from someone called Queen Jadis, or Magdalena. She knew where to reach me. She could be trying to get through here at this moment.

"Nothing we do can really protect him," said Carmen. "I just don't want them to hurt him again, like before, you know. Torture is so *humillante.*"

"Torture?" Luis hadn't said anything about that.

The doorbell rang. The dog went into a frenzy of barking and dashed to the door ahead of Sam. Two half-grown boys stood there. They wanted to know if they could ride the bike. "It's okay," said Carmen. "And ask them to take Molly for a run." Sam and the dog went out. The phone rang again. Dina answered, then bullhorned to the house the name of the caller. I looked at my watch. One of the kitchen women brought a tray with tea things and set it down on the coffee table. Carmen poured, offered me a cup.

"Did you say torture?" I asked again.

"*Pues*, torture just once," she said. "Then another time knocked around. Another time—." She stirred sugar into her cup.

"There was an accident, right?" I prompted.

"A year ago. The first truck. Forced into a wall." She gestured a whack with her hands. "I was there. It was an army jeep that cut us off. That's when Luis hurt his knee. I had a few bruises, nothing bad. The truck was, what's the word, total."

I sipped the tea. It was scalding, all the way down. Sam came back in and turned up the television. A brief news spot, about an apartment house fire in the city. Then the regular programming returned, some kind of a sit-com. The doorbell rang again. Sam was handed a bouquet of flowers. He brought it in with a touch of embarrassment. I understood. It was too much like a funeral wake, and all the more so when the bell rang again and a priest was admitted, wearing jeans and a collar. Carmen crossed the room to meet him, calling him Henri and kissing his cheek. He asked a few questions in a lowered voice, then waved to the house and was gone. Not much later another guy showed up, full faced and notably young, introduced to me as the pastor of the chapel next door. He was also wearing jeans but not a collar. His name was Ramón, and he also got a kiss. I looked at my watch again.

This continued almost without pause, the door, neighbors asking for news, the TV, the radio, the phone, with Dina belting out the names of the callers: Jews for Peace! Wycliffe Translators! Then the boys returned Molly, barking, echoed by every other dog on the street.

Carmen sat down beside me again on the divan and I asked her once more about torture. Oh "not the big stuff," she said, not "so far." He had been burned with cigarettes "of course," on his back and "other parts," and two fingernails pulled out, nose broken. "The big stuff is harder to talk about." She began rocking again.

"I think you are being remarkably brave," I said.

I meant it, struck by it, but she whirled to me, her eyes blazing. "Don't say that! It's not true. My insides are just a pot of mush."

I nodded, retreating. "I know. Me too." She touched my hand with her finger. An apology. Then Dina called her to the phone.

I stood and stretched. I needed oxygen. "Feel free to poke around," said Sam. He pointed to the spiral staircase. I climbed it, thankfully, making that pong-pong on the treads. They went up two stories, each with a landing under the well of the skylight, and doors into what must be sleeping quarters. Eight steps more and the stairs met a closed trap door. It was fastened by a big bolt. I slid it, pushed up the door and climbed out onto a flat roof. In its center rested the windowed cap for a pick-up truck, a 4 x 4, the "memento" Luis had saved after the smash. Sunlight entered the house through its windows. At noon it would offer shade. Clever.

Dozens of flat roofs spread before me, on and on up the hill, so close you could almost step from one to the other, filled with clotheslines and doghouses, here and there TV antennas. One roof was heaped with garbage, apparently dropped from the house above it, a nice neighborly gesture. Lots of movement below me, children, chickens and dogs. I heard amped-up *ranchera* from a radio. Then gunshots, one, two. I spun around. A woman a couple of roofs away was snapping out a wet towel. She hung it on a rigged-up line.

Back downstairs people were helping themselves to tortillas and beans. I wasn't hungry. I longed to call the Costa Rica number, but I couldn't possibly do it from this phone.

The doorbell rang and another person was admitted, a blond man with thick glasses, wearing running shorts. Sam announced him to the house: Smitty Dennison. "Just thought I'd drop something off," he said. He spoke with a soft husky voice and, remarkably, the room grew quiet enough to hear him. He held out a big bag of chocolate bars. "Energy aid," he said. "Custom free." He was rewarded with applause.

He looked at me. "Who are you?" he asked, a friendly question.

Carmen answered. "It's Teddy. Luis's oldest friend."

"Oh yes," he said. "Peterson. I've heard about you."

We shook hands and he left.

"If I'd known he was coming," said Carmen, "I'd have asked him to bring us some things. We're almost out of cheese and eggs."

I quickly offered to go. She recommended a market. I thought I could find a place to make my call, return after a quick shopping and leave for my flight. Carmen handed me a list as I pulled on my cap. "You're planning to stay here tonight, aren't you?" she said. "Please," she added, before I could answer. "It will help Sam. Henri was going to take a watch, but he has an emergency. There are others who would come in a second. But here you are. Like a godsend."

Should I tell her? There's this crazy possibility—I may be an extra danger, a fugitive on the lam. How silly it would sound, and truly just a possibility, pale against the darkness of her own reality. "I can't stay," I told her. "I'm scheduled to fly to Costa Rica."

Outside the house I fell instantly into a state of wariness, a distinct sense of being watched as I walked to the car. But of course I was watched, by a cluster of young boys smoking behind a bush, by a man with a wheelbarrow full of rocks, walking slowly past the house. I found a phone at the bottom of the hill in front of the *tienda*. It was inside a fiberglass hood that I would have to stand under. I was reluctant to do that, to shut off surveillance. But once inside, my head touching the top, I felt protected, just because my face was not showing. It was so irrational I didn't even try to account for it.

The ground around my feet was covered with trash and dog crap, but the phone was working, at least still hanging in place, and I got through to Costa Rica with my telephone credit card. I counted exactly nine rings before an answer, as Catherine had said.

"*Buenas tardes. Quién es?*" The voice was that of an adult woman, efficient and briskly cheerful. Not Catherine's.

"I am Ted Peterson, friend of Catherine Rodriguez. Have I reached her home?"

The cheery voice dropped to a dull whisper. It asked for my middle name.

"My middle name? Cavalier." Accent on the second syllable.

"*Pues. Bueno.*"

"Why did you ask me that?"

"Her instructions."

Just once I'd told Catherine my middle name, and now it was a code. "Are you calling from a secure phone?" the voice asked.

"I think so." How could I tell? "Has she arrived?"

"No."

"Have you heard from her?"

"No. Can you tell me anything?" the voice asked. "Where are you?"

"In Guatemala City. We got separated. Maybe she flew out three or four hours ago, maybe she's driving home with friends, I don't know. How long would it take to drive?"

"About fifteen hours."

Don't panic, I told myself, with panic tumbling around in my head like a gymnast. "When she gets there please tell her I called. I'll try again soon."

We hung up. Think, think. There was no point in going to Costa Rica unless I knew she was there. It was all guesswork. A phone book hung from a chain, ragged and dirty, a miracle of survival. I called the TACA airline and changed my flight to the next afternoon.

Then, still under the hood, I rang up Carlos Méndez, the best person of "influence" I could think of. He greeted me with his usual cheeriness. I told him about Luis. He seemed genuinely shocked. "A matey of yours, is it?" he said. "I'm so sorry." Did he know of anyone who could find out what happened? I asked. He said, "Hmm," then "hmm, hmm." He hated to get mixed up in this sort of thing himself, but he would find out something, if he could.

Then I told him I was a "little worried" about Catherine, that she had not arrived in Costa Rica as planned and apparently no one had heard from her. That's all I said, though it seemed like too much as soon as it left my mouth. He made some reassuring noises. "I shouldn't worry if I were you," he said. "Catherine is quite capable of taking care of herself."

I got back in my Bug and went to look for the market. As I stopped at a light a car pulled up across the intersection, in the driver's seat a woman with long dark hair. I didn't notice anything about the car, just that it was considerably bigger than mine and she sat a lot higher on the road. Her hair partly covered her face and I caught a glimpse of something blue. I tooted and waved, wildly. She raised her hand, to return the wave, I thought. Instead, she gave me the finger. The light changed and we drove on, in opposite directions. I couldn't believe I'd done that crazy thing again, see somebody who wasn't there.

Once in the haven of the store, I stretched out the errand, getting a measure of composure from the aisles of familiar products, picking things up just to feel them in my hand: Snow's Clam Chowder, Skippy Peanut Butter, Shredded Wheat—Niagara Falls still on the box. I added considerably to Carmen's list, used the store restroom, then drove back to the madness of 100 Garden Lane.

That evening there were ten of us as we sat down to eat at the big central table, including two people I hadn't seen before. One was a silent boy in his teens. He was from the neighborhood, someone told me, and had been doing his homework upstairs. No one seemed surprised at his presence, or at the appearance of an older woman addressed as *abuelita*, grandma, who consumed a plate of food and carried away extras in a paper napkin.

I had no appetite, and noticed that Carmen, too, only pretended to eat. Conversation was scant during the meal, though the phone still rang and continued ringing through the evening. Around 9:30, Dina and others left the house. Carmen didn't question my apparent decision to stay on for the night. She told me where to find an empty bed. She intended to sit up herself and listen for calls. I knew what she was hoping for, word from Luis himself: "I'm out. Come get me." I offered to take the first watch. I said I couldn't sleep anyway. Sam said he'd be down sometime after midnight to relieve me.

So now I was alone with the dog. It was quiet for once. I walked around and around the small space as time crept by. The place was as messy as the back of Luis's truck, with boxes of clothing and other supplies in a pile by the door. I poked through it, listening to a voice in my head, like an incantation: *Where are you? Where are you, Catherine? Where are you, Luis?*

I'd seen people go in and out of a door at the foot of the stairs and opened it. It led to a slot between this and the adjacent house, wide enough to permit a washing machine, a shower and toilet. The air was cool and damp. I stood there awhile, listening to the distant whirr of the city, while the voice in my head repeated its question, calling now into the sky. *Where are you, where are you? Dónde, dónde?*" I bolted the door as I went in. I'd found it unlocked, an oversight, I was sure.

Back inside I studied the spines in the bookcase. Three copies of Thomas Merton's *The Seven Storey Mountain*, two copies of *Gravity and Grace,* by Simone Weil. I recognized a whole row of books as my father's, now Luis's, books I'd seen every day of my young life in our house at Las Cavernas, the titles on the spines reading lessons in themselves, as I had once sounded them out. *Beyond Good and Evil*—that was fairly easy, but *Critique of Pure Reason* and *Varieties of Religious Experience* were unpronounceable mysteries. Certain names of authors were a muddle of letters, Nietzsche, Rauschenbush and Niebuhr. I'd been peeved to find out that *Children of Light, Children of Darkness* was not a story for kids.

My old Narnia series was there, held together by elastic bands. I left them where they were, too fragile. At the end of the same shelf was a book I'd never seen before in my father's collection. It was bound in black pasteboard, no outside identity. I opened to the title page. *The Revolution Betrayed*, by Leon Trotsky, translated and published in 1937, and in ink, "Property of T. Peterson." Tucked inside was a pamphlet the thickness of my little finger: *Kommunistiska Manifestet*, the *Communist Manifesto* in Swedish. It was signed inside, Teodor Gunter Peterson. My father's name, but also my grandfather's. The book must have been his originally. I couldn't recall ever hearing a discussion of Communism in our house, or Swedish Socialism, though it wouldn't have meant much to me as a kid.

Sometime after midnight I let myself drift off on the divan, then sprang awake to the growl of a motorcycle, right here in the room. It was Molly, in the middle of a long loud fart. She looked up at me, accusingly. I went to the door to let her out, but she ignored me, her head in her paws. That door was unlocked, too. I locked it, then questioned the sense of that. If Luis, or maybe Catherine, should show up, they might need instant access. So I unlocked it, and sat watching it for a long time. I listened. No footsteps. All I heard was an occasional claxon horn and the whine of distant trucks in low gear.

All this time the phone had been silent. If it took fifteen hours to drive to Costa Rica, they could have arrived there by now. This was a good time for me to call, while there was privacy at this end. I should, ought to, any idiot would, and I did, dialing the long row of digits. I let it ring, on past the designated nine times. No one answered.

Sam appeared around 2:00. He offered me his bed upstairs but I declined. He went outside to look around and when he came in, bringing a waft of outside air, we talked for a while. I liked his slow, dismissive speech and a gentlemanly slouch that pronounced him harmless. He wanted to know why I was in the country. That changes by the day, I said. I asked him about the people I'd met today, in a bleary-eyed effort to show interest. Smitty was a Mennonite missionary, he said. He taught peace studies at the Mennonite Seminary. Dina was attorney for several non-profits, not just this one.

"What about you?" I asked him. He was a cultural anthropologist, a teacher at a small college in Louisiana I'd never heard of, doing research for a book on ways the Maya adapt to oppression. He'd narrowed it down to one case study, Luis. That's why he was here, for daily observation. "Though I feel guilty taking up space. They need room for other people."

"What other people?" I asked.

"Anybody. This is a sort of Dorothy Day house," he said. "Radical hospitality." Didn't I know? "It's mostly Carmen's doing. She used to be a nun. You knew that." No. "She was raised in a conventional Catholic family, Ladino, but she got canned by the order. Too independent."

I glanced around the walls. I saw no *crucifijos* or in-your-face slogans.

"Preferential option for the poor," Sam said. "They've always lived this way, starting with the land invasion ten years ago." Invasion? He thought I knew what that meant, too. "Occupation of unused land by the homeless. This whole hill. At first all the houses were like the ones below us. Up here they've got electric and water, after years of wrangling with the city." He pointed out a photo I hadn't noticed, Luis and Carmen with their young boys in front of what looked like a one-room hut. "Open house, even then."

"Sometimes it's a regular looney bin," Sam said. He yawned, stretching his long arms. Kids come and go. They take in foster children, too. Three little girls are bunking with Carmen's sister now until this crisis is over."

"I found the doors unlocked," I said. "Is that policy?"

"Well, does anybody have a lock around here? Down below us the shacks have curtains for doors. Besides, what's the point? Military police broke in the front door here a year ago and searched the place. They thought this was a safe-house for Commies. Jardín de la Communidad, that has the right ring. They held everybody at gun point until they were done tearing the place up and then Carmen offered them a cup of tea."

Right at that moment, Carmen came downstairs, as if beckoned. She gave us a little silent wave and went to the front window where she stood for a long time, rubbing the dog's head. Finally she waved again and went back up the stairs.

Sam decided he was hungry so we foraged in the kitchen. My head ached. I knew I should eat something. We found the left-over chocolate bars Smitty had brought. "A little Zacapa Centenario would be better," Sam said. "Knowing Smitty, that's what he'd have preferred to bring."

"Why didn't he? I could use a little rum right now."

"You don't know? Luis is a recovering alcoholic? No booze in the house."

I thought I'd start wearing a sign: *No lo se.* I don't know. I certainly did not know this.

"He doesn't hide it," Sam said. "He got hooked at seminary in Boston. That's his joke. It probably started long before that."

"I'm glad to hear he's not perfect," I said, after a minute. I was afraid it sounded dismissive, but Sam said, "I know what you mean." Surely he was thinking what I was, what everybody must be thinking, that Luis was just out on a binge—actually hoping for that against other odds.

When Sam curled up on the divan, knees to his chest, I sat at the desk with a clean piece of paper I found there. I was too tired to write and decided to just make an outline of the last 24 hours. When the phone rang, my head was on the desk. I opened my eyes to "Wednesday, August 26, 1987," yesterday, with nothing under it. It was morning, shortly after 7:00. I grabbed the phone, sure it was for me. Carmen was already there, at the foot of the stairs. "For you," I told her. "Someone at Centro Medico."

We listened to her end of the call. "Oh...oh. *Bueno!* Oh, no. *Qué? Sí, pues.*" She hung up with a clatter. "They have him! He's alive! He's all right!" Sam and I cheered. I felt hope like a blast of sunlight. Carmen began turning about in the room, picking up her bag from behind a chair, grabbing a sweater. "I can go see him. The police brought him in. They found him lying in the road down in *El Basurero.*"

He'd been found in the dump?

"Unconscious," said Carmen. "Broken nose! Oh, God, not again the nose!" She brushed her hands over her hair, tucking it behind her ears. She asked Sam to call Dina, and Smitty, too. "Ask him to meet me at the hospital." She ran to the stairs. "I should find things. Toothbrush, razor."

"One of us should drive Carmen," said Sam. I knew he wanted to go. I said I'd stay by the phone until Dina arrived. Which she did, at that moment, smelling of perfume and cigarettes, all business, taking over the desk and dialing a series of calls to report the news. Two women materialized in the kitchen to make coffee and fry tortillas. In another hour Sam rang from the hospital. They were bringing Luis home.

THIRTY

I met them at the door, the four of them. Luis walked into the house under his own steam, barely ambulatory, Carmen hovering. He was wearing a knee length hospital gown, the kind made of paper, his muscled, hairy legs underneath, feet in paper slippers and someone's sweater around his shoulders. He put out his right hand to greet me. Two fingers were in splints. We did a gentle thumb lock. "Glad to have you back," I said.

"Thanks, ol' pal." His voice was hoarse. He moved his mouth in a smile on one side. The other cheek was stitched with black thread in a line from the middle of his cheek to his ear. His nose, that outsized feature, was swollen even larger, black and blue, a clown's monstrosity. Hair had been shaved away from the crown of his head, where a bandage was taped. The rest of his hair was out of the pony tail, hanging around his face. He looked like a mad holy man just down from the mountain.

Inside he unfolded himself lengthwise at the divan, slowly, brushing away help. "Can't sit. Balls hurt. That's the bottom line."

"Stop making jokes," scolded Carmen. "He's been doing that all the way home."

"Talking out of one side of his mouth, as usual," said Smitty. Luis gave a grunty laugh and caught himself. Carmen covered him with a blanket, fussed with pillows. One of the women brought a glass of water and a cup of tea. He sipped a little, then he wanted to call his mother and his sons, so Sam and Smitty and I went out to the front patio.

They told me what they'd learned at the hospital. His injuries were not life-threatening. The facial cut was clean and superficial. He'd been hit on the head with something, but there was no concussion. The police report was at the emergency room desk. They let Carmen read it. Drunk and in an accident, that's what it said. But the doctor suggested otherwise. The wounds were administered. "That was his word," said Sam. "Administered."

"Beaten up?" I asked.

"Maybe. His wallet is missing. But not drunk, according to the blood test. Of course, there was a time factor."

"What does Luis say happened?"

They both smiled. "He seems more concerned about what happened to the truck than himself," Smitty said.

A couple of board members arrived, and Carmen called us in. Luis was ready to talk. We gathered around the divan where he sat, propped up on pillows. Smitty and Carmen sat on either side of him.

He addressed us in Spanish, without energy, almost without expression. His throaty accent was markedly stronger, as if he were even more of an Indian. I had to strain to catch every word.

"All I want now is witnesses to what I remember, and to what I don't," he said. "No sympathy. Please. I just want you to know what I know, really know, and the sooner the better." He held a hand against his stitched cheek as he spoke.

After the arrest, he said, he was handcuffed and put in the back of an army truck, with two soldiers on either side of him. He was blindfolded. He took a measure of comfort in that. "Maybe it meant they didn't intend to kill me. If they did intend to, it wouldn't matter what faces I saw." They drove here to Guate City. He could tell that without seeing, he'd done it so often. They ended up on Avenida la Reforma. That was a guess, judging just by the sound of the traffic and the stop lights.

He mentioned a place called *la casa*, over by the dump. He thought maybe they would take him there, for "disposal." But they didn't go anywhere near the dump. He'd know, he'd have smelled it, he said. He was taken somewhere else, to another building, where he was led down some stairs, way down, three flights, where the smell was a fruity disinfectant, and he remembered that, from the "time before."

"Twice on the way down I got a gun butt in the stomach, to make sure I wasn't getting cocky. Then they took off the handcuffs and told me to undress, all the time yelling a bunch of insults. When they thought I was humble enough they started with the questions."

He was interrogated three times, he said, always blindfolded. "First they say they are going to explain the rules to you. The rules are that they will reel off names of people, and you say whether or not they are guerrilla supporters. If you don't cooperate, they will be forced to hurt you. Just an unfortunate necessity. I did happen to know some of the people they mentioned, but I didn't comply, so I was not cooperating. Various things happened after that. I've lost track of the sequence. The worst is that electric prod to the ass. The *batón*. You're bent over, your bare bum in the air. You fall over when it touches you. You shit. You hope you're dead."

Someone whispered "Ay, ay, ay," but otherwise we sat in motionless silence. Carmen, who was holding Luis's hand, whispered, "Please stop," but he shifted his position and went on.

He expected more trouble when he was brought in for the second session of interrogation, still blindfolded. This time there were two new men, at least two, judging by the voices. But for some reason they changed their minds. "They said they were going to give me a new chance. They wanted me to think things over." He was taken to a cell and left in isolation, for what seemed like hours.

At some point he was told to dress and led to another room, a longer walk. A guy was there who spoke to him in English. "From Ohio, he said. He took off my handcuffs and asked if I wanted a cigarette or coffee. I asked for water and got it. We can help each other, he said. He knew me to be an intelligent man—whoopee—with many friends. If I helped him I would be out of here in half an hour, a free man. He would see to it that I was driven safely home. He wanted the names of subversive cell groups, ones with munitions capability. Army buddy talk. I told him he was asking the wrong person. I'm not party to any of that. Then he told me to hold out my right hand and he began to bend back my fingers, one at a time, very slowly. I could stop it whenever I liked, he said, just by talking. Name some people. I refused, so he broke a finger. Then he began telling me that he couldn't vouch for the safety of my mother, my wife, or my sons. This country is full of bullies, he said. I said right, bullies paid by the U.S. Pentagon. I don't think he liked that. He broke another finger. He said he could protect me and my family and would do that, if I would just talk."

But then someone else came into the room. There were whispers, an argument. He couldn't follow it. He was led away, still blindfolded, to be shot after all, he thought. That was where his memory stalled. Maybe that's when he was hit on the head. He couldn't explain the cut on the face, or the statement by the police that he had been drinking.

"I have no memory of being set free or of what I might have done afterwards. The doctors said I was found on the street near the dump. I have no idea how I got outdoors, never mind all the way to the dump. Could be I was being taken to *la casa* after all, and somehow I slipped their grasp. I don't know. So, if anyone outside this group asks any of you if you've been told what happened next, there is only one thing you should say, without evasion. You don't know. You don't know because Luis doesn't know. None of you, or anyone you pass this on to, should feel any obligation to fudge that. There is no obligation to defend me. I need your promise." He ran his eyes across the group, waiting for visible assent from us one by one, then he lay back against the pillows. "I will now entertain questions from the floor."

"Oh, no you don't!" said Carmen. "*No más*, no questions." It was clear to me too that he should stop talking, and probably clear to everyone else. Except Dina. She was ready. Did he go to a bar or a liquor store after he was released? No. Did anyone try to force booze down his throat? Not that he recalled. "Where is my truck, that's what I'd like to know," he said. "What have they done with my poor truck?"

"Never mind the foolish truck," said Dina. She had other questions. But Carmen stood abruptly and began to sing the *Doxology*, loudly and not quite on key. That was the end of the conference.

We dispersed. Dina and others went to the office area to set up a relay of calls: Luis is home. At noon a doctor arrived to examine him. He was in good hands and I had a plane to catch. I gathered my stuff and sought out Carmen. "You mean you won't be here for dinner?" she said. "We're having a little celebration."

"I'm sorry. I'm due in Costa Rica," I told her—again—hoisting my pack onto my shoulder and grabbing my suitcase. "Please tell Luis I'll stay in touch."

I stopped first at the pay phone I'd used before and ducked under the hood, glad again, just as vapidly, for its offer of protection. It had begun to sprinkle, drops hitting the plastic like tiny pebbles.

In Costa Rica the same woman's voice answered. We went through the same rigamarole of identity before she told me that "she" had not arrived yet and they had not heard from her.

I didn't believe her. "Look, I'm coming anyway," I said. "Give me the address."

She hesitated. "If she didn't do that herself, I can't. I'm sorry. Can you understand my caution? You are only a voice. That's all I've got."

And what *I've* got, lady, is a number on a little piece of crumpled paper and a filthy telephone receiver under a plastic bonnet. I don't even have a name for *you*, no fancy middle name to tell me you're legit and not lying through your teeth. I sighed. "Please understand this question. Is she truly not there?"

I got a sigh in return. "I have no reason to deceive you, *Señor* Cavalier. Are you sure she's not *there?* If she's not here, chances are she's somewhere there. Let's just stay connected."

I waited fifteen more minutes, sweating it out in that most ridiculous hiding place in all the world, then cancelled my plane reservation again without making another.

Back at Garden Lane, the house was already filling with people. If Carmen was surprised to see me she didn't show it. More and more guests arrived, adults and children, fitting in where they could, sitting on the stairs and standing around in the front patio. It was as if the whole neighborhood had turned out. Luis, damp from a shower and in a change of clothes, lay on the divan among the pillows. Sam hovered about, guarding him from good-will huggers and hand-shakers.

Before we ate, we sang a blessing in a round. Ramón, the next door pastor, divided us into rangy quarters, struck a chord on his guitar and directed us with his plump hand. It took only a minute. The last word, "Lord," was *Señor*. As it happened, Carmen's voice carried that, alone and just under the note. One second went by and the word was repeated by someone else in the room, spoken, not sung, and then again by someone else. Sen-*yor!* A kid hit the table with a spoon, dum-a-*dum,* and a Latin beat took over, that one spoken word and the spoon, a sound that took on music and passed like a growing wave through the house and out into the patio. Some of the women began turning in wiggly little circles and children stamped and drummed on the table and the stairs. It didn't stop. I heard castanets, a *conga,* the *claves,* though there were no instruments, that I could see, just Ramón's guitar and the clack of silverware, a pot and a wooden spoon, boxes of cereal shaken, altogether an extremely loud, glorious sound. Sen-*yor!* Outdoors people were clapping and dancing. It went on for a long time before it drew to a close all by itself, softly, in Carmen's off-key solo again. Then a male voice on the patio yelled "Luis! Luis!" with a peppering of fire crackers, while dogs throughout the neighborhood barked and yowled and roosters crowed.

That high continued all around me on into the evening, while my own anxiety returned and took over. I moved about restlessly in the jubilant crowd, feeling poisonous, pale-faced, the carrier of a dangerous disease. Finally, I gathered my belongings and stopped by the divan to say goodnight.

"Why are you leaving?" asked Luis.

"You need the space. I'll stay at a hotel tonight."

"Space? There's always space here. But do what's right for you." His speech was still labored. He was wearing an old pair of granny glasses.

I said I'd check back tomorrow. Carmen, who was sitting beside him hugging somebody's sleeping toddler, walked with me out the door, still holding the child. "Listen," she said. "The girls are going to stay with my sister a little longer, so their room is still free. Clean sheets. No bed bugs. Private bath." She tried to smile. "Luis needs you, Ted. You and Sam. I know how this works, this torture thing. He jokes and talks. But he goes in and out of sadness. And shame. Why shame? I don't know. It helps him to have friends close by, people who know him well. You see?"

I said I did.

My assigned room, the "girls' room" on the second floor, was a tiny space filled with three narrow cots and a good two dozen stuffed animals, including a pink bear the size of a two-year-old child. The "private bath" was an old-fashioned commode, fitted out with a potty.

Clean sheets and towels were folded at the end of one bed. There was even an intercom over the door, in case I had a bad dream.

Downstairs the guests departed and the place grew quiet. The whole house seemed to be breathing differently. At least it had dropped its chin-up tension.

My mood changed again. Luis was indomitable, and so was Catherine. I was bound to hear from her soon, maybe even tomorrow. I listened to my Oscar Peterson tapes on the Walkman, *Night Train* and *Georgia On My Mind*, while I caught up in the journal notes, then fell deeply asleep among the animals. I dreamed of the boy, Manuel, and knew, in the dream, that my body would always remember him, whenever I crouched and made a lap. In my dream that seemed like a very good thing.

THIRTY-ONE

At six in the morning, I was just ready to step into the outside shower when I heard a voice, Carmen's I thought, in one prolonged high register note. I dashed inside, wrapped in a towel. Luis was on the divan and Carmen stood rigid beside him, with a cup in one hand and a dishtowel in the other. Both of them looked dazed. Sam was there, in the middle of the room, holding an open newspaper. "Page two," he said, handing it to me. It smelled of damp fresh air. The headline read *Mujer Muerta Encontrado en Carro López*. "Woman Found Dead in López Truck." Under that were two photos, one of a wrecked panel truck, half-buried under a mountainous heap of trash. The panel on the visible side was smashed in, but the painting of the soldier and his blazing gun was clear.

The second photo was of the interior of the truck. Without my glasses I had to hold the paper at arm's length to study it. A human figure lay sprawled in the back, face down, partially concealed by soccer balls and boxes. I made out a slender bare foot and what appeared to be a mass of dark hair.

I'd hardly begun translating the text when my eyes were drawn to the closing lines. Police had identified the woman from a *cedula*, passport, found on her person, as Magdalena Rodriguez Adrela, home address in Antigua.

If I gasped, it was covered by Sam's voice. "Who the hell is *Magdalena*?" He asked Luis, who answered, tonelessly, "I don't know." Carmen buried her face in the dishtowel. A roar started deep in my belly.

Another newspaper, still rolled, was tucked under Sam's arm. The story was repeated there, with the same photos. The text added that two empty gin bottles were found in the truck, according to police.

I walked away in my towel, up the stairs, two treads at a time, the iron cold under my bare feet, thinking only to get where I could release the roar. Halfway up, it began breaking apart into its component voices, grief and protest and anger and disbelief, all shouting at each other at once. When I reached the top of the stairs, anger was the loudest. It was a hoax, I was sure, a trick thought up by some deranged force, and I was the only person in the world who could get the ghastly joke. Nobody else in the whole country who read that newspaper story knew what I knew, who the person might actually be in the back of that truck.

Except Luis. If it was not a hoax, then Luis would know, and she, she would have known, too, of course. She knew. Knows? And if so, since we three, Luis, Catherine and I, each know what we knew and knew what we know, the whole freaking universe has just gone belly up.

I had entered the little girls bedroom and was talking out loud to the pink bear.

I had to run. Nothing else made sense. I skipped the shower and dressed in cutoffs and sweatshirt, the apparel of a sane and invulnerable man. By the time my shoes were on, I'd gained a measure of control. Luis and I must talk. It was essential, mandatory, to tell him what I knew. I owed him that. He owed me the same. Our present friendship might be altered forever, but we could honor our history. It was important to do it now, before Dina arrived, before the phone started ringing and the dog began to bark and the house became a looney institution.

I went down. Sam and Carmen were in the kitchen. Luis was on the divan, in his half-lying position, holding an icebag to the lump on his head. I said, "We need to talk." He said "Sure," and stood up, or halfway up. "Let's do it outside," he said. "I think the bad news has energized me."

Out in the patio we stood under the vine canopy, its leaves dripping with last night's rain. Luis was breathing hard from just that much exertion and I almost lost my nerve. I blurted. "I know who that woman is—in the back of the truck." I didn't say "your truck."

He was astonished. I knew he was because his first words of response were in Mam. Then he corrected himself, holding his hand against his stitched cheek. "*You* know that—you mean that Magdalena somebody in the paper? You *know* her?"

"No. Not Magdalena. Magdalena has been dead for a month."

"What are you saying?"

"I know her niece, her niece by marriage. I happen to know that she was carrying Magdalena's ID."

We stared at each other in a kind of paralysis, the portent of it rising around us in the misty air. I gave him the barest minimum of data: My language teacher, an "errand" to the hills, the checkpoint at the *derrumbe* when I held Magdalena's ID in my hand. I managed quite well, until it was time to say her name. I saved that for the end, and it came hard. It emerged in a whisper and I had to repeat it.

"Catherine Rodriguez," Luis said. He had taken off his glasses as I talked and was looking directly up at me, his eyes framed in the dark lashes, Alicia's eyes. "That strikes a bell. But I don't think I've met her."

"Win Hall never mentioned her to you?"

"Win Hall knows her?"

"They have a connection. Friends in common. Win was asked to check me out, for her—check with you. He followed me to your office, last Sunday."

"Oh, God, what a crazy coincidence." He began to pace the patio, his body moving like an old horse. "Win never mentioned her. Never asked me anything about you. I'd have told you that. Maybe he came to his own conclusions."

"I'd like to keep it quiet, if we can," I said. "I mean, her real identity, if it really is her."

"I understand. Ted, I'm so sorry you've been dragged into this craziness." He stopped in front of me, wrestling with a thought. He asked, "What part of the country is she from?"

I said "Wisconsin," before I realized he thought she was Guatemalan.

"U.S. citizen," he said. "That makes it totally different. This could be a case for the Embassy. Go to the Embassy."

"That's the last thing she'd want. Maybe the last thing I want. Or you."

"Then talk to Smitty. He knows the ropes on this kind of thing. He'll advise you. What time is it? Smitty goes to the gym early every morning. You can catch him when he comes home."

It was two miles away. My legs were still begging to run. I sprinted, all thought of vigilance flown. I met Smitty just outside the gate to his house, his jersey patchy with sweat. "Peterson!" he said, in his husky voice. We stood there a second or two, me panting, he blinking through steamy glasses. We both started to speak at once. "Have you seen—?" I asked. He said, "I read the paper at the gym. Is Luis all right?"

"As right as possible. Can I talk to you?"

"Come in." He opened the gate. "Everyone is still asleep," he whispered. "My wife and kids."

The front patio was cluttered with boy things. A basketball hoop, minus net, hung over the door. Inside, the space was similar to the López house, sunlit from a skylight. An orange cat came to meet us, pressing against my legs. We sat in the kitchen and drank warmed-up coffee, while I explained. I left out Catherine's name.

Smitty processed this calmly, his blond hair flopping over his forehead, a vestige of the towhead he must have once been. While I talked, he rubbed his glasses on the hem of his sweat shirt. Without them, his eyes lost coordination, one focused directly at me and the other off by just a hair. He looked anything but effectual, but his response was all business, with none of the concern for me that Luis had shown. I couldn't have handled that twice. Yes, he said, we should report it to the Embassy. "As soon as possible, if you're convinced this is a U.S. citizen."

"Except, how can we do that and keep it private?"

"I don't know. If there was a body in that truck it's probably at the morgue now. The police morgue here in the city." He asked me a question Luis had not. "Why was she carrying her aunt's ID?"

"For protection," I said. "She thought she was in danger. That's all I can tell you."

He accepted that. "In terms of your own interest right now, what do you want?" he asked. "Suppose it does turn out to be her? Do you want to know that for sure, or would you rather not?"

First I said yes, then I said no. No, of course not. God no, of course I'd rather not, I said, because that would mean she is dead, wouldn't it, and I'd rather she wasn't dead at all, for God's sake. "But she's missing. I think she is. I haven't heard anything." I pinched my eyes, apologized. "Look, what *I* want is not important. She has a son. If there's something to this then her son ought to be told."

"I have a friend at the Embassy," said Smitty, still all business, "a consular official. We help each other now and then. If she's in the morgue, he might be able to put a stop to the burial long enough for her to be re-identified. Did she get her driver's license here in Guate?"

"I don't know."

"If she did, her fingerprints will be on record."

"How much do you need to tell this guy?"

"Just what you've told me. Shall I? I can get him at home. Private call."

I agreed and he started dialing the phone. I glanced at a clock on the wall. It was 7:15. "It's okay," said Smitty. "He owes me big time. —Hey, Mauricio. This is Fred. Have you seen this morning's papers?"

He repeated my story to Mauricio, then relayed the answer. "He says he can't get involved until there's positive proof that this is a US citizen. He needs her name."

I shook my head, sorry now that I'd started the process.

"Must you?" Smitty asked the phone. "We have concerns here. Is there a way to do this under wraps?"

Mauricio, or whoever he was, gave a long answer, while I stabbed myself in the heart. Smitty listened, then talked to me again, hand over the mouthpiece. Yes, a name was necessary for fingerprinting. But a fingerprint match could take too long, since unclaimed bodies at the morgue get buried in forty-eight hours. Dental records might be hard to trace. And forget pathology. Things at the morgue tended to be disorganized. Things got stolen there, and lost. Even bodies got lost, or mislabeled. There might be another way to identify the body, if there was a next of kin available, someone eighteen or over.

"Her son Alex," I said. "But he's in Costa Rica."

"Can Mauricio call him?" Smitty asked.

I repeated the Costa Rica number, though not at all sure I ought to. Smitty passed it on. "Now we wait," he said, hanging up. "He'll contact someone at the Embassy in Costa Rica, who will take over with everything there."

"I'm afraid I've stirred up a hornet's nest."

"Mauricio knows how to do this right."

"But I think I should alert them in Costa Rica," I said.

He handed me the phone. The same woman answered there, her

voice now familiar. Maybe mine was too because she didn't request my middle name. "No word yet," she told me, before I asked. I explained that the U.S. Embassy there might call to talk to Alex. She wanted to know why. "Is there news?" Someone from the Embassy would explain, I said. I didn't mention the morgue.

I thanked Smitty. He brushed me off. "It's our job to keep those Embassy blokes busy. By the way, his name's not Mauricio, and obviously I'm not Fred. And he asked that we not tell anyone else about this, until he knows something for sure. I'd say not even Luis. That could be tricky for you." We walked outside. "As you know, there's a point at which this information may cease to be private, anyway," he said. He picked a half-deflated basketball out of a bush and shook off last night's rain. "Are you ready? The justice system is unpredictable here, but the police could pursue it legitimately. Luis could be indicted for murder."

"I'm sure he's aware of that."

"What if the son identifies his mother? Is he apt to bring charges against Luis?"

"I don't know."

"And you. How come you know about that ID? You could be questioned, at the least."

"I know. I'm a collaborator."

Smitty didn't comment on that. He dropped the squashy ball through the hoop over the door, an easy shot, and looked up at the hoop for a minute, squinting through his glasses. "You know that place in Ezekiel?" he asked. "About the wheel in the middle of a wheel?"

"I've heard the folk song."

"Right. 'De big wheel run by faith, and de little wheel run by de grace of God.' That's all of us here," he said. "Little wheels."

I wondered if that was what Ezekiel intended, but who cared?

Back at Garden Lane, I walked square into an argument between Dina and Luis. Volume on her part, quiet persistence on his. He wanted to visit the dump, check out the truck, make plans to salvage it. She was against it. "*Está loco?* Return to the scene of the crime?"

"What crime?" said Luis. "There's no crime."

"*No seas baboso!*" she scolded. (Don't be a baboon?) "The place will be teeming with police. An armed guard."

"Whatever, it's still my truck. Ours. It still belongs to *Los Rebozos*."

"No. It's evidence. There's a valid reason to arrest you again."

"They don't need a valid reason."

"If they decide that woman has been murdered...."

I thought it best to keep moving on upstairs, but Luis stopped me. "Ted. Dina has discovered something very interesting. She's called the police in Antigua." I turned and went back, heart tripping, feigning disinterested interest. "Really?"

"A woman named Magdalena Rodriguez died there a month ago. Age 50."

"Really," I said, again, and escaped.

I showered and changed and dropped a load in the washing machine, adding some house towels piled beside it. In the time that took, Luis won his argument. We would drive by the site. *We* would, all of us, that is. I was glad. I wanted to go, though I dreaded it. Dina assumed charge of the venture. We went in her car, a small sedan, she driving, Carmen in the passenger seat up front, Luis in the back squeezed between Sam and me. He had disguised himself at Dina's insistence, striking a scarface gangster pose with sunglasses and a wide-brimmed hat. "But my nose still shows," he said.

"Put your collar up," Dina ordered. On the way, she barked instructions. We were not to leave the car. We were not to make ourselves obvious in any way. Was that understood?

We followed the same route Catherine and I had taken when we drove last Saturday. I recognized landmarks along the way right up to the road approaching the dump, still lined with pedestrians, carrying stuff in and out.

"*La casa* is somewhere here," Luis said.

"The house? Which house do you mean?" I asked.

There was no answer. Dina stopped the car. We were not far from the spot where Catherine and I had stopped, and sat staring at the same appalling scene, heaps of multicolored trash spread over acres, the licks of flame here and there, the circling vultures, the smoke—that smoke from Hades—and the smell, the terrible eye-watering smell. But no wrecked panel truck in sight, not until a giant yellow Mack disgorged

260 T H E   R I S K   O F   R E T U R N I N G

its load and backed away. It had been blocking our view. "Ah, there she is," sang out Luis, as if a three-masted schooner had just appeared on the horizon.

Sam began snapping pictures out his window. The truck was upright, but tilting precariously into the hill of garbage, the mural on the visible side half-swallowed by it, as in the newspaper photo. The soldier with his red-blazing machine gun seemed to be standing on a pile of trash. I lunged forward, ready to scramble from the car and slog through garbage to look in the back of the truck. To see what? Just that space, among the books and the soccer balls and children's clothing, as if her body could have left an imprint there.

"Where the hell are the police?" ranted Dina. None in sight, and no armed guard, but plenty of activity. Several men, knee deep in garbage, were busy at work, one with a crowbar. They were removing the seats. On the side facing us the tires were missing. The broad snub-nosed hood was up.

Luis groaned, "*Dios mío.*"

"Let it go, *amigo*," murmured Sam. "Let them have it."

"Yes," he said, sinking back on the seat.

"Can we leave now?" asked Dina. She was already turning the car around. Out the back window I caught sight of something else, four-leggers, two or more of them, darting in and out of the garbage around the truck. "Dogs," I said, the word tossing itself from my mouth. Sam caught it. "And rats too, I'll bet," he said.

I tensed. Luis pressed his elbow against my side.

We turned around and drove back to the highway. "Does that help, Luis?" asked Dina, seeking him out in the mirror.

"*Qué?* Help what?"

"Does being here help you remember anything?"

"Remember?" he mused. "Remember, remember. Why yes, *sí pues*, now that you ask, it all comes back to me, in a flash. Let's see, how did it go? I was hit on the head by something and blacked out. Pow! I remember that, clearly, being unconscious. Then I was released from custody, still unconscious, found my vehicle parked somewhere, unguarded, what luck, got into it, though I couldn't sit down, dug out my keys, though they had been confiscated, and drove it, stinking drunk, in the middle of the night, and ran it into a mountain of garbage. Right there, at that very spot. *El basurero!* I remember, *distinctly*, seeing a bunch of little fires here and there and thinking I was in hell. Oh shucks, I said to myself, it figures. And then I crawled out from behind the wheel, injured but upright, *homo erectus*, and staggered down this very road. Possibly singing, at the top of my lungs. Yes, that's it, singing! Until I collapsed at last in a heap upon the hard, cold ground."

"Leaving that poor woman behind to her fate," Sam added. "That would be just like you."

"Well, that's my story, and I'm a-stickin' to it, by golly gee."

"A little over the top, pal," I said, "but we're right behind you."

"Stop that nonsense!" snapped Dina.

"So what do you want me to say when I'm on the rack?" asked Luis. "Or before a judge. Any way we slice it, it will just be my story."

"That's right," she bellowed. "Whatever your story, it's all you've got! The police have got a body and a suspect. You." (*Usted.*)

"Don't mind Dina, folks," Luis said. "What this hemisphere needs is more bossy Hispanic women."

"*Deja de decir pendejadas!*" she scolded.

"Did I hear that right?" I asked.

"Oh yeah. She said cut the bullshit. Or more essentially, tuck it in, fellows. Don't you just love her?"

"To pieces," I said, and was impaled by Dina's eyes in the mirror.

But she was right. We were just boys, horsing around like fools when it was impossible to play it straight.

THIRTY-TWO

That afternoon Dina came in with more newspapers. We looked through them together. The story of the panel truck had been repeated verbatim in two others, and twice already, Sam told me, on a radio news report. No new information, nothing about how the woman had died. No requests for Luis's side of things had come from any facet of the local media, not even, as Sam noted, from a moderate English language weekly.

In general, the telephone was ringing less often today, as if friends and supporters were afraid of what they would be told. Even so, the house was filled with the usual multi-activity. Henri, the priest, checked in. A family with five children used the shower. Somebody dropped off a box of clothes for distribution. I put it just inside the door where the other freebees were piled. Someone else left a strip of complimentary tickets to the symphony next month. I happened to answer the door for that one. I held those little red cards in my hand like admission to another form of life. Not everybody in this city was a guerrilla or a soldier or a loud-mouthed lawyer. Or maybe they were, and they still played the cello and the oboe. —And only an academic snob would think that was news.

Later three women sat in consultation with Dina around the table. "They're from GAM," Sam told me. He'd been listening in. "Grupo de Apoyo Mutuo. Women whose men are *desaparecido*. Or murdered."

"Why are they here?"

"Establishing bonds, I think. One of their founders was abducted and killed a few years ago. Along with her three-year-old son. Whose fingernails were pulled out before he was killed. To get her to talk, probably."

That was all I needed. "Let's get out of here," I said. We took Molly for a long run and a crap in an empty lot below the hill. When we got back, the GAM women were gone, and a group of six men arrived to see Luis. At least half of them were Mayan. This time I hovered, listening in. They were severing ties with Luis, backing off from the organization, making it official. Luis didn't argue. He listened without expression, then sent them away with his blessing.

He caught me watching. "Last year they wanted me to run for president," he said. "They were wrong about that, too."

"Sounds good to me," I said.

"Not the way *they* wanted it. Selling my identity."

He had enough to do, anyway, he said. Things needed fixing around here. "Want a job? We need a new sewer line." I told him I was good at digging. "We also need someone to open a school in the barrio," he said. "No pay, but lots of excitement. Interested?"

A part of me flew out to that like a bird that had just found its nest. I whistled a call, some call or other, not too badly, and he answered with another. But I couldn't accept, obviously.

Next a woman arrived to clean, pushing an upright vacuum cleaner with the roar of a tractor. I went outside again and swept the front patio, accidentally erasing a fresh hopscotch some kid had drawn on the cement. I found chalk and was repairing it when a long scream shot up the hill from the shacks below us, and then another. Four women with small children on their backs barged into the patio, breathless. A fight, with knives. Has anyone called for help? I asked. Yes, the padre. Claxon horns answered in the distance and the women ran into the house. Just another day at 100 Community Garden.

Still no word from Smitty. Nothing I could do but wait. I helped pull together a dinner and cleaned up afterwards, anything to stay busy. There was a radio there on the counter. When the dishes were washed, I searched the stations for sports news, found none, just soccer scores, but picked up other news around the world—an East/West accord on medium and short range missiles, a South African mine strike, Noriega in trouble in Panama. None of that seemed as important as what was happening here in this house and in my head. In the local news, the volcano Pacaya, southwest of the city, not far from where I stood right now, was active again and had developed a new cone. That seemed appropriate.

Halfway into the evening, someone phoned with a tip. Turn on the television. Elizondo, the politician, was scheduled to appear live on a local interview show and the topic was relevant. We gathered in front of the 12-inch screen, Sam and I and Luis and Carmen, the four of us presently in the house, or at least the only ones in evidence.

Elizondo looked polished and energetic. He was wearing a silky green shirt like the one he had on when he appeared with Mendez in the motel courtyard a week ago. A young woman conducted the interview. Carmen spoke her name, so I supposed she was a familiar face on local television. They were seated in what appeared to be an office, maybe Elizondo's own. In the opening long shot I could see a desk, tall plants, and the corner of a painting, an abstract in bright colors that I wished would show in full. I was still watching for it when the reporter asked her first astounding question.

She was wondering, she said, if she should discount something she had recently been told—that it was he, Elizondo, who had managed to free Luis López, the well-known leader of Mayan protest, from "police detention" after he was arrested near Quetzaltenango several days ago.

"Oh, apparently that is the case," said Elizondo, in his fine baritone. It was true, he said, that when he learned of the arrest he did make a few calls on behalf of Luis López. "And I'm happy to say it seems my efforts were successful." He said this off-handedly, as if telling her— us—well, yes, it does seem he was the one who had managed to coax a neighbor's cat down from a tree.

"Were you told why he was arrested?" the woman asked.

"For causing a menace on the highway. I supposed they meant his vehicle. I urged them to simply free him with an appropriate fine."

So, noted the reporter, he was willing to do López this favor, "even though he has been publicly critical of your campaign." Elizondo waved that away, with dispatch. "All part of what it means to be politicians, he and I. *Señor* López has a perfect right to be a critic. He's a champion of the indigenous population. As I am. My mother was once an Indian servant, and I'm very well acquainted with the problems of the Maya in this hemisphere. López and I take different approaches, that's all."

The camera zoomed in then full-face on the reporter, who appeared to grope a second for the next question. "According to the media, a woman named Magdalena Rodriguez was found lifeless in the back of *Señor* López's truck, after he was released from custody. Have you been privy to any further information about that woman?"

My blood pressure spiked, almost lifting me off the chair. "Of course not," Elizondo said. Now it was his face that filled the screen, in obvious disapproval.

Back to the reporter, who looked unfazed. "Any word about how she died?"

"No," Elizondo said. "No, and I believe that's a question for the authorities, isn't it, not me."

Until now there had been no vocal responses from any of us here in front of the set. Now Sam sputtered something disdainful, Carmen made an unspellable noise in her throat, and Luis said "Right." I heard a fourth voice as well, from somewhere up around the ceiling, in the same mellow baritone that was coming from the set. *Cat?* That was what it said, just that, and got no answer.

The reporter's face filled the screen again, wearing a thoughtful frown. "All right. Let me ask it another way. Apparently, Luis López was the last person to see her alive. That could be meaningful. In your opinion, do you think López is capable of murder?"

Carmen gave a hoot and Sam and I leaped to our feet. I thought he was going to smash the set. If he didn't, I would. Elizondo appeared shocked as well, for a second speechless, then indignant. "I don't like that question either," he said. "Who am I to pre-judge another man? Leave that to the courts." He stammered a little, then recovered himself. "Listen, no one hates violence more than I do. I take the commandments seriously. Thou shalt not kill. But am I capable of it? Yes. Of course. Are you? Yes. Ex-president Ríos Montt referred often to the rottenness of humanity, and Luis López is just a human being with weaknesses like the rest of us. Granted, clowns are apt to get themselves into trouble. But let's not start rumors. Rumors are also a form of violence."

"But aren't violent measures sometimes necessary?" asked the reporter.

"Of course they are. Yes, there may be times when we find it necessary to be the instruments of God's justice. But there are right ways to do that. Our Minister of Defense has declared a reversal of Clausewitz, not war as politics, as the slogan goes, but politics as war—our present, on-going war with subversive forces. And I say no, that's wrong. It's not a political war we are fighting, but a spiritual one—spiritual warfare—and we can win it by holding out God's reconciling love to the enemy. God's blessing, which means health and wealth and well-being. That's what the Good News party and I offer to this nation and to the world." He gave the little laugh I'd heard before, as if he had embarrassed himself.

And the interview was over. Sam turned off the TV. "Straight out of schmoodom! A set-up. Can he do that? Set that up on a major station?"

"He plays squash with the station manager," said Luis, matter-of-factly.

"But surely he didn't get you released with a phone call."

"He could. He's got friends in the military. Pew mates, so to speak."

"Who would have tipped him off in the first place?" asked Sam. My question, too, my big question, but I didn't say so, and Sam continued. "And why are you so important to him? Does he think you're an opponent? Gonna run for office?"

"I've said over and over, in public, that I'm not, but he doesn't believe me. He knows I represent a big hunk of the Mayan population who don't vote and won't, except for someone who will give them back their share of land. So I guess that makes me important."

"Well then, if he's smart, he'll try to make you a running mate," Sam said.

"Ha. It would never fly, and he knows it. He offers a top-down approach. It rewards those who conform."

I was listening to all this with one ear, while the baritone *Cat?* spoke over and over in the other. I heard it now with a background of other voices, many, outdoors on lighted terraces, and a marimba band playing the Guatemalan national anthem.

"Actually, I think you baffle him," said Sam. "You undercut the binary semiotics of identity."

"*Qué?*"

"Ha, gotcha. You defy easy classification. You're an Indian, but you live like a Ladino. You're highly educated, but who would know it? You're a Christian and a heretic, a peacenik and a threat."

Luis sent me his crippled grin. "Anthropology."

"Sam's wrong," I said. "You bad. Bad Indian. Play ball with high stakes. Sacrifice the young. Kill babies."

"And we discovered the zero. The value of nothingness. Could I run for office on that platform?"

"Okay," said Sam, "let's take this guy at his word. He hates violence, he says. If he knocks you off, that makes you a folk hero. So he decides to diminish you, with kindness. He hears you're in trouble. He gets you out of it. He tells the world. He looks good, you look bad. There's more than one way to victimize an opponent."

"But just a minute," said Carmen. "Luis is not a victim. He's not anybody's victim. He's never been."

A quick reaction from Luis. "Oh, I don't know. I think about that a lot. Maybe I am. How do you be a good victim? That's my question. How do you be wise and harmless when the wolves come around? There are people in the Pan-Mayan community who think my style is all wrong."

"And if your style gets you into even worse trouble, then what?" said Sam.

"Hey, at least I'll be in good company."

Carmen stood, or rather shot straight up out of her chair. "It's time for some tea," she announced. She walked to the kitchen, her head high, that classy bearing, now a body language of exasperation. I followed, mumbling something about helping.

She was reaching for cups from a shelf too high for her. "Everything all right?" I whispered, gesturing to help.

"Yes," she said, nudging me away. "I'm just so mad I could—bust. With Luis, I mean. Victim, victim. What's he think, he's going to rise again on the third day? And he won't defend himself. Never just plain I didn't do it. I didn't get *borracho*. I didn't pick up a *puta*. I didn't kill her. I didn't abandon her in the *basurero*. He won't say that right out. He just wonders if he's being wise and harmless. *Dios mío!* You know?"

She whacked down a cup, knocking it off the counter. I caught it. Oops, too much like a correction. Her eyes flashed at me as they had days ago when I called her brave. She filled the tea kettle with water and set it on the stove. "I know him," she said. "I know what he is trying to do. But sometimes he takes things too far. —Do you think he really is a clown?"

"Well, I suppose, in a way," I said. "Sort of like a holy fool?"

She took it as I meant it, smiling now. "*Sí pues,* but not so holy."

Back in the parlor area Sam and Luis were arguing. Sam wanted Luis to go on TV himself and tell his side of the story, and Luis found the idea repelling. His eyes had grown dull. I knew he must be in pain.

We drank tea in silence, then turned the TV back on and watched a replay of a Mexican mystery. It was very bad. In it, the detective wrote down all the clues on his fingernails and studied them while subtitles spelled their content. Finally, just minutes from the end, his eyes lit up with realization. "Motive, means and opportunity!" he cried, and out the door he dashed, out into blackest night, bleary-eyed, unarmed, all alone, no backup, straight into obvious danger, to save somebody from a certain fate, just in the nick of time.

Lying in bed later, I heard it again. *Cat?*

"Did he recognize you?" Is that how I asked it? What did she say? "I doubt it. My hair was very short back then." When was that, *back then?* And if he knew her first name, Cat, wouldn't he know her last? Then what did it mean to him that the woman, "that woman," in the back of Luis's truck, was also named Rodriguez?

THIRTY-THREE

In the morning, Luis and Carmen left for Xela to check on things at the office there, then to Las Cavernas to assure his mother and other villagers that he was all right. Dina chauffeured them, refusing to let them go alone. Sam and I agreed to answer the door and telephone while they were gone. Molly, our early warning system, went with them, so we were the front line of defense. If there was any trouble with "difficult drop-ins," Carmen instructed, call either of the *padres*, Henri or Ramón. And just hang up on any threatening messages. She said nothing about a police raid or a military invasion.

As soon as they left, I called Carlos Méndez. Before I could ask my question, he asked his. Had I heard yet from Catherine? No, I said. Then I asked my question and he said yes. Yes, he did call Elizondo and ask for help for Luis, and Zondo did intervene successfully, and Luis was freed, and bully that!

So now I knew for sure, it *was* my call that started the process. I had actually done something right, however accidentally. For one second I exulted. In the next second, Méndez-the-cheery was venting his shock and horror, his rage at that terrible story about the dump, that woman with Magdalena's ID, such a terrible disgrace for "poor Mag." But he had the answer, he said. It had been stolen, of course. Just days after Catherine moved out of the house the place was invaded. Yes, yes, one night. Neighbors heard noises and called the police. The place was ransacked. Papers and belongings strewn everywhere. A priest from the Cathedral had told him about it.

This was stunning news. "What night did it happen?" I asked. Monday, he said. I checked back. Where was Catherine on Monday night? With me at the *posada,* on the narrow mattress on the floor. No reason to tell that to Méndez, or tell him anything.

I spent most of the rest of the day writing, obsessed now with getting everything down. Sam was organizing his own notes, packing up his files. Otherwise we were not busy. The kitchen women did not appear, or kids to watch television. But as always in that house, even when nothing was happening, everything was. Bases loaded. I hovered by the phone, waiting to hear from Smitty and dreading what I might.

Three calls came in, one from a guy who offered to lend Luis his gun, one from an animal shelter trying to sell him a guard dog, *barato*, cheap, and another from a lady who wished to remind everyone what a son of a bitch Luis had turned out to be. Then Benita, Carmen's sister, called. She wanted to talk to "one of the women." No women here just now, I told her. She didn't ask who I was and I didn't offer. She said she hated to bother me but one of the little girls in her charge was worried about her *oso de peluche*. I didn't catch that. "Bear," she said. "It's a big pink bear in their bedroom." Would I mind very much checking on him—it?

"Sure, I know that bear," I said.

"You do? Oh, *bueno*. She just wants to hear that he is still there. She's worried that someone might steal him while she's gone."

"No problem. Tell her I was chatting with that very bear just yesterday morning and—what's his name?"

"Teddy. Teddy bear." That in English.

"Of course," I said. "Teddy is still here and feeling fine, but he misses her and hopes she'll come back soon."

"Oh, thank you. That's such a help." She said I must be a *taita*, a daddy. I said no, but I understood about "still there."

And who was she talking to, by the way, she wanted to know. "I'm Teddy," I told her.

Soon after, a message from Smitty. He bore it in person. Best not phoned, he said. The morgue agreed to hold the body another twenty-four hours. I braced for the next statement, but it was none of the versions I had prepared myself to hear. "We're out of it," Smitty said. "The Embassy, that is."

Was that good news? He thought it was. "That's all I can tell you. But the boy is here, the son, still in the city, at the Embassy, and he wants to meet you. Maybe he'll explain things. He wants you to carry a sign with your middle name on it. I don't know why."

I put on my Red Sox cap, visor up, and drove like a Guatemalan through Saturday traffic to zone ten, my hopes soaring. It was a bright afternoon, with racing clouds and a wind that blew the smog off the mountains. For the first time in this city, I smelled no trace of rancid smoke. It seemed like a good omen and I was not beyond omens.

The Embassy building, a concrete box bordered by a high steel fence, filled the corner at Avenida la Reforma and 7A Calle. I parked as close as I could and walked back toward the handful of people lingering at the closed gate, feeling silly with my "Cavalier" sign, printed big on a page from a canary pad.

A kid in a black sweatshirt and a Yankees cap came to meet me. The cap raced my heart, until I saw that it was much grungier than hers. As for the boy, here was Saint Paddy for sure, a round face with a splash of freckles, ruddy cheeks, reddish hair around the ears below the cap, and a light glow of early beard across his chin. A cherubic altar boy grown up. The Indian heritage was in his build. He was about five ten, a happy balance between his father and mother, but with the muscular Mayan physique, heavy shoulders.

"I'm Ted Peterson," I said, reaching out my hand.

"I know who you are," he said. His dark eyes, a gift from both parents, were unsmiling. "She told me about you in her phone call."

"She *called?*" Hope spiraled out of control. "When? When did she call?"

"Tuesday."

"Oh." The call from my room at the Santo Tomás hotel.

"I haven't heard from her since," he said.

God, what was the matter with me? We were talking about his mother. "Are you okay?" I asked. His answer was "Yeah."

"Let's talk inside," I said.

"We can't. It's closed. It's closed to the public on Saturday."

"Where's your Embassy contact?"

"He's gone. We met inside for a while in his office. Afterwards."

Where next then? A nice, safe restaurant. "Are you up to eating something?" I asked.

"I could use a drink," he said. "A shake, maybe. Could we go to McDonalds?"

McDonalds, of course. What kind of a venue do you seek after a visit to a morgue? "You know where to find one?"

"Sure," he said. "There's a new one here, just built." He probably knew how to get to every McDonalds in Central America.

He guided me through the traffic, as Catherine had done just a week before to the day, almost to the hour. The McDonalds we entered looked exactly like every one I'd ever been in, except it was smaller and almost empty. "Only rich people here can afford McDonalds," Alex said, as we chose a booth. It was an oddly irrelevant remark, apropos of nothing that mattered so achingly at the moment. In the same spirit we both ordered chocolate shakes, double thick, sixteen ounces. Better, I thought, than drinking beers at a bar, but not all that different. We sat without further talk, slurping our straws noisily to the bottom of our paper containers. I examined his face, bent over as he drank. What was he carrying, relief, grief or horror? He wore that blank look teenagers perfect for adults, and that's what I was right now, I supposed, just another adult. I prepared myself for the possibility that he would not explain a thing.

Finally he spoke, his line of vision just outside of mine. "I thought I would puke, but I didn't."

"Good for you." I waited.

"They gave us nose masks, and plastic bags over our shoes, the Embassy guy and me."

I waited again.

"He told me how they'd found her, in some guy's truck. In the dump."

"So it seems," I said.

He turned his straw upside down and squinted into it, up to the ceiling. "The truth is, I couldn't really tell, if it was her, I mean."

"I see," I said.

"I had no way to prove it, I mean." He met my gaze squarely now, as if my reaction suddenly mattered. "To them, I mean, the morgue guy, or the embassy guy. The face was messed up bad. I couldn't tell for sure."

"I see. Was she tall?"

"I thought so, but she was lying down. It may sound funny, but I haven't seen my mother lying down that much. I mean, she was in this body bag and they unzipped it. She was stiff. What do you call it?"

"Rigor mortis?"

"She had no—there were no clothes. Her arms were crossed." He demonstrated with his own, covering breasts. "Like, if there'd been clothes, I might have recognized something. I asked the morgue guy, where are her clothes, and he told me this is how she was found."

"When I saw your Mom last she was wearing—," I said. I couldn't tell him she was wearing his aunt's clothes. "My Red Sox windbreaker." I pictured it on her, zipped to the chin. "White nylon," I added, gratuitously.

"I didn't see that. There weren't any clothes."

"What about her eyes?" I asked, thinking to move the physical focus. But eyes? A dumb mistake.

He answered. "Half-closed. I couldn't see them. She—." He stopped. He paused a long time. "It could have been her hair, I suppose."

"Are you okay with this?" I asked.

He nodded, a duck of the head. "I don't know what to tell you. Maybe you could ask me some questions."

I was touched by this, beyond words. He was trying, after all, though he had no obligation to tell me anything. "Did anyone say how she died?" Wrong question again, probably the cruelest. I faltered. "This woman, I mean?"

"Not really," he answered, doing better than I. "The Embassy guy said they couldn't be sure without an autopsy, but it looked like she was beaten. I could see her teeth. They were broken, some not there."

A family entered, two small children and a grandmother type. The kids ran to separate booths and were herded firmly to a third.

"So you didn't know," I said. "If it actually was —."

"Actually, I *felt* it was. You know what I mean? But I didn't want it to be. Maybe that was part of it. I wasn't sure. Really. I'm not now." He slurped air noisily through his empty straw.

"Are you up for seconds?" I asked. He was. Strawberry this time, he said. He must own a bladder like a horse. I went to the cashier, glad for a brief hiatus as I waited in line behind the grandmother. I carried her tray of food to the children, then went back for Alex's second shake.

"So what did you decide?" I asked. "What did you finally tell them?"

He was ready for this one, maybe wondering why I hadn't yet asked it. "Well, first, I thought I was going to say yes it is my mom, just in case it really is, you know, but then I thought it might get into a police report and I didn't think she'd want that, because of how she was found, I mean. I knew I couldn't lie and say it really is my aunt, *Tía* Mag, because she died a month ago in Antigua and the police have got to already know that. And I knew if I said I don't know who it is, they'll dump her in that cemetery there near the morgue. *La Verbena.* Everybody knows about that place. It's where they stick the bodies of *putas* and other unnamed people." He stopped to take a shaky breath. "And I knew. I mean, I knew that what she would *want* is to be buried there, if she is really dead, you know, because that's where my father got put when my grandparents wouldn't claim him."

"Right."

"Do you know how my father died?" he asked.

"Just a little."

"How he was found, all that shit?"

"And your grandparents refused to claim him?"

"Yes. So he was buried at *Verbena.* My Mom told me he'd be honored to be there in that cemetery, with all the other victims. That's what I decided. I told them I don't know who this woman is. It's nobody I know. So she'll be buried in the same place with my father—if it's her."

I released a slow whoosh of air. "And they bought that, at the morgue?"

"Sure. They asked me to sign a form and I did."

"No questions?"

"Nope. I could tell nobody cared. They don't care who she is or what happens to her," he said, his voice rising, the first detectable edge of anger. "They took my word. The Embassy guy asked me if I thought my family would insist on an investigation. I just said no and nobody asked any more questions."

"But if she's an American citizen."

"But she's not. She switched a long time ago. Before I was born."

"She's a Guatemalan citizen?" Did she ever tell me that? I'd remember. The passport she'd shown me at the hotel was definitely U.S. Or maybe a fake, like Magdalena's. "I think you did the right thing," I said. "You did well." He didn't answer. Then he said, "If it's not my mother, who is it, anyway?"

"Was she wearing a bracelet?"

"What bracelet?"

"I gave her a snake bracelet," I explained. "She put it on her left wrist. Then we couldn't get it off." But surely, I thought, jewelry would be removed at a morgue. So they'd have to cut it, with wire cutters, and if they did, where was it?

"I don't know," he said. "Her hands—." He didn't finish. I knew. Rats and dogs in the dump. Move on, move on. "Did they show you any possessions?"

"They showed me a plastic bag. But it had only one thing in it, that blue thing like my Mom wears—wore in her hair, sometimes."

"Jesus," I whispered. "Where is it?"

"They took it back."

I shut my eyes, listening to the children, giving their grandma a hard time. Alex was watching me when I opened them. "Are you all right?" *He* asking me.

"What about the ID they found? Did they show you that?"

"The Embassy guy asked. They said the police have it."

Sure. The police would keep it. "There should be a small purse," I said. "And a big bag, woven, crocheted or something. She had those with her."

"I didn't see those. What about her other things? Her own passport and money and everything. All her fucking stuff, where would it be?"

I stared into the remaining fluff of my chocolate drink. "I've got her suitcase out in the car. You should take that."

"How would she end up in that fucking truck, anyway?" His voice broke, slipping from low to high.

"It's got to be a coincidence," I said. "A really crazy coincidence."

He finished his drink. "I'd better get going."

"Let me drive you."

"All right." To his friend's house, if I didn't mind. He was staying there overnight, then tomorrow flying back home to Costa Rica.

In the car he pointed me south, to the Avenue of the Americas, then dropped his face into his hands and sat that way as we drove. It was hard to imagine his pain. I wondered if I should touch him, but if I did, we would both fall apart. When he looked up, his eyelids were red but I saw no tears. Not for me to witness.

"You liked her, right?" he said.

"Yes."

"Were you lovers?" His mother's unwavering directness. It lifted my spirits. His spirits too, I sensed, the subject moving from possible death to some evidence of life.

" 'Ours is a high and lonely destiny,' " I said, keeping the present tense.

He looked surprised, then caught the spin and rewarded me with Catherine's smile, the real one. "She told me things about you."

"She did?"

"Yes, when she called. She said you lost your father, too, when you were little."

"When I was seven."

"No shit? I was nine." He looked at me again. "What about your mother?"

"Still alive. Though you could say I lost her too."

"You were sort of an orphan, then. And now I am, maybe. She told me, when she began making trips, not to worry if I didn't hear from her for long periods. She'd get word to me when she could. I think I'll believe she's alive."

" 'The presence of an absence,' " I murmured, not sure who I was quoting. "What are your plans for yourself? For the future."

"I'm thinking about the priesthood. Except I really like girls. And maybe I'll finish my father's book someday."

"What's it about. Your Mom was a little vague."

"I can't tell you much. It's about rich people here, how they influence the country."

"You've got his files?"

"Oh sure. We've got them locked away. My Mom said once she thought that was why he was killed. He was checking out some secrets, about people we know. Look, there's where you turn, on your left. Quick, left turn."

And here we were in Catherine's old neighborhood, where we'd been together one week ago. In the sudden quiet my VW motor seemed rudely loud. We crawled down the shady boulevard, lawns and flowering vines on both sides of us. I breathed in newly cut grass, refusing to raise my eyes to the machine gun nests. Alex pointed out the stone paved lane that led to his old home, as Catherine had done. "You grew up here," I said.

"Yup." He named the families as we rode by the gates, the Zamoras, the Riveras, the Flores, the Pieros over there. "Bunch of kids there. I played with them. Melanos there."

"The Melanos?"

"There at the green gate."

Old friends, Catherine had said. Did she say "old neighbors"?

"You know them?" asked Alex.

Met them, sort of, I told him. "Your Mom chose to ride with them to the airport." He looked confused. "They were at the same hotel we were, at Atitlán," I explained. "They were flying to Costa Rica. She decided to go with them, maybe the same plane."

I stopped the car. They could be back. They might be able to tell us something. "You go," I said. "They may not trust me."

He was already out of the car, trotting down the driveway. I watched him pause there, peer through the gate, lift a phone from a box on a pole, listen, hang up and trot back. "No one there. They're still away."

"I'll try later," I said.

"I'm kind of surprised she went with them, you know? They're sort of jerks."

"She said it was best, for everyone. That's what she told me."

He mouthed the word "best." I could see in his face the questions it raised, as it raised them for me. I wanted to tell him something more reassuring, a better way to end this meeting. "In fact, she seemed glad, sort of gay," I said. "That was my last picture of her, in their car. She was smiling. Gave me a funny salute."

"Oh, sure. She and my Dad used to salute each other a lot like that, sort of a take-off on the Exploradores. That's a neighborhood do-gooder thing."

"I know. Run now by that politician, Elizondo?"

"Sure. Zondo. His place was next to ours. Right there. He and my Dad were childhood pals."

"Your mother didn't mention that."

"Well, she sort of didn't like him. After my Dad died they weren't friends anymore. I guess she didn't tell you that either." He shrugged. "I didn't get it. To me, he was a nice guy. He'd always let us use his pool and stuff." He pointed down a lane. "Go there. My *amigo* is waiting."

We crunched onto a driveway filled with white pebbles, a black iron gate ahead of us, closed. Alex's hand reached for the door handle. I slowed to a crawl, suddenly worried about him, gripped by worry. He opened the door, ready to leap out. Into what? He was the heir of more than anyone ought to inherit, the child of parents who knew too much. Was he aware of that? I blurted: "Look, it's none of my business, but your mother's family, in Wisconsin. Do you know how to contact them?"

His smile became Catherine's again, the teasing one, as if I'd used the wrong verb tense. "I'll tell you my secret," he said, shutting the door. "I've never told my Mom, because she and her family, they're kaput. My uncle Kevin in Milwaukee, her brother and me, we've been talking on the phone for a couple of years. He keeps inviting me. There are cousins I've never met."

"That's perfect!" I said. "So what would you think of going to visit him, stay awhile, until things calm down around here?"

He didn't reply to that, patiently abiding my adulthood, I was sure, my parental over-concern. But he said thanks anyway, sincerely, and for the ride and the shakes and everything.

Somebody yelled. A kid in a sleeveless sweat shirt was walking toward us down the driveway, pumping his fist in the air. Alex jumped out. The gate opened automatically. The two met and gave each other a high-five that ended in a neck lock, a comfort I couldn't offer him. I watched them walk down the driveway in that tough embrace before I drove away, back to the green gate, the Melanos. I needed to know for myself.

There was no sign of life on the property, what I could see through the gate. No manned machine gun, no snarling mastiff behind a fence. I lifted the phone from its box on a post. A male voice spoke instantly, recorded. The Melano family was traveling and not available. Click. Not even an invitation to leave a message.

I spat into the phone. Not very effectively, not with one of those big globs people come up with in the movies, or with the aim of that old woman at Las Cavernas, who landed one at my feet. God, I don't even know how to spit, I thought, actually close to tears. I heard something then. I can't say it was another click, but it lifted my eyes to the top of the post, ten feet above me. My picture had been taken.

I'd forgotten to give Alex the suitcase. He and his friend were still in the driveway and the gate was still open. I met him as he walked to me, his face a question. I said, "You've got to go." I didn't wait for him to answer. "Get out of here, for your Mom's sake. Because she'd want you to. Go to Milwaukee. Go pay a long visit to your uncle and cousins. Do it for her. Don't wait."

His face grew serious as I blundered on. I expected him to blow me off, just an intrusive adult bastard. But I was misreading him again. "All right," he said, breaking in. "I'll go. I will. I promise. I'll call Uncle Kevin tonight."

"Go as soon as possible."

"I have to go back to Costa Rica first. I have to get a visa."

That was as far as I had the right to take it. "This is new to me, this business," I said. "All this anxiety. I'm not very good at it."

"Oh. He-e-ey!" He drawled out the word, as if I were the child. I thought it was a Catherine tease, but he was earnest. "You shouldn't worry. Everything's gonna be okay." He reached up and touched the visor of his Yankees cap, then brought his finger to mine, visor to visor. "But the Red Sox," he said, shaking his head sadly. "No hope there. Still under the curse of the Bambino."

THIRTY-FOUR

I drove around the city for an hour or more after that, aimlessly, slowly, into neighborhoods and out, almost hoping I'd be spied. I'd have welcomed anything concrete, specific, unquestionable. "Why don't you help me?" I heard myself ask my father, the old childhood resort. "That's what you're supposed to do."

I drove past the Parque Central, past the palace, then to the parking lot below the Cathedral, where we'd hugged over the gear shift of my red Cruiser. That was the scene I relived, that awkward hug, her softened face, our histories and a possible future blending for just a few seconds.

The alley was empty, the entrance blocked by a barricade. No cars, no sudden appearance of the brawny owner, or Catherine herself in some new disguise. I sat there a long time in that forlorn place, my head on the steering wheel. Nuts to the presence of an absence. She had to be alive. It was a necessity, not just a wish or a hope. There was evidence for it, after all, wasn't there? No bracelet. No tell-tale clothing. Just a headband—which could be anyone's. No bag.

Wait. No bag, no *Yertle the Turtle*. The bag could have been lost or tossed away by someone, somewhere, the worn-out old book along with it. Or it could have been stolen. Or not stolen. She could still have it. She could go back to the mountains, to deliver that map. It was exactly the kind of thing she would do, finish that errand.

Foolish thoughts. I knew only one thing. Dead or alive, she was missing. *Desaparecida*, at least to me. This is what it feels like. I thought of all the things people do when someone is missing. Call the police, trace steps, call everyone who might know something, tack a picture on a tree with that terrible question, *¿DÓNDE ESTÁ?* Or stand on a street corner with the picture in my hands. Walk around with it. Have you seen this woman? Really tall with a lot of dark hair. But I didn't have a picture anyway, not even Magdalena's, and if it were Catherine's own she would not want me to show it, and she would not—a shaft of truth I couldn't evade any longer—would not want me to know where she is, for my sake as well as hers, for everyone's sake. She might not have gone to the mountains, but wherever she was it was a place far beyond me. Let her go. It's over. She'll go her way and I'll go mine, just as she once predicted. We were never meant for the long haul.

It was turning dark and the rain had begun. It was not a good place to be, parked outside this deserted alley. I pulled away. Time to get going.

Back on 5a Avenida I got locked in the worst traffic jam yet, a lethal mix of exhaust, downpour and headlights. I settled in, resigned to be a small part of this creeping horn-blowing monster, when the car behind me, a green van, slipped in closer and shot its high beams into my mirror. I put up my hand to shade my eyes, all it ought to take to get a half-decent road hog to back off. The message was ignored. I pulled up into the space I'd been trying to maintain between me and the car ahead. The joker behind moved with me, all but riding the bumper of my Bug, a bully teasing a smaller kid.

Of course I wondered if my brashness of the last hours had actually drawn attention. Had I been followed all along, or just discovered? Two men in a green van, Catherine had claimed. I decided to stay in the middle of traffic. That was the safest place, if there were any intentions here beyond bullying. It was hardly likely they would do anything to cause a chain reaction accident. I stuck it out for a mile or so, then it was over. The van turned off at a side street, disappearing into the dark and rain.

Just as I reached Calle Marti I saw it again, behind me fifty feet or so, just visible in the thinned out traffic. It must have circled around on an alternate path. Calle Marti was a well-lit commercial boulevard. As they drew closer I could see two heads in the front. Oh, please, not a stupid car chase.

I considered pulling over to the side, getting out and flagging them down, yelling "Hello there! What do you want?" in unmistakable U.S. English. That would be stupid, too. Incredibly. My only recourse was to stay on this route, though I had no idea what kind of territory or circumstances lay beyond my usual turn-off. I crossed the bridge over the ravine and started the climb up the hill. When I looked back, a bus was passing the van, spewing its thick diesel cloud. It came between us, blocking my view, and theirs too, I hoped. I turned while I had the chance, not into Community Garden, but into the barrio below the hill. I was aiming for the white church, thinking the words "asylum" and "sanctuary."

But I'd trapped myself. It was a reckless mistake. The alley was thick with mud and so narrow I could have reached out my window and touched the walls of the houses, plywood, cardboard. A man with a sheet of plastic over his head pressed out of the way as I passed. I slewed, straightened, worried about hitting someone, a stray child. Two big dogs raced to my front tires, one on each side, barking wildly. I couldn't find the horn. When I did, it produced only the Bug's hoarse beep. I slowed, then saw the van coming behind me and ducked as headlights entered my back window. But there were no shots, just a sudden loud thump and a howl. The van stopped. I heard shouts and saw people running out of their houses. They'd struck a dog. It lay in the road in front of them, caught in their lights.

I plowed on to the end of the alley, pausing outside the church. It was dark, door closed. I turned up into the Community Garden lane, angry with myself, and drove the Bug into the patio as far as it could go behind the vines, then started on foot down the hill to the barrio, across the dark empty field. I had no idea what I meant to do, except not to be the one who walked away from this craziness. When I got between the shacks, everything looked the same. I'd found the right lane in the maze, I was sure, but the van was gone. Dogs, yes, but no dead or injured ones. A head poked out around a curtain door, then pulled back in as I approached. I stopped by a group of men, smoking. Did a dog get hit by a car here just now? They shrugged, silently. Did a green van come through here? Shrugs again. It was so dark I could see only glimpses of their faces as their cigarettes glowed. There were four of them. This was stupid too, stupid, stupid. Nothing was right. No right alternative. I climbed back up the hill, refusing to look behind me or listen for the sudden scurry of feet.

Sam was in the kitchen. "There's not much food," he said. He'd been eating beans out of a can. The sink was full of dishes. I washed a glass and drank some water from the *agua pura* jug.

I should tell him what happened. He had a right to know. "By the way," I said, as casually as I could fake it, "I think I was followed just now."

He was sawing through a hunk of hard bread and stopped. "No joke? Did you get a look at who?"

"Not a good one, no." I put some leftover coffee on the stove to heat. My hands were shaking.

"I half expect it myself, all the time," Sam said. "But it's a big risk, going after a U.S. citizen. Maybe they just meant to scare you. Yankee, go home."

"I got the feeling they meant to run me off the road."

"Ha. Sure. You have this unfortunate accident."

"And I die from the injuries?"

"No. You walk away unscathed, but never to be seen again. A clever way to get rid of a Yankee."

Or a Scandinavian on the lam. It seemed loonier than ever, too silly to mention.

"So what have you done to make yourself such a target?" Sam asked.

"I'll never tell."

He leaned back against the sink, his round-shouldered slouch accentuated. "Well, anyway, it's clearly time to go home. I'm ready, are you?"

I agreed, though I knew we meant different things. He meant home to his wife and girls, and to an established teaching position, with classes soon scheduled to start. I meant back to a half-furnished apartment, with no settled employment, and a mother who thought I was my father. But she still needed me. It was time to get back to her.

"I need to be with my mother," I said. That didn't come out quite right, but Sam said, "I know the feeling." He sawed away at the bread. "There's no excuse for me to be here now," he said.

I agreed again. He meant he'd completed his research, I supposed. For me it meant no longer waiting here for a call I had no solid reason to believe would come, no reason to fly to Costa Rica—none I could defend—and no longer a justified hunt for my father's secret. I'd found my essential facts, hadn't I? Met my *agenda?* And my moratorium, that convenient fantasy, waved at me vaguely from a distance, like a faded old flag.

"I hate to leave Luis in this mess," Sam said. "If I knew I was doing some good, maybe I could find a way to stay. But I don't think I'm helping now."

"And I'm certainly not."

"What's crazy is that we *can* leave," he said. "Just because we can. That's pretty miraculous."

I played with that, the permission itself, a roaring lift-off into the sky, peering down on all this perplexity and chaos, re-crossing the border without question. It still felt like abandonment, incompletion, but it was time to go.

Sam whacked the bread loaf on the counter and split it in two. We dunked it in the coffee until it was chewable. I found a can of beef stew I'd bought in that shopping and warmed it up. Someone had left a ripe melon on the doorstep, a small one, green and oval, and we ate that too.

THIRTY-FIVE

The next morning, as I was trimming my new beard growth, I thought of Pat Crane. I was half-dressed, standing at the only decent mirror in the house, over the kitchen sink. Sam was "observing" at the chapel next door, where the Sunday morning service had already begun with singing and shouting.

My beard had been returning unevenly, with a tinge of red, which brought Crane, the redbearded, to mind. I had promised I would connect with him when I left him at breakfast in the Chichi hotel. I knew what he wanted, an interview with another hapless MK for his dissertation. I didn't want to do it. By chance he was not yet back from wherever he had gone. That's what I hoped.

I needed a haircut, too, this mirror suggested. I considered shaving my head. At worst it would make me look like an aging street punk. Was my Norwegian *doppleganger* hairy or bald? I knew only that he had a beard, because Catherine had said so. I began to snip away at the new facial hair. Shaving would have been preferable, but the outlets were giving no power. Electric service had gone off during the night.

That little detail is significant, because it meant I could hear better without the noise of my razor, and I did hear something. I heard what I thought was movement in the room overhead, which was mine. I heard it again. Maybe Sam had come back. But I'd have seen him. It was hard to slip by anybody in this house and I'd heard no one on the noisy stairs. I stepped out of the kitchen and looked around. "Sam? *Hola?*" Nothing. The only sound now was outside the house, the singing and clapping at the chapel. I checked the doors to make doubly sure they were locked. They were. It was a minor deterrent, but we had agreed last night to lock the doors ("Nuts to Dorothy

Day") and I knew Sam had taken a key. In fact, he had forgotten and returned to get one, shouting to me. Where was I then? Out between the houses, pulling a wash off the line there.

Suddenly it seemed important to get some more clothes on. I abandoned the barbering and climbed the stairs with as much noise as I could make in my bare feet, enough to scare off a rodent. The scissors were still in my hand.

The door to my room was open, as I'd left it, and someone had been there. The contents of my pack and suitcase were all over the floor. My single impulse was to get out of the house as fast as I could, through the nearest exit, the roof. Then I saw a foot under one of the beds. It was a child's, very dirty.

"*Sale, tú,*" I said, depositing the scissors on top of the dresser. The foot retreated. "Come out, come out!" I sang. Don't worry. "*No te preocupes.*" I won't hurt you, kiddo. We can die of fright together.

A little girl emerged, slowly, head first. She stood up. She was tiny. It was hard to tell her age. Her face and lack of front teeth suggested six or seven, but her frame was the size of a three year old. Malnutrition. She must have slipped in when Sam returned for the key, and of course she headed for the room she knew held the toys. And my stuff? What was she looking for? I did a quick check. My wallet was on the dresser exactly where I'd left it, with a roll of mints and a pen. Her hands were empty.

A little girl in my bedroom was not a good idea in any country and I was half bare. I backed off as far as I could, assuming what I hoped was an unthreatening posture. "*Ahora es el momento de volver a casa,*" I said. Time to go home. I said it gently, anxious not to scare her any more than I supposed she was. She didn't leave. Instead, she said "*Ayuda,*" help, and turned to pick up something from the bed.

It was the black leather case that held my father's Bible. She had unwrapped it from the Wheaties box that had enclosed it. Sure enough, Jackie Robinson stared up at us from the floor. She tugged at the stuck zipper with her little fingers, grunting with the effort. What on earth did she think was inside? It was just something to be opened, I supposed, a curiosity, like a big black purse. "*Ayuda,*" she said again, pleadingly, and held it out to me. I shook my head no. She begged. "*Por favor.*"

Why not? When she saw what it was maybe she would leave willingly. I took it from her hands. As I fingered the zipper tag, my fingers felt the old sense of anticipation, remembering the piece of candy in the back pocket. Had she felt that, too? Maybe she did know, with some universal kid wisdom, that a surprise might be tucked into a case that looked like this.

I had to find out for myself. I applied force. The zipper split wide open and the whole back side of the case tore away. The Bible fell out and dropped to the floor with a loud clump. The child laughed, delighted at the performance. I picked the Bible up and showed her, see, just an old book, funny words, no pictures. I showed her the pocket in the back of the case. "*Nada*," I said. Empty.

I was disappointed and so was she. She let out a long "Ohhh." What could I give her instead? I grabbed the roll of mints from the dresser top and offered her one. She stuck it in her mouth and held up her hand for another. I gave her the roll. "Never take candy from a stranger," I said, in teacherly English. She laughed, though she couldn't have understood. I pointed to the door with a monster face. She ran, still giggling. I followed her down and out to the patio to make sure she was really gone. She turned in at the chapel, where the singing had risen to a new crescendo.

Then I searched the house again, downstairs and up, all the bedrooms, and yes, under the beds, before I returned to the mess in my own room and began straightening up. Lots of little girl things, doll clothes, crayons, parts of a Candyland game, all mixed in with my own belongings. The Bible had been damaged in the fall, the back cover half torn off. Reassembling it in the case, I saw something written on the rear flyleaf. The page was black and the writing was in pencil, my father's writing, the lead shiny on that background and hard to read. I brought it over to the window, squinting, tilting the page until the light hit it right. *Culpable.* In Spanish it would be Cul-PAB-lay, but it meant the same in both languages. Guilty. A date had been added at the bottom, 6/30/54. I read the word again and again, out loud, recording it in the air in case it should slip off the page and disappear.

I'd given up too easily. I hadn't done anything resembling a responsible search. My quest for "facts" was shamefully passive, and I knew why, the lingering, foolish fear that I would actually find something, and I was too easily persuaded that there was nothing to find, because that's how I wanted it. Now I knew there was *something*, and somebody else around here had to know what it was. Not Luis, or he'd have told me. He wouldn't lie. Nor would Alicia or Arturo. Maybe old Tomás Garcia, here in the city—I should try him again, though I hated to chance another linguistic tangle.

I pulled on pants and shoes and went back to the mirror in the kitchen, to my scraggly beard and hair, and so to Pat Crane. Pat did research. He dug into other people's lives. He'd dug into mine, my family's, and he'd found us, he told me, in some kind of an official government record. I couldn't remember the name of it. I had to call and at least ask him that, and go look for myself.

If he was in the city, he'd be at the Centenario Hotel. I dialed that. He was there. "Well, well," he said. "What a coinkidinky. I was just this morning wondering where one might be."

I told him one had a quick question. A question? Good. He wanted to see me anyway, "about a small personal problem." Not something he ought to discuss on a phone. Could I go there? He sounded a little desperate. He would be glad to come see me, but he was feeling rather poorly, not up to going abroad himself.

I was not happy about "going abroad" either, in that vulnerable Bug. But it was daylight, the sun was shining, the streets would be full of Sunday morning traffic. It even occurred to me, with an absurdity I should be getting used to, that thugs and assassins might not work on Sundays.

I finished with my hair, cleaned up the sink, and drove to the Centenario.

Crane's room looked the same as it did before, cluttered with piles of manuscript. He scooped out a place for me to sit on the unmade bed. He was unkempt himself. He was wearing the greasy cowboy hat and I had a hunch he'd been sleeping in his clothes. The god Thor gone to seed.

"Let's not lose a minute," he said. He sat down in the chair by the desk and uncovered a typewriter. It was a portable, a Royal that had seen better days. It looked like an old toy there in front of his oversized body. "Oh, my manners. I read about your friend Luis. How is he? That awful business. That lady in the dump."

He was rolling a thin sandwich into the typewriter, two blank sheets of paper with a carbon in between. He mouthed my name and the date as he typed them across the top of the page, his empty pipe bobbing up and down between his teeth. "And how are you faring?" he asked. "How's the *Red Badge?*"

"I haven't opened it since I got here."

" 'He had been to touch the great death!' " he quoted, his hands conducting a chorus. "And found that's all it was, 'the great death.' Something like that. You have a question for me. Ask away."

"It's about the archive you mentioned last week. The record of foreign visitors in the country."

He gave that some thought. "Oh, the *Archivo General de Centro America?*"

"That one. How extensive is the information there?"

"Mostly just arrival and departure of families. It's in microfilm. Your parents arrived in 1944, as I recall it, you got born somewhere in there and you and your parents departed the country in 1954."

"Nothing about my father? Not that he died here?"

"He did? Well, well. So who left the country?"

"My mother. I was already in the States."

"Well, let's get into that a little bit more."

He stared down at the typewriter keys, scratching his beard. I stared, too, at the paper. He'd typed my name in the upper case and the T key was malfunctioning, so I was (space) ED PE(space)ERSON. Whatever info he got from me, every time he typed my name I would be diminished by about a tenth of who I really was.

"Never mind that," I said. "You want to talk about something yourself, you told me."

"I did?"

"A personal problem, you said."

"Oh. So I did. Actually, it's not important. Now that you've asked. I get these moods, that's all." He rolled the paper up and down in his typewriter several times, the pages slipping and separating. He adjusted them, lined them up with industry, rolled them again, muttering, "No, no. It's nothing. Actually." Then he froze. He went absolutely still, hands quiet, face immobile, teeth clamped on his pipe.

"What's wrong?" I asked. I glanced around for the phone, ready to call for help. "Pat?"

He recovered himself. "Oh. Ignore me."

"What's the matter?"

A long drawn-out sigh. "You know how it is with dissertations."

"I don't."

"To be truthful, I'm lost," he said, spreading his arms limply. "Lost at sea. Lost my compass. Lost my—what's that other thing? Sextant. Not to bore you, but I don't know where I am. I'm becalmed. Drifting with the tide. You know how long I've been working on this thing? Nine years. Going on ten. And it just keeps swelling up like a bloated whale. I can't grab ahold of a thesis. Every expat, every MK I interview has a different story. There's no commonality. I'm at an impasse. Sorry to dump on you."

I fumbled. It was like finding the right words at a funeral. "Didn't you tell me you have a publisher? When we met on the plane?"

Crane pursed his lips around his pipe, then moved them into a big false smile, pipe in his front teeth. "That, my dear *amigo*, was an outright bald-faced lie."

"Ah."

"My apologies."

"Well, don't feel bad," I said. "I lied to you, too. I told you I teach at a particular school."

"Oh, yes. I forget which one."

"Me too. I made it up."

The pipe gave a farty blast and he shook with a spasm of soundless laughter. "Nevertheless!" he shouted, taking out his pipe and raising it over his head. "Nevertheless, Stephen Crane really is related to my great uncle!"

"You told me it was your grandfather."

He wiped his eyes. "It was Hart Crane, anyway. I mix them up. I'm not a real scholar, you know. Just a dilettante."

"And I'm a piddler." I tried to think of something comforting. "Lots of important people never got doctorates." I couldn't think of an actual real person and resorted to fiction. "Remember Jack Burden, in *All the King's Men*. He never finished his history dissertation."

"Oh yes. I don't recall why."

"The subject matter got too personal," I said. "He walked away from his research."

"Speaking of." Crane picked a notebook off the desk, glancing through it with a spurt of new industry. "Peterson, Peterson," the T audible, if muffled by the pipe. "Here we are. You and your family left here in 1954. And your father died, you say. So for you there were two losses then, weren't there, your homeland and a parent. How did you deal with that, one might ask?" The old Crane was coming back.

"Well, I didn't wet the bed or torture puppies."

"Up to that point, your father's death, what were your early years like?"

"They were good." He was not typing, I was glad to see. His fingers were not even on the keys.

"Not shipped off to a boarding school like so many MKs?"

"For a short while."

"Otherwise not neglected? Exploited?"

"Nope. Nor abused nor violated."

"Ever punished? Beaten?"

"Never."

"Not starved or neglected?"

"Never. Never sold as a sex slave. Fingernails never pulled out. Never sacrificed to the gods, not even once."

I'd gone too far. He was angry. He ripped the pages from the typewriter and threw them to the floor. "Right! You are absolutely right. And that is why I don't have a goddamn thesis!"

He picked up the typewriter, as if to throw it, but set it back down again with a bang. "Here's the truth of the matter. MKs and army brats, like you and me, are no worse off than any other middle-class kid. Oh, some have stupid parents. Who doesn't? Lucky kids, on the whole, the right color, right race, right religion, right size." He whirled to face me, the wretched typewriter behind him. "So what makes the difference in who they become? Why are some at home in the larger world, and why are some—?" He spread his arms helplessly.

"The lost children of Peter Pan?"

"Wow. That's beautiful."

"Your own words."

He didn't seem to remember. "Some are hard put to find their identity," he said. "So how would you classify yourself?"

"In flux."

"That doesn't help."

"I'd call it a thesis, myself." I stood and walked to the door.

"Hey, maybe it is. Don't go yet, please."

He looked forlorn. I went back and his eyes lit up, like an old lover. "You did come back," he said. "I mean, to this country. People do come back. I have that as record." He struggled for words, his hands moving as if he were picking up blocks he'd just knocked down. "Why do they? That's worth exploring. To look up a childhood friend, you told Luke. But is that the only reason?" He gave me his gnomish grin. "Are you here to reclaim your citizenship?"

"Which one?"

I could have given more thought to that, but Crane was sprinting ahead, full of new intensity. "To find something you think you lost? Dig something up? Rediscover family religion, by chance? Just a sociological question. Some MKs do that, I've been learning. Try on the old shoes."

He didn't wait for me to catch up and I didn't intend to. "I was with one just last week," he said. "Son of missionaries. Pentecostal, I think. Or Presbyterian. No, Nazarene. I mix them up. He'd strayed from the fold. He'd gotten away from the Lord, that's how he put it, and he's come back to find his childhood religion. He wants to convert me, too." He gave a whoop. "He invited me to a men's Bible class, at that enormous new church in the hotel district. Know the one I mean? Imported from California, I heard. Thousands of members, some of them wealthy citizens, this guy tells me. Government officials, military officers. There must have been a hundred men in this one class. It's all voodoo to me. Nice people, mind you, not strange. But the stuff they were saying. I made notes. I even bought a Spanish Bible from their book table." He snatched up a blue-jacketed paperback from the desk.

"I can hardly find my way around in this thing. *Deuteronomia*. That's what they were reading. Where is it?"

I reached for the book. "What's the passage?"

"Sir?"

"Chapter and verse."

"I have chapter 28 in my notes. Is that what you mean?"

I opened to it and handed it back, a show-off. Crane was goggle-eyed. "You know how to do that?"

I swiped my nose. "Years of practice." Well, I admitted, a Sunday School contest. I'd won a prize for rattling off all sixty-six books in the right order.

"Read it," said Crane. "Or do you know it by heart?"

I sat down to translate. It wasn't hard, taken loosely. "It says that if you worship the true God and obey his commandments your sheep herd will increase, your cows will give creamy milk, your bread will rise, and your grandchildren will multiply. However, if you disobey, you're toast. Crops will fail. Sheep get the mange. No grandchildren. No dissertation. No publisher. No job."

"Those guys play hard ball."

"That was written about four thousand years ago, if it's any comfort."

"Not much."

"I was taught that Jesus changed all that scary Old Testament stuff," I said.

"Oh yeah? Well, look what happened to him."

I riffled through the pages, hearing the sound as I always had, like a spate of gentle rain in the trees. My fingers stopped at the prophets. Major and Minor, whatever that meant. I felt suddenly defensive of the whole long crazy record, all the amazing voices, sane or obsessed, young upstarts and old cranks, speaking when no one was listening, which was most of the time.

Crane was riffling through his own pages, jowls in motion. "Where is it? It chilled my perpendicular. Here, got it, what somebody said in that class." He read aloud: "We should not be surprised at anything that happens to people on the wrong side of this equation. God himself will act in judgment. Our God is a God of tough love." He closed his notebook. "There's no middle ground, as I get it. If you're on the right side, you can expect to be rich, healthy and happy. That's what God wants. He especially wants it for this country."

"It sounds a lot like Elizondo." I stood to leave again.

"The politician, right. Somebody mentioned him. I think he goes to that church."

"He's *ubiquo*," I said. Catherine's word.

Crane shook with his silent, wheezy laugh through the pipe. "Well, put him on your prayer list. That's what somebody said. Pray for Zondo. He's got troubles. In fact, they prayed for him right at that moment. They called it a '*word* of prayer.'" That struck him funny, too.

"What troubles?" I'd gotten as far as the door.

"A nasty rumor. About some charity he runs."

"Exploradores?"

"That's it. Big charity. Some of the members are spies for the death squads."

"What?" I turned around.

"Spies. That's the rumor, supposedly. Why are you looking at me like that? Do you know something about it?"

"No. What else did they say?" I walked back to him, back again.

"In that word of prayer? I wasn't really listening. God did, one hopes." Whoop again. "Why do you look like you're going to hit me? Or hug, which is it?"

"I don't know," I said. "It's nothing. Thanks for the chat."

"Thank *you*," he said. "You've given me a thesis."

"I have?"

"Maybe. Have I given you something?"

"Maybe." Maybe, maybe.

"Well, amen to maybe. Maybe is better than nothing. Quick, let's celebrate with a nip of old Remy." He opened a drawer and pulled out a small flask and passed it to me. It was ancient, sheathed in cork. I took a quick swig. Crane held the flask to his own lips. "*Carpe diem, amigo!*"

"*Carpe momento,*" I said, my throat burning with rum and "maybe."

We passed it back and forth once more and then I left.

"Catch you later!" Crane called after me, into the hall. "We've really got to talk."

THIRTY-SIX

Sam was lying on the divan, knees pulled up, a pail on the floor beside him. Something had hit him while he was at the church. Not slain in the spirit, he said, just last night's melon.

"Do something for you?"

"Tell them to stop that infernal noise." They were still singing and clapping next door, now with an amped-up guitar.

"I'll tend to the phone," I said.

"No need. Disconnected. I pulled the plug." The phone cord lay coiled on the desk. I left it that way. The electricity had come back, so I brewed Sam a pot of tea, then went up on the roof to think. Preaching was starting now at the chapel, a male voice at top pitch, and voices responding, *""Hey-SOOCE! Hey-SOOCE!"* Then a burst of song and the wail of a neighborhood dog.

I stretched out on top of the truck cap, the sun-heated metal warm under my back. The sky was a clear blue, cloudless, except for a narrow white plume on the far horizon. The volcano Pacaya, I supposed, its new cone letting off steam. I watched it while I gathered my thoughts, picking them up like sticks from a little pile. All I wanted to do was look at them. Carefully. This was not a detective story with evidence that would fit on my fingernails. What I had was a maybe, a "word of prayer" and a second-hand report, not necessarily reliable, about a rumor, not necessarily true.

What did I really know? I knew Catherine had saluted me. She'd given me a Boy Scout salute when she took off with the Melanos. Was that just a playful gesture? I thought it was at the time, a kind of assurance that everything was all right. Or was it a declaration of danger? But how could I get that message? Because she had told me nothing to suggest that any members of the Exploradores could be a threat, and why wouldn't she have told me that? The Melanos were members, as she would know, because everyone in that neighborhood was a member, and surely she would know that Elizondo ran it, because Alex knew it. But she hadn't mentioned any of that either.

Could be it was just not important enough to mention, like the fact that Elizondo was a close neighbor. Or that they had ceased to be friends after Martin died. I was making too much of it.

What did I have in my hand then? A little pile of possibilities, that's all, a bunch of sticks. But something else *was* there in the pile, I was sure of it. "A crazy coincidence," Luis had called it, and I'd passed on those words to Alex, and wished I hadn't. Mystery writers did that to excuse the obvious use of coincidence.. But if not a coincidence, then what? Not a plan. It was too intricate, too dependent on too many things going right.

Careful now, careful. Back up. What do I know, without hearsay and speculation? I made a phone call asking for help, for Luis. That's what I know. And my concern was passed on to Elizondo. There's no doubt about that much. I made a phone call to Méndez and he called Elizondo. But that call may also have offered a crucial bit of information. *Catherine is missing. No one has heard from her.* That's what I said to Méndez. So that could mean that my call, *mine,* could be the common denominator in this crazy mess. I let out a yelp. The stick in my hand was a snake.

Wait. Far too dramatic. I was re-entering the field of guesswork. It was only a guess that Méndez passed on to Elizondo my concern about Catherine. Why would he, unless he happened to know that she and Elizondo were once acquainted, neighbors? Maybe he did know. Elizondo was an old friend, Catherine was an old friend. Even so, that wasn't enough, and how could I find out, and what did I think I would do about it, anyway, even if I could prove that what I was guessing might really be true?

I'd taken the process as far as I could. The snake was just a stick, after all, a meaningless scrap of an idea.

But then I heard it again in my head: "*Cat?*" And my own voice: "Did he recognize you?" And hers: "My hair was short back then." Something *was* there, I knew it, and I also knew I very well might not ever know what it was. The roar was back. I jumped up off my perch and began to howl with fury and frustration, my voice riding out over the roofs to blend with the shouts at the church and the baying of the dogs.

Then a sound from below, a loud slam, a door. I peered down through a window of the truck cap. A shadow moved, and moved again, then Molly's tail came into view, wagging. Luis and Carmen were back. I went down.

Molly was in the kitchen, slurping water from her pan. Sam was sitting up on the divan. He was holding his head, Dina was holding the phone cord. "Who disconnected this?" she asked. She looked at me, ready to maim. I was breathless and knew my face must be red and sweaty, sure signs of guilt. "Where are Luis and Carmen?" I asked.

"Still at the village." She examined the end of the phone cord, giving it a shake. She was wearing her usual attire, high-heeled boots this time, green stockings with an argyle pattern, and a short, tight skirt. "And you are expected. You'd better go."

Go? Yes, yes, she said, go. Where? To Las Cavernas, where else? Luis wanted me. Sam, too. Both of us. *Vos?* Go! "*Marchando!*" she ordered, sending me off the face of the earth with a flick of her thumb and forefinger.

"Go when?"

"Right now," she said. "*Ahora!*" We should get there in time if we started immediately. She would manage things here. She bent over to plug in the cord, her short skirt riding up over her beefy bum. I gave her a kick with the flat of my foot—whomp!—and she landed on her face under the desk, too surprised to do more than make a helpless squeak.

No, I didn't do that. I only wanted to, badly, another scenario more satisfying than the actual. She was still standing, right side up, un-kicked, the cord in her hand, unplugged.

"Get there in time for what?" I asked, at my nicest.

"I'm sworn to secrecy," she said, her voice lowered to what she prob-ably thought was a whisper. She shook the phone cord again. "So, *desembucha,* one of you, tell me, how did this happen?"

"*Solo Dios sabe,*" I said, with a deep shrug. Only God knows. Her expression placed me at the bottom of the evolutionary scale. I plugged it in for her, then sat down next to Sam. "*Marchando!*" I said.

He made a face. Neither of us was thrilled. But we both knew we'd do it. No chance of disappointing Luis and no possibility of remaining here with Dina. No discussion, even.

I drove, in and around and up the same mountains I'd climbed with the feisty spirit of Fern by my side—now with Sam, as corporeal as anyone could wish. He was quiet though. We both were silent, spacey in our separate fevers. By the time we got to the village Sam was feeling better, and my roof-top roar had reduced itself to a controllable state, about the size of a tennis ball, curled up right next to the pancreas.

We found the village quiet, all but unoccupied. Almost everyone had gone to the Sunday market in town and others, for some reason, were making themselves scarce. Even the dogs and roosters seemed more quiet than usual. Alicia and Arturo were there in the central courtyard with Carmen and Luis. The place had been cleaned up, the packed ground swept. I hardly recognized it, except for the lingering aroma no scrubbing could ever remove, wood smoke and baking tortillas. I breathed it in gratefully.

Alicia was dressed in a spectacular *huipil*, and Arturo, too, wore a sleeveless tunic, woven in stripes of the four cardinal colors. A red cloth was tied around his head. Carmen sat at the table, her arms deep in a big basket of flower blossoms, stirring them up.

"Fire ceremony," guessed Sam, pointing to the blossoms. That was it, the "surprise." Arturo, as village shaman, was offering a private fire ceremony for Luis. Carmen told us that. It was to be held up in one of the caves. It was Arturo's choice, Luis explained, throwing me a significant glance. I assumed he meant the cave he and I had tried to sneak into when we were kids, the one where they brought my father to be healed. I caught the same sense of excitement and importance the caves had always evoked, as if we were embarking on a long journey to an exotic place, not just up the hill.

Sam, too, was enthralled. He had been wanting to attend a fire ritual, but usually they were exclusive affairs. He bowed to Arturo. "A great honor," he said.

Something else was astir. For all the colorful preparations, the air was not one of festivity. Carmen was too quiet and I didn't like the way Luis looked. He'd lost weight, I thought, and the shadows under his eyes were deeper. "You don't look so hot yourself," he said, catching my gaze.

We were served anise-flavored sweetbread and the apple drink, and then it was time to start. There were six of us in the party, Arturo, Alicia, Luis, Carmen, Sam and myself, each of us carrying part of the supplies. The cave was half a mile up a steep path. Nothing was visible above us but trees and rocks and the far peak of the hill with a crown of mist.

I walked behind Luis, slowly, he and I a good thirty feet behind the others. He was using a homemade cane, still not able to straighten his body.

"Have you heard from Smitty?" he asked, as soon as we were alone. "Do you know anything more about your friend?" He didn't name her.

"Not much," I said. "All I know for sure is that she's not a U.S. citizen, and her son could not identify the body, or wouldn't."

"No kidding." He took a deep breath. "What does that say to you?"

"I don't know." I wanted to talk about the Exploradores and all the "maybes," but his own face, his body language, took precedent. "Something's going on here," I said. "Tell me what it is."

"Oh, it's nothing to concern you," he answered, with a flick of the free hand, fingers splinted. "I've been demonstrating a little anger. A couple of roaring fits."

My own roar murmured, in familial recognition.

"Belated reaction to the torture," he said. "That's not all. I wanted a drink so badly yesterday I threw myself into the brook. Not that water was what I needed."

I stopped in the path.

"It was that part in the rapids we were always warned about," he said. "It's been even deeper since the flood. I thought I might stay there, face down, but a couple of the men pulled me out. Shook me like a wet rat. Very effective CPR. So, they're all watching me now, afraid I might do myself damage."

"And could you?" I was afraid to ask. "Could you harm yourself?"

"I was wearing a backpack full of stones. I know that's not very original."

"My God, you meant it."

"Well, I thought I did. I wasn't planning to walk on water."

I jumped around him and blocked his way, grabbing his shoulders. "Tell me you won't ever do that again."

"I won't. Not a chance, anyhow. I haven't been alone since, not even to pee. It was an act of ultimate self-pity, of course. A betrayal of love, Carmen's, God's. My boys. This village. I won't do it again. And I'm not going back to the drink, in case you're wondering about that, too."

"Why did you do it?"

"Knowing I can't trust myself. Knowing they'll come after me again. It's only a matter of time. They won't kill me, you know. They'll just squeeze me for information until I give in. And I'm afraid I will."

But there are other solutions besides—. I didn't say it. What did I know? What the freaking hell did I know?

"It's more than that. Torture convinces you of a deep down evil in the world. Sometimes you can't stand that knowledge, or the fear. *Xob'il.*"

We stood there for a while. He seemed not present, looking up and beyond me, off toward the mountains. I was still holding his shoulders, facing him, wondering where he was. Then he said, "You can let go of me now, Ted." He was back, the person I knew. I released him. We began walking again.

"By the way, I should prepare you," he said. "This ritual is being performed for you also. I'm not the only degenerate around here."

He was breathing hard again already, and I was too, on a hill we had charged up as kids, probably running. We moved on, snail-paced, Luis stopping every few steps, holding his sides. "Get on my back," I said, stooping.

He was aghast. "Never!"

"Why not? You used to carry me. Everybody here is always lugging something or somebody around, on the back, on the head." I was determined and blocked his way again until he relented. He was no lightweight. I gave him the candles I was carrying and used his cane as we plodded along, now into a fringe of forest. A brightly colored bird flashed off a branch over our heads. "The Blue-throated Motmot," said Luis in my ear. We could hear other birds, hundreds of them, it seemed, and the voices of those ahead of us, the women also sounding like birds at that distance.

"Am I heavy?" Luis asked, as I gave him a hoist. "Or am I your brother?"

"Shut up," I panted. He was getting heavier by the second. It becomes part of you, I remembered, the load on the back. The thighs do the heavy work, my father explained. Mine were ready to give out.

"Everything OK?" Sam called. The rest of the party had stopped at the top of another rise and were waiting. Luis slipped off my back. They were at the cave, it turned out. I wouldn't have guessed it. The opening was concealed by bushes, a space between rocks so low I thought I might need to crawl on my knees. As a child, I'd seen it as a large mouth, looming and scary.

Arturo entered first and lit several candles, then the rest of us squeezed through. Inside there was nothing but a dim area about twenty feet in diameter, not much to see. It was certainly not one of the spectacular show caves in the area, with limestone stalactites and exotic rock formations. The floor was smooth stone, the ceiling fairly high, though there was only one spot, right in the center, where I could stand at full height, where my father might have stood, if he were standing. In the candlelight our shadows loomed against the walls, bobbing as we moved.

The only trace of an earlier human activity was a pile of ashes inside a ring of stones, not in the center of the space but at the farther side near a crevasse in the wall. Luis prodded me over there. I felt the draft instantly, the strong undeniable tug of a vacuum. "Speak into it," he whispered.

I put my face to the opening. My nose filled with an overpowering chemistry I couldn't identify as anything but wet earth, though I knew it was far more complicated than that. I heard running water somewhere in the deep dark distance, maybe an underground river. "*Hola!*" I called. My voice came back to me in multiples that lasted several seconds.

"The voices of the ancestors," said Luis.

"You believe that, of course."

"At the moment. This is not the time for academic doubts. Go with it. I told you, this is for you, too. Arturo said so."

"Oh yeah? Then it better be good."

Arturo was scraping the old ashes out of the circle of stones, speaking as he worked, explaining something to Sam and me, the uninitiated gringos. He was having trouble finding the right words.

"He wants you to understand what his role is," Luis said. "He says he only lights the fire and tries to read its message."

Arturo banked materials in layers over the scorched area of the last fire (how long ago?), starting with incense and dried resin. He built a tent of the wood about a foot high over that, then inserted wax tapers into it all around, with one at the top. The blossoms were piled around this, red, yellow, blue, white. Carmen and Alicia crossed themselves before they laid them out, murmuring "*Este, oeste, norte, sur*," the four cardinal directions.

Arturo said something else with Luis's help. "He says the fire will tell us each what we need to know."

What we need to know. It sounded good to me. I was open to anything at this point, sticks or snakes, burning wood or a whole burning bush, handwriting on the wall, a voice in a whirlwind. Purge me with hyssop, whatever works.

"Now we all kneel around the fire," Luis instructed.

We all did, shifting uncomfortably on the cold stony floor, Sam and I on one side of the fire, Luis on the other between Carmen and his mother. Arturo lit the taper in the middle of the stack, murmuring something in Mam. We held our breath until the wood caught. Flame and smoke were drawn distinctly toward that opening into the earth's depths, though there was still plenty of smoke around us. Arturo began to chant in Mam, no translation needed, the sounds of the words poetry enough. As he recited, he and Alicia added substance to the fire, a stream of sugar and a squirt of liquid that smelled suspiciously like Old Spice aftershave.

Arturo stood and gave us each a taper to offer to the flames. "These are prayers," said Carmen. "Or intentions." We stuck them into the sides of the little inferno, while Arturo's voice trailed on, with Luis's voice in tandem. "My grandfather used to say that violence in any form, even as thought, separates our parts, the spirit from the body. Healing is the uniting of the parts in right balance."

At some signal I missed, Luis now got to his feet and trotted, hobbled, around the fire, first in one direction and then in the other. Carmen followed next, then Alicia, then Sam and I, bent over to protect our heads, both of us holding back grins, knowing how silly we must look. Arturo poured more fuel on the fire and stirred it, then went to his knees again. We all followed, in our former places.

"What is he saying?" I asked Luis.

"He is asking if we wish to be restored to right intent. Those are the words, right intent, *intención justo*."

Arturo rose, but signaled the rest of us to stay down. He circled us again, his hand full of tapers, still muttering in Mam. "Now he is asking God to hear our prayers," said Luis. "He says our prayers must include forgiveness or we can't be healed." Arturo stopped behind the three on the other side of the fire. Luis listened again, staring at the flames, light shining in his eyes. "He wants to know if we can forgive my abusers." He stopped and turned to Carmen. "Would you like to speak first?"

"I forgive," she said, after a minute, her voice barely audible over the crackle of the fire. "But I will never excuse." Arturo nodded and touched her on the head with the tapers.

Luis next turned to his mother, asking the same question. She answered in Mam, also softly, but with a sharp edge in her voice. Luis translated. "She says she will forgive what they did to her son, but only if they come to her and *ask*." He touched her hand as Arturo touched her head. "To be really accurate," Luis continued, "the word in Mam my mother used means not just ask but *beg*. For mercy, that is. Abjectly. On their faces. Pleading. Writhing in shame."

Alicia looked at him, puzzled. I thought she might give him another whack.

Arturo took a step behind Luis and asked the question again. Will *he* forgive his abusers? He asked it twice, then a third time before Luis answered. "I forgive," he said finally. "I forgive myself for being an Indian, and I forgive my country for not forgiving me." Arturo tapped him on the head, then swept the tapers across his shoulders, down his arms and over his heart.

We were all handed another of the long slim candles, which we lit and stuck in the ashes, for Luis and Carmen and Alicia. The fire was burning low and our shadows on the wall were changing. Arturo walked around to stand behind me, more tapers in his fist, muttering just over my head. "He is speaking to you," Luis said.

"I know. What is he saying?"

Luis put his hand behind his ear and Arturo spoke more slowly. "He says, this ceremony is for your father, too. Because it didn't work before. It didn't work because—hang on here a second—because your father could not forgive himself. I think that's it."

"Himself?" I said, stupidly. The word *culpable* crossed my vision, in his handwriting, shiny pencil lead against a black page. Luis held up a finger. The two voices rode together again, his and Arturo's, Mam, Spanish and English bumping into each other, stopping, starting. Arturo repeated a series of throaty sounds, like swallowing air. Luis screwed up his mouth painfully, as if a word was trying to squeeze itself past his stitches. "I can't get an exact translation," he said. "It's a long word with four glottal stops." He looked at Alicia for help. She said something.

"It was a kind of *susto*," said Luis.

"Fright?"

"Or shock. Could even be shock of recognition."

But Arturo spoke again now, with new spirit. Luis listened, then leaned toward me, over the dying flames. "Ted. He asks if you will accept forgiveness *for* your father. Be his *nahual*. His shadow self. He says you can free his spirit."

"Free his—?" We were crossing the border into another world. I looked at Luis, Carmen, Alicia, the fire. My knees were hurting. I adjusted their pressure on the stony floor.

"Ted," said Luis, again. "Listen. This is just how Arturo sees it. It's his innovation. You can refuse, if it seems too strange. Too Indian."

I could feel Arturo's presence behind me, waiting patiently for my answer. I stared at the fire. I spoke to it. How about a little help here. Isn't that the whole idea? The cave room was silent, just the faint snap of the blaze and Arturo's elevated breathing. I got a message. This whole affair was really about Arturo, his *own* persistent guilt. He had carried my father bodily all the way up this hill, for a healing that had not worked. He had not healed him, not "freed his spirit," or his body, and for all these years he had been blaming himself. It was a guess, but a safe one.

"Too Indian?" I said. "But I *am* an Indian. I was born here, remember? I had a tapeworm. I'm an *Indio*. Tell him I accept for my father."

"Good shot," whispered Sam. Luis's face glowed with approval. He nodded to Arturo, who tapped my head three times with the tapers. Every hair follicle on my body responded. What remained of the tent of sticks collapsed. The fire flared but died down quickly, flames flickering around the base. We inserted new tapers into the hot ashes. They lit.

"Watch now," said Luis. "The fire will blaze again with a final message, if God has heard us, or an ancestor."

Arturo chanted, kneeling now over the fire, his arms spread in expectation. We watched. His voice died away. The fire was a red circle of ash. The flowers were gone, the tapers melted. I could smell incense and resin and burnt sugar. A minute went by. No flames. Arturo released a sigh and stammered something in his jumbled Spanish.

"He's apologizing for God," said Luis. "He says the air in here is too damp. The message is, I think—yes, he said inconclusive. *Ambiguo*."

Arturo hung his head.

"Nev' you mind there, Arturo, *mi hermano*," I said. He laughed, covering his mouth. We all laughed, wanting to reassure him, all of us feeling a little foolish. I imagined the sound sucked into the recess to the extending cave, along with the last finger of smoke.

Outside the cave, Luis answered my question before I asked it. "I don't know, Ted. I don't know what that meant, that guilty thing. I don't know why the heck your father should feel guilty about anything he did. I don't know any more than you do."

"But—."

"No buts, *amigo*. Time to lay your father to rest. Let him go. You hear me? Let him go."

The others were waiting to walk with us. Carmen and Alicia each took one of Luis's arms and slipped ahead of Sam and me. I could hear him chatting with his mother in Mam, with the little pops and gasps of air.

Back down in the courtyard Alicia offered to feed us, but rain clouds were already obscuring the mountains and Sam and I left quickly.

THIRTY-SEVEN

Sam was feeling well enough to drive. A good thing. I was sunk in thought, hunched over in my seat. He was energized. He talked as we wound down from the hills to the highway. We had just been part of "an anthropologist's dream," he said. What we had witnessed was an excellent example of ancient ritual as theatre, the best of theatre, a prepared script enhanced by the unpredictable. "What if you had said no to Arturo's request?" he said. The "shamanistic principle" would be challenged by the rational. As it was, my answer back there gave assent to the unexplainable, like Jacob wrestling with some part of himself and calling it an angel.

Whew. I listened, wishing I could do the same, lift the whole affair into another reality. My own reality at the moment was in following Luis's advice, put my father "to rest," once more "let him go." That's what I was trying to do. But I was succeeding no better than I had with Catherine.

"But now there's Luis," said Sam. "Let's talk about his case."

All right, I agreed. I sat up in the seat, relieved. Time to move the emotional focus. Luis was right about that, and he needed help himself, whether or not he would admit it. Concentrate there. "It's not an anthropologist's dream, is it?" I said.

"A nightmare. I've been sweating over this."

"I'm worried, too."

"So what have you come up with? As observable data."

"What's observable?"

"I mean Aristotle. But no speculation. I don't even want to start with a hypothesis, however damn right we damn well know we are."

"Understood. We're working with a high uncertainty coefficient here," I said.

He was delighted. "So you've noticed, have you, how a little language can help?"

"When you're discussing the unspeakable?"

"Fuckin' right, that's what I mean. So what have you got there, son? What have you got that's strictly observable?"

"We only know what Luis told us and even he said he doesn't know."

"So we've got nothing?"

I sorted through what I would call "strictly observable." When I was done, Sam knew a lot. He knew about Catherine, what I could tell him without betraying her confidence or slipping into the hypothesis that threaded her story. I told him about Alex's decision not to identify her—the decision itself a fact, though it was based in uncertainty. I told him about the Exploradores rumor, though it was actually only a rumor of a rumor. He listened well, muttering only "I be dog, I be dog," as I carried on.

What I did not tell Sam (and later I would remember this and be glad) was about the stick-turned-snake in my hand, because I had already filed that under projection, and I still didn't know if Méndez had mentioned my concern about Catherine to Elizondo, and even if he had it proved nothing.

Finally I said that I had only two completely observable facts that I could stand behind without question. "I made a phone call to Carlos Méndez, asking for help for Luis, and he told me he passed that on to Elizondo."

"So," Sam said, "it was your call that tipped off Elizondo. About Luis. Your call for help."

"And apparently he did help."

"And used it for his own benefit. The guy's a low-down punk of a skunk."

"That sounds like a hypothesis. Have we switched?"

"Yes. Let's hypothesize. For starters, what about Luis's version? About what happened after he was released from custody. Do you believe he doesn't know?"

"I do, absolutely."

"So do I. He'd have to be crazy otherwise. Even apart from the woman, why would he smash up his truck like that? But I wish to heck he would defend himself."

"Against what?" I asked. A real question.

"Well, you've got a point there. No charges have been brought. But even an uncorrupted court case could have bad ramifications. We've got to get some kind of help before that happens."

"What about a human rights group?" I answered that myself. They were already informed. Dina took care of that surely. Every organization that would justly be interested knew all about it.

"I expect they're being cautious," Sam said. "There's a history here, you know. Luis was arrested for drunk driving several months ago, and he really was that time. Enough to get the attention of a cop."

I groaned.

"More, there was a woman in the truck. He was just driving her to a clinic, but she was a street person, a prostitute. This one didn't hit the papers, but word got around and it didn't look good."

"They didn't take his license?"

"No. Just a fine. Besides all the other stuff they've been doing to him."

"Harassment," I said. "Would the Army bother to do that?"

"I've wondered myself. Outright atrocity is more along their line."

"We have no idea what we're getting into, do we?"

"No. And anyway, Luis would want us to stay out of it. Maybe we should just drop it, the whole idea."

We did, tried to, for a long time, driving along in the dark, letting the drum of rain on the roof take over. We were almost home, crossing the bridge and climbing the hill, when I heard Sam sputtering to himself and knew he hadn't let it go. He slapped the steering wheel. "I hate to leave the country without at least trying to help. Maybe we could just have a friendly chat with this guy Elizondo."

"Right," I said. "Maybe we could call his office tomorrow morning."

"Right. Let's just see where that takes us."

"Shouldn't we tell Luis?"

"Maybe better for him to not know."

"Not yet, anyway. Maybe afterwards."

"Right."

The house was empty, Dina gone. We considered going to a restaurant, but Sam was feeling woozy again. All he wanted was tea and toast.

"We must be crazy," I said, as we sat down with our cups.

"Crazy and presumptuous. But let's call the guy."

No chance of sleep. For an hour that night I read my Final Harvest edition of Emily Dickinson, skipping through here and there as far as page 248. *Tell all the truth but tell it slant*—her tricky version of *aletheia*. Definitely too much hypothesis there. So back to the baseball alphabet game. Category: Climactic moments in Red Sox history. But my mind was blank all the way to W—Ted Williams, of course, 1941. Final day of season, batting average a hair under .400. Manager offers chance to sit out meaningless doubleheader, with average to be rounded off at .400, which hasn't been done in a gazillion years. W plays anyhow, gets six hits, ends season at .406. A bat, a ball, and a little arithmetic. I could handle that.

Sam called Elizondo's office the next morning, squeezing it in before Dina arrived and commandeered the phone. He got an appointment with no trouble at all. Elizondo would love to meet with us, his secretary said, but there were absolutely no openings until the middle of next week.

Both of us would be gone.

"We need an advocate," Sam said. "Someone he knows who can get us in." I thought of Carlos Méndez, of course. I had that other question for him, anyway. I got the school office. He was out of town, would get a memo to call back.

"I'll try Smitty," said Sam.

Of course. By all means. Smitty would tell us what to do.

He did. It was don't. Don't do it. He was so adamant I could hear his husky voice myself through the receiver. "Too chancey. It could just stir up more trouble."

So we dropped it again. The usual stream of people began coming and going through the door. I did a laundry and started to pack. Sam and I answered the phone and took messages. So far there had been no "threatening calls," until the one that came in late that afternoon. Somebody laughed. That's all, just laughed and laughed, a strange laugh, squeaking like an old bedspring, like some fool bouncing up and down on a bed. I held out the phone so Sam could hear it, across the room. He laughed in response, maybe in spite of himself. It was meant for Luis, I supposed, but I took it personally, as foolish as that sounds, as if somebody in the world was aware of my state of affairs, my helplessness, debility, ineptitude. "I've changed my mind," I said to Sam, hanging up. "I'm gonna do it."

I called Bucky Treadwell. It was reasonable to think he might know Elizondo. Irony here, of course. My last cry for help at the Atitlán hotel had been to Bucky, but for that same reason I wanted him to hear my voice.

He greeted me with a "Ho, ho." I let that sit. "It's you," he said then. "Are you okay? Where are you?"

"I'm here in the city, at Luis's place."

"Need a lift somewhere? At your service."

"You really are a sonofabitch, aren't you?" I said.

"I am," he said, calmly. "But I'm not a dead one. What can I do for you?"

"Do you happen to know that politician, Elizondo Lupero?"

"Zondo? We've met. I've given him a ride or two. Why do you ask?"

"I want an appointment with him and I need an in-between."

"Very funny. I see what you want. But I can't do that. It's comparable to asking him for a favor. Favors are dangerous."

"Is Elizondo dangerous?"

"Of course. Like lots of politicians here. Why are you always getting yourself into trouble?"

I signaled a regretful negative to Sam: No go. He gestured acquiescence, went into his slump and said, "*Así sea,*" so be it, and I knew he had relinquished the whole idea again.

It made me furious, with Sam and everyone else—with Bucky for his arrogance, with Luis for inciting trouble, with Elizondo for being inaccessible. He knew something, this guy who kept saying *Cat* in my head, and I needed to know what he knew. But Bucky was not finished. He was still talking in my ear. "Good thing you called," he was saying. "My parents want to meet you."

"They do?"

"You asked me to ask and I did. The answer is yes, they knew your folks. They knew your father and they want to talk with you. I meant to tell you at breakfast in Chichi, but you went off to the hills with that woman. So why don't you drop over some evening? Come have a chat."

"I'm leaving the country in a couple of days," I told him.

"Then come tonight. Come to dinner. We eat at six."

"It's awfully short notice, isn't it?"

"No problem. I'll explain."

"Are you sure?"

"Just come, man. Trust me, it's okay."

This was not turning out right. I didn't want to do it, make yet another switch in focus. I was in a different zone now. I'd moved. I was in the Luis zone. I didn't want to have dinner with Bucky's parents and I didn't want to talk about my father, fire up everything all over again. Whatever these people might be able to tell me, the Treadwells, even if they know something more than a ritual fire in a cave, what is the point? It will just mean laying my father to rest again. Yet again. And I can't do it. —Have you got that? God? Somebody?

Sure. Got it. But to say no under the circumstance, considering it's one you have deliberately initiated yourself, would seem pretty rude, wouldn't it? To say nothing of possibly irresponsible? Considering, that is, what can you lose from what will probably be just a little polite conversation, anyway? Considering everything so far? —Have you got that? Teddy?

"What can I bring?" I asked Bucky.

"Flowers," he said. "Any flowers. My mother loves flowers."

THIRTY-EIGHT

The Treadwells lived in a middle-class neighborhood, south and west on the map of the city, a small concrete house. Muriel and Hugh greeted me like an old friend. They were both short and plump, in their seventies, I guessed. They were dressed in what my mother would call their "Sundays," though it was Monday, Hugh in a shirt and tie and Muriel in a silky print dress and a long loop of pearls. She had a blue-eyed rosy look that belied her age. Bucky himself was not there. He'd gotten a last-minute flight assignment and I was glad.

Their living room, like my mother's, was burdened with belongings, hardly room to move. I felt too big here, in danger of knocking things over, candy dishes and plants and knick-knacks. A dining table filled one end and a piano the other, a baby grand, a luxury for missionaries, though it was old, many ivories missing, as if that justified its presence. The top was covered with photos of Bucky and his siblings at all ages, the disturbingly wholesome family, as Crane had put it, now with the bunch of roses I'd brought in a vase among them. I sat down in an over-stuffed chair and immediately knocked to the floor the crocheted doilies on the arm rests.

"How's your dear Mom?" asked Muriel, and expressed shock at hearing she was in a nursing home. "What a gal she was!" she said. "And she really loved the Lord, I can tell you. And your father, too. Such a powerhouse. You've had wonderful parents, haven't you?"

I cringed inwardly at this effusion, but answered with something like a smile. I could hear my mother in Muriel's voice. My mother might have said exactly the same thing about her, with the same intonation. In fact, she reminded me a lot of my mother, though they looked nothing alike.

"We're hoping to talk about your parents tonight," said Hugh, a little stiffly. But we didn't. During an appetizer of V-8 and Ritz Crackers we covered earthquakes, unpotable water, transportation and strikes. They'd seen it all, they said. They'd been here for forty years, under Central American Mission. I asked about their children and got a long report. I felt ill at ease, reluctant to insert any questions and distrustful of any answers. They seemed nervous, too. Muriel kept glancing at the clock. Once she got up and went to the window, looking out into the darkening street. I thought they must be expecting another guest, but no one arrived.

Before we sat down to eat, Hugh asked me to select the "dinner music." I'd noticed that they owned an old stereo system and a large collection of LPs. I was pleased now at the quality as I looked through them. I picked Franck's D-Minor over Sibelius's Second, a hard choice. The D-Minor was a recording by the Chicago Symphony, one I owned myself. I listened for its lovely three note question as we moved to the table.

And the dinner was good, as North American a meal as it could be, mashed potatoes, roast lamb, green beans, out of a can maybe, but green. I found it comforting and said so.

"Muriel's the cook," said Hugh.

"I use a lot of garlic," she whispered. I nodded in conspiracy. It was an old oblique joke, garlic morally suspect, because the children of Israel had whined for it in the desert.

For a while we ate in silence, letting the music take over. Hugh said twice, "We should get started," and Muriel said twice, "Yes, we must." Finally, Hugh said, "But tell us something first. Tell us how you've fared, all these years. I mean you and your mother. How have you fared?"

"Fared?"

"Yes. How has all that happened back then played out in your lives? That whole terrible fiasco."

I set down my fork. It clattered on the plate. "What terrible fiasco?"

"Oh, my," said Muriel.

Hugh set down his own fork, more carefully. "Why, everything that happened before you left here, in 1954."

"I'm sure you think I know what you mean," I said. "But I don't."

"Oh, *my!*" said Muriel, again. "How can this be? Your mother, she never explained?"

"Never."

"Well, then," Hugh said, clearing his throat vigorously, "we have some quick catching up to do." He looked at the clock. "Let's get right at it." Still he hesitated, rubbing his chin as he looked at me. "Perhaps I should warn you. Some of what we have to say might be disturbing."

"Please don't get the wrong impression, dear," Muriel said, quickly. "We all loved your father. He was an inspiration to us all. He was a man who—."

Hugh broke into this with a hand signal of restraint and Muriel retreated, turning a key on her lips.

"Well, she's right," he said. "Your Dad had exceptional vision, a sense of the whole country, the interaction of things, the church, Mayan culture. He actually got to know President Arbenz and became a sort of consultant on Mayan concerns. He was in and out of the palace."

In and out of the palace. I heard it as a bit of poetry. I could settle for that. Why know more? I should stop this awkward conversation right now, just listen to the music, talk about earthquakes, eat roast lamb and fly away.

"On the other hand," Hugh said, "he made us nervous. He also argued for the validity of certain Mayan beliefs, and that ran directly counter to what some of us had been called here to do. You know, release people from the two-headed monster—Mayan superstition and Roman idolatry."

He spoke that line with dryness and looked at me to see how I received it. I smiled, in case it was another in-house joke. He paused to wipe up gravy with his bread, then resumed with his formal air, words carefully integrated with chewing, a man accustomed to talking.

"When we came here in the mid-forties, this country was a democracy. Things were good. Every freedom. Great promise. But in 1953 word began to spread that the Soviets were gaining a foothold in this hemisphere and Jacobo Arbenz, who was the President then, was falling under their influence. As missionaries it was our habit to stay out of politics, as you know. But then Arbenz started a program in land reform. He began buying unused land from international companies, like United Fruit, and giving it back to Indians."

"Excuse me, Hugh," Muriel said. "Remember the time."

"I am, I am," he said. He cleared his throat again. "Land reform. That was the forerunner, you see, of what had just happened in China in the Communist overthrow. Hundreds of missionaries had just been booted out of China. We thought that was going to happen here. Then in January, 1954—."

"I think I hear something, Hugh," Muriel said. She got up and went to the window again, twisting her pearls, then came back.

Hugh pulled a yellowed newspaper clipping from his shirt pocket and passed it to me. "I've kept this. I wonder if you've ever seen it." It was in Spanish, the name of the newspaper cut off, and dated in ink in the margin, January 29, 1954. That startled me. My birthday, when my father and I were here together in the city.

The item claimed that President Jacobo Arbenz Guzman had turned over to the press "certain correspondence and photocopied evidence" that had fallen into his hands, proving to him "the existence of a plot by the United States to overthrow the Guatemalan government." Added was a response in a U.S. State Department press release, stating that a denial of such allegations "would give the story a dignity it did not deserve."

"Let me ask you," said Hugh, as I started to read it again, "how would *you* have taken this, back then?"

Back then. I was tempted to say all I wanted to do was buy bubble gum back then.

"Which would you believe?" he asked. "The words of a Central American president, or the U.S. State Department? It would have been a rare American who didn't side with Washington, wouldn't you say? But your Dad wanted to find out more. He tried to get an audience at the U.S. Embassy, with the ambassador, but he never got farther than an aide."

Was this on his mind while we wandered the streets that January day, blowing pink bubbles, arm-wrestling in the *Parque?* I pictured him as he appeared to me then, thinner than I'd seen him, clothes too big, clowning it up and making me laugh.

Hugh was still talking. "But right about then," he said, taking a bite and chewing, wiping his mouth, "the Embassy itself began to send out warnings. A revolt was in the making, an uprising to overthrow Arbenz. A big peasant army was building at the Honduras border, headed for the capital."

"The coup," I said.

"Pending, yes. I ask myself often why we didn't confirm it, this story of an approaching army. But how could we? None of our contacts in the States seemed to know anything. Then in June, early June, a certain thing happened, and—. I'm sorry. I'm not the person to be telling you this."

Muriel shoved back her chair. "I think the taxi has arrived."

This time Hugh went to the window. "Yes. He's here. I'll go help him." He left the room.

"I hope you won't think ill of us for this little surprise," Muriel whispered. "He asked us not to warn you."

I heard a clatter outside and Hugh's voice, briskly, and then another male voice, muffled. In a rush, the old fantasy came into play. My father was about to enter the room, ducking his head under the frame of the door and giving me a wink. Never mind all this stuff, boy. Never mind the grave and the cave and the palace. Here I am.

The First Movement of the symphony had just ended, and I went over and flipped the record, so the English horn would announce his appearance. Just in case.

"He was afraid you wouldn't want to talk to him again," Muriel said.

The voices came closer. Now I knew who it really was. I went to meet him as he walked in with his cane.

"*Hola,* Teddy." He peered up at me over the glasses, as he had in his office days ago. There was something different about him, though he was wearing the same business suit, three pens in the breast pocket. I smiled, managing my best front. "*Buenas tardes, Señor* Garcia."

Hugh pulled out a chair for him at the table, across from me, and Muriel fussed over him, putting a pillow behind his back. "I'll get dessert," she said, and went into the kitchen. I offered to help. "No, sit," she said.

"I'm grateful to have a chance to speak to you again, Teddy," Garcia said, quite distinctly. "I'm afraid I was abrupt when we last met."

"No problem." I flicked my wrist.

Muriel came back from the kitchen with a chocolate cake on a pedestaled platter and the three of us watched as she cut it, murmuring compliments. We received our servings and began to eat. Garcia's hand was steady as he lifted a bite to his mouth. He chewed, swallowed, and hummed, that bee sound in his throat I'd heard before in his office, the whirr of a motor.

"Teddy," he said. "I hope you will try to understand. There are times when all you want is peace and safety, to eat breakfast, read the paper, take a walk, do your work for God without the threat of trouble. It doesn't matter how that comes about. If a dictatorship can restore the quiet, then that's fine. Revolutionaries, right or wrong, bring trouble. And one gets so sick of trouble."

It was an eloquent little speech and I understood it very well. Same papery voice, same sagging cheek, but he was speaking much more clearly. Even the saliva control seemed better. He speared another bite of cake. The old devil, I thought. He had exaggerated his infirmity in our earlier exchange, a convenient control of difficult circumstances. My mother had done that, too, and it always worked. She would have a bad day when it suited her purposes, sometimes a very bad day. Tomás Garcia was having a very good day.

"You surprised me, you know," he said next. "Gave me a terrible start. Like your father's ghost had returned." He smiled, successfully. "Even good Christians believe in ghosts now and then. *Vos?*"

I nodded. "I'm beginning to believe in them myself."

"There are things I am more ready to tell you now," he said. He took a minute to adjust the place setting before him, fussing with the silverware, glass, cup, before he looked up. "In 1953 I invited your father here to the city to help me start a Bible study group among the students at San Carlos. He stayed in my home while we got things going. A dozen boys joined the group." He stopped to whirr his motor again. "San Carlos was deeply polarized about the Communist threat and my purpose was to help the boys understand the Christian alternative to Communism. But Ted wanted them to consider both sides equally and debate it. This went on for several months."

He paused to fork a piece of cake and wipe his mouth. It meant setting down his fork and picking up his napkin. "One day," he said, and stopped to sip coffee, two sips with another "one day" in between. "This was June now, 1954. Ted and I were both at home. Two men from the U.S. Embassy showed up at the door, without warning. They had come to tip us off, they said. Someone in our organization was an informer for the Arbenz government. A student, one of our boys. That's what they said. One of our boys was being paid to finger government enemies in the student population. Paid to finger enemies. One of our boys. They named him. It was Roberto, the one Indian lad in our bunch. I was shocked, of course. And your father." He stopped, shaking his head. "Your father."

"He laughed," I said, without a second's thought. Of course he did. I could hear it.

"Yes," Garcia said. "He laughed. Not just that, he told the men he'd never heard anything so ridiculous in his entire life. I must say I thought so, too. But I didn't laugh. I knew better. And the men were annoyed. You are an American citizen, one said to Ted. Our job is to protect you from the threat of a Communist regime. *What* regime? says Ted, and the man says *this* one, this regime. Don't you know? President Arbenz is a Marxist, he says, a secret Communist. And Ted laughed again. Arbenz is not a Communist, he said. Arbenz is an out and out capitalist. How come people from the United States Embassy don't know that difference? I remember those words in particular. The men left and I thought that was the end of it. But this is when your father, when he began to—when he changed."

He said "*se torció*," that odd term he had used before, not just "changed" as humans might do, but "twisted," like a pretzel. He spit the word out with a spray.

I guess I made a sound of some kind. Muriel asked if I was all right.

"I'm fine," I told her, told them, the three of them, all looking at me. Then I took a sip of coffee and burned my tongue, which brought tears to my eyes. I blinked them away and glanced up. They were still observing me.

"Please go on," I said to Garcia. "I'm listening."

But he gestured to Hugh, who took over. "That's when your father began his rampage, as it seemed to us. He began to do extreme things.

He drove Roberto, the Indian student, hidden in the trunk of his car, to somewhere—he wouldn't tell us—where he thought he'd be safer. He was convinced the U.S. was making an egregious mistake and it was up to *us*, the U.S. citizens here in the country, to correct it. He went around everywhere, talking about it. He got up a petition in support of Arbenz and took it to the Embassy. I don't know of any missionaries who signed it, just some Mayan farmers and university people. He kept saying our Ambassador was lying to us. He wanted to take a delegation of U.S. missionaries to the White House, but no one would go. We thought he'd blown a gasket."

"Wait!" I said. He was going too fast. "What was he trying to do?"

"Stop the coup. He was trying to stop the coup. That's what I'm saying. He was trying to save the Arbenz regime—single handedly, as it seemed. I can't believe you've never known this."

"I can't either." The heft of it was hitting me now. I was in awe. The nerve, brass, grit, temerity, balls. There was no right word.

"But he didn't," said Garcia. He paused, studied his cake, set down his fork on his plate, dabbed at his mouth with his napkin and sat back. "He didn't succeed."

"A coup did take place," said Hugh. "Well, *some*thing happened. Planes zooming around. The palace bombed in the night. It was frightening. But just a farce, mostly. There was no big army. No popular revolt. Just a rag-tag gang led by some blunderbuss."

Garcia picked up again, reclaiming the story. "And President Arbenz resigned. To prevent a war, he said. The truth is his own army deserted him. That was the real reason. And a new regime took power instantly."

"With that blunderbuss as the president," said Hugh. "I can't tell you how he got into office, but our Embassy announced him as the great liberator."

"Whatever, whatever," said Garcia. "I'm not quite done. There's more I need to tell you." He was flustered. For a bad moment, his lips formed words without intelligible sound.

"Shall I do it for you?" asked Hugh.

"No, no." He suddenly rallied, holding up his good hand. "I will tell it myself. I must. That's why I'm here." He was addressing me directly from over his glasses, his speech clear and strong now. "It happened several weeks after the coup. You and your family had gone back to the States. While you were away, while Ted was away, word spread from the Embassy that it was Ted. Ted Peterson himself was the spy. —Ted. A spy. Working for Arbenz at the University. He was the one."

"Huh!" I said. Or maybe it was "Hah!" Or "Ha-ha." No one seemed to hear me anyway. Garcia had stopped again and Hugh and Muriel were looking at him, as if they expected him to continue. But he seemed finished, as before.

"Word spread amazingly fast," Hugh said. "The Communist missionary, that's how it went. The missionary spy."

Something else left my lips, a loud grunt, or another "Ha-ha." My father the spy. This was crazier than anything my child's mind had conjured—a crime ring or knocking up a village girl. This was what my father had "done," the secret that been part of me all these years, the extra arm I kept hidden in my shirt? An assumed enemy of the state? It was far easier to imagine him as an outright criminal.

"Maybe it's hard to catch the curse of it," Hugh inserted, misreading whatever my mouth and face were saying. "It was the wrong time in the country, you know, in the whole western world, to be labeled a Communist. Word spread to the hill country, like lightning, to the churches there. It caused a lot of distress and confusion. Most village people hadn't the faintest idea what Communism was. They just knew it was bad."

This time I said "Yes," remembering old Anna, spitting at my feet. *Kom kom* and a hiss. One of the "confused." She'd thought I was my father. Even so, I realized, she was the only person who had addressed me about it directly. Not even Luis. Or had he? He could have alluded to it fifty times, thinking of course I knew what he meant, no need to explain, and I with no idea. I'd been asking all the wrong questions. *Another* secret? *A personal one?* And it was not a secret at all.

"Las Cavernas," I said. "The people there. What did they think?"

"They stood behind him," Muriel said. "When he was fired, for instance. They asked him to stay on anyway."

"Fired?"

"Yes. *Despedido.* The I.F.F., his mission board, dropped him when they got wind of this. The village wanted him to stay on there anyway, your family. But that would have been awkward, of course."

"Didn't anyone come to his defense?" I turned from one to the other in the brief silence that followed. "To tell the truth," said Hugh, "we weren't sure. We didn't know what to think. He was so openly critical of the U.S. We were wary of taking his side. And things got very dangerous after the coup. When Ted came back from the States, he walked right into a viper's nest. Thousands of people were being rounded up and arrested, anyone who had supported Arbenz. Las Cavernas was searched."

"Luis told me that," I said. Looking for our fathers, his safe in the cornfield and mine away in the car.

"You weren't there, were you, dear?" Muriel said.

"I was in the States. But my mother. She must have been there."

"She was the one who told us about it. When your Dad found out, he went all over the countryside in his car warning other people he thought were in danger. Like people who had signed his petition. Your mother was worried because he was so sick. She sent out word to the missionary community. Some people in Xela tried to take him in, but he wouldn't stay anywhere, lest he bring trouble to others. He wouldn't even go to the hospital, the Presbyterian Hospital. That's what your mother told us. It was very hard on her, you know." She dropped her voice to an important whisper. "Godless Communism. What was she to think? She was deeply disgraced, of course, and frightened."

But "stood by her man," I thought she would say next, but she didn't. "She called us to the village. She was giving everything away, saying goodbye to us all."

"Even in the States he'd have been in trouble," Hugh said. "But, as it turned out anyway—anyway."

"He died," I said.

"Yes, dear," said Muriel. "God took him. Maybe it was for the best. "

I'd had about all I could handle from Muriel, the three of them. It seemed to be over, anyhow, in a loose-ended way. Garcia sat staring at his cake. Hugh settled into his chair and Muriel started for the kitchen with the coffee pot.

Then Garcia stirred. "The truth," he said. His voice was barely audible, his eyes still on his plate. "The truth is, I wanted him out of the country."

Hugh sat back up and Muriel came back to her chair.

"It was I," Garcia said. "I'm the one who started the rumor. I went to the Embassy myself and told them what I suspected. That Ted was a Communist. I did suspect it. I really did. He'd given me reason to think so. I still think so. He never said he wasn't. And Communist or not, he'd become a menace, to us all, to more than half a century of work. I couldn't let him carry on here anymore, you see? It was my place to make sure that he didn't."

He lifted his head, to find my eyes, I thought, but he didn't, not quite, because I had stood up. His focus landed somewhere on my chest, where it remained. "I'm sorry," he said. "I've been sorry for a long time. It is time for me to tell the truth. And so I have, I have now, all these years later. It's done and it's over. God be praised. It's over."

He sighed, dug in with his fork and went back to eating, attacking the cake with vehemence, his face inches away from the plate. I watched him. No one spoke. A long time went by, what seemed long. The symphony came to its glorious conclusion, all by itself across the room on the player. In the new silence, street noises drifted through the open window.

"Bullshit," I whispered, then again in a yell. "Bullshit! Over? It's *not* over! That's crazy! Are you crazy? You must be crazy! How can it ever be *over!*"

My arm shot out across the table and swept his plate, cake and all, out from under his nose. It flew across the room, suspended itself in a frisbee hover, then swooped under the baby grand and landed with a smash.

This time it really happened. No question. There it was, the evidence under the piano, the white plate in three pieces and a long smear of chocolate frosting on the floor where the cake had slid by itself. Garcia sat with his fork in hand, gazing at the empty space on the table in front of him. It was a despicable thing to do, worse than knocking him off his chair. I said nothing.

"Never mind," said Muriel, as if I'd apologized. She even smiled at me, gently at first, then widely, a whole lot like a grin. Then she laughed, a high naughty giggle. Hugh's face darkened in disapproval.

"Oh, Hugh, it's nothing," she said. "For goodness sake, it's nothing but a dish."

"I'll clean it up," I said.

I went over to do it. Muriel joined me, down on the floor, handing me paper towels, emitting more little snickers, as if she was used to adolescent explosions of anger. I began laughing, too, silently, shaking with it. We were under the piano together, on our hands and knees, under the gallery of well-adjusted children, Muriel in her flowery dress, pearls swinging. I wanted to hug her, but if I did I would cry, bawl out loud on her shoulder.

Nothing more was said. We carried the trash to the kitchen and I helped Hugh clear the table. Garcia sat with his head down, his good day spent.

I thanked the Treadwells, genuinely, for dinner and for keeping this story, like a strange, unwanted plant they had been watering until someone came to claim it. Then I walked over to Garcia's side of the table and held out my hand. He placed his in mine, his good one. It trembled, as it hadn't since he arrived. "I've often wondered if Ted could forgive me," he said.

"I'm sure he would." You, but not himself.

"I wish I could make it up to him," he said. I tightened my grip and held his hand still. He repeated himself: "*Digame*—you *must* tell me—if there is anything I can do."

Go back to the villages and tell the truth, I thought. Tell old Anna. But it was too late.

"What can I do, Teddy, *mi hijo?*"

I had to smile, put in my place again by that diminutive. "I'll try to think of something." And I did, instantly, as if I'd been brought directly to this point for this very purpose. I said, "I wonder if you know that politician, Elizondo Lupero."

I said it to Garcia, but Muriel answered too. "Zondo? Why, yes, of course."

"I've known him for years," said Garcia. "He and I have worked together on many a project."

"I knew his mother well," Muriel said. "She died a couple of years ago. He still misses her. He was such a momma's boy, you know."

I told Garcia I wanted an appointment, as soon as possible, within the next couple of days. Could he arrange it? Oh, most certainly, he said. "I'll call his office tomorrow morning. What shall I say it's about?"

I waded in carefully. "The Exploradores."

"Of which I am a long-standing member," Garcia said. My guess hadn't taken me that far.

"And I've volunteered for them for ages," said Muriel. "By the way." She looked at Hugh, who hadn't said anything yet. "There's a rumor. Have you heard it?"

I nodded. "Do you know something about it?"

"I know it's a tricky subject," Hugh said. "Are you planning to raise it with him?"

"I've been meaning to do that myself," said Garcia.

"Then join me," I said.

It was the logical, courteous thing to do, invite him. I looked at Muriel. Her face held a question. "Sure," I told her. "Join us if you like." I looked at Hugh.

"Oh, no," he said. "No, I think not. Thank you just the same." He was staring hard at Muriel.

I spent the rest of the night sitting up in my room among the animals, watched over by their glassy eyes, wide awake. Not to be able to talk with my father about what I now knew seemed a monstrous injustice. I even listened for his voice. I heard something all right, because there is always something to hear in this city, at any hour. At 2:00 A.M. the neighborhood around me was still awake. It came through the windows almost as scored music, a baby crying, the snarl of a cat fight. Cars and trucks hummed and whined at a distance. I even thought I could hear the mountains in a deep bass strum of their massive energy.

I dug out the letter he had written on the road, on his own picaresque tour in the Buick, and read it again, translating this time with a different clarity, the way I thought my mother would read it, in paraphrase. The early lines looked the same as I'd translated them a week ago, the allusions to Felipe and Tomás Garcia. Then the apology to my mother and the refusal to "change his mind" or "recant," which was understandable to me now. Why he still felt guilty was not.

Then where do we go next? It appears I am supposed to be a man with-out a country, off-shore forevermore. On the contrary, I own two [countries] and I love them both and refuse to give them up. I will always carry them on my back. They are part of me.

It becomes part of you, the load of wood piled higher than your head, the *mecapal* around your forehead and your thighs doing the heavy work. I was confident that was the image he intended.

Then the Swedish sign-off at the bottom and under that my P.S. and the Song of Solomon reference. I dug my father's Bible out of the suitcase and looked it up. The verses were 4:6-9. *Until morning come, and shadows flee away, I will get me to the mountains of myrrh, and to the hills of frankencense. Thou art all fair, my love....Thou has ravished me, my sister, my spouse....* It was underlined, with a note in the margin. *For H.* A love note to my mother.

There was nothing here, nothing to suggest shame and dishonor. Not in this final reading, with all the understanding I could now bring to it. Then why had my mother *saved* it? Just for that expression of love and the promise to me, I had to conclude. Then why did she *hide* it? Because of his refusal to recant? My guess was that she had hidden it back there in the village, when the soldiers came to search, stuck it in her sewing basket, full of needles and crochet hooks, and left it there, because there was reason to hide it in the U.S. too, as she saw it. And was she so terribly wrong?

This much I knew. Whether she was wrong or not, whatever was real or blown out of proportion, it was the letter, two sheets of onion skin paper, that had initiated this trip, got me on a plane, brought me here, led me to Catherine and Luis, sent me into the mountains, kept me here when I was ready to flee, when I was sure it was a mistake, as much as if the handwriting was my father's own big hand, pulling and shoving along my reluctant, equivocating heart and mind.

When I shut the Bible and looked up, he was there, seated on the bed among the animals, his presence filling the room, as it always had, anywhere. *Presente.* No, not a hallucination—I hadn't gone completely wacko—nor a stab at magic realism. It was just something I had to do.

I knew how it would go. We didn't greet each other. We didn't need to. We picked up in the middle. "I still don't get it," I said. "What is this crazy business with the guilt? How come you couldn't forgive yourself?"

"I thought you'd never ask," he said.

"I'm asking now. For what? You didn't hurt anybody. You didn't commit a crime. You didn't—." I stopped short of the list of possible evils I'd compiled. "You didn't cause the coup. You even tried to stop it. Think of that! You tried to stop a coup, for God's sake! You stood up against the greatest power in the world. How can you possibly think you are guilty?"

"Is it so hard, *raggmunk?* We're talking about *verguenza*. You know that word?"

"I happen to, yes. Family scandal."

"Nationwide, in this case. The country I represent betrays the country I serve. That makes me complicit. Is that too big a stretch?" He might not use that stretch idiom, but so what. That's as close as I can get to what he would say.

"Yeah but," I answered. *Yah*but! That kid word.

He corrected me. "Slow down. Yes...but."

"Yes...but. How is it personal? That's what I want to know. How did it get to your, your, your t-oo-ush?"

"If you want one word, it was the hubris."

I had never heard him use that word either, and the only voice I had heard it in recently was Catherine's. "Could you break that down a little?" I asked him.

"Too much," he said. "That's what it means. Presuming too much. Presumed right to control. Right to distort facts."

"But you didn't do that."

"We're talking about complicity. Unintended, but real. It stunk. Think about that."

I tried. I got a faint, rank odor from below. "Is hubris worse than sloth?" I asked.

"Same family," he said. "Just across the table. The eighth deadly sin."

"Okay, I get it. But if you're supposed to forgive somebody else seventy times seven, how come you can't do that for yourself?"

"Counting has nothing to do with it."

"I'm not sure that's a rational answer."

"It's not a rational subject."

"Well, what about reconciliation? Isn't that the whole idea, free and undeserved grace?"

"Free or cheap?" I thought that was what he said. "It doesn't change what happened." His voice was beginning to fade already. I raised my own, as if that would help. "Okay, try this. Can certain sins be forgivable, but not *excusable?*" (Thank you, Carmen.)

"Good point. I'll give it some thought. Gotta go. Sorry, Teddy boy."

"Wait, wait! Just one more question." I scrambled. What was the most important thing I could ask him? Were you really a Communist? Not that. Or a Marxist, or a Trotskyite, or a Socialist, terms I understood in very little depth. All of that didn't matter at the moment, anyway. I bypassed it to get to the question I didn't really need to ask, just wanted to. "Why did you and Mom leave me at that school and come back here without me?" Age seven again. I was chagrined.

"*Mi hijo, mi hijo!*" he exclaimed. "For your safety, of course. Why else would we do such an inconceivable thing? It almost killed me, not being sure I would ever see you again."

That was exactly what he would say. I knew he would. "I am such a bozo!" I breathed.

"Never mind, *elote,* we all are." I could hardly hear him now.

"Don't go yet," I said. "We're not done. I need your help."

"So you keep telling me."

"There's that P.S. Something you were going to explain to me. When I got old enough. Like right now?"

"Oh yes. About telling the truth. Truth is expensive, that's the point. Use it wisely and harmlessly."

"Jesus said that, I bet." (Luis had, I knew.)

"Or something like it."

"But what does it mean?"

"You'll know. The spirit of truth will guide you."

"Did Jesus say that too?"

"I think so. Or he would have if he'd thought of it."

"Yes. But," I said, with clear distinction. "How can you tell if it's the spirit of truth—or maybe some other spirit, of something else?"

He threw up his hands in frustration. "I don't know. Frankly, Teddy, I don't know what the heck I'm talking about. I can't even explain it to myself."

He looked tired, what I could see of him. I knew I should let him go, but I forced him back again. "Just one second more. Something I've been wanting to tell you." That was so, but I didn't know what it was until now. "You're a hero, that's what. A national hero. No, international. Worldwide. Did you know that? No? Well, you're *my* hero, anyway."

At that he came all the way back and grabbed my hand for an arm wrestle. He didn't throw it and neither did I. After all, we were almost the same age, in our prime, you could say, both of us with faces sweating, eyes bulging, muscles straining against forces far beyond us, then and now. We called it a draw.

"*Jag älskar dig,*" he said, and was gone.

It was 4:30. Firecrackers in the neighborhood announced the edge of dawn. I pushed aside the curtains on a window. The whole sky hung low in a vast pink cloud, tinting the mist as it rose from shacks on the hillside below. *Until the morning come and the shadows flee away.*

I padded down to the next floor and roused Sam in his room. "Let's go for a run," I said.

"You're even crazier than you look," he growled, and swung his legs out of bed.

THIRTY-NINE

It was now Tuesday, September first. Six days had passed since I'd last seen Catherine, seven since Luis was arrested. I made a note of that in my canary pad journal that morning. An hour later I made another, because Muriel called to confirm the appointment. Elizondo would gladly meet us, she reported, tomorrow afternoon, Wednesday, at 3:30. In his offices on Avenida la Reforma, Muriel, Garcia and me.

Sam had already gotten his plane reservations, also for the next day at noon, and I now nailed a flight to the States for 7:20 on Wednesday evening.

From this point, entries in the journal record became much more frequent. Because that's how things happened. In another hour that morning (10:15), Muriel called back, to say that Garcia was not feeling well and would not be coming after all, and would I mind terribly if she didn't come either? "Hugh prefers that I stay out of it. He thinks I'll talk too much." No problem, I told her, with mixed feelings. "Do what seems best to you." She said thanks so much and she would be praying for me.

So it appeared I would be doing this thing alone, without back-up, like that crazy TV detective, bleary-eyed and unarmed. I was processing that with a great deal of uncertainty when who should appear but my old shadow, Win Hall, the Texan volunteer who had checked me out for Catherine, popping in without announcement, just as he did at Luis's ruined office.

We met each other on the spiral staircase. I was going down and he was halfway up, pausing there, scratching Molly's ears. She was sitting with her haunches on one step and her front paws on a step above, nosing his leather jacket.

He'd just arrived from Xela, where he'd been all week, cleaning up in the office and making repairs. He looked exactly as he did when I first saw him on the Pan-American Highway, his big sunglasses now pushed up on his bald head.

Molly nosed his jacket again, and so did I in effect. I didn't know what she smelled on him, maybe the animal in the leather. What I "smelled," sharp in my nostrils, was his connection to the underground. He could know something about Catherine. I all but grabbed him by the lapels.

"I've stopped by to talk about Luis," he said, before I could make a fool of myself. "Things are serious. He's losing supporters already. Churches in England and the U.S. Two speaking engagements cancelled. We need to do something to clear up this mess. Have you had any ideas?"

I told him about tomorrow's appointment and invited him to join me, sure he could be just the right addition. I was ready to explain everything, even the unobservable facts, but we never got to that point. He couldn't do it, he said. He was on his way back to San Antonio, headed for the airport right now. He didn't know much of anything about Elizondo, but thought a chat with him could do no harm. "Get him to talk. He's a talker. Maybe he'll talk himself into helping."

Then he turned from me to Molly, lifting her Irish face and studying it for a moment, and said, "Catherine," as if he'd seen her there. "Catherine Rodriguez."

I felt my own face color in a rush of heat, as obvious as a teen-ager.

"Luis told me," he said. "When did you see her last?"

"At Lake Atitlán. She went off with a couple named Melano."

"The Melanos. I hadn't heard that."

"What do you know about them?"

"Nothing much. They seem to have slipped away, too. Like everyone else in the network."

I sat down on my step, which put our eyes on a level. "What are you saying? The Melanos have been part of the network? The store network?"

"I think so. I'm not sure about that, to tell the truth. I never met them."

"And Catherine?"

"Met her? No. I know only what Paco told me."

"Paco?"

"Or Parko, as we Yanks call him. He owns that parking lot. You were there." He reached into his pocket and slipped a doggy treat into Molly's mouth. She gulped it down and looked up for another. Her body gave a little quiver. "All gone," he said, patting her head. He looked at me as if he might pat mine. "What I know is that Catherine has had more than one reason to be careful. For years. Not just because of the store. You know about her husband?"

"Martin."

"What do you know about him?"

"An activist. Murdered. Catherine told me."

"Did she tell you how his body was found?"

"Not exactly. Compromising circumstances, I think she said."

"In his car in the dump? With a dead *puta?* She told you that, too?"

No. No, a thousand million nos.

"Odd confluence, isn't it? Martin's case is a well-known one in subversive history," he said. "Unsolved all these years, like so much around here."

"No ideas about who did it?"

"None. But Catherine knew. According to Parko."

Had she been trying to tell me that, too, without telling me, hoping I'd pick it out of the air?

"He was doing an investigation, you know—Martin was—into certain powerful families here, including some of his own neighbors," Hall said. Molly poked him again with her nose. "All gone, Molly. Sorry. Be a good girl."

"Here, Molly." I pulled her up to me where I sat and buried my face in her red coat. It was cool and smelled wonderfully familiar, smoky, like a village cooking fire.

"Good luck with your meeting," Hall said. "Invite another American. Someone Zondo wants to impress. I hear he loves Americans." He gave Molly a pat and took off.

I was running out of Americans. There was still Crane. He'd be a buffer, all right, a nice soft cushion of buffoonery. On the other hand,

Crane could be disarming. He could say exactly the wrong thing and it could be exactly right. I called his room. No answer, and no follow-up information at the hotel desk. Just as well. Maybe Thor knew when to stay out of things, like any cautious god, though it left me feeling oddly forsaken.

Late afternoon (4:30): Méndez returned my earlier effort to reach him and I unloaded the question that had been getting heavier by the hour. By chance, I asked, had he mentioned my concern about Catherine to Elizondo? Why, yes, he certainly had. Certainly. He thought Zondo would be interested. "And he was. He and her husband were old friends, you know."

"Yes. I know." So, the stick was a snake.

"Let me know if there's any other way I can help."

I was tipping, unbalanced, on the edge of inclusion, an invitation on my lips, when Méndez. said, "By the way, have you learned any more from Luis?"

"What do you mean?"

"What he was doing with that *puta* in the back of his truck. What on earth could he have been thinking of?"

That begged the question, several of them at once. "Don't believe what you hear," was all I could think of as a response, other than calling Carlos Méndez a slime-ball, or worse.

"Perhaps you know something I don't," he said.

"I know the man."

He said "Hmmmm," and I bid him another cheery-eerio.

I reported that and my conversation with Hall to Sam. He was packing up papers in his room. I watched him a moment, feeling regretful about his departure and unprepared for a solo performance. Shakespeare used to like to bring the whole cast back on stage at the end of a comedy, with bells and whistles. This seemed more like a farce, the Keystone Cops, say, with me alone on the stage and fully as confused. My biggest concern was less any baleful aspects of taking it on alone, whatever danger Bucky implied, as much as knowing how to do it right. Sam and I could have worked it out together. Muriel and Garcia, as old friends, would have offered a buffer; I could have let them take the lead. Win Hall, I assumed, would have offered a sharper sense of what questions to ask and how to press them, with an air of control that would match Elizondo's. Who will I be? A friend of Luis's, that's all, which could make any approach I took a prejudiced one in Elizondo's eyes. And he would be right.

Mid-evening (8:30 or so): Smitty arrived to say farewell to us both. He looked as benign as always, in running shorts, blond hair in his eyes like a kid. I made coffee.

"So, still planning to beard the lion in his den?" he asked me.

"I'd like it very much if you'd come and supervise," I said.

"No. I'm a sucker for a losing battle, but not this one. Tell me again. Why are you doing this? Why?"

"*Porque,*" I said. Because. Because sticks turn into snakes, that's why. Because there's no coincidence in this mystery. Because I've said goodbye a thousand times. Because there's a presence in an absence, a *presente.* Because how can I leave here without trying to do at least one thing that matters? Because all the things I can't do in this country have gotten stuffed into an encounter with one man. In fact, the whole blasted war here has been stuffed into one man, one lion, who is waiting for me in his den.

Those were the best answers I could think of, and they were far too self-dramatizing to state out loud. "I'm not sure any more," I said. "I'm just a little wheel in a big one, remember?"

"So is Zondo," Smitty said. "The trouble is, he thinks he's a big one." He was rubbing his glasses on the hem of his jersey. Without them the coordination of his eyes was off just a hair, as I'd noticed before. "He thinks he's supposed to be the next president. It's a divine calling. That gives him a lot to protect. It's too easy for somebody to say the wrong thing to him, and he's got the whole political-industrial-military oligarchy at his bidding if he thinks he needs it. It takes a pile of savvy to know how to deal with somebody like that."

Sam was quiet through all of this, listening, drinking coffee. Now he said, "So, Smit. Tell us. How should it be done? How would you go about it?"

"I wouldn't go about it."

"But if you did. If you decided to go talk to the guy yourself. How would you approach it—as a Mennonite, that is?"

"As a peace-mongering son-of-a-bitch?" Smitty hooked on his glasses and gave a swat to his hair. "Oh, just your basic non-violent approach, I suppose. Track two diplomacy. No incrimination. Go the second mile. You know, return good for evil? Offer your coat, your left cheek? No emotional hijacking. No implied guilt. No veiled threats. No power-based strategy. —How does that sound to you?"

" 'O brave new world,' " I said. Actually, it sounded a lot like my divorce agreement with Rebecca.

"And no tragic necessity." Smitty repeated that, looking directly at me, eyes in sync now behind the glasses: "No tragic necessity."

"Don't worry," I said. "I'm not that noble."

I felt rueful. I respected Smitty. I owed him respect for his judgment and know-how. But this was something I had to decide by myself, even if I had no ground to stand on. At the moment I thought if he touched me with his little finger I would fall over. But I was still standing. I think he understood that. He seemed to withdraw.

"Are you going to ask Luis what he thinks?" he asked.

"If he comes back before I leave, I will." I decided that now, at this second.

"And if he asks you not to do it?"

"I won't." I decided that, too.

That night I wrote down every question I could think of that might work as a lead-in with Elizondo. None looked right. Smitty's words, Win Hall's, Sam's, Bucky's, my father's, were flying around in my head like birds of dark and bright plumage. Finally, I just wrote, recording everything that came to mind, blurting it all out on the yellow canary pages, every scrap of evidence, every suspicion, conclusion, fear, intention, doubt, paradox, warning, every door that opened and closed itself even as I wrote.

From the desk downstairs I stole a big manila envelope from the office supply and sealed into it those pages along with the rest of all I had written, my record of the month. In the morning I gave the envelope to Sam to stick in his briefcase with his other papers. I told him I'd contact him in the States and tell him where to send it.

"Good reading on the plane?" he asked.

"The best," I said. "Feel free." And if for any reason I failed to reach him, I added, he should decide what to do with it himself. Maybe he could make it part of his book, the exciting, readable part.

So, Wednesday, September 2nd now: After Sam left at 9:30, I showered and finished packing. I tossed out some things, like a pair of worn sneakers. I considered throwing away my three tattered paperbacks, but couldn't. I'd read them half a dozen times or more and was seeing them now as old friends I'd never really understood.

With the buzz of the last zipper my luggage became the centerpiece in a survey of alternatives. It came down to whether or not I should leave it here, and if there would be time to come back and get it. If I didn't return here it would mean not seeing Luis and Carmen before I flew to the States. But coming back here to pick it up might not be the wisest move either.

All that fussy deliberation, I knew, was just a microcosm of the greater unknown, where the visit to Elizondo might lead, which I couldn't really address, because if I did, I would call and cancel the appointment. I chose to ignore the tap-tapping hammer in my chest.

The solution was to get rid of the suitcase. I didn't want to deal with it at the airport, anyway. I squeezed a few essential items into my backpack, along with my books and tapes and my father's Bible, and then, proud of myself for solving this simple problem, I left the suitcase with everything else in it on the pile of other freebees by the front door. Then I went out to the Bug and got the mask and all the stuff I'd bought at the roadside market, and added that to the pile.

I waited as long as I dared for Luis and Carmen, then wrote them a note, saying I'd be in touch later. I put it on the table under an empty cup, made sure Molly had water and food and headed out to beard the lion in his den. What did I know about lions? Just a faint recollection from a sophomore class in philosophy. If a lion could speak, we would not understand him, not unless we knew his "way of being in the world." A quote from Ludwig Wittgenstein. I also thought of Aslan, the lion king of Narnia, who spoke impeccable upper-class British English with a touch of Irish lace, and was the exemplar of everything considered good, but my appointment was not with him.

FORTY

Elizondo's office was on a posh strip of Avenida la Reforma, with tall palm trees and modern buildings. I pulled in at the address, a new high-rise with a sign in front bearing a huge Z, with businesses listed beneath it. The entering drive led down a ramp to an underground parking area. A gate stopped me, steel grillwork, ten feet high. A guard in something like a sentry box greeted me pleasantly and asked for my ID, which I held out to him through the window. He was wearing a blue cotton shirt with a *Z* appliquéd over the pocket and a shoulder phone. He spoke my name. The gate swung open. My Bug went in like a midget entering a castle and the gate clicked shut. Just inside the gate another guy spoke into his phone and a kid about sixteen appeared from somewhere. He gave me the stub of a ticket and took the car to park it in the depths of the garage, joining it with a score of other vehicles I could see down there.

I was standing next to an elevator. It dinged and the door slid open. The operator was wearing the same shirt and also a shoulder phone. "*Señor* Peterson," he said into it. We rode to the 6th floor. There I was met by a male receptionist, this one in a business suit, who chatted in English about the weather as he led me down the hall. We passed other offices, one with the sign *EXPLORADORES* on the door, another with *BUENAS NUEVAS*, Zondo's political party. We passed the restrooms and a cafeteria, and into a seating area, where he served me the first really good coffee I'd tasted since I entered the country.

Then Muriel arrived. My surprise was evident. "Last minute decision, or I'd have warned you," she said, dabbing at her face with a tissue. She was breathless and her plump cheeks were pinker than ever. "I hope you don't mind. I know I ought to be here. The Lord spoke to me."

"I'm glad you came," I said, not warmly, because I was not sure how glad I was. *Ought* to be here? The Lord apart, there was something too motherly in the tone. She was still wearing the flowery dress and the pearls, like a cliché of herself. I liked her better under a piano.

The receptionist brought in more coffee and behind him was Elizondo. *"Hola, hola, amigos!"* He gave us a comical bow. *"Tía* Muriel!" He kissed her hand. "My blue-eyed auntie," he said to me, with a wink.

I stood to meet him. "My pleasure, Mr. Peterson," he said. "From Boston, I believe. Red Sox fan?"

"Of course."

"I follow the Cubs myself. Just as frustrating."

He beckoned us into his office across the hall. "You are a friend of Luis López," he said to me.

"I told him that, Ted," Muriel inserted.

"Are you here as his emissary?" Elizondo asked.

"No, I'm not." I was grateful for the chance to say it, for Luis's sake. "Not at all. He doesn't know I'm here."

"How is he doing, by the way?"

"Hard to keep a good man down."

"Please take my regards to him."

The office was not the slick space I'd imagined, with maybe an eight-foot desk clear of work, save for one perfectly centered manila folder. Rather, it suggested old-timey comfort. The desk was messy, the furniture well-used. Plants filled a ceiling-high sunny window.

Other than some photos and his diploma from Notre Dame, there was nothing on the walls except that enormous knock-your-socks-off painting I'd caught sight of in the television interview. It was even better up close, a playground of leaping brush strokes in shades of terracotta. I stood admiring it, hoping I wouldn't be called on to come up with the name of the artist. But Elizondo was eager to tell me. His son had done it. His son, an adult now, was an artist, and that was all he was able to do. "Muriel knows Miguel," he said, glancing at her. "An eternal child, badly retarded. But he does these remarkable things with paint."

So now I was thoroughly disarmed. We sat down, Muriel and I side by side and Elizondo in front of us, four feet away. He wore a starchy white cotton shirt, open at the neck. He looked as if he had just showered and changed. I was wearing the only tie I'd brought and a shirt that could stand some ironing. My backpack, looking teen-aged and grungy, leaned against my chair.

A woman with a pad and pen came in and sat next to Elizondo. The male receptionist stood quietly in the open doorway to the hall. I wondered about hidden cameras, tape recorders. If so, they were hidden nicely.

"We have a very small window of time," Elizondo said. "I don't know how long. I've squeezed you in between appointments. So tell me why you are here." He looked from Muriel to me and back again. I saw us in his eyes, the strange duet that we were.

Muriel answered. "It's about the rumor, Zondo." I expected a "dear" but it didn't come. "It's spreading fast, and Ted here has heard it now. We're very concerned."

"*Ah, lo veo, lo veo,*" Elizondo said. "But which of the rumors are you referring to, *Tía?* That I'm a womanizer, that old one? Or that I've fathered seventeen illegitimate children, or that a drug cartel uses my whirlybird, or the most recent, the Exploradores is in cahoots with the death squads?"

The stenographer chuckled, but Muriel didn't. "You know which one, Zondo. You take it with a grain of salt, but people are bound to think any rumor has a basis in some kind of truth. People need to hear that you are dealing with it."

"Absolutely. I appreciate the candor," he said, to me, as if I was the one who had spoken. "So I will be candid, too." He turned to the stenographer. "Get this down. I am about to come clean."

The stenographer laughed out loud. I didn't, nor Muriel.

"*Tía*, forgive me," he said, soberly. "I know you want me to deny it, and I do, as any intention of my own. But in an organization as large as the Exploradores, it's impossible to control the private activities of all its members, or even to know about them, if I even should know about them. So here is what I can tell you. If I find this rumor has any basis in fact, I will do the right thing. I hope you will accept that as an answer. How about it, Mr. Peterson? What can I say to reassure my gringo friends?"

This was the entree, the one I hoped for, but it was too wide open.

I paused before it, one foot in. "I don't know yet," I said. That was the truth, at least, a far-reaching one. I took another step. "What I hear from others is concern about your affiliation with the military. The Exploradores may not be in cahoots with death squads, but the military certainly is."

"Oh, you're right about that," he said. "The military is much too powerful here. But the officers in my affiliation, as you put it, are Christian brothers. They see themselves as protectors of democracy. And as you also know, Mr. Peterson, it's your own country that has provided the training and resources, into the millions of dollars, that has turned our little army into the counter-insurgency force that it is. Because the White House knows we are key to holding back the threat of Communism in this hemisphere. —But you're not here to talk about that. Is there something else?"

Here we go. I jumped in. "I would like to talk about Luis López."

"Ah, I thought so. And so would I. Tell me what's on your mind."

"He's in an intolerable situation, facing a probable murder charge, for one thing, and he won't come to his own defense. I'm looking for a way to help him out."

"Understandable." He was thoughtful for a second. "First off, though, wouldn't you say, we need to acknowledge that Luis is the creator of many of his own problems?"

"Yes. He knows that."

"And in my opinion he is wasting his life on a lost cause. You've been staying at his house, I understand."

Did Muriel tell him that, too? Maybe, when she made the appointment.

"So," Elizondo went on, "I expect you've experienced first hand what it means to try to identify with the poor, as they say. Communism is not our biggest problem here, Mr. Peterson, or our oldest, by any means. Just the other day I was talking with one of your own congressmen. He's disturbed that our poverty level is so high and he's reluctant to vote for continued support unless we can prove that we are doing more to help the indigenous. I tried to explain. They refuse to be helped, or to help themselves. Missionaries know this, right, *Tía* Muriel? They won't vote. Over fifty percent of the population and they don't participate. They refuse to educate themselves, beyond, what is it, a sixth grade level, if that. Most don't speak Spanish. So over and over it comes down to a few rows of corn, malnourished children, and a bunch of useless languages. They *choose* poverty, and ignorance, and for five hundred years they have held this country back."

"Why, Zondo!" said Muriel. "Zondo, *dear!*" She remained seated, but she did sit forward in her chair and grow an inch or two taller. "*Tú eres injusto.* Are you forgetting your own *mamá?* Wasn't she an Indian? Indian through and through. But was she ignorant? Did she ever hold *you* back?"

"Oh, you are quite right, *Tía.*" Elizondo leaned across and took her hands in each of his. "But I am not condemning the Indian population. I am trying to save it, don't you see?"

He sat back up to include me. "In the U.S., Mr. Peterson, things are different. The indigenous there were disempowered early on. I don't know how you evaluate that, but you can't deny that it has meant a certain peace of mind all these years. And when you go back to the States you will expect the same comforts you have always known. Should you be faulted for that? Of course not. It's God's will, for all of us, equally. In a new Guatemala those riches can belong to the Indians, too, every village in every region, when and *if* they turn their back on the old ways and give themselves to a God of freedom and bounty. —*Verdad?*"

There was a clock on the wall behind him. I longed to look at it, and didn't, but as if I had, he said, "I know. Let's get back to Luis, you are thinking. And I am, I am getting back to Luis."

He paused, palms together against his lips and then went on in that formal, pre-constructed way, as if Muriel and I were a roomful of U.S. senators. So far he had not muttered a single *um* or *er* or *you know*, with not one extraneous hand motion. "I explained this to President Reagan a while ago and he found it very convincing. There is a reason God has not been able to bless us here as you have been blessed in the States. Look at what we have been harboring and tolerating for over five hundred years—the demonic practices of the Maya, still going strong in the mountain villages. Worship of the old gods, the jaguar and the snake, the gods of the lakes and the mountains. More than tolerate, we've *celebrated* this disgrace in jewelry and pottery and weavings. We've commercialized it in hyped-up tourism. Archaeologists have been exploring and protecting the so-called sacred sites. I believe there will always be war here, a spiritual war, until we wipe this abomination off the land. *Vos?*"

"I hear you, Zondo," said Muriel. "Do go on. We need to hear this."

Huh? Did she mean that? I wanted to look at her, but couldn't without being obvious. "We need to take the Gospel of love to these people," she said. "And that's what we've been trying to do, haven't we, all these years, Zondo, model Christ to them. And it *has* made a difference, hasn't it?"

"Not enough. There are still the hold-outs, millions of them. Five hundred years of God's patience. How much longer can it last? I fear for those people, what is going to happen to them, unless the Satanic bonds are broken."

"All right," said Muriel. "Now I see."

"And you, Mr. Peterson?"

"Do I see?"

"Yes. Tell me what you think."

"You really want to know?"

"Certainly."

"I think it's a crock of shit."

The secretary jumped in her chair and Muriel whispered, "Oh, my!" Elizondo gave his head a little shake, as if a fly had landed there. Then he smiled, not a big happy smile, but a knowing one. I had done exactly what he wanted me to do, exactly what I wanted to get him to do, reveal himself. Now I've shut him up for sure.

But I'm wrong. "Thank you for your honesty," he said. "Let me return the favor with something else I've just begun to realize. Are you acquainted with spiritual mapping? The Old Testament is full of it. The Israelites, when they listened to God, were able to pinpoint the geographic territory where pagan worship was most actively threatening, and now God is showing us the same thing, where those geographical sites exist in this country."

"Very interesting," said Muriel. "I hadn't thought of that."

"It's no different than any military intelligence, determining the location of the enemy. The best example I can give is Las Cavernas.

Here is a village where Christians have lived for many years, *but* a village surrounded by caves that have historically been the locale of pagan worship and rites. Rather than seal off those caves, shut them up as a gesture of rejection, the people of Las Cavernas have continued to permit them to be used, even today, for the old styles of worship—done in secret, true, but well known. And here's the thing. I have never heard Luis López repudiate this. And why would he? Part of spiritual mapping is learning what fruit the land bears. And what has Las Cavernas produced? Luis himself, for one, a sick and tormented man. And for whom was he named? A disgraced priest. And as you know too well, the village has not only produced a disgraced priest, but a disgraced Protestant missionary, a Communist."

"Whoa!" I shouted, shooting up my hand. The stenographer jumped again and the receptionist at the door took two steps into the room. Elizondo signaled him back. Now I do turn to look at Muriel, confronting her, not hiding my fury. Has she told him about my father, too? But she returns my gaze, clear-eyed and unflinching.

Elizondo resumes. "I know how unpleasant this must be for you, Mr. Peterson. But history proves it. Las Cavernas is a village under a curse. Things have not been good there for a very long time. Natural disasters. Poor soil, poor crops, poverty. And none of us can protect them from something even worse."

What the heck is he doing? Is he trying to bait me, or warn me, or threaten, or sincerely include me in a divine revelation? I don't know, I can't read him at all. I just know that the basis for anything I want to accomplish here, anything to do with Luis, has been poisoned. I could speak now. He has stopped talking, the opening is there. But it would be like addressing a madman in a world of his own fantasy. Is that what he's intended? I look at Muriel again. This time her eyes are fastened on Elizondo.

It's over, anyway. There's a light knock at the door. A woman enters and whispers to the receptionist, who signals Elizondo. "It seems our time is up," he announces. "I'm sorry to end this, friends, but my next appointment is waiting."

Muriel picks up her purse, gives Elizondo a warm kiss on the cheek and me a wave, and leaves the room. The secretary and the receptionist walk out as well. It's time for me to go, too, I tell myself, before I do something truly destructive, like smashing him in the face. Go, go, go, says my better, more sensible self. But I don't go and I don't hit him. That would precipitate Smitty's tragic necessity. I just stand there, alone with him, with no plan or strategy, for sure no power-based strategy. After about a thousand years have passed, I turn to leave.

"Please wait," Elizondo says. "Just a minute more." He moves in closer to me. No doubt he wants to hit me, too, and could, and get away with it, but his manner and tone reflect nothing at all of what has just passed between us. He is a different man. Same face, body, same white shirt, but different. "I believe you are the one who is worried about Catherine Rodriguez," he says.

I nod, barely.

"Was it you who called Carlos Méndez about her? When she went missing?"

"Yes," I say. "And he called you, I believe."

"Well, I'm worried, too. Have you heard anything more at all?"

"Nothing."

"We were friends once, you know. I knew her husband's family well, the whole tribe. We grew up together. I knew Mag when she was still living at home. Magdalena Rodriguez? You know who I mean? The woman whose ID was found in Luis's truck."

"Yes."

"That was not Mag in the truck, of course. I've been wondering if it could be Catherine."

"I've been wondering myself." I'm stunned that I've said it, but I'm glad. We're back in the real world.

"Actually, I wouldn't put it past her to take Mag's ID," he says. "Another persona. Cat's romantic obsession. She always fancied herself as some kind of a Mata Hari, you know. I used to tease her about her nine lives."

I want to hit him again. Walking out would be wiser but I know what I've got to do instead, all advice and warnings aside. Stay in the real world, as much as real means anything any more. Let that truth speak for itself, take us where it will. *Aletheia*. "I'd like to tell you what I know," I say.

"Please do."

"First of all, I know that Catherine was carrying Magdalena's ID."

"Oh. —So it could be Catherine."

I have no way to read that. "It could," I say, carefully. "But Magdalena owned several fake IDs, and her house was ransacked right after Catherine left."

"Carlos told me that, too," he says. "What else do you know?"

"It's unlikely that Luis could have driven his truck into the dump, or anywhere, after he was tortured."

"And that's something you know—for a fact?"

"Not actually. Call it a reasonable conclusion, drawn from verifiable circumstances. The *batón* to the balls."

He considers that. Maybe we're sharing the same physical sensation. "So you think someone else drove it there," he says.

"Any idea who?" I ask.

He shrugs. "The police? They did seize his truck, when they arrested him. They intended to trash it."

"That's something you know?"

"So I was told."

"But maybe somebody had a better idea," I say. "I have a sort of hunch about this, just a *capricho*, but it makes sense to me. Shall I tell you?"

"If you wish."

"I think it was the scheme of someone who's been having a problem with both Luis and Catherine. Luis is a nuisance, let's say, a challenge. And Catherine, well, she knows too much. And suddenly the chance arrives to deal with them both at once—disgrace Luis and get rid of Catherine."

"—Rid of?"

"But maybe it doesn't work. Maybe things go wrong. There's a screwup. Like the wrong murder. Or maybe, please God, no murder. But wrong body. Wrong ID."

"What do you mean? That it might not be Catherine?"

"I don't know," I say. "It's just speculation. I have a few pieces but I don't know how to put them together."

"Well, by chance do you want to know what I think?" he asks.

"I do, of course."

"I think it's a crock of shit."

He tosses me a little smile and I toss it back, grimly assenting. I should have predicted that. Then he asks, "Are you alone with this theory, Mr. Peterson?"

And I should have predicted that too. I need to be careful now, about who else I involve. Sam is the only person I could have told and I recall that I didn't because it was not observable data. And Win Hall, I could have told Hall, but I didn't. And not Luis, certainly. There's no one else.

"I've never explained it to anyone," I say. "But it is in writing, I can tell you that for sure, and it's possible someone else has read it, or will." He says nothing—face, voice or body language, but I know what he's got to be wondering. *Donde?* Where is it? So I answer. "I sent it off. By now it's somewhere in the States."

He thinks a moment, eyes on my face, then shakes his head. "In all truth, I think your theory is flawed, Mr. Peterson. Too cumbersome. Too hard to pull off. Who would attempt such a thing in the first place?"

"Someone with the right connections? Someone with the influence to carry it out?"

"It would be a bit hard to narrow that down, wouldn't it?" He smiles, a real grin. "You'll need to do a little better. Try again."

"Someone with a lot to protect?"

"Lots of people like that around here." He shakes his head again.

"Then how about some skunk," I say brightly, "some low-down, cock-sucking son of a puta? Some ass who thinks he's doing the will of God?"

His eyebrows shoot up and he laughs. "Now that's more like it," he says.

But now he backs away from me, just a little, raises his eyes to the door, which is behind me, and then down to his watch. His next appointment is surely waiting. He can stop this interchange any time he likes, but he's the one who keeps it going. He raises his eyes to mine again. "I think you would like to name this despicable person," he says.

I don't want to answer that. I don't think I should. Every ounce of good sense is warning me not to. But it's as if the real world has led us both to this point, a place where he has the right to ask the question and expect a frank answer, the confirmation of what he already knows.

"I think it's you," I tell him. "And you're not surprised."

"No. A bit horrified, shall we say?"

"I have no proof, you understand." I'm sure he knows that, too. "Just my phone call to Carlos Mendez, and his to you. And your history with Luis and Catherine."

"What you know of it."

He glances again over my shoulder. He's shorter than I, but he can see comfortably whoever is behind me. It could be his secretary signaling or he may be signaling someone himself. What I see, over his head, is the painting on the wall. The colors are moving, swirling, as if sending a frantic signal. Get out! Run! Or else it's just doing what some abstracts are supposed to do, move, race all over the canvas.

"Then, there's that odd coincidence," I say, "Martin." Marteen, as I've pronounced it. "How his body was found, in the dump in his smashed car, in the same framed up circumstances. I'm sorry to mention that incident, but you can't blame me for my own spiritual mapping."

He doesn't appear to make the connection. "So what is it you plan to do with this *absurdidad*? Start yet another rumor?"

"I could," I say, fascinated for an instant with the power. "But I hope I won't stoop that low. I'm not trying to get anyone else in trouble. I just want to get Luis out of this mess." He's listening, so I blunder on. "How about an agreement? I won't spread a rumor that has no proven basis—since, as I've heard you say, rumors are a form of violence. And you think of a way to give Luis a break from this one. You know, with another television interview, maybe, or a story in the right newspaper. You want to set the record straight, new information has come to light, Luis has been framed—that sort of thing."

His throat bobs in a chuckle. "I'm not Luis's guardian angel, but has it occurred to you I might do that anyway, just to help him out? Provided new information comes to light—that sort of thing."

"I feel sure you can find a way."

"And if Luis gets himself into even more trouble, will you think I'm the culprit?"

"I'll certainly wonder. And if something happens to the people of Las Cavernas, I'll also wonder."

We've been avoiding a steady eye-to-eye confrontation, in an odd show of Guatemalan courtesy, both of us respecting the cultural taboo. But now our eyes meet and hold. "So was it you?" I ask.

"You amaze me, Mr. Peterson. What gives you the right to ask that question?"

"I've presumed the right, I admit." A bit of hubris, true.

"If I'm guilty, God will be my judge," he says.

"But God doesn't vote." No, too snide. "Just a consideration," I add.

"All right, Mr. Peterson, let me ask *you* a question. Are you a believer? Where do you stand, personally, in matters of faith?"

"Where will I go if this plane goes down?"

"Something like that."

"What gives you the right to ask?"

"A presumption, I admit. In these days of bodily peril it's best to make sure one's soul at least is secure."

"That could be taken as a threat."

"Well, if it were, I don't suppose it would scare someone like you, would it now?"

"Oh, it would, actually. It does." I feel the truth of that in every part of my body and whatever I can designate as my soul. "*Xo'bil.*" That comes out right, as sho-*beel*, with the startled catch of breath in the middle. He looks puzzled.

"Mam word," I explain. "Scared half out of my pants—Luis's translation. And you. You have a lot to fear, too, don't you, even someone like you."

"Then you and I have a lot in common."

"True." I am in the lion's den and at the moment the lion and I understand each other very well. But it's still his den. His eyes shoot over my shoulder once more. This time I turn my head. Two men in uniform are standing in the doorway, watching us.

"Goodbye, Mr. Peterson. It's been good to meet you."

Elizondo is reaching out his hand. It's cold, I notice, as our skins touch. Mine is sweaty.

"You might add this little scene to your written record," he says.

"I will." I give him a brisk Boy Scout salute, grab my pack and walk out, past the two soldiers. They're young, in camouflage, trousers tucked into boots. On their red berets three arrows point down over the left eye, the Kaibile logo. We greet each other nicely. I walk down the hall, alone as far as I know, past the other offices, and slip into the men's room. It can be a trap, I'm aware of that, but there's no choice. I sit there in a stall as long as necessary, five minutes, maybe ten, in a full-blown panic attack, sweating, heart pounding. Someone comes in, hard heels on the hard floor, while I stop breathing. I hear a long piss in a urinal and the flush, and the feet walk out.

The truth is expensive, as my father might say, and I haven't given a thought to "wise" or "harmless," or Smitty's track-two diplomacy, or going the second mile. Maybe I offered my left cheek, I don't know, but I also can't say Elizondo smited me on the right. I only wanted to nail the guy, and though he may be guilty as hell about something, there's not an ounce of solid evidence that it's anything I've implied. To him, this is a spiritual war. I need to get that straight.

In a few more minutes I leave the stall. I wash my hands and face, taking my time. No one else comes in, certainly no one with weapon raised. Out in the corridor people are moving about busily. Hardly anyone glances my way. Not a uniform in sight.

When I get to the elevator, the door is open, the same operator on duty. "Peterson," he says again into his phone. He stands with his back to me. He knows I'm harmless, I bet, never hit anyone in my life, never carried a weapon. No gun in my pack. He's not going to shoot me, either. Nothing so messy. No, by God, this is a *spiritual* war.

Anyway, there's a camera on watch, blinking its red light over the door. I run my hand across my barbered scalp and offer the lens a pro-file, first one side, then the other, just for the record. I may not have done anything right, but at least I know who I am, and it's no one in the military computer system. Not a Norwegian, I tell the camera, and not just a Swede. Indian, by birth and tapeworm. Citizen of the Americas. Son and *nahual* of Communist missionary. *Amigo* to Mayan clown. Lover of girl guerrilla. Unreconstructed post-modern piddler.

"Well, *pues*," says the camera, blinking away. "Whoopdeefuckindoo!"

The elevator stops and I step off into the underground garage.

FORTY-ONE

No one was there, neither of the two men who had met me when I arrived, though I could see activity down in the parking well. I couldn't see my Bug, but Bugs can hide, and there were still a lot of cars down there, including a small bus, and a couple of vans, dark ones. Maybe they weren't green, but I wasn't about to get particular. The gate to the street was shut. Of course it would be. A big two-tone brown car was idling in the exit lane with someone in it. I looked around for a pedestrian egress, just in case, and didn't see one.

Then the driver-side door of the brown car opened and Muriel Treadwell climbed out. She waved and walked over to me. "You're still here," I said.

"Yes, Ted. I'm afraid there's a problem." She looked neither smiling nor sweet. Before she could say more, the elevator dinged and slid open. A blue-shirted guy stepped out, the one who had greeted me inside the gate when I arrived. "Ay, *señor*," he said. "It's you. I am looking for you, everywhere."

I held out my ticket stub but he didn't take it. "Humblest apologies, *señor*. *Perdone, perdone*. Your car. Your car is not here. Someone steal."

"What?"

"Someone steal your car."

"My Volkswagen? Someone *stole* it?"

"*Sí*."

"But why?" It was the only reasonable question.

The guy threw up his hands. *Saber, saber*.

"It's true, Ted," Muriel said. "Someone drove off in it, just a few minutes ago."

"Did you see it happen?" I asked her.

She shook her head no. "I hadn't come down yet. I stopped at the Exploradores office."

"Then how—?"

The attendant began to explain, talking rapidly, in Spanish and bad English. They had brought up our cars, he said, the *señora's* and mine, because they thought we were leaving. The motors were running, and "some *hombre*" hopped into mine and drove away. "Zoom! Like that."

"Some guy? Who would, for God's sake?"

Don't know, he said. He waved his hands, repeating *muy ocupado,* very busy, very busy, didn't see.

It couldn't have been more phony. "But I've got the stub," I said. And what about all that security? Telephones. Cameras. "There must be cameras here," I said. "Are there cameras?"

"*Sí.*" The guy pointed out three, explaining something, jabbering.

"Did you call the police?" Just thought I'd ask. He screwed up his face as if I'd told a bad joke.

The elevator bell dinged again and two women stepped out and stood there, Hispanic women in business suits. Muriel waved to them briefly. The attendant spoke into his phone and a motor started up down in the parking well.

"Is your car rented?" Muriel asked me.

"Yes, of course." Who was going to call the rental? I didn't care. I just wanted to get out of here. I started for the gate.

"Oh, wait. We take you home, *señor*," the guy said. "*A dónde vas? Where do you go?*"

"No, no," said Muriel. "I'll take him. I told you I would."

"*Bueno, señora, gracias.*"

We walked over to her car. I was immensely relieved to get into it. The interior felt like the fortress I needed. It was huge compared to my Bug, a Plymouth Fury, 60's style, a little beat up but still intimidating, with the long broad front and a trunk big enough to hold a grown man. But no room for my knees, which were against the dashboard. I was sharing a bench seat with Muriel, and it was pulled as far forward as it would go so her feet could reach the pedals. The steering wheel was in her lap.

"Where to?" she asked.

"Airport, if you please. You know how to get there from here?"

"Well, I'll give it a try," she said.

I took that as a playful put-down: I've only lived in this city for fifty years, Teddy boy. She drove to the gate, stopped, gave a little toot, the gate swung open and we entered the traffic of Avenida la Reforma. We were north of the airport, not far from an entrance to the terminal. My watch said 4:35. Plenty of time and now no car to return. I checked my mirror. The traffic was terrifying, as usual, but no dark vans behind, no green ones, no vans at all, nothing that looked menacing. No shadowing, no car chase. I sat back. "I'm grateful to you for this," I said to Muriel.

She gave a quick smile. "We're not there yet." Her eyes were on the road, her chin lifted to see out the windshield. "Do you understand what's going on?" she asked.

"Yes," I said. "For one thing, I think my car is going to find itself in an unfortunate accident."

"That's the plan," she said.

"And I will apparently leave the scene unscathed. Somehow never to be seen again. Am I crazy?"

"No, no, you're not crazy."

"But here I am safe with you."

She glanced at me with the same brief smile and back to the road. She was not a good driver, nervous. Her plump foot was heavy on the brake, and we were hugging the right edge, too close. My leg and arm muscles tensed, driving for her, holding back the obvious irony that I could still be in an "unfortunate accident," however unintentional.

"I feel bad about all this, Ted," she said.

"I know," I answered. "I know you do."

"I'm sorry." She looked suddenly tired, I thought, or older, as old as she was, as old as my mother. Her face seemed gray, no longer the pink glow of upstairs. Tell me you don't really agree with him, that ominous nonsense, I wanted to say. To my dismay, a tear slid from the corner of her eye down the line of a wrinkle in her cheek. She wiped it away with her finger. "I just trust the Lord to understand."

I didn't press her for more. It was better not to distract her. She was clutching, braking, accelerating. I braced my knees against the dashboard and shut my eyes. In a few minutes I felt the car turn right. I looked. We were headed west, as we should be, right into the sun, misty with coming rain. The airport would soon be on our left. So far good.

"Best," said Muriel. "Sometimes we have to do things we don't want to do, you know, because it's best. Best for all."

Oh ye gods, don't talk, just drive, I thought. We were passing Aurora Park and the entrance to the zoo. I watched, wary of a left turn in her hands. But she didn't take a left. She kept on going, past the logical turn, hands gripping the steering wheel, more tears rolling down. I wondered if she could see well enough. We entered a cloverleaf, which led us onto Avenida Bolivar, going north, a busy highway, with traffic at a speed that was destined to take us quickly away from any possible access to the terminal, as it was doing with every second. It was a strange mistake. I hated to ask. I had to. "Why are we here?"

"Because I don't have a choice," she said, grimly. "What else can I do?"

"Can I help?"

She answered by taking an exit. I thought she intended to find her way back, but with another turn we were on 7A Avenida, still going in the wrong direction. Maybe she couldn't read signs. "Are we lost?" I asked.

"No, no, of course not," she said, panic in her voice.

Things were beginning to look familiar, unpleasantly so. I knew where this road ended. I had come here with both Catherine and Dina. Already an odor was sneaking into the car, a very particular odor, smoke, a very particular smoke with the stench of hellfire. *El basurero.* "The dump," I said. "The *dump?*"

"No, no, dear!" Muriel said. "Not the dump. *La casa.*"

"The house? What house?"

"*Para disposición.*" She was looking around as she drove, braking, shooting ahead.

"Disposal? House for disposal?"

"Yes. Everyone knows about that."

Except me. I had heard it mentioned, I recalled, by Luis, but never explained. And now I knew. There are notions your mind turns away as unacceptable, that have no place in the work of the brain, as reality or metaphor, logic or wild imagination. But this unacceptable notion was a determined one. It knocked again. *Tap tap tap,* then louder. *Bang, bang bang!* Open up, idiot! I opened.

"Delivery," Muriel said.

She was still glancing around, both sides of the road, at the shacky houses made of plastic and tin. I glanced around, too, while I took it in, wholly, along with the smoke that now filled the car. I was being delivered. *Muriel Treadwell* was delivering me—to *The House for Disposal.* I was not to be chased by another car, nothing so predictable. I was *in* the car. Not a green van, not a white one, not an army jeep—a U.S. suburban sedan, driven by a parental figure in a flowery dress and pearls, a veteran missionary of forty years, a volunteer and vigilante, a Christian soldier caught up in a war—a spiritual war. Someone who would ordinarily never do this or anything like it, who had no capacity for it, who was apologizing, in tears. It was as if my own mother were turning me in, most regretfully, to be sure, but knowing it was "best"—best for all. It was a wonderful, ingenious twist of events, even laudatory, and terrifying as hell.

I had no intention of letting it happen. I could overpower her easily and grab the wheel. I could pull up on the emergency brake. I could leap out of the car. That was it. Leap and run. I reached for the door handle.

"Oh, poo-ey!" said Muriel, straining up into her mirror. I turned to the back window. A small sedan was pulling up close behind us. Someone was trying to pass. This was the time to jump. I opened the door, ready to go. But Muriel gunned and jerked the car in a tight ninety degrees on to a street at our right, so suddenly only a machine this heavy could stay upright. I was thrown back in, the door slamming. A horn blew loud and long behind us. I looked again. The same car had followed us and two people, two women, the driver and passenger, were signaling with their hands over the roof. Back, back, go back. Muriel waved into the mirror with a helpless gesture and kept on going, not speeding now, but not slowing, zig-zagging from one short block to another, as if trying to find her way. The area was jammed with buildings, homes, factories, pedestrians, people carrying things, to and from the dump, traffic. I watched for another place to jump, my door ajar.

The car behind kept up, closer to us now, very close, the women still signaling. I recognized them. They were the ones who had come down in the elevator to the garage while we were standing there. They looked frustrated. Muriel was not getting a message.

"Pray, Ted, pray!" she said. Then our car entered an exit. But it was not our exit, nor our entrance. There was the sign, hardly avoidable. NO ENTRAR. "Stop!" I shouted. "Wrong way!" She pushed on, not even slowing. Four, five vehicles approaching us swerved out of our path, in a blast of horns. Two cars skidded over to the side and stopped, one just missing the car behind us—those women. They had actually followed us. Now with a surprised screech of tires, we angled into the traffic of Avenida Bolivar, as illegally and insanely as it could happen in any country in the world. I looked back. Our followers were not martyrs. They were nowhere in sight.

"Whew!" Muriel said. "I think we're okay." She took several deep breaths. "We can go to the airport now."

I didn't ask. I didn't say a word. At the clover leaf, which she maneuvered with proper skill, I looked back again. Still no sign of the women. In minutes we were at an entrance to the terminal, where we picked up a ticket for parking and found a slot for the car. Muriel turned off the motor.

"There," she said. "There. Oh, my goodness, my goodness. I didn't know what to do. I just asked the Lord to lead."

"Adventurous Lord."

"Well, we know that, don't we." She fanned her face with her hand.

I was hot and breathless, too, as if we'd run the distance on foot. "When did we start to be followed?" I asked.

"Oh, right away, right away. They were two cars behind us the whole time. Elena and Maria. I know them well. We're on the Exploradores scholarship committee together. They were making sure I took you to the right place."

"For disposal."

"You didn't see them following us?"

"I didn't know their car. Will they rat on you now? Will you be in trouble?"

"No, no. Everyone knows I'm a terrible driver. I'll just say I was confused. I tried to seem that way. Did I succeed?"

"Superbly."

"I had to throw them off. I'd have come right here to the airport, but then they would know where I was taking you. I was so worried about that." Her eyes were watering again. "Promise me something, Ted. If you ever have the chance, please don't tell Hugh what I just did with the car." She wiped her eyes.

I swiped at my own with my sleeve. "I have no idea how to thank you," I mumbled. She gave me a tissue. That made me laugh. "Come in with me," I said. "Get a cup of coffee."

"I should go home and start dinner. When is your flight?"

"I've got plenty of time."

It was starting to rain. We ducked together for the entry, me holding her umbrella as she trotted along beside me, like a guardian angel in motherly drag. She came no higher than my shoulder. The terminal was more crowded than I'd seen it in my two prior visits. I found an empty table in a corner of the cafeteria, as far as I could get from the one where the Melanos had sat. I got the coffee while Muriel composed herself. She was still damp-eyed when I got back. She said, "I'm sorry, Ted."

"Before you say that again, I need to know what for."

"You don't know?"

"Everybody in this country thinks I know what they mean."

"Oh, my." She covered her mouth. "But you said—. This whole time I thought you knew what was happening. What could you have thought? You must have thought—. Did you think I was really going to—? Oh, dear, dear. And when I lied to Zondo, right in front of you. Didn't you know?"

"You lied?"

"I was deceptive. I played along with him. I was trying to smooth things over, don't you see? And then you said that about, about a crock of—."

"Shit?"

"Yes, thank you. And with those boys at the garage? I thought you understood what I was trying to do there. I had to make it look like I could be trusted to—do the errand."

"All right, I see that now, but." I was weary of the buts.

"It's terrible. The whole masquerade." She fought for words. "Hugh and I have known the truth for weeks. So have a lot of others, members. We've been trying to save the organization, without getting people hurt. So we haven't been openly critical. When you said you wanted to talk to him, do you see what a dilemma that presented? Hugh didn't want me to come, but I had to. I was afraid you'd get yourself in trouble, and I was right. What on earth did you say to Zondo after I left?"

"Nothing special—other than exposing the CIA. Disarming the entire military complex, the political industrial something or other oligarchy. Like, you know. Sort of."

She laughed, trembly. "No wonder you're in trouble."

"When did you find out about my car?" I asked.

"They told me right away, the garage boys. They know me, I come here so often. I think they're on the fence, probably scared to death, poor boys."

"And the two women?"

"Oh, they're *in* on it for sure, up to their ears. Guilty as —."

"Hell?"

"Yes, thank you." She sipped her coffee. "This is not a bad country and Zondo is not a bad man. You know that parable about the sower? The seed that falls on thorny ground?" She carried on with that for several minutes, developing the whole lesson for me, as if it were the explanation to everything. I let myself fall back into its soft, prickly bed. "But there's lots of good ground here, too," she said, finally, with a preachy ring. "Where everything flourishes, even a hundredfold." I couldn't think of a profound response. I probably said, "Really," or "I see."

She picked up her purse. "Hugh will be waiting."

I reached for the umbrella. "I'll walk you to the car."

"No, stay here, please," she said. "Go to your gate and stay there until you board. I'll be all right."

"Not a chance," I said.

She begged me. "Stay here, please. No one is going to hurt me. Zondo's mamá would haunt him the rest of his life. He knows that."

I went with her anyway, holding the umbrella over her head. "This is what my own mamá would want me to do," I said.

She kissed me goodbye. "Say hi to her for me. She's quite a gal, you know."

"You're quite a gal yourself," I said, then stood in the rain and watched her drive away.

Back inside I found the same bank of phones I'd called Community Garden from a week ago. At that time Luis was missing, now he was the one who answered. "Ted. Are you still here?" He sounded pretty good, I thought.

There was a lot of noise in the background, voices and laughter. "Who's that?" I asked.

A group of students, he said, from the Netherlands, there for the week. "They're very loud, I know. Neighbors may complain. Where are you, anyway?"

"At the airport. This is probably not a secure call, if it matters."

"What the heck difference can it make, anyhow? Why are you calling?"

"I'm just saying a better goodbye."

"Goodbye? Listen, Buddy, you better get your butt right back here."

"I will. I just have to take care of a few things at home, spend some time with my mother. Then I'll come back, open a school, dig a sewer line, whatever you want."

"But there's another reason. Somebody left something for you here, hanging on the doorknob outside. It's a jacket, a windbreaker. There's a name on it, attached with a safety pin. Theodore Cavalier Peterson. I think that's you. —Ted? Hello? Are you there?"

"Describe it."

"White nylon. Big red B on the back. Boston? Red Sox? I'm not a fan or I'd keep it. —*Hola?* Are you still there? Say something."

"Is there a hole in the right side pocket?"

"Let's see. Yep, a hole. I can put my hand right through it. Is it yours? —Speak up. What's the matter?"

"It's mine. Is there a note or anything?"

"Nope. Wait, I'll try the other pocket. Yep. There's a piece of paper in it, folded. Shall I open it? Huh? Can't hear you. Speak up. I'll open it, anyway. —Jeeze. The handwriting is terrible. Big scrawl. It says 'Gracias, it worked.' That's all it says. It's signed. Love. Hey, it's signed with love. From Jadis. Jadis? Who the heck is Jadis?"

"You know that, dummy. The White Witch of Narnia."

"Oh sure, sure. But how did *she* get your jacket? —Ted? *Hola.* Are you still there?"

reaparición

noun, fem.

reappearance or return

NOTES FROM THE AUTHORS

Why a second edition? Henry James is the only novelist we know of who decided to revise his previously published work, but it's a safe guess that many other writers would like the chance. Thanks to Wipf and Stock Publishers, we have the opportunity to keep this story alive and kicking. We see the reader as a partner. Just as a play is not complete until it's performed, a novel is not finished until it has been read and processed. Over a hundred people have offered us wise and gracious feedback.

First of all, those who began walking with us at the very beginning:

Dennis Smith, our in-country collaborator, expert in all things Guatemalan, including the right cuss words. His pages of help could be a book in themselves. Any mistakes are ours, not his.

Eugene Garber, who regularly gifts us with the highest standards of creativity, criticism, and friendship.

Liz Phillips, sharp editor, good neighbor and faithful cheer leader when the going got tough. Every writer needs a reader like Liz.

Jeanne Murray Walker, whose keen literary sense so often renews our hope in the power of story and word.

Matt and Nancy Samson, our eyes and ears among the Maya, providing us with essential data (Sam Matthews' "observable facts") and good instincts, as well.

Virginia Stem Owens. Want the truth? Ask Ginger, and gain a laugh or two while you're at it.

Dave Pollock, with his expertise on third culture kids.

John Wilson, Harold Fickett, and the members of the Chrysostom Society of Writers who have listened to us read session after session.

Wilson Roberts and Diane Esser read our first completed draft, as did Ned and Patricia Trudeau, Scott Nelson, Margaret Black Mirabelli, and Jerry Gill and Mari Sorri ("A little more work on the ending.") Others who have read the book in various stages of completion and graced it with their responses: Tom Bourne, Tim Doherty, Doug Frank (who knows a lot about fathers and sons), Dan Carroll, Alice Schrade, Gary Dorrien (who knows a lot about everything), Todd Nelson and JoAnn Stevelos (good eyes and ears), Zoë Nelson, T'Chaka Sikelianos, Kris Nelson ("Scoop that cake right off the table!"), Robert

Brenneman, Carol and Charles McCollough, Gary McLouth, Bob Bady, Virginia Garrard-Burnett, Andy Schindel, Scott Teems, Randy Wilburn (who also gave us *aletheia*), Chris Robinson, David Noller. And former students, now our teachers: Anne Averyt, Cora Jane Barnes, Doug Kane, John Erickson, Priscilla Leavitt, Pat and Sears Eldredge, Paul and Lynn Pickens, Arthur and Esther Pope, and Andy Conrad.

Thanks to Ed Atkeson, our designer, the most laid-back person we know, and Susan Novotny and Jessika at The Troy Book Makers. You've been great to work with.

Others who have contributed along the way: Sara Parker, and the Scotchmer family, Karla Ann Koll, Bill and Joyce Peck, Antonio Otzoy, Tom and Ava Navin, Maribel Smith, Randall Shea, Grace and Juan Par, Michael Collier, Eugene Mirabelli, Karisari, Bev Taylor, legal advisors Jeremiah and Jeremy Manning, Cliff Sanders, who gave us the tapeworm story. And how can we thank Glenn Thorp enough for offering us his father's story?

Ted Lewis, Rick and Kitty Ufford-Chase, Tom Driver, Anne Barstow, Walt Chura, Fred Boehrer and Diana Conroy have offered us living examples of peacemaking and radical hospitality. Tom and Margery Melville were often on our minds, with their unwavering courage in truth-telling.

And special thanks to the unaware contributor of "Whoopdefuckindo," who shall remain nameless.

To all others who have joined the conversation over the years, advised us, published reviews, endorsed, or in any way promoted the book, initiated events, attended readings, provided hospitality, and helped us to see our way into a second edition, our deepest thanks: Larry Kinsman, Rick Spalding, Virginia Mollenkott, Pat Hanlon, Lian Xi, Kathleen Henry, Bill Jersey, Frankie FitzGerald, Jim Schaap, Eugene and Jan Peterson, Luci Shaw, John Hoyt, the McColloughs, Bob Begiebing, the Grieders, Joan Allen, John Buchanan, Marion Bean, Paula Huston, Lana Cable, Benji Smith, Eugene Mirabelli, Harry and Sharon Seelig, Patricia Lee Lewis, Maureen Moore, Jacqueline Sheehan, the Grations, Cora Jane Barnes (again), Warren Farha at Eighth Day Books, and Martin Marty's windowsill.

Novels can be—often should be—historically thin, but the heft of factual substance had better lie behind them. Dozens of scholars and journalists have informed us through this process. At the very beginning, *Harvest of Violence: The Maya Indians and the Guatemalan Crisis*, edited by anthropologist Robert M. Carmack, one of the first books on the subject, awakened us to the current Guatemalan dilemma. Carmack's own chapter, telling the story of his personal encounter with the forces of violence, launched us early into the heart of the long conflict. Also, early on, Mark Kline Taylor's *Remembering Esperanza* sparked our imaginations, again with the personal side of scholarly research. Though the book bears the heady sub-title, *A Cultural-Political Theology for North American Praxis*, it introduces itself by Taylor's own coming-to-terms with the "other" in his life and work.

Other reliable resources over the years: Dennis Tedlock, translator of the Popol Vuh; photographer-journalists Jean-Marie Simon and Paul Jeffrey, Marilyn Anderson and Jonathan Moeller; Latin American historians Susanne Jonas and Virginia Garrard-Burnett; anthropologist David Stoll; *The Magic of Ritual*, by Tom Driver; the hard-hitting poetry of Julia Esquivel and the novels of Francisco Goldman. Note also Goldman's superbly true report, *The Art of Political Murder: Who Killed the Bishop*?

For more in the long list we recommend *The Guatemala Reader: History, Culture, Politics*. Greg Grandin, Deborah T. Levinson, and Elizabeth Oglesby, eds. (Duke University Press, 2011). Add a fact check that includes the month of our story, *Closing the Space: Human Rights in Guatemala*, May 1987-October 1988, an Americas Watch Report.

Two events in Guatemala framed the context of our story. Of primary importance are the facts surrounding the coup of 1954. Hugh Treadwell told Ted that he'd heard of a book proving the direct involvement of the CIA in the overthrow of Jacobo Arbenz, Guatemala's president. Hugh was referring to *Bitter Fruit: The Story of the American Coup in Guatemala*, by Stephen Schlesinger and Stephen Kinzer, which first appeared in 1982. Catherine also alluded to this book in one conversation with Ted, when she told him it had taken twenty-eight years (1954-1982) for the truth about the coup to be published. Those facts are amplified in Stephen Kinzer's 2014 publication of *The Brothers: John Foster Dulles, Allen Dulles, and Their Secret World War*. An equally important source is *Secret History: The CIA's Classified Account of its Operations in Guatemala 1952-1954*, by Nick Cullather, based on documents declassified in 1992.

The second event is the "Year End Offensive" that began in the fall of 1987. On their drive into the hills on that fateful trip to find Isabel, Ted and Catherine watched helicopters flying in and out of the western mountains. Later, in the hotel at Lake Atitlán, she explained that buildup of arms as a campaign to "liquidate guerrillas" and CPRs (Populations in Resistance, citizens displaced by government violence) by the end of the year. For that reason she was bringing a map of safe routes to new locations to be picked up by Isabel's brother. You can find further information about this campaign in *State Violence in Guatemala, 1960-1996: A Quantitative Reflection* (Ball, Kobrak and Spirer). It continued off and on for six years, including aerial bombing that killed hundreds of civilians, and was only partially successful in dispersing the insurgency.

A lot has happened in Guatemala since 1987. On December 29, 1996, a "Firm and Lasting Peace" was finally signed in Guatemala City, officially ending 36 years of civil war between insurgent forces and the Guatemalan military government, but the reforms it proposed, including the rights of indigenous people, were scuttled by political maneuvers. Our documentary, *Precarious Peace,* covers aspects of both the war and the struggle to end it peacefully. Available from Vision Video.

In 1999, the Commission for Historical Clarification, established by the United Nations, confirmed the military's overwhelming responsibility. The report also charged the U.S. government with using the CIA to support the Guatemalan government's systematic use of state terror against its own citizens. On March 10 of the same year, President Bill Clinton, on an official visit to Guatemala, publicly stated that Washington "was wrong" to have supported Guatemalan security forces in their counterinsurgency campaign.

The legacy of the long civil war still holds sway in the country, manifested in vicious drug trafficking, criminal gangs, femicide, and deadly para-judicial retaliation. Mayan rights are still a deeply dividing issue. For reliable updates, we recommend reports from Human Rights Watch and the Guatemalan Human Rights Commission. And religious groups continue to play a mixed role of blessing and curse. For varying perspectives on that, note *Re-Enchanting the World: Maya Protestantism in the Guatemalan Highlands*, by anthropologist C.Matthews Samson, Robert Brenneman's *Homies and Hermanos: God and Gangs in Central America*. Also, *City of God: Christian Citizenship in Postwar Guatemala*, by Kevin Lewis O'Neill, and *Securing the City: Neoliberalism, Space, and Insecurity in Postwar Guatemala*, edited by O'Neill and Kedron Thomas.

Recently the arrest of wartime president, General Efraín Ríos Montt, on the charge of genocide and crimes against humanity, bolstered hopes that at last the stonewall of impunity is breaking down in the courts. That hope was modified by two developments. The Constitutional Court voided the conviction on a technicality, and the Attorney General, Claudia Paz Y Paz, who brought the charges, was deposed from her position.

However, witnesses in the Montt trial were able to put their stories on official record, and outspoken resistance is generally more possible in the country, as evidenced, for instance, in the founding of "Plaza Publica," an on-line investigative journal.

We've been asked dozens of times if we intend to write a sequel, which we accept as a nudge toward a happier ending. But the sequel we would like to write goes far beyond this story. How about a happy ending to our world-wide, human capacity for cruelty and greed and grandiose illusion? No need for a plot there. We all understand what it means and we would all like to write it.

Hasta la vista, compañeros,
—Shirley and Rudy Nelson
  2013-14